"An inspiring account of bravery and fortitude in the face of cruel injustice. Heartbreaking and beautifully told, Waites pulls you in and doesn't let go. This story and its characters—some real, some fictional—will haunt you for years to come."

—Lenore Borja, author of
*The Last Huntress (Mirror Realm Series Book I)*

"I finished the last page…feeling like I'd witnessed something that mattered…[It] is one of those rare books that pulls you in with the promise of a personal story and ends up handing you a mirror…I recommend it to readers interested in the intersection of faith and ethics and those interested in historical fiction and World War II narratives."

—Salina Coria, *Reader's Favorite Book Reviews*

". . .a powerful and moving account of the damage wrought by family shame and governmental and institutional cruelty where the reader is ultimately gratified when the rats are exposed and good triumphs over evil. A necessary and well told contribution to the story of Byberry and a meaningful tribute to the patients locked behind its walls who exist only in memory."

—Deirdre Fagan, author of *Find a Place for Me*

"*TFO* takes the reader on a wild ride inside the Philadelphia State Hospital at Byberry. . . Its Philly-centricities and mannerisms provide a realistic backdrop any Philadelphian would recognize. With the right balance of fiction and documented facts, the reader is treated to an experience that ranges from horrific to heartwarming, and it comes to a satisfying conclusion. This one is hard to put down."

—John Webster, author of *The Philadelphia State Hospital at Byberry: A History of Misery and Medicine*"

"*The Faithful Ones* is a haunting, heartfelt tale of a sister's quest to uncover the mystery behind her brother's wartime experience. Based on a true family story, Waites offers a captivating look at the cost of family secrets, and the power of love and loyalty."

—Ellen Birkett Morris, author of *Beware the Tall Grass*

# the faithful ONES

A Novel

KATHLEEN J. WAITES

*Published by:* Invictus Press

ISBN Paperback: 979-8-9989691-0-2
ISBN eBook: 979-8-9989691-1-9

Author Photo: Jennifer Johnson
Interior Design: Creative Publishing Book Design
Book Cover Design: Sheri Williams

*For Edward F. Hohlfeld, and all the invisible and unacknowledged heroes of the greatest generation, and for Mary Hohlfeld Joyce, whose devotion to Edward's memory and honor inspired this story.*

"If the mystical truth that comes to a man proves to be a force that he can live by, what mandate have we of the majority to order him to live in another way? We can throw him into prison or madhouse, but we cannot change his mind"

—William James, *The Varieties of Religious Experience*


"Catholics drafted for an offensive war, of whose justice they are not fully certain, must under pain of mortal sin, become conscientious objectors . . . They are bound in conscience passively to resist the tyranny of their government preferring prison or the concentration camp to participation of such a war"

—Rt. Rev. Barry O'Toole,
*The Catholic Worker* –November 1939


"Truth is so hard to tell, sometimes it needs fiction to make it plausible."

—Francis Bacon

# Table of Contents

# PART ONE

# Escape from Bedlam

*Winter, 1942*

Ed craned his neck. It looked like a twelve-foot drop. Maybe a little more. It didn't matter. It was escape or die. He banged the lock with a piece of broken floorboard until it finally gave. Nothing mattered but moving, not thinking. Running, not staying. He'd make the jump and then he'd run until what was left of his heart gave out, until the gruesome image disappeared. Joseph. Poor, innocent boy rammed over and over by a monster.

"My God, my God, why hast thou forsaken us?" Where was God? The boy's eyes screaming desperately, while Ed, a silent, furious, unwilling witness tethered to a sink, was unable to save him.

I won't leave you. He had promised. But he'd had to leave, hadn't he? Buster would have taken Joseph to the restraint room by now. Patients called it the dungeon—a black room behind a locked door crammed with rows of arms and legs chained to foul-smelling cots in the dark. Poor, poor boy. Buster could assault and shackle whomever he wanted and then lock them away for safekeeping. In this place, Buster was God, and he would be coming back for Ed. It was now or never.

He had to free himself from the sink first. Leaning back, he lifted his feet and kicked at the rusted legs of the sink, his will compensating for what he lacked in physical strength. His desperate arms tugging and twisting and pulling at the cuffs until he thought they would be torn from the socket, and then, miracle of miracles, the rusted pipe gave way. Fevered and frantic and shaking uncontrollably, his hands slid free. Tip-toeing his way through the haunted dayroom, lit only by the shaft of light coming from the toilet room, he located the window with the broken lock.

I won't leave you. But he had no choice. He'd return with help. Surely, Father McGuire would help them.

Early evening, but dark as death as far as the eye could see. Dark as death behind him, too, as the lights guarding the building were blessedly dim. Ed leaped, falling to the hard, frost-encrusted ground with a thud. He toppled over, his right ankle smarting from a twist upon impact, but otherwise unscathed. While the wind churned and whistled, he heaved himself up from the ground and bolted, only a thin layer of Army wool between the soles of his feet and the frozen ground. The cold bit his face and ears. Behind him, through the open window, something flapped and clattered. Ahead, somewhere, lights and freedom and help for Joseph.

Keeping to the shadows alongside the asphalt roadway, he slowed down to skulk past the guard house. The guard's head tipped forward, his earflaps moving rhythmically to his snores. Ed ran. Ran as he had done as a boy, arms and legs pumping, heedless and reckless and free, the wind rushing through his hair. Not feeling the unyielding earth beneath his feet, not seeing the boy's body-splitting, heart-splitting agony. Not looking behind but ahead to safety and home. To the priest, and mother, and little Mary, and innocence, and home. Baptized by rain, he prayed the lingering stench of evil away.

On Roosevelt Boulevard, he headed south. Car lights washed the dark street. The driver, not seeing Ed until he appeared apparition-like through his rearview mirror, not seeing a desperate running man with a bruised soul, but a ghost. The driver shook his head in disbe-lief. It must have been a trick of the eyes.

Home. Home. God, help me make it home.

He ran, cold snot dripping into his mouth and down his chin, clenched lungs begging for air while his heart willed him forward. Running and sniffling, thin socks sliding, he lurched past Grant, at last to Pennypack Park and over to Frankford and east to Aramingo. He slowed to bend over, gasping, clutching his aching side. Glancing up, he saw the boy's terrified face in the headlights coming toward him—Noooooooo. The wind buzzing saw-like through his ears, and a car swerving and screeching alongside him as he stood and ran on, ignoring the driver who yelled out the car window for him to get the hell out of his way. The bold outline of the railroad trestle finally coming into view, and with it, the promise of Port Richmond and safety, and protection at last from the relentless slap of wind.

Upon reaching the trestle, he stopped to catch his breath, his lungs and eyes burning. He wiped the snot crystals with the cold, drenched sleeve of his shirt. Stifling a howl of pain, he dropped his knees onto the frozen concrete and tried to find God. A sudden clanging sound and a voice behind a light weaving in his direction jolted him. "Who's there? Show yourself!" Ed leaped up. He charged back toward the opposite end of the trestle, the light and the voice disappearing into the dark behind him. He was close enough to smell home, but no, not yet—the boy—he had to get help for the boy first. He hoofed his way to Memphis Street. To the church and the priest and help for Joseph.

Within sight of the rectory at last, Ed yelped in relief. His exhausted legs trembled as he stumbled up the steps and leaned his benumbed hand on the doorbell. A light flickered on. The door opened, and a haloed Father McGuire appeared on the doorstep.

"Father," Ed gasped, choking back tears. "They'll be after me, Father."

"Ed?" The priest ushered him into the vestibule. "Ed Hohlfeld, is that you? My dear boy! What in the world?" A bare bulb from above him glared down at Ed, exposing his ashen face, his sodden clothes, his gaunt, shuddering frame.

"Help me, Father. Please, you have to help me. They'll take me back there. I can't go back there, Father." He shook his head and clenched his hands. "Evil, Father, it's evil, pure and simple, and I'm dying in there. I had to run away. From that place. I had to. But they'll be coming for me, Father. You have to help me. And what he did to that boy, you can't imagine, Father. Buster's a monster. Plain and simple, and we have to help the boy. Father, please."

"Where, where are your shoes?" The priest stared at Ed's wet, tattered socks. "What? What boy are you talking about?" The priest's head curved around the partially opened door, his eyes scanning the darkened street for signs of a boy.

Ed's eyes cast about the vestibule for an answer. Where to begin? They scanned the rectory's cream-colored walls and glistening oak floor, settling finally on his own shoeless feet, seeing himself as the priest must. A deranged and desperate man. But Father McGuire must know. He must know what had happened to him at boot camp. The priest must know about Ed's having been sent to the state hospital. Surely, his mother would have told the parish priest. But told him what exactly? Ed's mother *didn't know* the truth. How could the priest understand anything? How could Ed even begin to explain it all to him?

"I . . ." The priest started to say something and then paused. "Following you?" He opened the door wider to survey the street beyond the church, a stream of car lights in the distance spraying the damp darkness. "I think I need to call someone at the hospital for you, Ed. Come in and calm yourself. I'll fetch a towel. Tea? You're overwrought, my good man."

So, he knew about the hospital. But what did he know exactly? The priest patted him on the back, then quickly removed his hand and slyly wiped off the pungent moisture on the side of his cassock.

"Let me make a call and get you some dry clothing, Ed, and something warm to drink."

The priest was glad he had the rectory to himself, thankful Mrs. Harrigan, the housekeeper, had left for the night. With her, there'd be no end of questions.

"No. You don't understand, Father." Ed shrieked and jumped back, picturing the ambulance, and Buster leering at him like a trapped animal.

Backing away from the priest, Ed turned and scrambled down the steps and back into the black, wet streets. Ignoring the cars, the night, the panic, he made his way to Aramingo, and back through the railroad trestle to Tulip, toward Somerset Street and home. His ears clogged with wind, his feet and heart benumbed, Ed ran. His father, then—he had to get his father to help him. He prayed he could make his father understand.

## Chapter 1

# "Land of the Free and Home of the Brave"

*Fall, 1941*

Beneath snowy furrowed eyebrows and a white and blue star-studded top hat, the man's piercing eyes peered at him, his gun-like finger pointed directly at Ed's heart. The #54 trolley wheezed forward. Ed turned from the window and shook off Uncle Sam's unsettling glare. He concentrated instead on the spindly city trees that grew like miracles through the cracked concrete. He might sketch one from memory when he got home. Supper first, though. His stomach growled. His mom's bean soup, gurgling in the cast iron pot, waited for him. When the trolley finally slid to a halt at the corner of Tulip and Somerset, Ed sprang from his second-row seat. His lean six-foot, one-inch frame dipped slightly to clear the rooftop. He tipped his cap at the driver and skipped down the steps.

"You got it, Mac," the driver said before the trolley pitched and rolled away. He knew Ed's name, but everyone was Mac or Ma'am to Pete, the seasoned driver with a ruddy face and ready grin.

Ed was a trolley regular, ever since bagging the job at Heinz's Manufacturing a few months before. He was lucky. Jobs were hard to come by, and it paid a decent wage. His dad's accident down at the docks left him crippled and out of work. His older brother Sam was already working at Heinz, and Ed was glad they could chip in and help support the packed household that included five girls under thirteen.

When the trolley pulled away, Ed glanced across the street. It was Friday. Willy's taproom was already hopping. He caught sight of Chappy Lafferty standing outside with Spike and Shorty, friends from their Richmond neighborhood. A cigarette hung on for dear life from the corner of Chappy's mouth, his stubby fingers cradling a mug of beer.

"Ed," he beckoned with his other hand. The cigarette danced up and down with his lips. "C'mon over. Have a few. Weekend's finally here." He raised the mug of beer in a mock toast.

"Thanks, Chap. Not tonight." Ed drew a figure in the air. "Sketching. Maybe tomorrow?" Chappy gave him the thumbs-up.

"Right. See you tomorrow morning at the baseball field then? St. Anne's boys want us to umpire their game, remember?"

With a wave good-bye, Ed turned toward home. "I'll be there, Chap." Best buddies since grammar school, Ed and Chappy made an odd pair. Short, stocky, and square, Chappy had a boxer's body to go with his ready fists. Good thing he was a happy-go-lucky kind of guy. When he wasn't, Ed was there to step in and pull him out. Ed was the calm to Chappy's storm. He hadn't seen much of Chappy during the two years he and Sam did their stint in Roosevelt's Tree Army. The CCC job got the Hohlfeld brothers out of the city. The job came wrapped in a patriotic cause that thumbed its nose at the Depression and made Ed proud. It also put much-needed dollars in Ed's pocket, most of which he sent home to his mother.

"Ed! Edward!" Her pigtails flying and arms flapping, Mary pumped her legs like she was headed for the tickertape at the end of a race. Ed dropped to one knee, his black lunch pail falling to the split sidewalk. He pushed his wool beret to the back of his head and swept a feathery spray of sand-colored hair from his forehead.

"Hey, baby girl." A broad smile revealed the snaggle tooth that made Ed self-conscious. His chiseled jaw and warm hazel eyes did their best to make up for the flaw. Nearly nine, Mary wasn't much of a baby, but her face brightened when Ed addressed her that way. With a final whoosh, Mary landed in the circle of Ed's outstretched arms. She squealed and giggled as he hoisted her up and spun her around. After gently delivering her back to the uneven pavement, Ed leaned over to retrieve his pail, and brother and sister walked hand in hand as they made their their way home to 2313 Somerset Street.

"Where's Sam? Guess what Mom made for supper?" Not waiting for his reply, Mary posed the last question as if it were a surprise, even though ham-less bean soup was pretty much standard Friday night fare. Most suppers were meatless these days, except for sirloin steak Saturday. Their father got the steak, along with his weekly, wife-approved quart of beer.

"Sam stayed late to get in a little overtime, and yup, I bet I have a good idea." He reached into his pocket to fish out two pennies, pressing them into Mary's delighted hand. "Is it bean soup?"

Mary gave a little jump and squealed her thanks, closing her right fist around the pennies. Her other hand was still tucked inside the shelter of her big brother's.

"I think I'll use my pennies to buy Yum-Yums. Nah, I'm gonna get two soft pretzels instead and give one to Agnes. Yum-Yums do sound better, though. There, I made up my mind."

Ed was bound to listen about Elizabeth being mad at Rosemary for "no darn good reason" and a host of other child-world worries. While Mary chattered away, Ed breathed in the familiar sights and sounds of his working-class neighborhood. He waved to the Kelly sisters playing jacks on the stoop. A few older girls skipped rope on the sidewalk across the street, and a swarm of boys shouted and dodged cars as they chased their ball. All kept an ear cocked for Mom's suppertime call. Ed sighed. He had a job, a meal, a bed, and a pastime he loved. No girl yet, not the right one anyway, but there was still time for that. It was the darned war news and the likelihood of being drafted that dampened his spirits. Ed couldn't count on asthma to get him a pass like it did with his older brother Sam, who was, unlike Ed, gun-ho about this war business. While they got along well enough, the brothers never did see eye-to-eye on politics, or faith, for that matter. His best friend Chappy was elated when he got Uncle Sam's postcard. Couldn't wait to start killing Nazis. Not Edward Francis, so named after St. Francis of Assisi. Nobleman turned warrior turned peacemaker, Francis had the guts to give up everything. Ed took that to heart. The man said "No" to what the world wanted and "Yes" to his conscience. What would it take to have that kind of courage?

Returning to the crisp fall day and the bubbly girl beside him, Ed waved to Mrs. Simzak perched precariously on her top step. "How are you doing, Mrs. Simzak?"

"You didn't happen to see my Harold, did you?" She sniffed the air, keeping a keen eye on the gathering storm clouds to the east as she shook out a threadbare rug. She also slyly glanced up the street for signs of her errant husband, who was likely celebrating Friday payday at Willy's.

"Nope, sure didn't, Mrs. Simzak. I'm sure he'll be along soon enough, though." Mrs. Simzak's grimace told Ed she wasn't so sure.

She turned her attention to Mary. "Little Mary's sure growing up, ain't she?"

When Mary beamed and waved hello, Mrs. Simzak half-smiled. Now that was something to see.

Mary returned to her prattle. "And anyway, Edward, Anna wants a kitty-cat, but Mama said no, no more mouths to feed, and Anna bawled her head off, and it made me cry, too, even though I don't want a kitty cat at all. I'd rather have a horse, but I know I can't ever have something so big as a horse, and I didn't want Anna to get even more upset . . ."

Chuckling to himself, he leaned over and held her gaze. "Uh, huh, okay, well, remember Mary, Anna is younger than you. Up here." Ed pointed to his head. What Ed didn't say was that Anna would always be a child and Mary would have to be the one to look out for her. "She's older than you, but she's not a big girl like you, Mary. She doesn't understand. Maybe we can draw her a picture of a kitty-cat later tonight during your art lesson to make her feel better. What do you think about that?"

Ed relished his alone time in the makeshift studio he shared with his brother Sam, but he didn't mind giving Mary the occasional lesson. Art materials were hard to come by these days. The brothers took an old dining room server and made it into a painting easel and sculpting table and scavenged for drawing pencils, paints, and brushes at thrift stores.

Mary sighed. "Oh, okay, I guess that's a good idea, Edward. But will you draw something for me too and help me copy the Arabian horse I saw in your big picture book?"

"You betcha." Ed squeezed Mary's hand. As they inched closer to home, he scanned the horizon. A storm was on tap, all right. Dark clouds hovered in the distance like a tease, as if unable to commit. "So, little Miss Mary, how did school go today? Did you get good marks?" He expected a "yes" and a "pretty good," and that would be the end of it. Instead, Mary saw it as a green light to gossip.

"Guess what, Edward!" Mary's voice rose with the telling. "Eileen Carmichael got sent back to the coat closet by Sister Mary Dolores today. Sister was mad as a hornet's nest. That's the second time this week she got into trouble. Big, big trouble." She stretched her arms out to demonstrate how big.

"Oh no! Really? What did Eileen do to get into so much trouble with Sister Mary Dolores?" Ed listened patiently, while picturing himself comfortably settled in the living room with his *Catholic Worker* newspaper.

Mary's brown eyes widened. "Sister Mary Dolores pointed her clicker at Eileen's head and clicked it three times like this." Mary let go of Edward's hand and raised a pointed finger to demonstrate. *Eileen Carmichael, keep your eyes and hands to yourself, young lady. Why are you looking at your neighbor's copybook?* Then she found a folded-up note to Regina Papernik on Eileen's desk and called her a bold article and sent her straight back to the coat closet until the end of the day!" Pleased with her performance, Mary examined her brother's face for a suitably shocked reaction.

Ed clucked his tongue and shook his head. "Well, yes, that's just terrible. Poor Eileen. She must have been mortified."

"What's mortified mean?" Mary pulled on her pigtail and knotted her brow.

"Well, that's just another way of saying really, really embarrassed."

Ed smiled at the memory of Sister Mary Dolores's delighted face when he presented her with a smoothly sanded homemade pointer for her classroom. Father Murphy Turkey Sourpuss had told the nuns there was simply no money for such frivolous items, so Edward got to work. He carved pointers out of old broomsticks. For the Christmas holiday he built a Nativity stable with scraps of wood he'd collected from work sites. And to brighten the nuns' dull classroom blackboards, Ed painted elegant Scripture verses bordered by vibrant red, violet, and yellow flowers. He enjoyed pitching in at St. Anne's. Made him feel like he was part of something bigger than himself, like when he was in the CCC. His buddies razzed him about it. Called him 'Father Ed'. He thought long and hard about whether or not he might have a vocation but couldn't quite come down on the side of yes.

When they arrived at the familiar white marble steps, Mary was still prattling.

"Then Rosemary cried and said I was being a goody-two-shoes because Sister picked me instead of her. Sister said if I am very good and go to Mass every day as I have been, I can be her helper next week, and when I grow up, I'm going to be a nun just like Sister Mary Dolores. What do you think about that, Edward? Aren't you so proud of me?"

Ed chuckled. "Sure, baby girl, but we'll have to see about your being a nun when you get older." An errant ball bounced in front of Ed. He picked it up and tossed it back to Mario who was playing handball with his brother.

"Wanna join us, Mr. Hohlfeld? Sergio could use a little help." Mario smirked at his brother. Ed knew the boys looked up to him. He listened without judging and didn't talk down to them when they confided in him about family and girl troubles. He knew his easy way with folks would be useful skills in the priesthood if he ever decided to go in that direction. "If"—a little word with a big meaning, his mother would be quick to say.

"No, thanks, Mario. Another day?" Mario shrugged in disappointment. Ed returned to Mary and her concerns.

"Listen, Mary, I think it's grand that you want to be Sister's helper and become a nun. But it sounds like Rosemary may be a little jealous because Sister chose you instead of her. She's your best friend, isn't she? Maybe it's not such a good idea to brag about being Sister's helper if it hurts your friend's feelings. Remember, do unto others. . .?"

Mary's tongue fell silent. She wrapped her arms around Ed's waist. It didn't stay still very long. "Oh, Edward, I'll try to do better. Honest, I will. I won't brag and hurt my friend's feelings anymore. Well, I'll really, really try not to. But I can still be Sister's helper, can't I, so long as I don't brag?"

Ed cradled her head with his broad hands and chuckled. "Sure. Now go and play until supper. But keep an eye on the sky. It looks like that storm may break soon, and you don't want to get caught in it." With a tug of Mary's pigtail, Ed sent her on her way.

Ed bolted up the steps and through the front door, calling to his mother to let her know he was home. The aroma of homemade soup wafted through the house.

"Sam's working overtime, Mother. Won't make it for supper."

Alice Connolly Hohlfeld scooted to the doorway of the kitchen, which was little more than an attached shed at the back of their narrow row home. Roughly fourteen feet long and twenty feet wide, the house offered two small bedrooms up and two down, and in it, the German Irish family of eight made do. She wiped her hands on her striped apron and smiled shyly. In moments of self-consciousness, she had a habit of combing back stray hair from her forehead with her fingertips, a habit that Ed had picked up. An attractive woman, she wore her faded brown hair in a neat bun. Ed could see the Depression's wear and tear in the crinkles on her face, if not in her erect bearing.

"All right, dear. Mary insisted on meeting you at the trolley stop again. I hope that was all right."

"It was fine, Mother." Ed removed his faded twill jacket and hung it on the coat stand in the hallway before stooping down to unlace his Nettleton work boots. "She's down the street playing with Agnes and the others."

"Well, that's good. Any men's club meetings at the church tonight?" His mother had a hard time keeping track of his and Sam's busy schedules. She rested her shoulder against the wall and looked briefly back at Anna to ensure she was still safely sitting at the small square table. "I haven't had a chance to collect the mail. Would you mind?" With that, she turned back to her iron stove and stirred her soup—carrots, potatoes, cabbage, and navy beans in a tomato soup-based brew. Meatless Friday.

"Nope, no meeting tonight, Mother. Nothing much going on, but I promised Mary that I'd give her an art lesson."

"I do hope that girl's not being a pest."

Ed chuckled. "No, just talkative is all." Ed walked down the long, narrow hallway and into his mother's kitchen, with its spotless, green linoleum floor. Before Christmas, he and Sam had installed it as a gift to their mother. The first time she saw it, she pulled her apron up over her face and wept with joy. Ed took one of her favorite sayings to heart. "We may be hard-up, but that doesn't mean we can't be clean. Cleanliness is next to godliness." Both he and Sam were fastidious in their personal grooming, and they kept their shared bedroom spotlessly clean. They trotted off to work in pressed pants and shirts and kept their Sunday shoes polished.

Ed's empty stomach gave him another nudge. "Soup sure smells good."

"Aw, go on with you now, Edward, m'love. Supper will be ready soon enough." She picked up her ladle, wiping her moist forehead with the heel of her other hand. "Why don't you wash up? There're soda crackers in the tin if you're starving. It's good you have a night off, then. No Church work to do."

"Do you need more coals on that fire?" Not waiting for an answer, Ed leaned over the coal bucket and scooped up a few bricks with the hand shovel. His mother quickly opened the door, and he placed them atop the red-hot embers in the stove. Then he made his way to the sink. After washing and drying his hands, he reached into the cupboard and pulled a few crackers from the tin, leaning against the new icebox. "Yup, it sure is nice to have a free evening. Thanks, Mother." He held up the crackers and gave her a peck on the top of her head. "I'll fetch the mail. Maybe relax and read my paper."

Munching on the salty wafers, he ambled over to stand behind Anna. Of the five Hohlfeld girls, Anna was second eldest after Alice, now married and gone from the house. That left Ronnie, Anna, Mary, and Agnes. Several years older than Mary, Anna was a sweet child who would never grow up. Ed patted her head and watched her color in the balloons and clown figures he'd sketched for her. His mother's manner was to act mildly annoyed at interruptions in her kitchen, but she was more tolerant with Ed. She sometimes grumbled about the time he invested in the Church, but he knew she was proud of him. Mrs. Hohlfeld's oldest son was her north star and the one she hoped might be a priest. He understood this even though she never expressed it. Every Irish mother wanted her oldest son to be a priest and elevate the family in the eyes of God and the Church. Their tight-lipped family didn't discuss expectations. Nor did they talk about problems and family matters. They just got on with it. Except when it came to politics, and then only in controlled tones between the boys and Edward senior. In recent weeks there'd been some tense, late-night political discussions prompted by war-related news headlines and radio programs. War loomed on the horizon as certain as winter, especially given the German torpedoing of the USS Reuben James. The old man had a special stake in these developments, fearing there might be a backlash against him and other German immigrants. He stood solidly behind the war and a man's duty to serve. He also had little patience for Ed's qualms about violence. Quite apart from debates about German aggression and the merits of war, the Hohlfelds kept their concerns, alongside family secrets, safely stored in the family closet. They met adversity and problems with a fierce combination of German and Irish stoicism.

After squeezing Anna's shoulder affectionately and commenting on her beautiful picture, Ed looked over at his mother. "Where's Pop?"

"He's over speaking to Mr. Callahan. More war talk, I suppose," she said with a dismissive wave of her fingers.

Ed made his way down the hallway and to the front door. He leaned outside to retrieve the mail, hoping his *Catholic Worker* had arrived. It had. Ed scooped it up, along with a handful of other pieces of mail. Setting the bills and letters atop the corner table, he picked up his newspaper. Though he read the *Philadelphia Bulletin* faithfully, he was more eager to read the editorials on war and non-violence in Dorothy Day's *Catholic Worker*. His post-Depression life was finally on an even keel, his family's income stabilizing. Now he worried about Europe's war becoming theirs and turning it all upside down.

He slumped down into his father's cracked brown leather chair that sat across from the Victrola, one of the family's few treasures and the center of the family's nightly entertainment.

Ed's *Catholic Worker* lay on his lap. He decided it could wait, along with the decision that weighed on him: could he serve his country as a soldier? More to the point, could he, in all good conscience, kill another man? He seesawed between duty to country and obligation to conscience. Although he'd taken the matter up with his friend and spiritual advisor Father McGuire, he came away with a heavy question mark, along with the priest's assurance of support whichever way he went. He closed his eyes to the problem and let his mind drift. Ed's simple life worked for him. His job at Heinz gave him a steady paycheck, but he was happiest working in his art studio. Any other spare time found him at a St. Anne's Men's Club-sponsored event or meeting. He enjoyed building the game booths and painting signs for the church carnival. Over a few weekends, with the help of Chappy and a few scrappy St. Anne's boys, he fashioned a much-needed baseball diamond for the school. It was a gem. When Ed first clapped eyes on the abandoned lot, a jungle of weeds and trash piled atop uneven dirt, he threw up his hands in dismay. Chappy just scratched his head, waiting for Ed to lead the way. Robbie, Joey, and Frankie, handpicked by Father McGuire to assist Ed and Chappy, stood around helplessly.

"C'mon, Father," Frank protested. "Give us a break. This is gonna take a miracle." Ed had to agree. But the priest had presented him with a challenge, so he set to work. They cleared the field of bottles and candy wrappers, newspapers, and garbage and pulled weeds until their hands were blistered and raw. They flattened the dirt with shovels and rakes. Finally, the field started to take shape. Ed crafted a perfectly measured baseball diamond of 90 feet between the bases, with a raised pitcher's mound 60 and one-half feet from home plate, just as it was in Shibe Park, home to the city's beloved Phillies. For the batting box, Ed and Chappy built a backstop from old fencing wire and poles the boys retrieved from a seemingly abandoned property, a task that gave them a thrill. Ed cautioned that this detail shouldn't be shared with the parish priest. Topping it off, they anchored each of the bases and pitching rubber, and Ed chalked perfectly straight baselines and a squared batter's box.

After the magical field was finally completed, the boys' grumbling turned into bragging and pats on the back. They completed the work on a muggy July night, just as the sun was taking a final bow behind a ribbon of clouds. With a flourish, Ed re-chalked and put the final touches on home plate. Then he stood up to indulge in a long, well-earned stretch to get rid of the kink in his spine before clapping Chappy on the back and shaking his hand. Suddenly recharged, after another blistering hot day of physical labor, Robbie and Frankie started tossing an imaginary ball around, feigning hits and running around the bases. Summoned by Joey, Fr. McGuire strode out to the field. His eyes widened, and his jaw dropped.

"Ed, how in the world. . .?"

Frankie zoomed in from third base, breathless and gleeful. "Hey, Father, whaddaya think about our new field? Ain't she just a peach?"

Smiling at the memory, Ed woke from his reverie. He yawned and stretched his legs and arms. The sudden movement sent his newspaper, along with the mail that sat on the corner table, skittering onto the floor. He leaned over to push together and scoop up the scattered envelopes and pages of the newspaper. Page four of *The Catholic Worker* lay open and aslant on the floor. He paused, drawn to the editorial byline "Infallibility of Conscience" from Bede

Jarrett's series on "Meditations for Layfolk." His eyes settled on the second paragraph:

*But while in this way I am completely under the domination of my own conscience, I have to remember that in consequence, I cannot move until my conscience is sure. I may not act until my conscience is really determined: I cannot act, that is, when my conscience is in doubt. The reason of this principle is that were I to do so, I should in effect be saying to myself, I don't know whether this is right or wrong, but I am going to do it anyway. Obviously, this would be altogether a disrespectful attitude to God, a complete disregard for the law of God. Yet, on the other hand, it is surely very difficult to make up one's mind determinedly on all points that have to be settled by conscience . . .*

Ed sucked in his breath, whistling it in release. Conscience. Doubt. He's talking to me. For some time now, Dorothy Day had been calling for a revolution of the heart. For followers like Ed, Jesus' Sermon on the Mount was more than just an empty prayer from the pulpit, and Ed was a peaceful man by nature. Sure, he'd gotten into his share of scrapes with neighborhood toughs, but only to defend himself and his brother or a buddy—a shove here, a punch there. He stood his ground, but he never started a fight. But killing? His heart bucked at the thought. But pacifism was a bold stance to take in a pro-war country, and Ed was a patriot, after all. He didn't want to let his country or his family down, so he'd been wavering. Once he decided . . . once Ed knew for sure, well, there would be no turning back. Deliberation was the key. But he'd been deliberating for months now. Maybe he'd find the answer in this article. He'd scour the paper and read the entire editorial more carefully after supper.

Ed returned to the assorted pieces of mail. A yellow postcard addressed to Edward Francis Hohlfeld slid from the pile. His eyes landed on it unwillingly, like a fly on sticky paper. Through blurry eyes, he scanned the key phrases: "The President of the United States . . . having submitted yourself to the local Board . . . are hereby notified you have now been selected for training and service in . . ." His heart tilted. He stood up. His breath came fast and unevenly as he skipped down to a separate line that read, "U.S. Army." The date and other details blurred. His eyes darted around the front parlor, looking for help. There was none. Willing the postcard away, he stuffed it into his shirt pocket.

His mother popped her head through the kitchen doorway, her voice jolting him. "Edward. I'll be putting dinner on the table. Can you go down the street and get the girls? I don't know why your father should be gone this long, but we best not disturb him."

Ed cleared his throat. Found his voice. "Yes, okay, I'll call the girls in now, but I won't be staying for supper, Mother." His thoughts were spinning. His stomach no longer talked to him.

"Well, why in the world not? You have to eat. You must be starving."

Ed hastily re-laced his boots and grabbed his jacket. "The church . . . it's something at the church. I forgot. I have to see Father McGuire. I have to take care of . . ." He threw open the door and left his mother standing in the doorway to the kitchen, her hands open in a question that wouldn't be answered until later that night. Outside, the wind blustered, pushing the troubled clouds and Ed to a decision.

*Chapter 2*

# The Priest

Mrs. Harrigan gave the counter one last swipe with her dishrag, casting a critical eye around her kitchen to be sure she hadn't missed anything. A portly woman, she must have been a looker at one time, if you could see past the gray stripes in her thinning hair and the sag in her mid-section. Birthing eight babies, two stillborn, can do that to a woman. She had a patrician appearance and carriage though, evidence of her roots in the North before the troubles took her family's land and wealth. Her bewitching green eyes, complemented by pale skin and a small sharp nose, once had the boys pining after her. Now she used what remained of her assets to cast a spell on the widowed butcher and get a fairer price for the rectory's meat.

"Your dinner is on the stove, Father. Father Murphy's eaten already. He's gone for the night. Shall you be wanting anything else then, Father? Sure, I can stay a bit longer if you need me to."

Father McGuire strode to the sink to pour himself a glass of water, relieved that it was Friday and the end of the day. He turned to face her, speaking between sips. "No, Mrs. Harrigan. You may go. Thank you. I'm looking forward to a quiet evening off. Are you sure there were no calls for me from the Chancery?"

Although he was still just a rectory priest and not yet a pastor, John McGuire was definitely on his way up. His Irish charm drew people to him. It was his talisman. His two years of seminary study in Rome also served him well. Nearing 80 years old, Pastor Murphy was slowing down and relying on the younger priest more. The bishop had taken notice, giving John a place on the all-important fundraising committee. The chancery plum would come only after he'd greased the palms of several officious priests and labored on tedious chancery committees, all while staying on the right side of the archbishop. Ambitious, John saw a bishop, maybe even a cardinal, in his future.

"No, Father. There were a few calls for Father Murphy but none for you," Mrs. Harrigan said, flashing him a bewildered look as she donned her coat and tied her flowered kerchief under her double chin.

John's frank smile reassured her. "Well then, that's all right. Have a good evening, Mrs. Harrigan. Mind the storm."

She hung her black pocketbook on the crook of her arm, picked up her umbrella, and negotiated the opening of the kitchen door that always stuck when there was moisture in the air. "I will, Father. Good night. I'll see you at Mass in the morning."

After Mrs. Harrigan muscled the door shut, John exhaled a noisy breath. Finally, the rectory to himself. He set his glass down and tugged at his white collar to loosen his cassock, bidding good riddance to another day of parish work. The school's problems were mounting. Textbooks were in short supply, and the nuns were stretched thin across classes one through eight, but there was no money to purchase books or hire lay teachers. The nuns would have to make do without them. Well, with the war coming down the pike, Americans would all have to make do and bear their portion of the burden.

He collected his dinner of overcooked cod, boiled potatoes, and peas from the stove and took it into the formal dining room, as if the shining mahogany table and unlit candelabra might magically transform his pedestrian meal. Mrs. Harrigan cooked the way she cleaned, thoroughly and without mercy, but his hunger overcame his diffidence. At the end of the school day, a group of eighth-grade rowdies had prevailed upon him to play a little pick-up basketball, and his competitive edge pushed his "Sure, boys but only for a few minutes" into more than an hour of vigorous exertion. As his sainted mother might say, he was no longer a spring rooster. He had some manly face to save though, and he hoped his show of athleticism might entice a few of the boys to the Church's non-paying job at the altar. Early morning masses were tough on the young ones, and the pastor's dour personality didn't help. By the end of the day, John had worked up an appetite that even Mrs. Harrigan's cooking couldn't ruin.

As if it had been waiting for hours to unleash its fury, a surge of rain pelted the rectory roof. Glad he didn't have to make any evening visits, John forked his way through the bland dinner, the day's newsreel playing out in his mind. He'd been hoofing it all day, starting with Communion rounds in the parish and visits to the sick at Nazareth Hospital, where he'd had to perform the last rites on two dying patients—may God have mercy on their souls. Thankfully, neither was from his parish, or they'd have to be added to the funeral masses already scheduled in the coming days. Lunch was followed by Confirmation lessons and a visit to imploring nuns concerned about their meager classrooms. He admired his friend Ed's decorative handiwork on their blackboards. Reminded the nuns that these were hard and anxious times but with everyone pitching in, they would, God willing, manage.

With increasing frequency, John found himself being pulled away from his administrative duties to counsel parishioners still stumbling from a protracted Depression and now contending with the prospect of war. The sacrifices were bound to mount. God help them. Today, it had been the husbands of two young mothers and the son of a widow that were called. The nation needed men, and so the Church had a responsibility to support a country headed to war. Whether or not it satisfied Thomas Aquinas' criteria for a just war was being endlessly debated in the pages of Dorothy Day's *Catholic Worker*. In recent months, John had scanned its pages, peppered with fretful letters from thoughtful men in search of their moral bearings.

The wind moaned at the door like a puppy trying to get in, and the rain retreated to a steady drumbeat. John wandered back to the kitchen with his empty plate in search of dessert. Where did Mrs. Harrigan stash the rest of that apple pie the Italian baker donated? A quick glance around the room found a thickly sliced piece sitting on a dish on a shelf above the stove and waiting for him like a prize in a carnival booth.

"God bless you, Mrs. Harrigan," John said with an air-blessing. He eagerly picked the plate up, along with a clean fork, re-boarding his train of thought about war and conscientious objectors. Still standing, he brought the fork to his mouth and savored the first bite.

John considered himself an open-minded man. He perused the *Worker's* pages for answers. Not so for Father Murphy, whose jaundiced eye saw the columnists of the *Worker* as socialists stirring up an unpatriotic anti-war brew. While the pastor refrained from giving John an actual directive to cancel his subscription, his judgment was rendered in stony silence, a raised eyebrow here and an accidental toss of the paper into the trash can there. His Sunday sermons made it eminently clear: Peter Murphy stood firmly with the bishops who sided with the pro-war Roosevelt Administration and popular opinion on the matter. Thanks to Franco, and the Church's own longstanding antipathy toward communism, the bishops lined up on the side of war. Or, certainly, they did not stand against it, too blinkered even to consider Rev. Barry O'Toole's theological arguments and appeal to Matthew 5:1-12. Well, wasn't it always so? 'Blessed are the peacemakers for they shall see God' and all the other Beatitudes were merely principles to aim for rather than laws to be obeyed. Or so John decided, in his fervent desire to get off the seesaw of debate and square his conscience with fealty to Church authorities.

The war was a touchy subject, and John dared not discuss his misgivings with the pastor or anyone else. He had talked the matter over with one or two of his keen and more circumspect acolytes, Ed Hohlfeld and Bob McCann. He was in no danger there, after all. Those discussions came under the aegis of friendship and private counsel. Over a few drinks, he had broached the topic with three priest friends who got together to play cards on Sunday nights at the end of a long day of baptisms and masses, but even here, John stepped lightly. He was not surprised to learn that while they weren't gung-ho, they did come down on the pro-war side. For John to challenge them or the Church would be career suicide. John had to keep his eye on the prize. A Monsignor's cap did not seem far off, and, maybe, one day, who knew? Back to Rome? Perhaps Cardinal in his future? Bolstered by his mother's hopes, he lived for thirty-seven years with the promise of a special calling, and he felt certain his elevator did not stop at the first floor of parish priest.

An incessant doorbell followed by several loud knocks at the front door jolted John, and his plate smacked to the floor. Pieces of

China flew everywhere, and the last chunk of apple pie with them, onto Mrs. Harrigan's spotless floor.

"Oh my God, she's going to kill me," John said aloud as he strode to the door, wondering who had the gall to intrude on his precious Friday evening off.

Annoyed, he strode to the vestibule. "Coming, coming," he called as he opened the door. "Why, Ed, what in the . . ."

"It's happened, Father," he said, the rain drumming down on his hatless head. "They've called me up. Can you help me?"

John McGuire had hoped it wouldn't come to this. He didn't want to embarrass the Church or call attention to himself at a time when his carefully constructed career might be left hanging in the balance. He ushered his drenched friend into the vestibule and contemplated how he might help the young man, as promised, without risking his own promising career.

## Chapter 3

# The Die is Cast

"That's it? Said his hands were tied?" Chappy drummed a matchbook on the chipped oak bar, his eyes peering anxiously into Ed's.

"Yep. Said he spoke to the bishop. Did what he could, but non-military CO status is hard to support, especially for Catholics. The Church ain't on my side." Ed raised his glass at Nick, the bartender, and held up two fingers with his other hand.

"And did he," Chappy pressed him. "Do what he could?"

Ed shrugged. "He's a priest. I'm guessing he did." Ed's feigned nonchalance masked his terror. He was aware of his responsibilities to his family and country, but why must they come before the obligation to his conscience? And why wouldn't the Church back him up? The only conclusion he could draw was that this must be God's will like Father McGuire suggested.

"Comin' right up, Ed." Nick hollered over the barroom din.

On the other side of the bar, a group of men playing darts whooped and hollered. Ed drained his beer and tried to slow down his thoughts. Like a fly in the kitchen that didn't know where best to land, his mind flitted back and forth. It landed, finally, on something the priest kept saying.

"The question you must keep before you here, Ed, is, what is God's will not what my will is. In some matters, those in authority *do* know best." It was a different tune compared to the one the priest had sung in their previous conversations. Maybe he was right. Maybe this was God's way of telling Ed what he wanted of him, even if his gut gnawed at him and told him otherwise. There were lots of guys like him. He'd read their letters on the editorial pages of *The Catholic Worker*. But who was he kidding? Even if the Church did support his CO application, his family couldn't go without his weekly pay, and they sure as hell couldn't afford the $35.00 monthly room and board fee at the Catholic CO camp they'd just opened in New Hampshire. That was out of the question.

Nick grabbed the men's empty mugs and spun around to fill them from the Schmidt's tap. As he set them down, he joked. "Not like you to have more than one or two, Ed. Why so glum? Girl broke your heart?"

"Something like that." Ed gave him a wry smile. Nick walked away, chuckling.

"Well, you tried, buddy. You tried." Chappy clapped Ed on the back. "What else can you do? At least we'll be going together. Might be in the same unit. That's something." He gestured to the draft card in his wallet.

Ed nodded absently.

"Look, Ed." Chappy wiped beer froth from his upper lip after taking a long swallow. "I respect you because I know you're a good man." He paused, his eyes wet from too much drink or tears. Ed couldn't tell which.

"The best. You have a good heart." Here he thumped his chest and almost fell off the stool. Ed reached over and steadied him. He'd been drinking when Ed got there and was still going strong. "You're sincere and all. I get that. You want to do the right thing. But this religion stuff you take way too serious, buddy. Have to take it with a grain of salt. The stuff in that *Worker* paper . . . I don't know. I tried to read it and all like you asked, but I can't figure out whether they're asking people to be saints or pinkos. Know what I mean? Who the hell can be a pacifist? That stuff ain't meant for regular guys like us. You think way too much, buddy. 'Blessed be the peacemakers?' Are you kidding me? It's war. Men have always gone to war, and we're on the right side here, Ed. Freedom and democracy. You see that, right? He clapped Ed on the back again before returning to his beer.

Funny thing was, on this point, Ed agreed. Fascism was evil, and men had always gone to war, and for far less righteous reasons. But that didn't mean Ed could. Ed suspected he wasn't like other guys. He'd known ever since he was a little kid that he was different, and it wasn't just because of his strong faith. His father taught him how to stand up for himself, sure, but he thought with his head, not his fists. His conscience was his compass in matters of right and wrong. How could it be God's will for him to be a soldier when he felt in his heart that war and killing were wrong? He hoped his best friend would understand his dilemma. But Chappy didn't get it. Ed kept trying, and they continued to argue until Ed was as drunk as Chappy. The long night ended on a sour note. They stumbled out of Willy's and went their separate ways. On the walk home, Ed tried to brace himself for what lay ahead. He already knew where his father stood. The old man scoffed at Ed's qualms. Ed was too soft. Ed owed something to the country that had taken in his father and mother's family.

"Besides, you're half-German, son. Remember that. You're vulnerable. Look at what happened to Adolf Voss." His dad was right about

31

that. A few nights before, Ed and his father had been playing cards on the front stoop when federal agents flashed their badges to Mrs. Voss before carting her good-hearted husband away. They watched helplessly as Mr. Voss's shocked face disappeared into the back seat of a black car. They didn't know where he was taken, and they hadn't seen him since. Their neighbor was a stand-up guy who had never broken the law.

But before he came to the U.S., he was a member of some German organization. German aggression in recent months brought the group and its members under scrutiny. It had something to do with a new law called the Smith Act. Seemed to Ed that these days the American government was paranoid, finding criminals in innocent immigrants who were just trying to be good Americans. The government started targeting and rooting out suspected foreign agents. It seemed like a catch-22 for German Americans: to register was to be singled out, attracting government scrutiny. Fail to register and, well, it's deportation for you, buddy, naturalized citizen or not. It didn't seem fair. He feared the law might hurt honest, hard-working people, especially since the seizure of the Britain-bound USS City of Flint by the German Navy the year before. Like kindling to a fire, the attack heated up the war and fearmongering on the Homefront. Both his father and Adolf Voss had strong roots in America. They despised Hitler's power-grab in Europe. It gave German Americans a black eye. Ed hoped Mr. Voss was okay. He was a good man. Generous, too. Ed shook his head, recalling how Mr. Voss came over with homemade sausages for the meat deprived Hohlfelds last Christmas. And his father's counsel echoed in Ed's head. "These days, you must *prove* you're *American*, son. Religion? Faith? Why, let the priests take care of those matters."

Ed surveyed the black sky. He finally reached his stoop, a little woozy from the beer and the train of thoughts running back and forth between two tracks in his head. If Ed couldn't get his own father to come around, what made him think Chappy could understand. No, Ed was on his own. He would have to put his misgivings aside. He would obey the law and report for duty. The choice seemed to have been made for him. God's will be done.

*Chapter 4*

# "When Freemen Shall Stand"

The train squealed and whistled its way south beneath a powder-blue autumn sky. Two solitary puffs of cloud in the shape of a man's perfectly coiffed mustache peered down at him. Ed wondered what type of bird he might paint to complete the picture. It would have to be bold and graceful. A falcon, maybe an American Kestrel. Blue-gray wings with a brown back and tail. A Peregrine would be larger but not as colorful. Aiming his pencil at the blank paper on his lap, he started with the wings and tried to quell his smoldering anxiety.

The revelry on this boot camp bound train had finally morphed into a hum of chatter punctuated by nervous laughter. One guy was whistling. Al Jolson tunes mostly. "For Me and My Gal" and "When the Red, Red Robin goes bob bobbin' along." George from Staten Island told the guy to "shut up, already," but others liked it and told George to pipe down. Whistler, they called him now. "Hey, Whistler, give us an Ink Spot tune." When he started on "I Don't Want to Set the World on Fire," they yelled. "That's Hooey. Give us some Benny Goodman." He happily complied, and started whistling, "Sing, Sing, Sing with a Swing." Another guy chimed in with a harmonica, and a third pulled out a couple of spoons and started thumping on the metal-framed seats. The drummer was a small, wiry guy with wispy blonde hair. They called him Popeye because his eyes protruded, the whites of his eyeballs too large for the eye socket. He seemed unfazed by the ribbing. Used to it probably. A New Yorker from Queens, he told Ed. Boy, he sure could bang those sticks. A couple of other guys started singing and swinging in the aisle until several unanticipated tunnels and sharp zigzags sat them down. The horsing around broke up the tedium of the ride and kept the train-car fear and uncertainty at bay.

Ed watched daylight ebb through the train window and let his pencil fall slack in his hand. His seatmate Frank snored quietly. Heat rose from the bowels of the train and blasted through the cars. The sweat on his trousers and shirt glued Ed to the frayed leather seat. He shifted slightly, careful not to drop his sketchpad. The piquant citrus of Old Spice mingled with sweat wafted in the air. Ed wasn't the only Old Spice man on the train bound for Camp Crofton in Spartanburg. He took a Lucky Strike from his pocket, tapped it twice on the seat in front of him, and placed it between his lips. After lighting it, he took a long pull, letting the smoke permeate his hungry lungs. He exhaled in short, quick bursts, tucking the cigarette between the fore-finger and thumb of his right hand, his free hand fluttering upward to push the stray locks off his forehead.

"Hey, buddy, do you have another smoke?" Frank sat up. He yawned and rubbed his eyes awake. "My gal made me give them up. Thinking I might just pick it back up 'til we get back from this here mess." Like most of the other guys, Frank boarded the train with bravado, laced with a healthy dose of humor and goodwill.

"Sure." Ed secured his own cigarette between his lips and took the pack from his left front pocket, shaking it until a cigarette popped up, and Frank retrieved it. He slid the pack back and pulled a book of matches from his pocket and handed them to Frank, a fellow Philly man. The men chit-chatted and smoked. Frank wondered whether or not the Phillies would ever get out of the basement and if Boom-Boom Beck, the oldest member of the team, should pack it in. Frank pointed out that the Eagles were headed in the same miserable direction. They'd already lost to the Giants twice, and the season was just getting started. Ed told him about his job at the factory and, when asked about the doodling on his pad, admitted that, yeah, he liked to draw, and he painted some. Frank asked questions, but he did more talking than listening. He was working for the Reading Railroad in Port Richmond when Uncle Sam tapped him on the shoulder. He'd just turned twenty and was married less than a year. His wife was pregnant and due in the coming weeks, so naturally, Frank worried about her and the baby. She'd been on bed rest for two months. He'd have to find a way to call her from boot camp and hoped that wouldn't be a problem. Although they had a small apartment, they decided it was best for his wife to move back in with her folks until the war ended. Her two sisters did the same when their husbands joined the Navy.

Frank paused, taking a long pull from his cigarette. He exhaled. "Goddamn, it's hot. Ain't it? For early November? It's like fall high-tailed it for a few days. How much longer you think we got to go?"

Ed glanced out the window and shrugged. "Heard someone say not too much longer once we hit North Carolina. Almost there."

Ed leaned back and propped his knee against the window. He was dog-tired, but his legs and arms felt tingly, like they were on red alert. Felt like this since he left the induction center with orders to report to Camp Crofton. He'd managed to tuck a sketchpad and pencils in among his personal belongings, along with a photograph of his nine-year-old sister, Mary, who insisted he take it so he wouldn't forget her. He smiled, remembering.

"Oh, sweetheart, don't you worry. I could never forget you." Ed slid the photo into his bag. They were standing at the front door. He cradled Mary's head.

"Be sure to help Mom when I am away." His eyes and voice softened. "We'll see each other soon enough. Now, you keep working on your sketches, okay? I'll check them when I get back."

Tears sprang to her eyes. Mary nodded. "I promise. And I'll write you stories about what's going on at home, so you won't be lonely without us. Mom said I could. What do you think about that, Ed?"

I think it's a swell idea, Mary. But I might not always be able to write you back, so don't be disappointed, okay? The truth was he didn't know what to expect. When he gave her a goodbye squeeze, Mary held on tight.

"Heard this Quaker guy talking back there." Frank jostled him from his reverie, motioning to the rows behind them. "A few seats behind? Other side."

Ed turned and followed his thumb. "Oh, yeah?"

"Small guy, black hair. Wearing spectacles. Bookworm type."

Ed recognized the man with whom he had exchanged a few pleasantries at the Maryland stop. "Huh, don't say? A Quaker?"

"I'm a Protestant myself," Frank said smugly. "You know, you got your Protestants, your Catholics, and some Jews too, a 'course. Those are square religions. I don't get this Quaker business at all. Know what I mean?" Frank threw his hands in the air like he was brushing away a pesky fly. He didn't pause for a reply.

"Why, did you know they don't have no ministers or religious services? Just sit in a room and mostly don't talk? Now, I'm not prejudiced, mind you. I have to work with all kinds down at the railroad. Believe you me, Jack. But there's something strange about that. Dontcha think?" Assuming agreement, Frank continued. "Where do these Quakers get off? That fella says he applied for something called conscientious objector status, and he's waiting to hear back. What the hell does that even *mean*? He won't fight those Krauts, he says. Don't believe in killing for no reason. Can you beat the hell out of that?"

Frank paused and eyed his seatmate. Ed wished the guy would fall back to sleep. What would he think if he knew Ed's heart moved him in the same direction as the Quaker's? Ed pulled his knee back down and straightened his back. He took a final drag and dropped the butt, crushing it with his shoe heel on a floor already littered with butts and candy wrappers. He glanced out the window before finally turning back to Frank.

"Well, I respect a man who stands up for his beliefs, Frank. Every man has to live with himself and his conscience. Don't he? You think that's an easy road he's taking, the whole American country against him and all? He won't be getting off scot-free either. Has to do an alternative service of some kind if they approve his request. Has to pay for it out of his own pocket, too, unless his church picks up part of the tab."

Frank gave Ed a sidelong glance, suddenly uncertain of Ed or maybe himself. The muscular shoulders, which didn't match his round, cherubic face, puffed up in reassurance. "Huh, well, maybe there's something to that, but if Franklin D. Roosevelt himself says he needs men to stand up for the good old U.S. of A., I just don't know how a *real* man can turn his back."

Ed left the discussion at that, grateful when Frank finally slid back down in his seat, pulled his cap over his eyes, and fell into a cave of slumber.

For most guys, it was that simple. My country 'tis of thee sweet land of liberty was enough to settle the question, even if this sweet land was about to join a world gone mad with violence. Ed got it. The Nazis had to be stopped. Roosevelt was right when he referred to Hitlerism as evil itself in his Labor Day address. But for guys like Ed, it was not quite that simple. Turning his head, he eyed Chappy sitting a few rows behind and on the other side of the train. He had avoided Ed when they boarded at Fort Dix. He was still a little sore, but they would be okay. They went too far back not to be. Chappy might not understand his peace-loving friend, but he'd always have his back, and Ed would have his, even on the battlefield if it came to that. His body winced, unable to picture himself shooting another man. Thinking wasn't helping. Ed had to stop thinking. "Ours is not to wonder why, ours is but to do or die." Hell, where did that come from? The pulpit? Had he learned it in school? Maybe this was exactly the answer he needed. Not to question. Not to doubt. Just do. He suddenly felt very tired. Stretching his long legs, he slumped back and gave himself over to the clackety-clack of the wheels. His fingers reached beneath his collar and tugged on the St. Christopher Medal that hung around his neck before tucking it back inside. Then he crossed his arms and delivered his exhausted mind over to slumber.

Ed was floating alongside an American Kestrel against an indigo sky when the train whistled and screeched to a halt, jolting Ed awake. He sat up and rubbed his eyes. Frank gave him a hand-up, and he made his way to the aisle. His back felt like a knotted rope, and his legs were cramping. It was a relief to stand and stretch and move again. He grabbed his bag and followed the trail of sluggish bodies down the steps and into the fresh air. The men lit cigarettes to pass the time. A couple of the guys lay down and stretched out on the damp ground.

Most, like Ed, paced and made small talk for what seemed like an hour but was probably just minutes, until a line of buses pulled up, and they piled aboard. As the bus rumbled through a guard post at the entrance to the camp, Ed gazed through its front window at a half-moon and a shower of stars pinned against the black drape of sky, nothing like the one in his dream. He glanced at his watch, a gold Gruen given him by his father and mother on his 25th birthday. It had belonged to his grandfather. "The best in German design," his father said when he gave it to him. "And it looks just like the one Fr. McGuire wears," his mother cooed. Ed blinked away the memory and held his watch to the moon's pale light. It was 8:03.

"All right," the genial driver announced as the bus rattled to a stop at the end of a long, winding roadway. "Home, sweet home, fellas. Good luck!"

A rush of movement and sound followed as guys scrambled out of their seats, yawning, grunting, cursing, and hoping to find a bed at the end of their long journey. Ed stood up when he saw Chappy amble down the aisle. His friend paused, clapped his shoulder and half-smiled as he pushed Ed forward and down the steps. He and Chappy joined the other men who shuffled and waited in the shadow of a lone flagpole surrounded by dust and open space.

Out of the dark, someone yelled. "What the hell's a guy gotta do to get a bed in this town?" It set off a round of snickers and jokes. Within minutes, a wavering flashlight with a husky voice behind it arrived like an apparition. The flashlight, flanked by two soldiers, led Ed and the others on a short march to an endless row of two-story gray and white clapboard structures several hundred yards from where the bus had stopped. Ed looked back and watched the red taillights of the bus wink and disappear along the twisty road back to freedom. He shuffled a Lucky from his pocket, leaning over to offer one to Chappy before lighting up.

"Welcome to 3rd Platoon Company B of the 32nd Infantry and BCT, basic combat training," the voice behind the flashlight barked, scanning the sea of expectant faces. "This is your goddamn unlucky day because you drew the short straw and got me. I'm Stanley Kaczynski, your drill sergeant. Let's get started on the right foot, fellas. I'm the bastard who will make your life miserable in the coming weeks. It's my job to turn you raw recruits into soldiers in record time, and so help me gawd, that's what I'll do, or I'll kill y'all trying. I'll be with you, morning, noon, and night, so get used to this sweet voice and pretty face, fellas." He aimed the flashlight at his pockmarked face that was anything but pretty and turned it back toward the recruits. Noting the rash of red tips from lit cigarettes, his bark turned into a low growl. "Y'all best put out those cigs."

Ed looked around, relieved to see he wasn't the only one to have lit up.

"Pvt. Sellers will lead you to the processing center where y'all get a pretty new haircut and trade in those civvies for the uniform of the U.S. Army. Now, I want to hear a loud and clear, 'Yes, Sergeant' when I call your name." He ticked off names, pausing after Ed called, "Yes, Sergeant" in response to "Hohlfeld."

Ed's hands grew clammy. Why did a pause come after Ed's reply?

"Holmes, Robert," Kaczynski elongated the name, making it sound like a dirty word in need of correction. Ed recognized the man as the Quaker his seatmate Frank pointed out earlier.

"Yes, Sergeant," Holmes's voice came from somewhere behind Ed.

Kaczynski took three long strides to the left, brushing past Ed, and planted himself in front of the Quaker. Ed looked back and saw a slender man who stood maybe 5'7". Holmes looked even smaller in the hulking shadow of the sergeant.

"Now, Holmes, what was I saying before about recruits and soldiers? Oh, wait a minute," he said, glaring at the man and holstering the clipboard under his arm like a concealed weapon. "You're not aiming to be a soldier at all, are you, Robert Holmes? What in the Sam-hill are you doing here with the rest of these guys that'll be busting their asses to prove themselves worthy to be in this here Army? Putting their asses on the line for Uncle Sam and democracy around the world. What did you just hear me say? Huh? Why are you standing here with these men?" The air trembled. An owl hooted in the distance.

Ed cringed. Clearly, the sergeant knew who the soldier was and why he was here. This moment was an opportunity to make a point to the rest of them.

"I'm IV-E, a conscientious objector, sergeant. I'm waiting for my alternative service camp assignment. There was a problem with my paperwork. It was held up, and I was instructed to report here. Thou are tasked with turning recruits into soldiers, Sergeant."

A few men snickered. Others leaned forward to get a better look.

The man had a funny way of talking, but Ed was struck more by his composure.

A miffed Kaczynski glared at the CO, leaving no doubt as to which man would prevail in this exchange. "Are you a smart-ass, Holmes? Have a special way of talking, do *thou*? Think you're smarter and better than everybody else here, huh? Special, maybe? Think you shouldn't have to put your life on the line to preserve our rights like every other able-bodied man in the country?"

The sergeant had no business shaming the man. Back in his neighborhood or down at the plant Ed might step up and defend him, but here there were different codes. He wasn't in the old neighborhood. He was in this sergeant's army.

Holmes' voice quivered, but he held fast. "No, Sergeant, I'm a Quaker, sir, and we don't believe in violence. We have a long history of following our conscience, of Social Witness and Peace . . ."

"Shut up." Kaczynski spat at the man's face. "Get the hell out of my sight, you yella belly. You make me sick. You don't deserve to stand in the company of these men. Now, see if you can follow this." He snarled, aiming an angry thumb at one of the privates behind him. Holmes picked up his bag and moved away from the sergeant. He glanced back and shook his head as if to apologize, not for himself but for Kaczynski, and marched into the darkness.

Hours later, head shorn, Ed lumbered into their barracks, still rattled from Kaczynski's treatment of the Quaker. He reached up to push his pesky locks from his forehead, only to find stubble.

Sgt. Kaczynski flipped on a light switch, waved the men in, and gestured toward the thin rolled-up mattresses and the two rows of cot frames. Each cot came equipped with a mattress, sheets, and a green woolen blanket with U.S. Army stamped on it in black letters. He stationed himself at the top of the barracks, furthest from the latrine, and proceeded to demonstrate the proper way to make a military rack. He tugged the sheets under the mattress with the proper 45-degree corner until not a wrinkle showed and then did the same thing with the blanket, placing a pillow in a clean case with a dust cover over it at the top of the bunk. At the conclusion of his demonstration, he took a quarter from his pocket and threw it on the bed and got the required result as it bounced on the perfectly flat, tight surface. Then he demonstrated how to arrange their boots at the side of the bed and showed them where and how to hang their personal belongings.

"I want everyone's space to look exactly the same, no variation, no deviation. Got that?"

A chorus of "Yes, Sergeant" followed.

Ed shifted his weight several times to stay awake during the demonstration, glad to be at the opposite end of the barracks. His body ached to drop onto his bunk and disappear into the black and forgiving world of sleep. Instead, Kaczynski ordered them to follow suit.

"Once you find your assigned racks, drop those duffels in there," he ordered to no one in particular, while pointing to the footlockers that sat at the bottom of their bunks. "Then I want to see you make them up."

Ed rolled out his mattress and started working on his bunk. It was second to the end and nearer the latrine, just like it had been in CCC camp. He had done fine there. Liked it even, he thought, as he measured, straightened, tightened, and tucked. It was regimented there as well, but he had woken up each morning to build roads and bridges not to kill other human beings. Maybe he could speak with the major. See if there was another way around this. He would see what Chappy thought about that idea. Or not. He scanned the barracks and found Chappy in the middle on the other side, right across from Whistler. Chappy acknowledged his buddy with a mock salute. Ed grinned. It felt reassuring to have his best friend here. Even so, Ed fretted. He'd had to comply with the law, but his conscience could not be so easily salved. What would he do when push finally came to shove?

Kaczynski made them repeat the rack-making process four times before he was satisfied, railing the entire time about the men's slowness and stupidity. Ed sneaked a look at his watch. It was 1:30 a.m.

"All right, start shutting it down," Kaczynski barked as he made his way to a doorway into his private quarters at the back of the barracks. "Tomorrow, after roll call and drills, you'll report back to the induction center. Fill out some forms—insurance and benefits to dependents and the like. Take a test to tell us what the hell you have to offer Uncle Sam and this war effort. We're going to be at war, fellas. Mark my words." His eyes swept the room to ensure that his words were, indeed, marked. "By the time I'm done with you, you will be good and ready for it because you *will* be needed on the battle-field. Lights out in fifteen. I want to see fresh shaves in the morning. Reveille at 0430."

When his head finally hit the pillow, Ed noticed an uprooted brown spider scurrying back and forth on the ceiling who couldn't seem to settle on a spot. He examined the support pillars that held up the barracks. Pine. A soft wood, but sturdy. Looks like the building was hastily erected. His eyes drooped. Within minutes he was half-dreaming and back in the bosom of his Port Richmond home, tucked away in his studio in front of a fresh canvas, pencil in hand and a palette of colors before him. Somewhere though, at the back of his dream, a shadow crept up. He watched as it eclipsed the palette.

*Chapter 5*

# Sergeant Kaczynski

Morning came like an icy cold bath on a January day. The long day was a blur of lines and paperwork. Ed kept nodding off during Captain Sweeney's orientation lecture on the "Do's, Don'ts, and Musts" of camp life. A large map of the 167,000-acre-camp behind him, Sweeney pointed out the post office and service center, the stockade and chapel, and an assortment of other buildings. Except for the chapel on Sunday, he informed them, the men were not at liberty to visit any of these places until they completed basic training. Every waking hour would be spent in the company of their NCO, their drill sergeant, whose job it was to teach them how to do everything by the numbers: how to make a rack and wear the uniform properly, how to stand at attention and salute an officer, how to drill, march, and fire a rifle.

"Consider your rifle your battle buddy, recruits." The captain at the front of the room made a lame stab at humor, telling them that until they were trained on the M1 Garand they would be issued an RB. "Your own rubber ducky. Ha, ha, ha. "

Ed winced. His two years in the CCC had prepared him for Crofton's 12-hour-day regimen but not the prospect of becoming cozy with a firearm. He uncrossed his legs, rubbed his eyes, and lit a cigarette. He scanned the auditorium filled with fresh-faced recruits. There was no stopping the war machine now, Ed glumly realized. Would all of them see action? How many would make it back? The guys in the barracks had been speculating about where they might be sent, but "over there" somewhere was a foregone conclusion if you believed the papers and the gossip. Recruits were waking up to the reality of what it meant to be in Uncle Sam's Army, far from familiar patterns and people. Homesickness within sight of home was one thing. Across an ocean in the midst of battle, it promised to be quite another. Ed's hand reached up and finger-brushed the nubs of remaining hair on his newly shaven scalp.

In the days that followed, every minute was accounted for. Time was no longer a private matter in a rigidly controlled world of sameness. Same haircut, same clothing, same activities. No space for individuality or chance to catch up on lost sleep. He'd have to learn to get by on less. After the bugle sounded first call at 04:30, Ed stumbled from his cot. He grabbed his shaving kit and followed the trickle of men to the sinks in the latrine. Six small white sinks sat against a drab wall. A frameless mirror and naked light bulb hung above each one. The cold cement floor startled his feet and legs to life each morning. Nearby was a large open area with showerheads. The urinals and toilets, as well as a single metal washing tub, lined the far wall. After morning roll call came calisthenics—the jumping jacks, push-ups, and squats. A 5-mile jog-hike through peach fields followed PT, and all of this before breakfast, with Kaczynski harping at them the whole time to pick up the pace.

"Man up," Kaczynski yelled. "You're not even carrying packs yet or running the obstacle course." He spun around and ran backward, taunting and barking. "What? Some of you girls didn't get your beauty sleep last night?" He was a barrel of a man, thick through the chest and waist, with biceps punching their way out of his crisp khaki shirt. His hat was round and wide-brimmed in the front. It looked down on a square jaw and thunderous voice of the iron-willed man who wore it.

Ed's head and legs throbbed. It seemed like every muscle in his body was screaming at him to slow down, to rest, to think. To think. Fat chance of that with Kaczynski driving them like cattle on a range. The mild fall was good and gone away, and the day was gray and chilly. Weighed down by utter exhaustion and a troubled heart, Ed dragged his body through the gray dawn. Did God really want him to be a soldier? Was he testing his faith? His head felt foggy. On Sunday, he would go to the chapel for services. Talk with the chaplain. Then he'd speak with Kaczynski. No, that wouldn't work. He'd put in a request to speak with the officer in command regarding a "personal" matter. Explain his misgivings. Maybe see if the military could reconsider his status. Yeah, that'd make more sense. He'd have to do it soon. He would explain that he was a man of faith who couldn't be a party to killing. That's it, he decided. That's what he'd do. The prospect of taking decisive action cleared his head and lightened his load. Ed picked up his pace.

During company time on the third morning, Kaczynski strode into the barracks and called the men to attention.

"All right, now, here's the drill, so pay close attention. I want you to grab your duffel bags . . ." Popeye, three cots away from Ed, moved toward his trunk, only to be halted abruptly by Kaczynski's stinging rebuke. "Not now, you idiot. Did I finish giving the order? Did I?"

Popeye froze. "No, Sergeant."

"No, I did not. Now the barracks just lost 15 minutes of personal time tonight, thanks to you."

The barracks moaned in unison, shooting dirty looks in Popeye's direction.

"Grab those duffel bags and throw them in a pile here," he snapped, motioning to the open space in front of him. "Then step back."

Ed looked over at Chappy, who raised a bewildered eyebrow before throwing his mud-green bag down onto the painted cement floor. Ed and the others did the same, making a small hill of identical Army-issued bags before returning to their respective places.

Kaczynski pulled a pocket watch from his trousers and pressed a button. "All right. Beginning now, you have one minute to locate and retrieve your duffel bag and stand back at attention."

The men hesitated, a few moving toward the bags uncertainly. A guy they called Tiny, who bunked next to Ed, tugged at his ear. "What the hell is he talking about? They all look the same. How can we . . ."

"That's 5 seconds." Pause. "10."

That led to a mad scramble as the men pushed and shoved one another to the pile, frantically trying to find their bag. Ed saw Chappy take an elbow to the head that knocked him backward. He reached out and pulled him up with one arm while his other arm riffled through the pile. Tempers flared. In the melee, Ed tripped and fell forward. He sprang up and lunged back to the bags. He thought he had found his until someone behind him grabbed it.

"Hey, that's mine. Give it here." Turned out it wasn't his or Ed's. Maybe six or seven guys had moved away from the pile with their bags. How many minutes had elapsed? They would get nowhere this way. Out of the corner of his eye, he saw a big guy. Stu, they called him. He was pummeling someone. Whistler? Ed's hands kept frantically searching, vainly trying to help the other guys when they identified their bag while warding off frantic knees and elbows. Seeking his own duffel, Ed inadvertently knocked Popeye down. "Sorry, buddy." Ed paused to help him up. Another scuffle broke out. Someone yelled, "Get off me, you bastard!" The whistle blew. Confused, the men hustled back to their places. A jumble of bags lay strewn on the floor.

Kaczynski snorted and ordered all of them to throw the duffels back into the center. Then he held up his stopwatch and clicked. "Again."

The drill went on for nearly 30 minutes until Kaczynski made his point. Work with and not against one another. The unit's success depended upon the individual's ability to forsake his own goals for the sake of the group. It was necessary to work together. If you grabbed your bag, what good did it do if others in the team were left behind? If the team didn't win, even if *you* won, you lost. If a guy's uniform didn't comply with the gig line or a quarter didn't bounce from his cot, the barracks got zapped with 100 push-ups or docked personal time. All were punished for the mistakes of one. They had to learn to look out for one another. This was a mandate Ed could live with. It was the killing part that troubled him.

Two weeks later, Ed's request to meet with Major George Hanson, the commanding officer, was finally approved. When he arrived at HQ, Ed saluted the officer correctly, as instructed, and was told to stand at ease. He felt anything but at ease as he examined the wall behind the major's desk. It held a large poster filled with precise specifications and instructions for the marking of soldiers' caps, duffel bags, helmets, and combat boots. These were just the regulations for uniforms. There was a procedure and rule for everything. He shifted his uneasy gaze back to the man behind the desk.

The major had salt and pepper hair and sported a Clark Gable mustache. He was probably 50, maybe 55, but trim and fit. His recently smoked pipe sat forlornly in an ashtray on his desk, giving off a pungent scent.

"Where do you hail from, soldier?" He leaned back and folded his hands behind his head. He wasn't as begrudging with the term as old-school Kaczynski's was. The sergeant insisted on referring to them as recruits until the successful completion of basic training. Only then did they become bona fide soldiers.

"I come from Philly, sir. Northeast part. Port Richmond, sir."

"That so? Not familiar with that part of the country. Settling in okay, are you?" Not begrudging *and* amiable! Ed took this as a good sign, and a wave of optimism passed over him.

"Yes, sir. Just fine. Thank you, sir."

"What can I do for you, soldier? Got a wife back home about to have a baby? A trace of a smile played around his mouth. He was in a chatty mood and talked on a bit about the merits of an Army career and how some people said it didn't go well with family life, but he disagreed. He was a lifer with a wife and five kids back in Omaha who were preparing to move south. It had worked out just fine. Hard but doable. But with the country going to war to defend democracy, of course, it highlighted the hazards and costs, and blah, blah, blah.

Ed's mind wandered in and out during the major's monologue. He knew the major had given Frank permission to call home. His wife had given birth to a baby girl. She named her Frances. Frank teared up when he told Ed about her. They were in the barracks a few nights after they arrived, bent over a card table squeezing in a hand of poker before lights out. Frank, Chappy, Whistler, Popeye, and Ed. Ed could see Frank was distracted. He wasn't his usual raucous self, slamming down cards when he got a flush or full house. "There, suckers," he'd say. But tonight, Frank was already out of the game. After Ed's hand folded, he lit a cigarette and offered one to Frank, who shifted his chair away from the group.

"What's up, buddy?" The game was heating up, and the other guys were arguing about a point of order.

"It's Susie. The baby. She had a . . . a girl." He held the tears in check, but his voice quivered. "Frances, she called her Frances. I just hope I get back to see her."

Ed slapped him on the back. He leaned in, careful to whisper. "Hey, Frank, that's terrific news. Congratulations." He wasn't expecting a girl, Ed realized and had probably never imagined himself as a father to one. Hadn't likely considered the fact that instead of holding his newborn, he'd be holding a rifle either. Maybe he had to see it as holding a rifle because of her.

"It'll be okay. You'll get through this. You'll get back to your baby girl." Was he saying this to Frank or himself? "Who's got the cigars? We should be celebrating."

The spell was broken. Frank grinned, "Yeah, Ed, you're right. A celebration." He stood up and thrust his arm upward. "Hey, guys," he shouted. "I'm a father. First time. My wife had a baby girl. Frances. But I don't have any cigars."

The guys at the card table let out a cheer. Pretty soon, the whole barracks hopped on the celebration bus. It was a good excuse to let off steam. Bret Hinton, a cigar smoker from upstate New York, produced some King Edwards. Even Kaczynski, who sprang out of his private rooms when he heard the ruckus, offered a toast and a pat on the back to the new father.

The major was winding down his account of Army life with a family, snapping Ed back to the present and the task before him. "So, soldier, is that it? Are you here about a family issue?"

"No, sir," but I'm troubled."

The major tugged at his earlobe. "Why is that?"

Coiled behind his back, Ed's hands trembled. Beads of moisture popped out on his forehead and upper lip. He tried to remember the script he'd prepared in his head. Tried explaining how he thought he'd made a mistake by not standing by his Catholic faith that told him it was wrong to kill. How he was respectfully requesting that his classification . . .

Cutting Ed's recitation short, the major's tone shifted. "Have you been classified IV-E, Hohlfeld?" His hands came from behind his head and braced the desk. His friendly demeanor evaporated.

"As what, sir?"

"Did you submit an application for and receive classification as a conscientious objector?"

"No, sir, I did not receive conscientious objector status, but if you let me explain . . .'"

"What about an I-O?"

"What? No, sir. My classification is I-A." But . . .."

The major's cold voice cut Ed off. "Well then, no ifs, ands, or buts about it. You're here. Decision was made. The board classified you as I-A. That's the end of it. You belong to the U.S. Army, son, and I can't treat you any differently than another fellow, can I? Give you special privileges the guy next to you don't get? Treat you like a prima donna? What would that do to platoon morale?" His face and voice hardened.

"No, sir, I don't think I'm asking for special privileges. I'm a man of faith who opposes violence. I'm ready to serve my country, sir. I just don't think I can kill."

"What kind of men do you think the other guys in your platoon are?" He gestured toward the window behind him and the camp beyond it. "Those are men of faith, too. Are you a coward? Is that what this is about?"

Ed paused to consider the question. "No, sir, I'm not a coward, and I can't speak for anyone else. The others have to follow their own conscience. I'm just trying to follow mine." There. I've said it. Relief flooded him the way it did when he made the sign of the cross and walked out of the confessional box.

"Dismissed." The major turned back to the papers on his desk.

"Sir, I . . . if you'd just let me explain . . . I want to serve, see, but I'm a Roman Catholic, and the teachings . . . my conscience . . . just won't let me . . . If I could just do something that didn't involve killing." He sputtered like a car engine threatening to break down. He knew very well what his conscientious objections were based on, but in the face of the officer's dismissive and contemptuous tone, his mind kept drawing blanks. It didn't matter anyway. Maj. George Hanson was no longer listening. He was good and done with Ed.

"Too late for that. I said, dismissed, soldier. The matter's been decided. You better get the hell out of my sight now, or you'll find yourself in the stockade." He aimed his pipe at Ed after taking two furious puffs. The private, who had stood behind Ed during the interview, escorted him from the office and to an outer door.

Ed trudged back through the dirt to the barracks in a fog. A redtailed hawk dipped and swerved several times in the distance, finally swooping down and disappearing in the brush. Victory. The hawk ascended gracefully, his prey securely in his mouth. Ground squirrel? Chipmunk? Ed had played his last hand and lost. What now? Where could he turn? He had to talk it over with Chappy, but not just yet. He had to think.

At roll call the next day, the sergeant paused after calling his name. When Ed replied, Kaczynski repeated his name, dragging out each of the letters. "H-o-h-l-f-e-l-d. What kind of name *is* that?" His voice was tight and menacing. Ed struggled to summon his voice.

"German."

"What's that? Can't hear you?"

"German," he said, with heat. His temple throbbed, and his hands felt suddenly clammy.

"German, what?"

"Yes, sorry. German, Sergeant." Get a grip, Ed told himself. He's working you.

"What's that, princess? Couldn't hear you."

In the crisp early morning air, a yellow warbler in the scrawny tree in front of the barracks sang *sweet, sweet, sweet*. "German, Sergeant."

"Louder."

"GERMAN, Sergeant!"

"That's right, H-o-h-l-f-e-l-d. German. You got another stake in this war? Is that what this conscientious objector bullshit is all about? You love Krauts or something? What about sauerkraut? Ya like that? Or are you just a plain chicken?"

Ed's heart sped up, and his head swirled in confusion. What the hell's he talking about? What's he trying to do? Where's this coming from? It must be Hanson. He stood, uncertainly, in the spotlight of Kaczynski's fury, and a blanket of troubled stillness settled over the platoon. He must've spoken with the major. Recalling Holmes, he steadied himself.

"No, Sergeant. I'm an American, Sergeant. Half-German and half-Irish."

"Are you a cowardly American, Hohlfeld?"

"No, Sergeant."

"Then by gawd, I don't want to hear any more about your belly-aching conscientious objecting bullshit. You got that H-o-h-l-f-e-l-d?"

"Yes, Sergeant."

"Good." His voice thundered. "When we're done here, I want that latrine cleaned with a toothbrush. Top to bottom. Bottom to top. Ya got that, H-o-h-l-f-e-l-d? Now, get your American ass down on the ground and give me a hundred. Drop."

Ed fell to the ground. He willed his stunned body to move up and down while his mind tried to make sense of the exchange. By the time he was finished, Kaczynski had moved on to another guy because his shirt was not buttoned properly, and a third who had fallen into line a minute or so late. The entire barracks paid for the infractions later that night. Personal time was confiscated.

During their hike the next day, Kaczynski was wound up.

"Move it, move it, move it. You sissy sons of bitches." He kept sidling over to Ed. His contorted face was an explosion waiting to happen.

"Let's see just how American you are, Hohlfeld. Pick it up. Pick it up, you son of a German bastard!"

Ed swallowed his taunts. He kept his head down and his feet moving. He couldn't let this guy get to him, break him. He had to tough it out. The sergeant's animosity would blow over. It had to. Ed would bide his time until he came up with another plan. He couldn't ignore his nagging conscience, and there had to be a way for him to be in this man's army and be true to himself. There just had to be. Right now, he had to survive Kaczynski.

Later, Ed found his way to the mess hall. It was orderly but loud as the men tried to make themselves heard over the clatter of tin plates and trays. The chow line moved slowly in a room that consisted of rows of wooden picnic tables. Lunch consisted of milk and a plate with brown meat in one slot, peas in the other, and lumpy potatoes in the third. Ed took a mouthful of peas and speared the meat, noting how the guys from his barracks walked past his table and avoided making eye contact. Chappy edged up to him and took a seat.

"Son of a bitch. That's not right." He settled in next to his friend. "About your name and all. What the hell was that about? You do something to get his attention, Ed? Huh?" Chappy bent over his chow and started swallowing large forkfuls of peas.

Ed shrugged, feigning indifference while his guts roiled. "I went to see the major."

"Goddamn it, Ed." Chappy smothered his fork with the thick curve of his hand, filled it with potatoes, and swallowed hard. "We talked about this. Didn't I tell you to let it go? You're in this. I'm in this. We're all . . ." and lifted his fist and motioned to the mess hall. "In this. I get it. I do. Your conscience and your soul and . . . all that. But the brass will not let a good man like you go. They're going to need as many men in the field as they can get. This is bigger than us, Ed. Bigger than you and your goddamned principles."

His comment caught Ed's fork mid-air. He slammed it down and glared at his friend.

"No, Chap," Ed said with finality. "You don't get it. I can't let it go. I think I messed up. If I can't stand up when push comes to shove, what kind of a man am I? Huh? When a thing is right, it's right, and when a thing is wrong, it's wrong. Not for you, maybe, but for me. There ain't no in-between. I told the man I can't be a part of killing. Why can't they give me that? Huh, why can't they?"

"I always said you were too stinking stubborn for your own good, Ed. Bite you in the ass one of these days, that stubbornness of yours, if you don't watch out."

The clatter in the mess hall masked the intensity of the exchange. They fell back to their food. Ed sipped his blackstrap coffee and pushed his disgusting fish-eyed pudding over to Chappy, who ate most anything.

"Thanks, buddy." Chappy softened. "Look, Ed, I'm on your side. I am. But I'm saying this for your own good. These guys, well, they have you by the balls."

"Right now, I think this war has us all by the balls," Ed added with a laugh, puncturing the balloon of tension that filled the air.

Chappy joined in, relieved to put the spat behind them. "Well," Kaczynski's just working you. It'll blow over. Maybe you'll figure something else out, or maybe they'll come around. Just keep your nose clean. Huh? It'll be all right. We'll go get shit-faced when this is all over. Right?" He forced a hopeful smile.

"Yeah, sure. Thanks, Chap." Ed pushed his plate away and pulled out a Lucky, tapping the end twice to secure the nicotine before bringing it up to his mouth. He hesitated a moment before lighting it. "What a mess over there, though. Huh? Poland, Yugoslavia, now Russia. Sonofabitch Hitler is on the goddamned warpath. So much death and destruction. For what? Power? Domination? What the hell's wrong with the world?"

"Beats the hell out of me." Having inhaled his second dessert, Chappy shrugged and then burped long and hard.

Hours later, Ed's head was curled beneath the urinal. He clutched a toothbrush between his cramping fingers, its bristles aimed at the crusty seams in the porcelain. His neck and back screamed at him. His uniform stank with sweat. He was dog-tired. His left hand acted like a relief pitcher for his more efficient right one and helped ease the ache in his upper arm.

"Okay," he said aloud. "Last one. Nearly done." He'd been at it for hours and couldn't wait to throw off his filthy work clothes, stand under a hot shower and throw on a pair of clean undershorts. With the motion of the toothbrush, his mind kept running back and forth over the problem. Chappy said he'd come up with something else, but so far as he could tell, there was no something else.

Ed longed for the luxury of personal time. He missed the simple things. Hoofing it around the city, playing baseball or having a beer with the guys, watching an image take shape on canvas. Times when he felt solid in his body and clear in his mind. He never did get to finish that hummingbird drawing. His mind's eye could see the brush strokes of green, gray, and red he would use when he got back to it. If he got back

A whoosh of an opening door and thud of boots startled him. When he heard a whistle, he assumed it was Whistler. It sounded like an old-time favorite, "Ma, I Miss Your Apple Pie." He was about to say something when the whistling stopped.

"Well, if it ain't the Nazi loving Kraut."

Stu. Ed ignored his comment and turned back to the task, dipping his brush in the bucket of bleach and water beside him. He heard the flush and squeak of boots moving across the wet floor in Ed's direction. For a moment, he wondered if he should stand up and face him down. No, too confrontational and risky. If Kaczynski didn't have it in for him, it would be a different matter. He kept scrubbing.

Stu's shadow loomed over Ed. At 6'3 or 6'4 and broad-shouldered, he flaunted his linebacker bulk.

"What can I do for you, Stu?" Ed kept his voice even. He'd managed bullies bigger and tougher than Stuart.

"You better watch your step, Hohlfeld." His ears were tiny, way too small for his wide face and newly shaven head. "I'm sick and tired of paying the price for your crap. You hearing this, Hohlfeld? Kaczynski's got it in for all of us because of you, and I'm sick and tired of paying for it. You better figure out which side of this war you're on, asshole, and make the man happy." He spat again and moved toward the door. "I sure as hell hope I don't find myself in a ditch over there with *your* kind, Kraut." The door closed with a thud.

Ed sat up, his back against the wall and knees drawn up. He dropped the toothbrush in the bucket and rested his head in his weary arms. It'll blow over, Chappy had said. He wondered. For the life of him, he couldn't figure out what to do. That wasn't right. He knew what he *had* to do. He just didn't know *how* without causing a stink. A problem was something you looked at methodically and with a clear head. If you looked into it long enough—the whys, the wherefores, and so on—you came up with a solution, a way forward. When things stayed fuzzy, you prayed. Usually, an answer came along just when you least expected it. That's how it worked. That's how it had always worked in the past. Now he felt like he was all alone, behind the wheel and flying blind.

The door banged open. Ed looked up to see Kaczynski's uniform looming over him.

"Ten-hut." Ed sprang to his feet and stood at attention, the tired toothbrush resting at his side.

"Sleeping on the job, Hohlfeld?" he sneered.

"No, Sergeant, I was just finishing up."

"Didn't look like that to me," he said, inspecting the crevices. "Again," he ordered as he walked out. "Tomorrow, you start on the barracks floor."

*Chapter 6*

# Mary's Star-Spangled Day

"But Mommy," Agnes whined, I don't like to have my galoshes on. My feet get too big."

"Hush, now, Agnes. It's cold and snowy. You'll catch your death if you don't." Mrs. Hohlfeld stooped over to help Agnes tug the red rubber boots over her shoes, while also casting a sharp sideways glance at her older sister Mary. "Mind you now, Mary, look after your sister and be sure to keep those hats and mufflers on."

"Yes, sir." Mary pursed her lips and saluted, hoping to bring a smile to her mother's pensive face. A stuffed sausage in an overcoat, Mary waited patiently for the usual drama that came with getting Agnes out the door. Pretending to be a soldier like Ed didn't make her mother's mouth smile, and her eyes were far away. Mary wondered what she had done wrong. Then her mother blinked and came back. She reached into the pocket of her blue and white checkered house-dress and pulled out some coins.

"Here are your twenty pennies, Mary, love. Keep them safely in your pocket 'til you get to the factory. That should get you twenty pretzels, half-baldies, half-salties to sell. Ronnie earned $1.00 yesterday.

Another $1.00 today, well, that'd be a help." Mrs. Hohlfeld bent over and clutched Mary's shoulders. "You *are* my good little soldier, Mary. You always are. I'm counting on you. Remember that."

She pulled the door open. With the flat of her hand, she coaxed Agnes out of the warm house and into the cold day. Weighed down by winter clothing and her mother's expectations, Mary trod lightly on the icy surface a few steps behind her sister.

Tucking her basket beneath one arm, Mary reached for Agnes's gloved hand and marched her in the direction of the kids' makeshift playground to meet Rosemary, Mary's school chum. From there, they planned to head over to the pretzel factory on Frankford Avenue. Rosemary promised Mary that she would help her sell the soft pretzels. Mary knew a shortcut, although it would take them through a rundown neighborhood that her mother warned her to avoid. But taking it would give the girls more time to play before it was time for Saturday afternoon confession. Confessions could last hours, depending on the line and the sins committed during the week. Mary shared her scheme with Agnes, giving herself a mental pat on the back for being a pretty good planner. There would be lots of shoppers on Saturday. Mary pictured the pretzels flying out of her basket. Her mom would be so very pleased.

"Mom doesn't like us taking the twisty way without Alice or Ed or Sam. Remember?" Agnes glanced up at her older sister with a question mark on her ruddy face.

A pale sun peeked through the slate-colored sky. Yesterday's snow had turned to speckled slush on the city street, with melting bits and pieces of children's hastily erected snowmen strewn on the sidewalk like so many dismembered dolls. Mary patted Agnes' head and sucked in the cold air.

"Well, we're going to do it just this once because we have to hurry and sell our pretzels and make Mom happy. Don't worry. I know the way." She let go of Agnes's hand to press her sister's shoulder reassuringly. "C'mon, let's hurry. Rosemary's probably there already."

Mary wanted very much for her mother not to be so sad. Mary felt sad, too. The house felt lonely without Edward. She missed meeting him at the trolley stop and seeing him hunched over the easel in his art studio with a pencil or brush in his hand. Every night before bed, she said the same prayer: "Please, dear God, keep Edward safe and bring him back home from the Army as soon as you can. That's number one. And bless Mom and Dad, Sam, Alice, Ronnie, Anna, and Agnes. Oh, and my cousins. That's number two. Help Agnes not to be such a crybaby and make Ronnie be nicer to me and Agnes. She can be pretty impatient sometimes. That's number three. And help me to be good and be a better help to Mom. That's number four. Oh, and one more thing. I would love to have the green dress I saw in Axes department store window. I could wear it to church for midnight Mass on Christmas. I promise that I'll be very, very good. I'll keep on saying my prayers every day and every night before I go to bed, no matter what, and I'll do whatever Mom asks without complaining. Well, not too much complaining, because I would sure love to have that dress. If it's your will, that is. Amen, and thank you, dear God."

"Mary, Mary, over here." Mary looked up to see her friend Rosemary huddled behind an empty train car, trying to keep warm. Rosemary stood up. One mittened hand struggled to push back the blond curls that came tumbling out of her woolen hat. The other mitten waved hello to Mary.

Mindful of icier patches, Mary and Agnes broke into a cautious run to the boxcar to join Rosemary. A group of fourth-grade boys from St. Anne's were scrambling up and down the hill with their cardboard sleds, trying to get a few more rides from yesterday's smattering of snow that was now mostly ice. They landed in snow puddles at the bottom, screaming with laughter.

"Hiya, Rosemary," Agnes chirped.

"Hi, Agnes." Rosemary's smirk asked Mary if she really had to bring her little sister along.

Mary dismissed her friend's silent dismay with a shrug of her shoulders. "It'll be okay. Let's go."

"Hey, whadda you guys doing? Dontcha know this is boys' territory? You wanna ice-knuckle sandwich or something? Ha, ha. Ha, ha."

Ignoring the boy's taunts, Mary nudged them both forward and picked up her pace. They had to get moving if her plan was going to work.

Rosemary twisted her face into a question mark. "What should we do afterwards?"

"Dunno. We can't play hopscotch. Too icy. We could go back to Agate Street and wait for the coal train from Port Richmond." Mary and her sister sometimes hunted for loose coal near the tracks that fell from the lumbering boxcars. Their dad often rewarded them with potatoes cooked over hot coals. Yummy.

Rosemary was less than thrilled. "I can't wait until summer. How many months?"

"Too many. Come on." Mary strode ahead, the other two following dutifully behind. The pale sun was playing peek-a-boo with the clouds. Sniffing the air, Mary was sure more snow was on the way. Maybe it would keep on coming for Christmas. Yay! Snowballs. Snowmen. Sledding. Maybe her mom would let them stay out after supper.

"You sure you know the way?" Rosemary pouted.

Mary had taken this route several times with her sister Ronnie. "Yeah, I'm sure." But she eased her pace and fell back into a walking rhythm that better suited Rosemary and Agnes. Agnes was glad to get her big sister back. Mary smiled and patted her head.

Mindful of splatters from passing cars and the huckster's wagon, the girls trudged after Mary who led them through the unfamiliar streets. By the time they were a block or so away from the pretzel factory on Frankford Avenue, Agnes's energy was flagging. "My feet are tired, Mary. Can we go home now?"

"Oh, but we're almost there. See?" Mary pointed to the large white sign hanging lazily and slightly askew from the brick building less than a block away. The EL thundered overhead, and Mary had to shout. "How about a piece of pretzel? Would that make you feel better?"

Mary had already decided to take one of the pretzels and divvy it up among the three of them. She didn't think her mother would mind if they sold all the others. If they bought twenty and sold nineteen for a nickel a piece, they'd earn $.90. Well, maybe she could talk the pretzel man into giving them one free pretzel. Then they would be able to sell all twenty and give her mom a whole dollar. She'd seen how her mom coaxed the butcher for a better cut or an ounce or two extra and thought she might be able to do the same thing.

The scent of fresh-baked soft pretzels seeped through the doorway, waking up Mary's tastebuds. She licked her lips. Mimicking her mother, she raised her forefinger.

"Okay, you guys wait out here while I go inside and buy the pretzels. I won't be long."

Closing the door on winter, Mary entered the warm, sweet-smelling pretzel store. She joined the short line. Before it was her turn, she arched her head toward the front and read the nametag of the man at the counter, P. Johnson. When it was her turn, she smiled and used her most polite Catholic-schoolgirl voice. Please, Mr. Johnson, may I have, and thank you, sir. Mr. Johnson collected her money, packed up the half-salties and half-baldies in a paper sack, and handed them over to Mary. Mary stepped away from the counter and proceeded to inspect them. She found what she was looking for and got right back into the line.

When it was her turn again, Mary held up the pretzel. "Look, Mr. Johnson, this pretzel is a little banged up and puny compared to the others, and I probably won't be able to sell it for a nickel." In fact, the pretzel was slightly smashed and noticeably smaller than the others.

Mr. Johnson frowned and rocked impatiently on his heels. Mary imagined smoke curling out of his ears, like the kind she'd seen coming from the cartoon bull at the movie theatre. Mr. Johnson's bushy brown mustache huffed and puffed and blustered. Mary hoped he didn't lean over the counter and attack her with his face.

"Lookie here, girlie, I don't have time for this." He gestured toward the line behind her.

"You see these people waiting?"

It was lunchtime, and the doorbell rang every time someone came into the store. But Mary held her ground, hoping her Hohlfeld doggedness would win her a free pretzel. "But sir, I won't bother you anymore, honest. Could I just trade this pretzel in for another one?" Experience had taught her that, once touched, a pretzel couldn't be returned.

Mr. Johnson squinted his eyes to inspect the pretzel more closely. He seemed to forget that his spectacles hung on a cord around his neck. Just then, an older man at the back of the line shouted. "How long is this going to take? C'mon already."

Mr. Johnson wavered, Mary's prized pretzel hanging in the balance. "Oh, all right then. Don't bother me anymore, little girl." He grabbed another pretzel and shoved it at Mary. "Go away, already."

Mary was triumphant. On her way through the door, the bell jangled, and she placed the fresh baked pretzel in her basket with the others.

"Finally," Rosemary said. "I was just about ready to come in and get you. What took so long?" Agnes, who had been entertaining herself with a stray puppy, perked up when she saw her sister.

Mary grinned and held up the deformed pretzel. "I got a free one just for us." She divided it into three parts, being sure to give each one a portion of the thick center, soft and still warm from the oven. The three girls walked slowly as they savored and chewed.

Mary swallowed her last bite. "All right! Now let's get this show on the road." This was what Edward always said when he was getting ready to make homemade root beer in the backyard. She couldn't wait to write a letter to Edward and tell him about how she and Agnes had helped their mom today and gotten a free pretzel to boot.

By early afternoon, a light snow started to fall. Frankford Avenue was humming with shoppers, street vendors, and clumps of sailors and army men. The girls settled in front of Buttons department store, a good ten blocks from the pretzel factory, and the nearest hot dog and pretzel vendor nearly three blocks away. Posters were taped to store windows telling people to buy war bonds and ration food. In one, an angry-looking man in a blue top hat with a big white star glared at Mary. He had knotted white ropes for eyebrows, and his white hair spilled over his shoulders where it joined his scraggly beard. The block letters under him said: I WANT YOU FOR THE U.S. ARMY. She knew Edward was in the Army, but she hoped he didn't have to be anywhere near that angry old man.

Sales went slowly at first, as slow as molasses in January, Mary thought, remembering what her mother would say when Mary took too long at her chores. A couple of ladies in fur coats walked by them with turned-up noses. At the pretzels or the girls, Mary didn't know which. A man in a black top hat and fancy coat rushed by, ignoring Mary's "Mister, please, would you like to buy a pretzel?" When jackhammers started "ratatatatatting" on the other side of the avenue, Mary figured it was time to move. Rosemary shouted over the noise and pointed to a spot down the block, but just then, two sailors came over and bought a pretzel each. Then a bunch of construction workers came along, and before Mary knew it, all their pretzels had been sold. Mary pocketed the nickels and pennies, imagining the look of pleasure on her mother's face.

The snowflakes that grew bigger came faster. They swirled between the tall buildings and kissed the pavement. The girls giggled with expectation as they threaded their way back home. Rosemary said maybe they could make sleds out of cardboard to slide down the snowy hill at the bottom of Somerset. Agnes forgot about her feet for a minute and piped up, asking Mary if she would help her make a snowman when they got home. She promised not to tell their mom about taking the shortcut. Mary assured her they would. They might even have time to collect coal, since the Reading Railroad train to Port Richmond would have gone through by now. All in all, it was turning out to be a pretty good day.

Rosemary took the lead because Agnes was tiring and slowing down. Mary stayed back to encourage and distract her. They were almost at Rush Street, a stone's throw from Tulip, when two boys suddenly appeared from an alleyway and planted themselves in front of Rosemary with folded arms.

"Where do you think you're going?" The tallest one inched closer to Rosemary's face. Agnes whimpered, and Rosemary glanced back at Mary with frightened, slightly accusing eyes. They looked like they were a little older than Mary and Rosemary. The quiet one was wearing a hat with earflaps. He was blowing bubbles and rocking on the heels of his rubber boots. The other boy brought his arms down to crack the knuckles of his gloveless hands. His nose was red with cold, and white flakes of snow were settling on his hatless head, but he didn't seem to notice. He adopted a fierce pose, jutting his jaw and twisting his face, just a breath away from Rosemary.

"Did you ask Daniel's permission to pass through? You don't have my permission to walk through this neighborhood. You have to pay. How much money you got, huh? Give me a nickel. We'll let you go through for five cents." He stuck out his hand and turned to wink at his silent partner.

Mary's heart thumped wildly. She wondered if everyone could hear it. Agnes started to cry, and Rosemary sputtered. "I don't know . . . we didn't mean to . . ." Tears sprang to her eyes. If the boy's aim was to scare her to death, he had succeeded. Mary had seen bullies like this before on the playground. Letting go of Agnes's hand, she dropped her basket on the pavement and rushed forward to step between Rosemary and Daniel. She heard Edward's voice in her head. "Fighting is wrong, Mary. Do you hear me?" But her friend was in trouble. She was sure Edward would want her to stand up to a bully.

"Hey, you leave her alone. Who do you think you are anyway? We don't need your permission to walk . . ." An arm came up and grabbed Mary by the shoulder. A second arm joined it, and Mary felt herself being shoved backward. She thrust her hands into Daniel's face and felt his breath on her neck. Snow was swirling all around her, and then the world disappeared. When it came back, Mary lay atop Daniel on the snowy sidewalk. He was trying to protect his hatless head from Mary's flailing arms.

"Lemme up, lemme up, you crazy girl." He squirmed and wiggled, stunned by the girl's ferocity and strength.

Mary heard Agnes wailing somewhere behind her, and Rosemary was pulling and yanking at Mary's shoulders. She relaxed and let herself be pulled up. She looked around, dazed, noticing that the other boy had slipped away. Daniel sprang to his feet and took off, disappearing into an alley as quickly as he had appeared.

"Mary, Mary, I was so scared." Wrapping her arms around Mary, Agnes pressed her tear-stained face against Mary's shoulder and cried some more.

Out of the corner of her eye, Mary saw two ladies appear across the street. They were carrying shopping bags. One of the women called out: "You children lost or something?"

Still stunned from the encounter, Mary hesitated. Then she found her courage and her voice. "No, ma'am, we're fine, just had a little accident."

"All right then, you girls better get on home. Don't worry your mama, now." The ladies turned and started walking.

"No, ma'am. We won't," Mary called across the street before turning her attention to Agnes. "Shh, it's okay. Stop crying, Agnes." Mary's head pulsed. With the back of her mitten, she wiped blood away from her nose.

"You sure you're not hurt?" Rosemary picked up Mary's hat from the ground and brushed the snow from her coat. "I was scared to death. I thought that boy was going to clobber you. And then you pushed him away, and the other boy just ran off. And then you both were on the ground, and then. . . are you sure you're all right?"

Rosemary's commentary roused Mary, whose mittened hands were shaking. Her faltering voice came out in spurts. "I don't even remember how I got there. He just made me so mad." She reached over to wipe Agnes' tear-stained face with the fat thumb of her mitten. "I was so afraid he'd take our money." Remembering, Mary panicked. She pulled away from Agnes to remove her mitten and reach into her pocket for the coins. "Still there. Whew. Good thing I have deep pockets."

"I'm glad, too, Mary," Agnes squeaked. "You were so brave."

Mary shrugged but secretly imagined how Edward would be so proud of her. Bending down, she scooped a handful of snow and placed it to her nose to wipe the blood away. "C'mon, let's hurry. Probably too late to go to the coal yard now. Agnes, remember to keep your mouth shut. Okay? We don't want to worry Mom."

Agnes's eyes grew large. She shook her head back and forth. "Nuh, uh, Mary. Honest. I won't tell."

"Good girl." Mary grabbed Agnes's mittened hand. The three girls broke into a cautious run back to Tulip Street. Mary knew Agnes was likely to spill the beans sooner or later. She wasn't sure how she'd explain the escapade to her mother. But she had the money in her pocket, and the snow was falling faster. Her ho-hum day had turned into a star-spangled-banner exciting kind of day, and she couldn't wait to write Edward a letter and tell him all about it.

## Chapter 7

# The Turkey and the M1Garand

*Dear Edward,*

*Thank you for the St. Francis of Assisi Medal. Mom put it on a chain, and I wear it on my neck every day. Do you still wear your St. Christopher Medal? Mom said it's sure to protect you from the bad guys. Guess what? Mom cut off my pigtails, and now I have a pageboy. Did you get my drawing of the Taylor's Bulldog? Samson looks mean but he's not. I gave him half my peanut butter and jelly sandwich and the rest of my apple, just like you always did. Mom got mad at me. Ronnie doesn't go to school anymore. She got a job at the soda fountain. Mom said she has to help out now that you're not here. Sam has a new girlfriend. I think her name is Elsie, and Mom doesn't like her. That's what Alice said. Sam shined his shoes and left them outside the bedroom door. It was nighttime, and Anna thought it was the potty. Number two! He got so mad. Sister Madeline said I'm the best speller in my class. I hope I win the spelling bee. Do you see the Nazis? Sister says they are very bad. I hope they don't hurt you. Come home soon so you can make root beer. I drew a picture of a Thanksgiving turkey just for you.*

> *Love,*
>
> *Your little sister,*
>
> *Mary Hohlfeld*

*P.S. Sister Marian says we could write a letter to a soldier who is lonely or doesn't have any family. Do you know any? I'm getting all my friends together one night every week so's we can write letters to our soldiers. But you will always be my bestest and most favorite soldier!*

Mary had drawn a turkey on a separate page and colored it in with her crayons. Ed lay stretched out on his bunk, holding the letter and picture up to the light, his arm cradling his head. He brought his thumbs up to his eyes to clear the moisture, glancing around to make sure none of the other guys noticed. Turning back to the letter, he re-read the shit-in-Sam's-shoes scene and chuckled. He read the letter a third time. What his sister said was true. He did give part of his lunch away to stray dogs. Mary watched and copied everything he did. He chuckled again. Little bugger.

It was a laid-back Sunday night. Guys lounged around the barracks in their civvies, trying not to think about Monday morning's marching and drilling. The outside temperature had taken a dip, and the wheezy radiator was chugging to keep up. Chappy, Whistler, and a few other guys were still duking it out at the card table. Frank was writing a letter to his wife, and Popeye was foolishly wrestling with Stu. Both men emitted grunts and groans, punctuated by threats of what they were going to do to "those Krauts" on the battlefield.

"Just get me over there," Stu said menacingly when he had Popeye pinned to the floor. "I'll show those suckers. I'll blast them into kingdom come." He jumped up and feigned shooting a machine gun. Some of the other guys joined in.

"Yeah, look out, Krautheads! Americans are riding to the rescue."

Popeye, briefly released from his opponent's grip, went back in for more Stu-punishment.

"Go, on, Popeye, you are one crazy son-of-a-gun. You can take him." Popeye's supporters fired Stu up even more.

"Something amusing you're reading there, Hohlfeld?" Tiny, sprawled out on the bunk next to Ed's, was reading Stephen Crane's *Red Badge of Courage*, having lost his shirt in the barracks' poker game the previous night. The book led to a discussion about violence and manhood the night before and ended with Ed asking to borrow the book when Tiny was done.

Tiny slid his horn-rimmed glasses back up his nose and laid the book on his chest and asked again. "What's so funny?"

Tiny and Ed had hit it off from the beginning. Neither was a favorite of the sergeant. Both were Catholic and liked reading books, although Ed enjoyed biographies and books about art and history, while Tiny preferred novels. Ed was tall and muscular with dark hair and movie star looks. Tiny, a bespectacled bookworm, was slight and sandy-haired.

"Letter from Mary. My little sister? Telling me about our Anna, who took a shit in my brother's dress shoes." Ed laughed aloud, again picturing the look of exasperation on Sam's face.

The grunts, groans, and boasts escalated in the background. Tiny smiled at Ed's story from home and picked his book back up. "Wish I had a little sister to get a letter from."

Tiny was an orphan. Told Ed he was left on a convent doorstep when he was barely three years old. By a twist of good fortune, he ended up an only child in a well-heeled Catholic home. It was love at first sight. He was small and fair-haired, like the son the Gallaghers lost to polio a few years before. They named him Richard Gallagher, but the only name he'd known was Tiny. His adoptive father was a businessman who traveled a lot. His mother devoted her life to Tiny and his education. She was devastated when he enlisted in the Army. Both his adoptive parents were. Tiny told them he was lucky to be an American and a Gallagher, and he wanted to join up to show his gratitude. Prove his manhood and loyalty to them and the country. Ed and Tiny had gotten into a few testy arguments about pacifism but always came away shaking hands, respectful of one another's view.

Ed smiled. "Yeah, Mary's a good kid. A little strong-willed but smart as the dickens."

"Ten-hut." When Kaczynski suddenly stepped into the barracks, Ed dropped his letter and sprang to attention along with the rest of the men. Mary's turkey drawing slid to the floor next to Ed's bunk. Except for the sound of Stu and Popeye's labored breathing, the barracks turned still and hushed. Kaczynski paced up and down, eyeing each of the men before finally saying, "At ease, men."

"You're past the halfway mark, recruits. How sharp do you think you are? How physically fit? How battle ready? What grade would you give yourselves as a unit so far, huh?" Kaczynski was in an uncharacteristically playful mood, maybe because it was the end of the weekend. By contrast, drills during the first couple of weeks had been intense, and Kaczynski had come down hard on the entire barracks for every minor infraction. He'd been consistent with his promise to *ride them rough* and *make them ready* for the next stage. But the men tolerated it and met his challenge.

"You," he said, nodding at Whistler. "What would you say?"

Lou Crawford whistled with perfect pitch and didn't miss a note, but when he spoke, it was a different matter. He was soft-spoken, his speech halting

"I, geez, Serge, I, I don't know what. . ."

"You don't know, Crawford? Take a wild guess. Let's have a grade."

He glanced down, up, down again. His voice wavered. "Maybe, I don't know, maybe a B, Sergeant?"

"B, a B?" Kaczynski said in astonishment. "Hmm. What do you say to that, Masterson? Do you agree?"

Stu's chest swelled. "Nah, Sergeant, an A. I'd give us an A."

Kaczynski's bellow reverberated in the drafty barracks. "You must be shitting me. You guys are full of crap. You rate a C, tops. You need to whittle down those gigs, fellows. Pick it up on your march. Get your asses through the obstacle course faster." Kaczynski scanned the two lines of recruits to ensure they got the point. "Y'all hearing me? Still have a ways to go. Wouldn't you agree, Hohlfeld, a C?" He planted himself in front of Ed.

"Yes, Sergeant. We have a way to go. But I agree with Whistler, a B, maybe a B-," Ed said, getting caught up in the playfulness of the moment.

Kaczynski snorted. "Oh, you would, would you." He might have dropped it there and resumed his jovial banter, but then he noticed it—Mary's drawing that had slid onto the floor. The turkey's bright red neck stuck out from under his bunk. "What the hell is this, Hohlfeld?" Kaczynski scoffed. He leaned over and picked up the paper. "Is this what you do with your personal time? Play with crayons?" He held the drawing aloft and waved it.

Ed sensed Frank's discomfort to one side of him, Tiny's on the other, and Chappy's across the room. These were his only allies since Kaczynski had smeared Ed's name and challenged his loyalty. Stu continued to take pot shots, and except for Chappy, Frank and Tiny, the other guys steered clear. Didn't want to be guilty by association.

Like lightning, the flame of indignation started in his toes and shot up through his body, ending in his inflamed cheeks.

Ed sucked in his breath. "No, Sergeant. I mean, yes, I sketch as a hobby, but my sister sent me that drawing. A Thanksgiving turkey," he added, and instantly regretted it. The fewer details, the better. Kaczynski used personal information like ammunition for his next attack.

"Ah, ain't that sweet, fellas? Hohlfeld here gets pictures from his little sister. And he likes to draw. Where's *your* crayons, Hohlfeld? Can we see them?"

It was one thing for Kaczynski to ride him. It was quite another to get personal about it. He wouldn't be baited, though. That's what Kaczynski wanted. There was a bigger fight at stake here, and Ed still didn't know how it was going to play out. He couldn't lose his footing because of the sergeant's cheap shots.

"Pencils, drawing, I don't give a shit, Hohlfeld. It seems right sissi-fied to me. Not most fellas' way of preparing to face an enemy on the battlefield. Maybe you should be drawing a chicken, huh? Cluck, cluck, cluck." Some of the men joined in the clucking, to Kaczynski's delight. Other guys just held their breath. Ed didn't take the bait. Kaczynski finally grew tired of the game and tossed Mary's sketch on Ed's cot. Turning on his heel, he spat a final comment over his shoulder. "If you'll excuse me, I'd like a few words with the *men* here."

His heart thudding, Ed swallowed hard.

"All right, now listen up. Fun and games are over. As you know, gentlemen, this week you'll be trading in your Rubber Duckies's for the real deal, the M1 carbine. Y'all carry that baby with you wherever you go. Y'all drill with it. Sleep with it, and by gawd, y'all learn how to shoot it. Tomorrow, I'll introduce you to your new companion.

After drills on the obstacle training course, you'll fall out in the full pack." The barracks groaned. That meant laying out their full field equipment on parade grounds and, worse, having to carry the extra weight on their long march.

"Day after, we head out to the shooting range and get you up to speed on those babies. When it's all over, and every single one of y'all can hit the damned target, maybe I'll bump your grade up to a B."

"And a boost in pay grade to go with that, Serge?" Stu chimed in, to a round of snickers and laughs. Kaczynski's glare shut them down. Fun and games were over. Another soldier might have found himself on latrine duty for the wisecrack, but the sergeant prized Stu's gutsiness.

"By the time I'm done with you, y'all be tough enough to spit nails and eat razor blades. Y'all hearing this? Then y'all be in A-ready territory. That okay with you, Crawford?"

"YeeeeeeeeYes, Sergeant."

Damne it, then y'all be soldiers. Y'all be fighting *men*." He glanced back at Ed before continuing. "Y'all be good and ready to outrun, outsmart and out-kill those Krauts by the time you ship out. Whose hearing me?" His voice rose, and his eyes narrowed as he made one last sweep of the two lines of men in his charge.

"Yes, Sergeant," the men thundered back.

"What's that?" he repeated, cupping his ear.

An even more animated "Yes, Sergeant" followed.

"Dismissed!"

The men erupted in cheers at the prospect of a gun in their hands and the end of boot camp in sight. Threats against the Krauts followed, along with tough-talking boasts and a few titters aimed in Ed's direction.

"Lights out in twenty." Kaczynski strode through the barracks and disappeared through the doorway to his quarters.

Tiny shook his head and shot Ed a sympathetic look. Frank looked away and got caught up in the chest-thumping and enemy insults. Ed didn't even want to clap eyes on Chappy. He stormed into the darkened latrine, glad to get away from the commotion and have the small space to himself. A shaft of light spilled into the room through the small window, enough for Ed to examine his face in the shadowy mirror above the basin. His hands gripping the porcelain, he stared intently at his image. A black ribbon of ill-will was wrapped around his head, and he had no way to cut it. His right fist flew up and pounded the wall next to the mirror until the skin became separated from his knuckles and dark red drops bubbled up. He brought his hands up to cover his mouth and released a muffled cry before wrapping his left hand around the injured one. Then he sucked in his breath and counted, one, two, three, until his heart stopped racing, and he could think. He turned on the faucet and let the icy rush over his raw knuckles, gritting his teeth until the stinging passed. Then he splashed it onto his face and neck.

Ed wrapped an unused cleaning cloth around the injured hand. Kaczynski was hell-bent on breaking him. That was clear. Did he really believe he could fashion a soldier out of humiliation and mind-games? That he could bend a man to his will and make him into something he wasn't? Or was he just a sadistic sonofabitch? Ed had to go with the option that gave Kaczynski the benefit of the doubt. He was just doing his job the only way he knew. He wasn't out to destroy Ed, just to mold him. He believed in America's cause and his God-given mission to ready his men for war, and he had no idea what to do with a guy like Ed.

By the time Ed found his way back to his bunk, the hubbub had died down. He had a few minutes left until lights out. He grabbed his sketchpad and pencil from his footlocker and, wincing with pain, started to sketch a dove with an olive branch in its mouth. He ignored the barbs and snickers of the men as they headed to the latrine. He very nearly cried when Chappy walked by and squeezed his shoulder.

The next morning Ed stood at parade rest with the rest of the platoon under a sky of slate.

Kaczynski stood at the front holding the rifle aloft. "Here it is, recruits. Your M1 Garand is the newest, most reliable, and accurate gas-operated semiautomatic weapon designed for the U.S. infantryman."

Ed's rifle rested butt down in the dirt in front of his right foot. The temperature hovered around 35 degrees. It had just started to drizzle. The weapon in his hand felt cold and strange, but Ed had to admire the light brown leather sling and the dark burnished wood with streaks of black running through it. The neat steel trigger and scope. A work of art almost, if it were idle and behind museum glass.

"She's 43-inches long and weighs nine and half pounds for easy carrying in the field."

Yeah, Ed thought, and easy killing.

"With very little kick and an eight-round clip, she's an infantry-man's best friend." Kaczynski slapped the black butt of the rifle. "This here is a steel plate that's useful as an effective weapon in hand-to-hand combat." Then he demonstrated how a soldier who was out of ammunition might swing the rifle around and aim its steel butt at the body or head of the enemy. He stepped back, pleased with himself, and resumed.

"Your bandolier contains six clips of 48 rounds. It can do a lot of damage, boys, a lot of damage." His cheeks glowed with pride. "Down the line, we'll concentrate on how to use this baby." He held the rifle in front of his puffed-out chest, the bayonet beneath, as he traveled from one end of the line of men to the other. "Take a good look, men. This is the infantryman's best friend."

Not mine. Ed shook his head. Not mine.

"Any questions?" Kaczynski barked into the chilly air, looking right, and left. The men were mute. Maybe they were as awed by the real deal against their shoulder and the task that lay ahead as Ed was. "Well, then, recruits, ten-hut! Present, arms. Right-shoulder, arms. About, face. Forward, march."

In spite of his internal debate with the sergeant, Ed's movements were measured and precise during their march past the peach fields under a light morning drizzle. Kaczynski couldn't possibly find fault with his soldiering or how he maintained his personal space and wore his uniform. Or in the crisp way he carried out his tasks and followed orders. As they neared the firing range and the incessant popping sounds grew louder and more intense, Ed's mind stilled.

Kaczynski divided them into groups. With the assistance of two other sergeants, he reviewed the basics: how to line up the scope from a prone position, squeeze the steel trigger with the upper part of the forefinger. How to reload the chamber and rest its steel butt snug against the shoulder. Ed stood behind Stu, Chappy, Whistler, and Frank, attentive to his instructions. The target would be 50 yards, then 100 yards, and so on. As far as his eyes could see in both directions, there were targets and rows of soldiers with rifles. Behind them, the occasional jeep roared by with more ammo or instructions from the duty officer.

A menacing sky was still plugged up, but the drizzle had turned into more of a steady patter. Raindrops bounced against the brim of his helmet, and beneath it, Ed observed the guys in his group as they followed directions and went through their paces. He kept the rifle several inches from his body, passing it back and forth between his hands like a hot piece of coal. Beads of sweat joined the raindrops on his forehead and upper lip. He wiped them with the back of his hand, only to have them reappear. Ed wasn't surprised to see Stu and Chappy take to the M1, hitting inside the black after the first couple of rounds and earning rare praise from Kaczynski. But Whistler had a harder time of it. He couldn't seem to keep the scope clear of moisture or the rifle steady against his shoulder. His shots landed mostly in the white or missed the target altogether.

"You need glasses, soldier?" Kaczynski's insult made Whistler more anxious. By the time Whistler moved to the back of the line, the sergeant's good mood had evaporated, and Frank's ho-hum follow-up performance stoked the flames of his irritation. Ed sucked in a deep breath as he watched Frank's hunched shoulders skulk to the back of the line to join Whistler. It was Ed's turn, and Kaczynski was good and wound up.

"All right, Hohlfeld, haul your ass up here and let's see what you can do." Kaczynski glared at him through the steady drum of rain. Thunder sounded in the distance.

Over Kaczynski's order, the words from *The Catholic Worker* editorial reverberated in Ed's head and made their way to his mouth in a whisper: ". . .bound in conscience passively to resist the tyranny . . ." He cradled the gun and felt a tremor in his hands and arms. "Resist the tyranny," he muttered.

Kaczynski glared at Ed. "What? What the hell are you mumbling, Hohlfeld? I gave you an order. Get into firing position now, or I'll slap a gig on you and send you to the stockade so fast it'll make your head spin."

Ed's moment of truth had arrived. He stared straight ahead, avoiding the crosshairs of Kaczynski's hard eyes.

He raised his voice. "Sergeant," I can't fire this rifle." His knees felt wobbly, and his lips trembled, but his words did not waver. He felt the drip, drip, drip of raindrops sliding from his helmet down to his nose and eyes. He suppressed the urge to wipe away the moisture. "I'm sorry, Sergeant, but I can't fire this rifle. I respectfully request to be excused from firing my weapon." In Kaczynski, he saw the face of his disapproving father.

In three furious strides, Kaczynski was looming over Ed. Spittle flew from his lips. "You lily-livered son of a traitor. Get your coward's ass up there *now* and shoot that rifle. I gave you a direct order. Are you disobeying my order?"

Pulsating with rage, Kaczynski leaned in. He was so close that Ed tasted his sour cigar breath. They shared the same raindrops that started coming faster, harder, and colder. His arms and legs trembled, and his rifle fell to the ground. Except for the pinging of raindrops on his helmet, all sound was blocked out. It was as if he and Kaczynski were in a pantomime. The two of them together, sealed in a deadly dance. Ed's voice quavered. "I'm sorry, Sergeant, I am. But I respectfully request . . . I can't shoot this rifle, sir, I . . ."

Kaczynski cut him off, seizing Ed's rifle from the ground, thrusting it hard against Ed's torso, demanding that he pick it back up. "Believe me, I'll deal with your insubordination later, Hohlfeld," he said tightly. "But right now, you *will* pick up this damned rifle and take your position. You *will* fire it."

Ed's arms and hands hung helplessly at his sides. His eyes were transfixed by the violent twitch in Kaczynski's cheek. The sky crackled and roared somewhere in the distance. A sudden change in air pressure finally opened the throttle on the black clouds. The rifle rose, like a demon, obscuring Kaczynski's red, contorted face. Somewhere beyond him, Ed met Chappy's stunned eyes. Ed's hands flew up to his head only to be shoved aside by Kaczynski, who kept thrusting the rifle butt at him. Ed half-turned to step back, only to feel a crushing weight fall against his shoulder.

"Hey, hey now, that ain't right," one soldier mumbled, and the line moved forward and circled the two men, alert but hesitant in the face of Kaczynski's fury and his rank. The men's energy buoyed Ed. He straightened himself to face Kaczynski down, only to see the rifle's black steel butt glinting and coming down toward his head, all new and shiny from the rain. The rifle came crashing into his skull again and again. His frantic hands were shoved aside, helpless to defend against it, until liquid—thick, metallic, warm, and baptized by rain—slid from his forehead and seeped into his open mouth, and his body went slack, crumbling and twisting and collapsing, finally, face-first in the mud.

## Chapter 8
# Black

Cloaked under a dark blanket, he lay pinned like a helpless, overturned insect. Save for the wheeze of some sort of machine and the "rap, rap, rapping" of a wild bird trapped inside his chest, he sensed little sound or movement. In the distance, hushed voices came and went like an erratic volume on a radio console in another room. He strained to open his eyelids. After several tries, he surrendered. His head felt like lead. The effort to lift it exhausted him. Where was he? His waking mind probed the other parts of his body. His right thigh twitched. The twitching spread to his calf and foot and toes and jumped to the muscles in his other leg, up to his torso, and into his arms.

Images flickered. A little girl, arms outstretched, scampering along railroad tracks, a white collar with a gold crucifix dangling below it and swinging from side to side, the red contorted face of the devil brandishing a pitchfork. No, not a pitchfork. A heavy instrument or a tool with something sharp extending from the top. Like a projectionist, he steadied the image. A bayoneted rifle. He gurgled, tears welling at the back of his eyes. He freed two of them. They slid out of his left eye, settling in the folds of his earlobe. As if doing a jigsaw puzzle, he started arranging bits and pieces of memory into a picture he couldn't quite see: a noisy Army mess hall, Chappy's slanted grin, a swirl of red mud.

The fingers of his right hand fluttered and fell, fluttered, and fell, until he willed the ball of his hand to open. Like a crab's legs, his fingers began crawling tentatively and sideways. Cool cloth caressed his fingertips and hugged his palm. The rapping in his chest eased. A bed. He lay on a bed. The rapping resumed when his hand moved, instinctively upward, only to meet resistance. After several unsuccessful attempts, his newly awakened hand slumped onto the bed. He turned his attention to the other hand. Same thing. Heart pounding and blood coursing, his body strained to move. His eyes wouldn't stay open. He twisted this way and that until, spent, his limbs relaxed. Black.

A firm hand lifted his wrist and held it. Black.

His eyelids winked once, twice, three times. Bits and pieces of overheard conversation floated in and out of his hearing. "Change that IV bottle . . . slant-eyed bastards . . . trauma . . . 2,000 dead . . . U.S. at war." America Attacked? Was he having a nightmare?

"Can you hear me, son?" Icy fingertips lifted his eyelids. A flash of light stabbed his eyes. With effort, he summoned his voice, but like a benumbed limb it failed to obey.

"Do you know where you are, Private?"

He couldn't find his voice. In the dark, Ed thought, in the dark.

*Chapter 9*

# The Highway

Trees, telephone poles, and wires stretched into the flat horizon as far as Ed could see. The MP's military cap turned away from the windshield to address Ed.

"Rumor has it you're a Kraut sympathizer. That right?" He raised his left elbow atop the seat, flexing his bicep to advertise the blue wool arm brassard with large white letters, MP. Not waiting for an answer, the MP dropped his arm and turned his attention to the taciturn driver who was battling an uneven gravel and dirt road, headed north and away from Camp Crofton. He lit a cigarette and snickered.

"Told ya, Powell. Guy from his platoon named Stu said he was a chicken-shit Kraut. Ain't that right?" He jerked his thumb toward the back seat. "Stinks in here. Don't it? Smells like Kraut with some stinkin' Jap mixed in." The MP at the wheel didn't reply. Disapproval or indifference, Ed couldn't tell. Ever since the car pulled away from the Army base, the MP in the passenger seat had kept up a steady stream of insults aimed at Ed.

In the camp hospital, the medical staff treated Ed with the same brusqueness. He winced, remembering how he'd had to adjust his eyes to focus on the cold white coat and clipboard.

"You were in a coma. In and out of consciousness because of the head injury." The doctor said this matter-of-factly. "Should be all right, soon enough." He stood at the bottom of Ed's hospital bed. The nameplate on his breast pocket read Capt. W. Parsons.

Ed felt woozy. "What? A coma? What happened? I . . . I don't understand." His head felt like an empty cartoon bubble. His voice came thick and slow. Beneath the thick white bandage, his head throbbed.

Dr. Parsons fidgeted with his clipboard before jotting something down in his notes.

"There may be some memory problems for a while, Private. Should get better." Ed's question had apparently sailed past him, like a long ball gone foul and quickly forgotten.

"But what, I mean, how . . .?" He struggled to fill the bubble with a string of words that made a sentence.

"What about the headaches? How often?" The doctor stopped writing and looked squarely at Ed for the first time.

"What? I . . . headaches? Yes, sometimes . . ." Ed flushed, as though he'd just admitted to having done something wrong. His words came haltingly. "Sometimes, they're, well . . ." He searched for the word, "Intense."

"Yes, quite normal." The doctor flipped through several pages of notes on the clipboard and resumed writing. "In time, they should pass. You may experience some depression and anxiety as well. Maybe some emotional outbursts."

Depression and anxiety? Emotional outbursts? Ed's sluggish mind struggled to catch up.

"The bruises on your shoulder and upper back have healed nicely, though. No fractures." He dropped his clipboard onto the silver tray alongside the bed and performed a cursory inspection of Ed's torso.

"Report said you got into an altercation with your superior officer. Became belligerent and refused to follow orders."

What the hell is he talking about. . .? "No! I mean . . ." Ed strained to remember. It wasn't like him not to follow orders. Something tugged on his memory. Something to do with the sergeant. At the firing range. It hurt to concentrate, and he couldn't bring the memory into focus. The doctor leaned in closer. His pencil-thin red eyebrows, that looked as if they had been painted onto his forehead, bore down on Ed's face. Pulling a penlight from his pocket, he pried open and inspected one eye, then the other. Thick fingers returned the penlight to his breast pocket and unraveled the gauze that cradled Ed's head, before removing the padding beneath. He set these on the silver tray next to a copy of yesterday's *Charleston Mail*. Questions buzzed in his head. How long had he been in a coma? Where was Chappy? Was he all right? What about Tiny and Frank? Have they shipped out? Did they know he was in the hospital?

Ed's torso shot forward when the doctor's dense fingers grazed the bruised area.

"Tender?" He lightened his touch before pulling back.

Ed nodded uncertainly.

"A fight? No, I don't remember a . . . well, yes, something, some kind of, something happened . . . yes . . . I . . . think . . . I can't . . ." Here he stumbled, and his mind shut down. Like a faded and horribly wrinkled photograph, this part of his memory couldn't or wouldn't be deciphered. A detail here, a detail there, but he couldn't fit them together. He didn't want to get anyone into trouble, but he felt pretty sure he'd been attacked. Maybe by a member of his platoon? Stu? Ed wanted to challenge the doctor's claim. He had to find his way out of this bubble first.

The doctor straightened and stepped back to the foot of the bed. Retrieving his clipboard and pen, he made a final notation. "Well," he hesitated. "You'll have to take that up with your commanding officer." His voice was flat and indifferent. He avoided looking at Ed, his eyes glued to the clipboard.

"Do you know when that might be?" The doctor turned and walked out of the room. Ed's unanswered question fell to the floor with a thud.

Awake now, Ed felt like he lay at the bottom of a deep ravine. He could see people walking back and forth on the lip above, but they didn't seem to see or hear him. He'd lost days, maybe weeks. One? Two? More? Like a hyena ready to pounce, panic sat on the bottom left corner of his hospital bed. Ed looked away from the fiend. He took long breaths until his stampeding heart slowed to a trot. His restless eyes searched the room, settling on an older *Charleston Daily Mail* that he'd tossed aside in frustration a few days earlier. Blurriness made it difficult to read. He grabbed the paper and forced himself to focus. Churchill's address to the joint session of Congress shouted triumphantly from the headlines. My God, the world's turned on its axis. Pearl Harbor attacked? The country gone to war while Ed lay in a hospital bed?

The headache woke up. Ed could feel the slow, steady romp atop his head. Soon it would turn into a pounding drumbeat. He steadied himself. Wait until it's gone, he urged himself. Then you can close your eyes and ease your head onto the soft pillow.

Like a phantom, the doctor reappeared.

"What happens next, Doc?

"Not up to me, Private." He checked Ed's eyes and the wound on his head. Then he made a few notes in the chart and slipped out of the room.

He never did see an officer. Just the MPs who arrived in his hospital room with a pair of handcuffs and orders to escort him to a federal court in Philadelphia.

"But what . . . I mean . . . I don't understand. This has to be a mistake." Ed blinked hard, as if by doing so, he could banish the two MPs and disrupt the string of events launching him into an uncertain future. He was swept up in a tornado with no idea where or when he might touch down to safety.

The stocky MP scowled but stood quietly. "No mistake," the other MP said evenly. His long, narrow face was blank. Ed detected a tic in his left cheek.

In the days since, Ed had been tugging at the strings of his memory. Did he get into a fight and assault somebody. No, he was sure he hadn't. But *he* was under arrest. A prisoner of war, the MP said, because of failure to follow orders. That couldn't be right. What would happen to him? To his family? They depended on his pay. A court? He must be in serious trouble.

Now, sitting handcuffed in the back seat of a Military Police car, Ed strained to make sense of his and his country's fate. The MPs chatted amiably in the front seat, freezing Ed out. He trained his attention on the flat, dusty landscape that sped by, grateful for the hypnotizing rumble of the car wheels. The morning was gray and thick with fog, mirroring the events of the days and weeks past. The headaches made everything worse. Sometimes they left his body stiff with pain. His mind went on furlough, and his eyes wanted to turn off the blinding light. In the hospital, he'd been woken up by nightmares, hyperventilating and drenched in sweat. A beast was charging him, its snout smoking and hissing, its hooves pounding. He tried desperately to run, but his feet and legs were stuck in red mud.

Memories started trickling back, but there were gaps he couldn't fill in. He remembered meeting with an officer to request a transfer or change in classification. Was it a General? No, he didn't think so. There were no bars on his sleeve. Something else. A leaf. Was it silver or gold, major or colonel? He couldn't remember. What was his name? Ed recalled salt and pepper hair. A pipe. He'd told him he couldn't kill, but he never said he wouldn't serve. He'd never disobeyed orders. Had he? Ed Hohlfeld, who had thrived in the Civilian Conservation Corp? No.

But something bad had happened. A scuffle with a commanding officer, the doctor said, but how could that be? Had he hurt someone? No. But he had been seriously hurt. Straining to remember he saw something black. A face? No. A rifle butt. The more he tried to remember, the more his head pulsed. Ease up, he told himself. It'll come back. And it did, in bits and pieces and in spite of the roaring ocean in his ears. Chappy, whispering in the cafeteria. "Stop making waves. It'll blow over." What? What would blow over? Rain. Something crashing into his head. A face bearing down on him in the rain, all twisted and black and terrifying. When he got to this point, his body trembled, warning him not to go there. Stay out of the rain, his body said. Stay out of the rain. A rush of anger spurted up from his bowels. He squeezed the sides of his head until it passed.

A box inside a box, inside a box, inside a box. Headed into an uncertain future with no clear memory, his life felt like a riddle. He had to talk with an officer or someone in charge. Who? A priest? No, a lawyer. He had to get to the right person and tell his side of the story, and then it might all be sorted out. What *was* his side of the story? Right. Legal representation, but who, and more importantly, how do I find it? Who would pay for it? What must his parents think?

Did they know what was going on or where he was? That he'd been hurt? That he was in trouble? A sudden rush of shame shot through his body. Chappy's warning came back to him. *It's gonna bite you in the ass someday, Ed, your stubbornness.*

"What have you done?" he whispered to his reflection in the window. "What in the hell have you done?"

A loud thwack, followed by the vehicle's careening off the roadway, jolted Ed's thoughts and threw his body forward.

"Damn it! Blasted tire. Are y'all doing okay?" Corporal James Powell yelled as he slid the long snout of the green Packard to a halt on the shoulder of the road. "Watson?" He turned to Ed in the back seat. "What about you, soldier?"

Ed nodded, reddening slightly. Disapproval, then, not disgust.

"Nothing this hard head can't handle," Buck Watson crowed. He tapped his forehead with his knuckles to show his head had won in the minor collision with the passenger side window.

After tugging on the safety brake, Powell sprang out of the car to assess the damage to the right front wheel. Watson jumped out and joined him, both heads disappearing from Ed's view. After both soldiers stood up, Watson clambered toward the boot to get the jack, snickering in Ed's direction as he passed. Powell stood up and stretched his back before opening the door and ordering Ed out of the car. Awkwardly, without the aid of his hands, Ed pushed himself forward and, refusing Powell's arm, lifted his long frame and stepped out unsteadily. His uniform sagged, the belt barely holding up his pants.

"I got this, Chief," Watson called to Powell as he hauled the jack and lug wrench to the front of the car. "You keep an eye on our P.O.W."

Ed's blood surged. Without thinking, he lunged toward Watson. "You don't know what the hell you're talking about. You got this all wrong. I'm a red-blooded American, damn it . . . I'm . . ." Powell's Billy club came down fast and with precision against Ed's shoulder. He pitched forward and fell to his knees, his arms and hands splayed in the gravelly dirt.

"You cowardly son of a Kraut bitch," Watson yelled, dropping the jack, he aimed the lug wrench at Ed. "I'll break your yellow-bellied head in two. Do us *all* a favor."

"Simmer down, George. I got this," Powell said, shielding Ed from the irate man. He stowed the Billy club and zipped up his jacket.

Tall and slender as a reed, Powell had an easy, sure-footed way about him. He didn't brandish his power. Ed liked to think that he had worn that same kind of easy authority when he'd served as sergeant in the CCC. The memory opened the door to a flood of pleasant images. Digging alongside his men, grabbing a beer with Sam at Ju Ju's beer joint, swing dancing with that pretty blond woman. What was her name? Tina, Tammy? Tillie, that was it. Tillie. Said she was a sucker for handsome men in a uniform. Didn't mind his snaggle tooth and liked his dimple. Made him blush when she praised his dancing. Why were these memories clearer than those of the last weeks?

"Y'all don't want to do something dumb and lose that brassard, now. Go on back now. I'll take this turkey for a stroll."

With the back of his hand, Watson swiped the angry spittle from his mouth and strode back to his station. The traffic was minimal. A fuel truck crawled past, honking hello to America's soldiers. The bearded driver gave a mock salute as he passed. Four military jeeps followed dutifully behind, looking for a safe place to pass on the two-lane road.

"C'mon fella," Powell instructed after spitting a wad of chewing tobacco. "Sorry I had to use a little force there but better me than

Watson. Let's take a walk back behind those mossy-looking trees. I need to take a leak."

Using his elbows to pull himself up, Ed dusted himself off as best he could. His heart sped up. He glanced in the direction of the trees and back at the MP's impassive face. Maybe his assessment of Powell had been wrong. Would the MP use this as an opportunity to teach him a lesson? He looked down helplessly at his cuffed hands. Bracing himself, he traipsed dutifully alongside the MP, averting his eyes when Powell unzipped and let loose.

Ed fixed his gaze on a massive, knotted oak. From a distance, it resembled a club-footed, multi-limbed monster that had finally made peace with the forest after years of struggle and strain. Moist South Carolina air soothed the winter chill. The kind of day that would be taken as a sign of early spring up north. An unexpected wave of home-sickness passed over Ed. Mom's fruitcake. Lugging the tree home on Christmas Eve and staying up late to decorate it when the girls were in bed. Mary and Agnes still believed that Santa decorated the Christmas tree. Can you beat that? He fought off the urge to bend over and heave his breakfast of coffee and burned toast. He cut his eyes in the direction of the car and the trees beyond, until the heaving waves in his belly receded. Moss hung like narrow twisted wizards' beards from the plantation trees, their long limbs leaning across the roadway like they were shaking hands with trees lined up on the other side.

Ed snapped back to attention when Powell sighed and announced, to no one in particular, "that felt damned good." He walked back towards Ed. His dark brown eyes scrutinized Ed's. He hooked his thumbs inside his belt and squared to face him.

Ed craved a cigarette. He straightened his back and met the MP's gaze. Bring it on, he thought. Bring it on. Whatever it is.

Powell shifted his eyes to gaze wistfully at the forest. "Grew up in a shack outside Greenville." His voice was slow and thick as maple syrup. "Had us an outhouse, but the rats liked to call it home." He looked down and chuckled. "Anyway, out of doors feels like home to me." He gestured to the forest as if he were introducing an old friend. "Me and my younger brother did a lot of scrambling around the countryside. Did us a fair amount of squirrel hunting, too. Always felt right sad killing the critters, but once Pap was gone, it was our job to get that food on the table. Pretty soon, you get good and used to killing a living thing." He fell silent for a moment and then turned back to Ed. "What about y'all?"

On full alert still, Ed wasn't sure where this was leading or what he was being asked. Was the MP asking him about killing?

"Need to take a piss or a shit? We got a long drive ahead of us."

Relieved, Ed lifted his shoulders, indicating the manacles on his hands.

"Yeah, I see y'all's dilemma there. Listen, I unlock these, no funny business. Get me?"

He gestured to his firearm, having left the Billy club back at the car. "I won't hesitate to use it."

"Of course not. I'm not the criminal you think I am."

"Okay, then." Powell leaned over and opened the cuffs with the key he had pulled from a short chain he kept in his pocket.

Ed shook his hands to restore circulation in his wrists and, turning back towards another tree, closed his eyes, unzipped and let go. Not just the piss he'd been holding in but the emotion that had been building up. After he zipped up, his shoulders started to convulse. He bent over, placing his freed hands on his thighs until his knees collapsed, and he fell to the moist ground.

"It's okay, soldier."

Ed felt a warm paw across his back. A flash of hope surged through him. Maybe, just maybe, with the grace of God, it would be okay. If he could just get to the right person and get a fair hearing, he could take whatever punishment they had in mind for him and put things right. If he could just get a fair hearing, he could straighten this mess out and get his life back.

"I saw your St. Christopher Medal peeking out your collar there. And I heard some stories back there at the camp." He held the manacles up and, almost apologetically, gestured toward them. "You seem like a decent man. Don't know what all you got yourself into back there, but . . ." He grimaced. "Seems like to me your sergeant was out of line, clubbing you with your own rifle and all. But this man's Army has its rules." As if uncertain, he glanced away.

The memories flitted in and out, like unfocused images in a camera lens, until they started to fall into place. That was it. The rifle. He'd refused to shoot it. Been clubbed. A furious Sergeant Kaczynski. The picture wasn't entirely complete, but at least he could see it. Ed *had* disobeyed his order. Remembering now, he clenched his jaw. Well, he would have to face the music, whatever it was. He stood up straight and squared his shoulders, managing a shy smile of gratitude for Powell's sympathy. First, though, he'd have to return to the car and Watson's hard eyes. Ed tucked the Medal back inside his shirt collar.

"Don't advertise it, but I'm as Catholic as the pope, just not as pure."

Both gave a short laugh. Powell placed the cuffs back on Ed's wrists and locked them. "Me, too," he said. "Had them a big debate back at St. Mary's, my home parish? Some thought it wasn't right, that Christ wouldn't want it, the killing and all. The war."

He paused and stuck a new wad of tobacco in his left cheek before continuing. "Turn the other cheek and all that. Sure as hell were well-meaning people, including one of the young priests in the parish that helped my family out a time or two. Father Donovan. Heard they yanked him from the pulpit. Others, well, they called him and his kind unpatriotic. I don't know the answer." He looked upward, as if he expected Jesus to appear and offer one. "But the country sure seems to think it's the right thing to do, going to war and all, and, well, here I am," he offered, almost apologetically.

"Following your conscience?" Ed offered.

Powell screwed up his face, "Yeah, something like that."

A mourning dove cooed softly in the distance. Ed wished he could shake the man's hand. He nodded instead.

Watson's shrill whistle ended the conversation. As they made their way back toward the car, Powell whispered: "Don't mind him. He's revved up and a little hard-headed. That attack on Pearl Harbor, well, the Japs killed a lot of Americans over there. A lot of destruction, planes, warships. Whole base demolished. Made soldiers jittery and hopping mad. It's Roosevelt's way or the highway now. Get my drift?"

Ed nodded. He certainly did. The question was, where did this highway lead?

# PART TWO

## Chapter 10

# Home, Sweet Home

*1942*

"Hey, Ronnie, what the heck's going on with Mommy and Daddy?" The sisters were unclipping clothespins to collect the chilly, cardboard-like laundry from their backyard clothesline.

Ronnie shrugged, which was not her typical know-it-all response, and walked back to the house. "How should I know?"

Mary trailed her older sister through the back door and into the kitchen, peppering her with questions and getting nowhere. "Ronnie! Why aren't Mommy and Daddy talking? Will Sam ever come back home?" Mary set the clothespins aside and dropped the basket onto the kitchen table for sorting and folding. "C'mon, Ronnie, *please.*"

Unmoved by Mary's pleas, Ronnie waved her off and headed toward the stairs. "Your turn to fold!"

Mary stomped her foot. "Not fair, Ronnie Hohlfeld!" she called back, all traces of polite wheedling gone. Something was wrong in the Hohlfeld house, and Mary was determined to get to the bottom of it. But how? She set her mind on figuring it out while sorting the household clothing. That's when she always did her best thinking. She began with the socks and her mother's aprons. They were the easiest. Underclothing was next, followed by the girls' blouses and play pants. She left her father's shirts for last. They were always the hardest.

How could Ronnie not know what was going on? It would be just like Ronnie to keep a big fat secret from Mary. On second thought, maybe Ronnie really didn't know why their parents were so glum. Neatly setting her father's trousers on a hanger for her mother to iron later, Mary sighed in frustration. Ronnie was so annoying. These days she was more interested in the high school boys who hung out at the playground than she was in what was going on at home.

Did it have something to do with Edward? Their house had sure been a lot quieter since he'd left for the Army. Her mother dismissed Mary's questions about Edward with a wave of her hand, or *I'm busy now, Mary, or go and light a Votive candle for your brother, Mary.* She couldn't ask Alice who was hardly ever around anymore. She quit high school to work at Woolworth's so she could help out at home. Her oldest brother Sam slipped in and out of the house like Peter Pan's shadow, so Mary hardly ever saw him. Know-it-all Ronnie said Sam was spending most of his time with his new girl-friend, Elsie, and their mom didn't like Elsie because she wasn't a Catholic, and that's why Sam wasn't around so much anymore. Her father mostly stayed in the parlor with his head bent over the *Bulletin* newspaper. He stopped asking Mary and Agnes to listen to the "Fibber McGee and Molly" show on the Victrola with him. He listened to boring news reports and told them to go outside and play. Her mom and dad were both acting strange. Instead of talking with one another at the supper table, they spoke in tight whispers behind their bedroom door.

Mary tried cupping her ear against it but couldn't make out what they were saying. Once, she was sure her mom said, "Oh, oh, oh." It sounded like she was hurt. Mary didn't know how, though. Her mom didn't look hurt when she came out of the bedroom. She just looked sad. Instead of singing her favorite Irish song, "When Irish Eyes are Smiling," when she was dusting or making supper, her mother wore tight lips under a bonnet of gloom. Mary didn't know where that saying came from, but it sure did fit. It seemed like their whole entire house was under a gloom bonnet. Like Captain Midnight on the *Captain Midnight* show, Mary was picking up signals. She just didn't know how to decode them.

These days the only thing Mary knew for sure was that ever since Edward went away, their house felt all crooked. A sorcerer had cast an evil spell on 2013 Somerset Street, and Mary wasn't sure how to break it. All she could do was wait for Edward to come back home from the Army. She picked up her clothes basket and walked upstairs. Yes, Edward needed to come home and make things right again.

*Chapter 11*

# City of Brotherly Love

Philadelphia stretched its torso west to the freshwaters of the Schuylkill River and east to the Delaware, the city's shipping channel and a stone's throw from the Atlantic Ocean. An industrial workingman's city, it rose from the shoulders of the southern states and spilled into the lush farm country of Bucks and Lancaster Counties to the north and west. At the first signs of his hometown—smokestacks jutting from the roofs of brick row homes, packed trolley cars, and squared city streets—Ed's heart pitched. Apart from a short stopover in northern Virginia, the car trip had been grueling and tense, worsened by MP Watson's overt hostility. Anticipation of the hazards that lay ahead kept stabbing at Ed's insides, like measured jolts of electricity. When he spotted William Penn's landmark bronze statue standing majestically atop the tower above City Hall, his nerves steadied.

"That's William Penn's statue up there," Ed blurted out. "Did you know he was a Quaker and a pacifist?" A rush of satisfaction at the memory of this important fact about his hometown swept over him. The irony that Ed was being returned in chains for championing the same cause did not escape him.

"Shut up, Hohlfeld," Watson barked. "I don't want to hear your Quaker conscientious objector bullshit. I'll be damned glad when they send you to prison, and we're finally rid of you."

The surge of lightheartedness fell to the car floor with a thud. Prison? Ed couldn't imagine he'd be sent to prison. He wasn't, after all, a criminal in any real sense. He couldn't imagine how his objection to killing could be construed as a criminal act. And yet, and yet, here he was, his fate resting in the hands of a judge at the Federal Court-house-Post Office Building that sat between Chestnut and Market Streets. Surely, if justice lived, it was in the U.S. federal courthouse in his Quaker hometown, wasn't it?

Cars and buses crept past as Powell slid the car alongside the curb on Market Street, close to the 9th Street entrance. Pedestrians scurried back and forth, seeking the shelter of a heated vehicle or building. A blustery day, it came as a shock on the heels of a mild southern winter. Powell and Watson climbed from the car. Powell stretched and adjusted his uniform while Watson hungrily eyed a long-legged brunette. Her skirt billowed beneath her winter coat as she hurried to catch a bus at the end of the block.

Powell opened the back door and waved Ed out. Ed stood and took one final long drag from his cigarette before flicking it to the sidewalk. In a gesture of pure magnanimity Ed would carry with him in the dark days and months ahead, Powell had purchased a pack of Lucky Strikes for Ed. Against the vehement objections of his partner, Powell also removed Ed's handcuffs. After stepping out of the vehicle, Ed straightened his belt and made sure his cap was sitting at the correct angle before holding out his wrists to the MP. As they approached the Courthouse, he tamped down his apprehension with a whispered prayer and breathed in the welcome air of Philly and home.

Ed was acquainted with the seven-story concrete building that stood on a two-acre plot in the heart of city center. In his younger years, he had dreamed of studying painting at the Pennsylvania Academy of Fine Art some blocks away. Hard times and a family in need of a steady paycheck had other plans for Ed. Flanked by Powell and Watson, he scanned its understated Georgian architecture. Except for the striking Sculptures and Reliefs flanking the entrance on the main floor, the federal building's face was plain and impassive. Ed didn't remember having seen this Edmond Amateis' chaps-clad, boot-wearing cowboy before. Surrounded by cacti, he was delivering a letter with one hand while holding his western-style hat in the other. But Ed believed in his message of public service. In giving back to the community. Glancing upward, he saw UNITED STATES COURT HOUSE in large block letters, and a chill shot through him.

The sudden weight of being escorted, handcuffed, into the courthouse came like a punch to Ed's gut. A rogue wave of shame followed. His pulse started sprinting. His mind jammed, like a needle on a scratched record. Trapped in a time warp that left him awake but not fully conscious, he moved robotically through the high-ceilinged foyer, across the tiled floor and into an elevator. Throughout, the MPs stood like long shadows on either side of him. When the elevator dinged and spilled him into a bustling hallway, he didn't register which floor they were on. He was marched down one hall, which turned into another, and then another. He ended up seated at a table in an over-heated, high-ceilinged room next to an Army officer he'd never met before. From a pedestal at the front, a United States flag greeted him. He trained his eyes on the flag, hoping it would unstick the needle and slow down his heart. He was a captive. Of the building's stateliness. The handcuffs. The armed officers of the law. The gravity of his predicament. Instead of waking from a coma, Ed was awake in a nightmare. He heard voices through the tunnel of his ears, but their words reverberated like echoes in the distance. He closed his eyes and opened them again. The flag steadied him. His heartbeat slowed. Suddenly, a voice boomed, and Ed crawled out of the tunnel.

"Edward F. Hohlfeld? Well?"

Ed tore his eyes away from the flag. A jowly man glared at him from behind a bench on the raised podium. A mane of cotton-white hair framed his flushed face. Heat? Alcohol? Anger? A gavel rested in front of his right hand. He took off his gold-rimmed glasses, blew on the lenses, and wiped them vigorously with an oversized handkerchief.

The needle jumped. "Sorry?" Somewhere behind him, there was whispering and titters. He felt the uniform beside him turn in his direction.

"Stand up, Private, and answer the judge," the uniform hissed.

The lieutenant was all business, square-jawed and rigid as a pole. A poker face matched his cold voice.

Ed stood. He steadied himself against the table edge.

"According to this report, you refused to follow the orders of your commanding officer. Refused to perform your duty. Got into a scuffle with your platoon sergeant when he gave you an order to shoot your rifle. You are insubordinate. You have refused to serve your country as required by law. What do you have to say for yourself?"

Disgusted, the judge vigorously wiped his lenses, checking them for spots against the overhead light. A large wart between his eyebrows made him look menacing. Like a troll Ed remembered from a children's fairytale. What was it? Something about a Billy goat.

"Sir . . ." Ed summoned his voice. He rummaged around his mind for the right words.

"Your Honor," the officer prompted.

"Your Honor," Ed corrected himself. "I don't think . . . that's not exactly right." Or was it? Yes, there was an order . . . the rifle . . . Sgt. Kaczynski. His arms hung by his side. His fists clenched. Unclenched. He had to find a way to explain himself.

"Well?" the judge briefly looked up before returning to his eyeglasses. He wiped them with the intensity of an irritated parent spanking an unruly child.

Powell's words of caution at the pit stop flashed before Ed like a neon sign: "It's Roosevelt's way or the highway." Where exactly would this highway lead?

Ed waffled. He was tired, so tired. He'd never felt this tired, this numb. This weak.

His father's admonition returned. "Pacifism is the coward's way out, son. It's no choice for a man." Kaczynski insisting that he take up the rifle. The Army telling him to kill. Their code, their laws. Not God's laws, a small, battered voice squeaked. *It*—the voice—was *Ed's*. His heart, his soul, his gut. If he had just done what *they* wanted, he wouldn't be in this jam. All he had had to do was hang his conscience up on a hook like a painting, something to look at and admire. All he had had to do was swallow his honor. Just until the killing was done. Then he could take the painting down and go back to his life. But what kind of life would that be?

He stood rooted like a wind-whipped tree, bent but unyielding.

"I did not attack my sergeant, your Honor, but I did refuse to shoot my rifle, Sir. I mean, your Honor. I'm guilty of that. But I won't kill. I can't kill, your Honor. See? I'll gladly serve. I'm a patriot. But I won't kill." Soft and halting at first, his voice grew louder and stronger as he spoke. "My conscience and my faith tell me to turn the other cheek. Like Jesus did. I can't go against my conscience. I'm bound to be faithful to it. I don't think that report you have there," he gestured toward the file that lay open in front of the judge, "is exactly right, your Honor. I don't remember hitting the sergeant. I don't think . . . but I was hit, though, see? My head . . ." Here his memory and his voice failed him. He turned his hands upward to state the plain and simple truth. "I can't kill, your Honor,"

"Oh, balderdash, soldier. You mean you won't comply with the law." The judge's voice dripped with scorn. Satisfied with two sparkling clean lenses, he hooked the glasses behind his ears and tucked his white handkerchief beneath the black robe. "That issue was resolved when you complied with the draft. The Roman Catholic Church *permits* but does not *require* its members to be non-violent. I'm sick and tired of you cowardly, socialistically inclined men traipsing in and out of my courtroom. Whiny able-bodied men refusing to perform their national duty. Why, it's an outrage. You should be ashamed of yourself." His eyes narrowed. "Are you a German sympathizer, Private Hohlfeld? Well?"

The judge's question struck his heart like a poisoned arrow. Glints of light bounced off the judge's newly cleaned eyeglasses, making it difficult for Ed to see his eyes. Shaken, he stammered, "A *German* sympathizer? No, absolutely not . . . of course not . . .I'm an American citizen . . ."

"Your Honor," the Army lieutenant prompted.

"Your Honor." Ed's voice shook with indignation.

The judge snapped back. "Don't take that tone with me, young man. Your commanding officer suspects you of having mixed loyalties. You are German, are you not? Don't you have a relationship with one Adolf Voss, who is now in federal custody?"

The courtroom started spinning. The memory of his good neighbor Adolf being carted away by federal agents flashed before him. Ed couldn't make heads or tails of the allegations. Was the judge suggesting he was a spy, or was he just trying to bully Ed?

"Yes, your Honor, I mean, no. I'm American. Half-German, half-Irish." He wasn't sure which question to answer. "I know Mr. Voss, yes, of course. He is. Was a neighbor of ours, a friend of my father's . . ." What was the judge getting at?

The judge leaned forward. "So, you admit to having consorted with this German patriot?"

"No. That's not right. You're bamboozling me. I'm an American. My father is . . ."

"That'll be enough, Pvt. Hohlfeld." The judge cast one final withering glance in his direction. "Where sir, is your patriotism?"

He answered his own question with a peremptory shuffle of papers and pounding of the gavel. "In accordance with the Selective Training and Service Act of 1940, I hereby remand you to the Philadelphia State Mental Hospital as a Prisoner of War until further notice."

The judge stood up. "Get this coward the hell out of my courtroom."

Ed's stunned body slumped forward against the table. Just where would this highway lead?

## Chapter 12

# The Quaker

The sticky city kissed the open spaces of the country hello at Philadelphia's northeastern edge. Walter Sinclair steered his uncle's '37 pea-green pickup off of Roosevelt Boulevard and into Bucks County. An elongated driveway, saluted by a line of blossomless cherry trees, led him to a cluster of faded brick buildings. Walter eyed the rows of four-foot by two-foot windows traversing the main story of the principal structure. He imagined the good he might do on the other side of those windows. A Quaker pacifist and a newly designated conscientious objector to war, Walter requested a transfer from his original assignment at Buck Creek Camp, to Camp #49, the Philadelphia State Hospital.

While he had no training for the job of hospital attendant, he thought he might be better at flexing his heart instead of his biceps. He also had a truckload of empathy for the downtrodden, having been taken in by his mother's only brother, the owner of 150 lush acres in Lancaster County. Walter grew up a farm boy, but his aunt and uncle nurtured Walter's loftier ambitions. He had an unwrapped college degree from Swarthmore College to show for it, too. The war had sidelined his law school plans, at least for the time being. It also placed his engagement to Sally Mae Hope of Akron, Ohio, on indefinite hold. She was an ace, though. He knew she would wait for him.

The sun kissed her auburn hair on that summer day he met her. It was early morning, the grass still gleaming from dew. Home for summer break, Walter stood perched on a twenty-foot ladder. He was slathering a fresh coat of red paint on the broadside of the barn when a soft chuckle drifted upward. Turning gingerly to face the ground below and trace the source, he clapped eyes on a pixie. Her long hair was tied back with a bright turquoise bow. Freckles dotted her turned-up nose.

Gazing upward, her hand blocking the sun, she shook her head. "My, my, Aunt Bessie *did say* thou had quite the pompadour." She lifted her other hand and pointed to her own shiny chestnut locks. "I've seen others, but thy pompadour sure beats the band." Another tinkle of laughter.

"Like it, eh?" Walter set the paintbrush across the top of the large can and swept his hair back. He was, he had to admit, rather vain when it came to his sandy mane. He pulled a red-checkered handkerchief from the side pocket of his overalls to wipe the sweat from his brow and collect himself. A cloudless powder blue sky blessed the barn and the farmland beyond it. "I'm Walter. Thou must be Emma's daughter." Emma was the sister of his uncle's wife and the only one of the four sisters who lived out of state.

"I am. I've been hearing my aunts sing thy praises for so long I decided I had to come meet this model of good looks *and* virtue." Stepping sideways into a spot of shade, she lowered her hand and hooked her thumbs on the belt around her slim waist. She kept her head tilted upward, as if she didn't want to take her eyes off of Walter for fear he'd disappear. Her sea-green cotton dress flapped in the soft breeze.

Blackbirds twittered good morning from the maple trees framing the barn. Walter couldn't see the color of her eyes. If they matched her dress, he knew he was a goner. Chuckling to himself, he took the plunge, stepping down from the ladder and into a summer romance he hoped would last a lifetime. Fortunately for Walter, Sallie Mae was equally smitten. He was a lucky man. She was a patient woman and an avid letter writer. While completing his alternative service, Walter planned to coax the flame of their love with his skillful pen.

When he reached the hospital guardhouse, Walter pulled up the hand brake and waited in line. He'd have to return the vehicle after the interview. Assuming it went well, and he was approved, he'd make the return trip to the Byberry hospital and his first post-college job by bus. He'd already said his good-byes to Uncle Henry, his mother's only brother, and Aunt Bessie, Henry's wife of thirty-five years. He could never thank them enough though, for saving his young life and giving him a future.

Walter never really knew his father, a shadowy man with long sideburns and slicked-back hair who came and went in the night to claim his mother's body. A scar on his left cheek widened his face into a steady leer, and a signature Chesterfield cigarette hung perpetually from the corner of his mouth. Walter couldn't summon an image of his father without seeing the flash of red, followed by swirls of smoke rising from thin purple lips and enveloping his face. The only feeling Walter had toward the man, who only ever called him *boy*, was dread. Then again, Red's Boardinghouse, where Walter had lived as a child, was home to men with scowls for faces and, excepting his forlorn mother, women with ruby lips and syrupy voices.

Walter was isolated and lonely as a child. He lived among adults at the boardinghouse because Red had a soft spot for his mother. Walter and his mother slept in the attic, which was a large, low-ceilinged room divided in half by a thin partition. Lily, his mother's friend, lived on the other side. She was nice to Walter. Always patted him on the cheek and gave him black licorice. One night, Walter woke up to the sound of an infant crying in the adjoining room. Walter perked up. A quasi-baby brother or sister? How exciting. He would be less lonely with a little tyke around the boardinghouse to look out for. Walter could teach him how to tie his shoes and throw a ball. What if it was a girl, though? Well, he supposed he could teach her to throw a ball and tie her shoes. He pestered his mother for days. He wanted to visit the baby, hold the baby. His mother became irritated. Told him to be quiet and stop asking.

"What baby? Babies aren't allowed here." He was pretty sure he hadn't imagined the crying infant. But he never did see the baby. It stopped crying after three nights, leaving Walter with a sick sorry feeling in his belly and a burning question. Should he have snatched the baby and run away to his uncle's farm? Lily was still there, but she was a lot quieter and less inclined to pat Walter's cheeks and give him licorice. Walter's hopes for something like a sibling were good and gone.

One day, he woke up on the twin mattress he shared with his mother and knew she was gone, too. Probably for good this time. She loved him. Walter was sure of that. But she had faraway eyes and a restless spirit, and she loved him enough to give him away. She left him a tiny silver locket with her picture in it, a picture from long ago when her gray eyes weren't so sad and her skin not yet sallow. He pulled on his trousers and undershirt and slipped into the closet where he set to counting the cracks in the plastered wall. When he awakened from his trance or sleep, he couldn't tell which one, he put on his tattered woolen sweater and slipped down the stairs and out the front door. This was the quietest time of day at the company house, as his mother called it, which woke up in the late afternoon and didn't go to sleep until breakfast. He sat on the porch steps waiting, and his aunt and uncle finally showed up as he sensed they would, likely summoned by his mother.

They didn't say much. His uncle squeezed his shoulder when he squired Walter into his rusted pick-up, the old one before he purchased the '37 Chevy. His aunt folded her hand over his on the drive back to their Pennsylvania farm. Even then, they had seemed old, or maybe tired. Disciplined, sturdy folk, they were getting on in years, and Walter now regretted that he was no longer there to milk and herd the cows and see to the heavier labor. Yet they were the ones who had encouraged Walter to pursue his dream of going to college and starting his own life. They were Quakers. Hardworking, peace-loving farming people who were humble and quiet in their ways. Walter loved them dearly, but the scales of justice summoned him. Someday he would be an attorney at law with a family of his own.

When it was Walter's turn, the insouciant security guard's pencil located "Walter Sinclair" on a sheet of paper in front of him and pointed the way forward.

"Why, thank thee, sir." Walter tapped the brim of his gray Fedora. It sat atop his golden-brown pompadour that he kept close-cropped at the sides, just the way Sallie Mae liked. As he drove forward, he imagined himself in his new role as an attendant at the state mental hospital. A sudden quickening of his pulse signaled his jumble of excitement and anxiety. He adjusted his silver-rimmed spectacles and surveyed his home for the foreseeable future, noting the flat, well-manicured landscape and the buildings that fanned out in front of him like a fleet of ships.

Located just outside the city, the institution was surrounded by farmland. Walter was not daunted by its isolation, though he might have heeded the menace in the languor of cherry trees, stripped and bewitched by the heavy hand of winter. Or the menace of the caged windows that revealed themselves only upon closer inspection. No, this CO assignment would not daunt him. For Walter, it was an opportunity to be a force of good in the world.

Walter's eager tires crunched over the thin layer of frosted roadway that curved to the right and took him to the administration building where his fitness for the job would be evaluated. Sound of mind and body, and 6'3" and 185 pounds, he was a good candidate for a job that needed strong, able-bodied men to manage the disturbed patients. Thankfully, too, it was an acceptable arrangement with the Friends Committee, charged with having to provide financial support for the church's conscientious objectors. The hospital had agreed to pay a small portion of the $30.00 monthly room and board fee and give him $2.50 for personal expenses. Not much, he knew, but Walter would get by. His aunt and uncle would likely send a dollar now and again, and that'd help. If all went as planned, he would secure the attendant position. His swelling heart imagined how he might serve the good Lord and care for the feeble-minded and spiritually desolate. What a wonderful opportunity for a young man who had disavowed violence to still serve his country and kinsmen. Yes, hopeful healer Walter Sinclair thought, some good might be done here.

## Chapter 13

# "In God is Our Trust"

Ed fidgeted in the hospital admitting area. Sat forward. Sat back. Crossed his legs. Uncrossed them. Sat forward again, trying to focus on something besides the jam he found himself in. The robins' egg blue walls were decorated with framed landscapes. A pine forest with sunlight seeping through the trees. A rainbow arched across a cloudless blue sky. The serene images did little to quell Ed's anxiety, with the judge's ruling still ringing in his ears. A P.O.W. for refusing to follow an order? For being half-German? And why was he being sent to a state mental hospital? "Until further notice." What did that mean exactly?

The waiting area of the Philadelphia State Mental Hospital was located off a long hallway, not far from the front entrance and on the other side of the main double-doors. Shifting his tense limbs, Ed's eyes searched the hallway for the source of the incessant pop-hiss-bang noise. They settled on a heater on the other side of the doorway, apparently on its last legs and doing little to warm up the chilly air. White and green uniforms bobbed up and down in the distance. The MPs who had escorted him from the courtroom stood dutifully on the other side of Ed and nearest the door to the outside. Powell had removed the cuffs, so Ed pulled his jacket tighter and rubbed his wrists. Out of habit, he slipped off his soldier's cap, folded it neatly, and tucked it into his belt. He ordered his rattled nerves to stand at ease. They were not inclined to obey. A movie reel of the courtroom played over and over again in his mind.

Startled by the judge's ruling, Ed felt unmoored. From outside his own body, he watched the MPs march him from the courtroom. He saw himself screaming, a long silent, horrifying scream, like the painting he recalled seeing in his art book. A distorted face—hand clapped on ears, mouth agape, eyes rounded in terror. Ed forced himself to shut the picture down. He tugged at the St. Christopher medal around his neck, sliding it back and forth between his fingers. He tried to pray. "Our Father who art in heaven . . . Hail Mary, full of grace, the Lord is with thee . . ." He tried to concentrate. But his mind insisted on returning to the courtroom scene.

His nerves were still jumping, but the fog on the window of his mind started to clear. The judge's ruling didn't make a lick of sense. The injury to his head and his faulty memory hadn't helped. But this? Sentenced to a mental hospital? It, *this judgment*, he thought bitterly, was what was insane. Where was the justice in it? The Army lawyer hadn't mounted a defense. Had he? Or had Ed blanked it out? He couldn't be sure. He felt as if the game that was his life had been played and lost without him. He was left alone on the field with twitching muscles and the slow, steady boil of defeat in his blood. Calm and reason. He kept repeating the words in his head. It was critical to check the emotions bouncing around inside him like jumping beans. Maybe the doctor will help me. The doctor will see I'm perfectly sane, that there's been a big mistake here.

"GOD TOLD ME! GOD TOLD ME! God told me. God told me. GOD told ME!" A hysterical voice thundered from the other side of the doorway. Ed's head turned toward the commotion. Half-dressed in a long, pasty green shirt with no pants, a patient stood on a bench across from the hissing radiator. A mop of gray, stringy hair draped his face. He spread his arms Moses-like and preached his dark Word. "You WILL all DIE!" His eyes swept up and down the length of the corridor, finally settling on the waiting area where Ed sat.

"I AM HIS PROPHET. GOD TOLD ME! DOOMED, YOU'RE ALL DOOMED! GOD TOLD ME!" He aimed a crooked finger in Ed's direction. Then, as if sprinkled with pixie dust, his body slackened. He shook his head from side to side in disbelief or wonder and grew sullen.

"But the garden and mother said the flowers, and she got so angry, angry, angry, but I didn't hurt mother the flowers." As he spoke, the prophet again grew agitated and belligerent. Attendants emerged from some unseen place. He bellowed at them, ignoring instructions to get down from the bench. "NO, I WILL NOT. HOW DARE YOU! I AM HIS PROPHET AND GOD TOLD *ME*." This way and that way he thrashed, until a husky man in a white uniform hauled him down and threw him, face first, onto the floor, his gray head inches away from the hissing radiator. The man wrapped a straitjacket around the prophet's upper body, hooked it, and clapped a mask over his face. Then he yanked him upright. From a ring of keys, he selected and inserted one into a locked door further down the corridor and steered God's prophet rather forcefully through the door, restoring restive quiet to the area. The door thudded shut behind them.

No one else in the waiting room seemed fazed. From his post at the door to the outside, Powell shrugged. Ed shook his head. Crazy. The guy's plumb crazy.

He leaned forward and cupped his face in his hands. *This* was wrong. The doctor would surely see this. It couldn't—wouldn't—go uncorrected. The heel of his left foot started pumping, dispelling Ed's bottled-up energy. He reached into his top pocket for a cigarette, held it up, and glanced over at Powell. In a few long strides, Powell was leaning over Ed with a matchbook, striking it with the thumb and middle finger of his right hand.

"How's it going, Chief?"

Ed gave Powell a half-smile and nodded. "Appreciate it." Ed felt so grateful for this long merciful moment of something so achingly human. Like-mindedness? Sympathy? Understanding? They locked eyes. Then Powell turned up his hands slightly, as if to indicate his helplessness in the matter of Ed's fate and marched back to his post.

Ed studied the door to the outside world where the MPs stood. His heart pitched. Freedom. He longed to leap up and push past the sentries, throw open that door, and run like hell as far and as fast as possible. Back down the long, elegant roadway that led to the hospital, past the barren cherry trees, and south on Roosevelt Boulevard. Home was so close he could taste it. It couldn't be more than fifteen or twenty miles away. He saw himself grab a beer with Sam at Willy's, lift Mary up and twirl her in the air, find that girl Tilley and take her dancing. Everything would be back to normal. Everything would be fine. The Army had to see they'd made a terrible mistake and assign him a duty on the Homefront. Maybe they were just trying to teach him a lesson. That must be it. They wanted to test him or scare him. He kept on coming back to the same bald fact, though. His sentencing made no sense. No way he belonged in this place. A looney bin? His parents, his family—did they know? What did they think?

If he gave into his impulse and ran, all bets had to be off though. He would be AWOL. That would be the end of him for sure. No, he couldn't risk that, couldn't risk worsening his situation. This was a crisis he had to face. He'd done nothing wrong. Well, refused to shoot his rifle. That was all. Right? He climbed out of his silent misery and glanced at the young man sitting across from him, guessing that he, too, sat waiting on the doctor. Pale and slender, he didn't look like he could be more than sixteen years old. His straight black hair fell over his right eye like a spray of ravens' feathers on a white canvas. He had a delicate, perfectly proportioned face. His slender nose was framed in translucent skin, high cheekbones, and oval eyes. His left eye looked up at Ed, like a wary cat circling his leg and trying to decide whether to trust him. Ed sensed the trembling of the young man's limbs. His hands were buried under his thighs, and beneath his coat, he was wearing long, checkered flannel pants that looked like pajama bottoms.

"Are you a soldier?" The boy's left eye blinked up at Ed once, twice, three times. His fingers brushed back the black hair, revealing cobalt eyes that looked as if they'd already seen worlds of pain. His right cheekbone was dark and swollen. It was severely bruised, maybe even broken.

"Err, yes, well," Ed paused, uncertain. "Name's Ed." He finally leaned over and offered the young man his hand.

Tentatively, the young man extended his right hand. He had the long, narrow fingers of a pianist or a surgeon. Angry red slashes criss-crossing the inside of his left wrist winked up at Ed.

"J...J...J...Joseph," he stammered. The cat had decided to nestle in the safety of Ed's gentle presence.

Ed shook the young man's hand warmly, waves of compassion passing over him, but at a loss for something else to say.

A nurse holding a sheet of paper appeared abruptly from the doorway to the doctor's office. "Pvt. Edward F. Hohlfeld?"

Ed raised his chin and nodded, mechanically pushing his hair back from his forehead. He stood, casting a final glance back at Powell. Then he bent over the young man. Searched for the right words to say, as if everything depended on them. "Nice to meet you. Take good care, Joseph."

Joseph's eyes softened and smiled.

The nurse gestured impatiently. "Doctor Windsor will see you now."

Ed slipped his hand into the corner of his right pocket. His fingers slid across the thin silver cross in his pocket. The St. Christopher Medal he'd worn since his Confirmation slapped against his chest. For some reason, words from the national anthem came to him, "In God is our trust." He took a deep breath and exhaled. Once inside the dimly lit corridor, the nurse unlocked a door and led Ed through it.

## Chapter 14

# Buster Keating

Walter's heart sagged a bit as he trudged the one-quarter mile from his cottage on the women's side of Route 1 to Men's B Ward on the opposite side of the street. At 5:45 a.m., the sky was inky black, and the pleasantly frosty air smelled like Christmas. His lungs woke up, white spirals of breath signaling a temperature that hovered around zero. He buried his chin in the plaid, hand-knit scarf around his neck, a gift from Sallie Mae's parents and a good sign that they'd accepted him as their future son-in-law. When he reached his destination, he looked up to see traces of crimson streak across the horizon, minutes too early for him to be baptized in the light of the new day.

But it was the darkness that stayed with Walter, given the stunning news reported in yesterday's *Bulletin*. Two million civilians dead. Exterminated, according to the president of the Jewish American Congress. Wiped from God's good earth by Hitler's evil henchmen. What a staggering number. How was it even possible to kill that many human beings? Two-thirds of Jewish Poles gone, simply gone. Poland swallowed up, and more countries slated to follow. Coerced like obdurate animals into Hitler's ever-expanding tent. Accounts of Nazi massacres had been trickling out in the news for some time now, but nothing like this, nothing on this scale. Walter's heart wept.

The heaviness slowly receded as Walter called up the memory of Sallie Mae's recent letter and their more hopeful future. Its lavender scent and sweet words of love.

*We splurged on our ration of gasoline this past weekend. Took a drive to Cuyahoga Valley National Park and snow-shoed our way along the lovely Tree Pine Trail. Oh, I think of thee daily, Wally dearest. Remember the time we walked barefoot in the brook behind the farm last summer, slipping and sliding on the mossy stones until we both fell in?* He smiled. Sallie Mae was the only one who got away with calling him Wally. *How I wished thou were here with me. The sun smiled on us the entire time, and I thought of thee when I spied the snow-white head of a magnificent bald eagle sweeping across the sky. I thought of thee when I breathed the sweet piney smell and saw the hemlocks. I imagined the day we would be together again. Oh, I hope it's not far off when we can finally walk this trail as husband and wife . . .*

His smile faded. No, not today, Sallie Mae. Your blue skies are no match for this black cloud. Two million human beings murdered by a madman. Walter shook his head. In the wake of this horror, his work with the sick and forsaken took on renewed meaning. He would answer Hitler's destruction in the only way he could, with his fervent commitment to compassion and service.

Walter reached the heavy outer door on the east side of B building. He paused to scrape the soles of his work shoes on the mat. The dark grout, porous and chipped from the elements, made the surrounding brick unstable. This can't be good. Walter made a mental note to report the problem to the hospital administration. Removing one glove, he pulled two keys from his pocket. The ice-cold metal stung his fingers, but he managed to insert the deadbolt key. It clicked, and he shoved the steel door open. A blast of warm air and an overpowering stench greeted him. What in the world? Trying to ignore the foul smell, he walked down the dimly lit corridor in search of a staff member. Further down, a door creaked open, and a figure emerged from the shadows.

"You the new guy?" The burly man sounded like he had a mouthful of marbles.

"The new attendant, yes. I'm Walter Sinclair." He extended his ungloved hand eagerly when he reached the white uniform. Shadows played on the walls. Two lights blinkered out.

Another was on its way. A thick, sweaty paw met his. Walter pulled his hand back and instinctively wiped it on his pants leg before removing the glove on his other hand.

The paid attendant had the girth of a Sumo wrestler as well as a good two inches on Walter's six feet plus frame. The heavily creased cowhide-like face matched his marbly voice. Tufts of curly gray hair stood out on a massive skull. Up close, Walter noticed that the man's mouth had more teeth than it could reasonably handle. They were also misshapen and stained yellow. Walter struggled to look past the man's less-than-attractive appearance.

"Well, Mr. Walter Sinclair, I'm Buster Keating. Keating, not Keaton. I'm funny, but not that funny. Ha, ha, ha." He'd obviously used the line many times before, and it still tickled him. A clipboard hung by his side. He didn't seem to notice Walter's hand-wiping or tentative smile. Walter let both go slack and removed his outer clothing, throwing the items over his arm.

Walter nodded. "Yes, Keating. I'll try to keep that in mind."

Buster appraised Walter, rocking back and forth on his heels as if to emphasize his height and seniority. "The Supervisor will check in with you later. Mr. Gerald Frank. Hoity-toity kind of fella." Buster briefly placed his fingers around his nose to demonstrate. "Not hard to miss in this place. Wears fancy suits like the doc. Oh, and you'll need this."

Buster produced a clipboard, scanned it, then pushed it into Walter's uncertain hands.

"And this is. . .?"

"Patient names and numbers are listed on those sheets. See? Won't do you much good, though. Who the hell can keep track of 300 and some crazies, huh?" Buster drifted off, scratched his left buttock.

"Surely, you jest, Mr. Keating."

"Good one! *Shirley*, I'm not." Keating guffawed, amused by his joke. "Let's see, oh yeah. No gambling or smoking on the ward, and if Doc Windsor or one of the bigwigs shows up, just stop what you're doing, see? Stand at attention. They like that. Your keys are hanging on the board in the office. Yours is number 55. Don't forget to sign the sheet of paper when you take them out. Return them at the end of your shift. Sign again." He cleared his throat and shrugged. "Guess that's pretty much it."

Walter didn't quite know what to think. His brief stint in the incontinent ward before being assigned to Ward B had been rough. He thought it was due to a temporary shortage of staff and supplies. The incontinent ward had been filthy, and the stench, overpowering. Many of the patients were naked, their skin smeared with feces. There was a critical shortage of clean sheets and blankets, forcing patients to sleep on soiled mattresses. The supervisor blamed the shortage and lack of staff and supplies on the war effort. From the looks of it, Ward B might not be much different from the incontinent ward. Worse, there had been no training to speak of, just a few directions about procedures for managing patients. What was Walter walking into?

The men's nakedness in incontinent A ward had shocked Walter's Quaker sensibilities. It wasn't seemly. The poor fellows hugged the walls for safety and warmth. With no furniture to sit on, they meandered around the day room in a daze like wounded animals left behind by the herd. Walter had hustled from duty to duty like a manic robot, leaving him little time to think about the situation. Didn't even have time to pause and take part in yesterday's collective national mourning for the Jewish dead. What a suffering world over there, and in here, he thought. And what in the world did Buster mean by 300 or so patients and only two attendants?

"Who will be working this shift beside us?"

Buster Keating smirked. "Ha, ha, ha. No can do, pal. You and me are on our own today. Two other guys got canned. Got us a couple worker-patients. They help out with mopping up the shit and piss."

So, it wasn't much different from the incontinent ward. Walter couldn't help but notice that something seemed to be wrong with Buster's nose. It was horribly bent, and thin purple rivers crisscrossed the bridge as though seeking an exit. Buster didn't breathe so much as slurp breath through his mouth.

"Four attendants whittled down to two for more than 300 patients. Why, that's outrageous." Walter expected sympathy or at least a nod of tacit agreement. Instead, he got a shoulder shrug of indifference from Buster Keating.

"Are thou at least going to show me around?" Walter had a mind to take the cretin to task, but the less time he spent in this revolting man's company, the better.

Buster snorted, ignoring his question. "You can put your things in there." He motioned to a door behind him that led to a small office. "Nurse should be along soon. Doc Windsor may come by sometime during the shift. May not. Who knows? He's a card, that one. You met him? Always good for a joke."

Buster's downright insouciance left Walter speechless.

"Nah, you'll be fine," he said, finally returning to Walter's question. "Pretty simple. Get from one building to another in the tunnels. Seen those yet? No? Gotta map here somewhere." He checked his pockets, and then he laughed and held up his hands as if he were surrendering to the police. "Hell's bells. Guess not. Just check the office. Should find one there. Patients sleep in the two wings in the basement."

He pointed toward the stairs at the end of the hallway. "Kind of a long walk to the dining hall. Move them in, move them out. Keep them quiet. That's the job. Then you got your day room, first floor on the other side. And your lockdown. Called the Restraint Room. That one's across from the office, see?"

He looked back in the direction of the office that Walter had passed. "The key to the office is on your ring. The others you'll figure out. Half the locks are broken and don't even work anyway. Ha, ha, ha. That's the way it rolls around here. Pretty simple. Need to keep a close eye on the troublemakers in the dayroom. Fights always breaking out. We keep the most violent ones tied to cots in the Restraint Room. Elopers or troublemakers, one of the two. Keep them on lockdown. Make sure they're not up to no good."

Walter ignored the double negative, which irritated him to no end. His aunt, a former schoolteacher, was a stickler for correct English. She'd invested a fair amount of time undoing the linguistic damage of Walter's early haphazard schooling. But the man's careless attitude toward the patients rankled him. In the incontinent ward, he'd at least been given a tour by an attendant who took his job seriously.

"An eloper?"

"Yeah, ya know, the guys that try to escape. E-lopers, get it?" He chuckled.

"Well," Walter paused, adjusting his eyeglasses. He missed the security of his Fedora that always steadied him. "How am I to know what to do? What's the routine? Is there a set of instructions for me to follow? What about medication?"

"Nah, ain't got much in the way of medications. You kidding? Too many. When they get really wound up, they get the straitjacket or the hydrotherapy. Seal them in an ice-cold tub. That shuts them down real good. Tie them up with these." He produced what looked like leather handcuffs. "Short of straitjackets. Most everything's broken or fallen apart around here."

Walter's eyes widened. He felt his lower jaw fall. Buster seemed not to notice, or else he was taking pleasure in shocking the new attendant.

"Rules?" Buster winked. "Don't kill the patients. That's rule number one. Sometimes it can't be helped, though. Ha, ha, ha. Rule number two? Don't let them kill each other."

Walter recoiled. Is the man deranged?

Ignoring Walter's frown, Buster added, "Whaddaya gonna do? Crazies."

He paused, stretched his arms, and farted unceremoniously before continuing. "Just last week, a guy stole an iron rod from the laundry room and beat another guy to death in the dayroom. See what I'm saying? Some of the crazies get mean. You got to be just as mean. Be on the lookout for homemade weapons, too. They don't get no silverware no more. A few of the quieter ones have spoons. Most make do with their hands. Can't trust them with silverware. Too goddamned many of them to watch."

An ear-piercing shriek from somewhere beneath them, followed by a thud, interrupted his monologue.

"What in the world?" Walter stammered, adjusting his eyeglasses. What kind of hospital *was* this?

Buster frowned. "Don't pay that no never-mind." He returned to his speech with a dismissive wave.

"Watch out for the sneaky bastards. Took a blade from one guy who had it hid in his ass. Can you beat that to hell? Just let them know who's boss. Let's see . . . what else? Be extra careful in the dayroom. Find some shackles and a few camisoles in the closet there." He nodded over his left shoulder toward the office.

Walter stood speechless, stunned by the man's crudeness and cruel indifference.

"I carry a homemade gadget myself." To illustrate, he reached into the pocket of his white pants and pulled out what looked like a chunk of rubber hose. He slapped it against his thigh. "Got some buckshot inside. But if you're the queasy kind you can always put a couple bars of soap in a sock. Works pretty good. Don't leave no marks."

He eyed Walter to see if his rant was having the desired effect. Walter didn't cooperate. Apart from the single frown, he remained stone-faced. Didn't want to give Buster the satisfaction.

"Oh yeah," Buster added. "Wet towel's also handy in a pinch. Just soak it, twirl it around it a few times 'til it's good and tight. Then put the patient in a chokehold. That settles the suckers down quick-like. Don't leave no scars, neither. Know what I mean?" He snorted.

Walter's stomach flip-flopped. He had no illusions about the patients. Obviously, they were mentally ill and no doubt unruly sometimes. That's why they were here. He understood that he'd have to restrain them physically from time to time. But violence as a method of dealing with them? The very thought of harming a patient in such a way troubled Walter. The fact that he was a conscientious objector seemed to have eluded Buster. Or had it? Perhaps Buster was just exaggerating. Testing out the new guy. Ribbing him, as it were, though the rubber hose sticking out of his pocket was real enough.

"Most of them are out of it. Ya know what I mean. Duh." Buster twisted his face, stuck out his tongue, and let it hang to the side of his mouth. "Welcome to the Bughouse! Have to get going," he announced suddenly, after checking his watch. "They'll be going to breakfast in the dining hall soon. We got to file them in and out. Then we got to get them back to the day room. Break up fights. Keep order and all that. Herd them to and from lunch. Same thing with supper. Then beddie-bye. Drop your stuff in the office there and have a look around."

Walter nodded. "Well, thank thee."

"See you in ten, Conch. Look for me. I'll be the one carrying the big stick. Ha, ha, ha."

He slapped his pocket and turned away.

Conch, the pejorative slang word for conscientious objector. He had taken notice.

"Oh, hold on." Buster turned back. "If we're lucky, the new guy gets here next week. Other one? One they fired?" He made a motion with his hand to his mouth. "Had a problem with the sauce, know what I mean? Spent most of his time sleeping it off in the office. Me? I'm way more careful." He pointed to what appeared to be a flask in his other pocket. "Keep it out of sight when it counts, and don't fall asleep in the supply closet." He bent over and clapped his knee. A thunderous har, har, har, har trailed him down the hallway.

Walter adjusted his spectacles, shifting his weight from his right foot to the left. Had Buster been exaggerating? Joking? He planted both feet, searching for grounding. How is it possible for two men to look after more than 300 mentally ill patients? He understood his assignment was to work with the more violence-prone patients because of his height advantage and muscular build, but he assumed he'd get instructions on how to employ other, non-violent ways of managing them.

He unlocked the office door and stepped inside. After pocketing his gloves, he hung up his jacket and scarf on a rickety coat rack in the corner. He found the board with sets of keys, all numbered. He signed the sheet and grabbed #55. A locked closet door stood at the back of the office. Supplies? He held up his ring of keys, and after trying three of them, he came to the right one. The door pinged open. He found a shelf of worn and damaged cuffs, assorted straps, and worn-out straitjackets. Walter picked up a straitjacket. Examined its straps and locks with tentative fingers. Disgusted, he placed it back on the shelf.

Shutting the door, he turned to explore the rest of the office. A broken swivel chair, an intact straight-back wooden chair, two file cabinets, and a desk strewn with papers. He glanced at the copies of patient histories. These were mixed in with a map of the buildings and tunnels, request forms for patient supplies, and instructions for securing cuffs on patients. He stuffed one of the instruction sheets in his back pocket. Well, he'd better get to it, he decided, with a renewed sense of purpose. He tried arranging the desk papers in some kind of tentative order and switched off the light before locking the door behind him. Maybe he'd see to organizing and filing the papers after his shift wound down.

As he drew nearer the door to the patients' quarters, the stench he encountered when he first entered the building intensified. It smelled like a lethal mixture of dead bodies and human waste. Like poisonous gas. Like Hitler. He sucked in the air and wavered momentarily, pulling his arm up to cover his nose. Finally, he exhaled, jiggling the lock on the heavy metal door. He coughed, trying not to breathe in the noxious air. Then he let his arm drop and stood erect.

A man had to stand up to such things. He had chosen this path, and, by God, now he'd walk it. He pushed the door open and stepped inside.

*Chapter 15*

# Welcome to the Bughouse

Ed's dilated eyes probed the dim overstuffed room jammed with rickety metal cots. His mouth and throat were parched. He hesitated to ask the churlish attendant for a drink of water.

"Over there, loon. Welcome to the Bughouse." He snickered, pushing Ed forward and onto a cot, separated only by inches from the cots on either side. It creaked and slid under his sudden weight. His left bicep still pulsed where the nurse had jabbed him. He shouldn't have yelled at the doctor. Ed couldn't make the doctor understand that his being here was all a big mistake. Ed wasn't crazy. But the doctor wouldn't listen. Too late now. Flashes of light danced in front of his eyes. The world slowed down. His limbs moved sluggishly, as if through an undercurrent in the surf. His sense of smell, more acute, registered the rank odor of piss and sweat. Nausea floated up from his belly and into his throat. He couldn't remember when he'd last eaten. It was just as well. If only he could quench his thirst. He leaned forward and set his feet squarely onto the floor to steady his stomach. In spite of the woolen Army socks, he was permitted to keep, the cold cement floor bit his feet, the sensation making its way by slow locomotive to his brain.

The admitting attendant's nameplate read *Rob Simpson*. When he took his shoes, Ed's heart slumped. How could he ever take flight now? His duffle bag was also confiscated. "For thafe-keeping." The man's front teeth were missing, making it difficult to understand the directions he spat out. "Thlothes ofh, ofh!" His body reeked of alcohol. A massive belly hung over his belt like a boulder at the edge of a cliff. He thumped Ed on the back, barking at him to "huwwy it the hewl up. My thift's about up."

What time was it? Seven? Eight? Ed had lost track of time, his precious Gruen collected and placed into "thafekeeping." Ed wondered how safe, and if he'd ever see his grandfather's watch again. Rob also collected Ed's Army uniform and black Rosary, the one his mother gave him for his first Holy Communion.

"Thorry fella," Rob held up the cross. "'Han't let you keep a weapon now, can I?" He'd ignored the St. Christopher Medal that hung around his neck. At least Ed had that.

After being stripped naked, he was shoved into a communal shower under a ragged sprinkling of cold water. Like a parched, wounded bird, his upturned mouth collected a few drops. The pungent smell of the other men's bodies was stifling. A sliver of soap passed between them. The showerhead stopped trickling, and a tattered green shirt and drawstring pants were thrust at his torso. Steered into a corridor, Ed was still stuffing his second leg into the pants when a high-pitched, heart-stopping scream suddenly rang out and almost tipped him over.

"AAAEEEYYYYY, AAAEEEYYYYYAAY." Ed scanned the mass of bodies and located the screamer several feet in front of him. He was clutching his upturned head like a bottle top he wanted to remove. The piercing scream ricocheted against the walls. Other men started to moan. Attendant Rob wrapped what looked like a rolled wet towel around the man's neck and pushed him to the floor. Ed squinted. Tried to bring the picture into focus. Then checked his instinctive urge to intervene. He was too unsteady. The man gurgled and sputtered with the tightening of the towel, his legs splayed and kicking. His body finally surrendered to the attendant who pulled him up and thrust him onto a bench. Rob clapped an iron mask around the screamer's mouth. The moans died down, replaced by a soothing baritone voice. Ed turned. He spotted the patient-singer behind him.

"When our heads are bowed with woes, when our bitter tears o'erflow, when we mourn the lost the dear, Jesus' son of Mary hear!" The grey-haired man beside Ed started to weep.

Another one, further back, cursed, and told the singing man to shut up.

Now confined to what looked like an overpacked dormitory, Ed lifted his feet from the cold floor onto his filthy cot and lay back. Sat up again. He leaned over, trying to shake away the fuzziness. He had to make sense of his grim situation, figure out how the day had gone so terribly awry. He rubbed his sore arm. His chest and arms were trembling from cold, or shock, or both. In the fog of his brain, he tried to remember. Stupid, stupid, stupid. He shouldn't have lost his temper. Shouldn't have pounded on Dr. Theodore L. Windsor's desk. Shouldn't have shouted at him about injustice and constitutional rights. Stupid. Stupid. Stupid. But the smug doctor in the fancy pinstriped suit demonstrated a maddeningly blasé attitude about the unfairness of the judge's order. He waved a dismissive hand and pronounced Ed's sentence, a king sending his lowly subject to the dungeon.

The doctor had seemed reasonable at first, sympathetic even. Ed calmly tried to explain that there was nothing wrong with him. He was not insane. He just couldn't bring himself to fire his rifle. His conscience wouldn't let him. He hadn't attacked the sergeant. The doctor had to understand this. The sergeant had assaulted him. Why had the Army sent Ed to a mental hospital? It made no sense. It was all wrong. Couldn't he see that? He'd been railroaded. See? That's what was crazy.

When Ed mentioned the sergeant, the doctor's face hardened. His seeming goodwill evaporated. He shuffled some papers and checked his watch. He picked up a glass of water on his desk to take a long swallow before setting it back down. He cleared his throat.

"The fact is, Private Hohlfeld, you have been adjudicated. I'm afraid these . . . ahh . . . these deviant and violent tendencies of yours . . ." He garbled the rest of his statement, as if even he knew the court's judgment made no sense.

Ed's hopes for a fair hearing crashed and splintered into the iceberg of reality. His respect for authority and his faith in justice spewed out to sea. He leaped from his chair and aimed his taut body over the desk. Shouted over the doctor's empty words and feigned show of sympathy. Behind him, two attendants appeared. They muscled Ed out of his office and through a tunnel to another building. In a room called "Reception," they held him down while a nurse stuck a needle into his right bicep. Within minutes, Ed's body fell limp, and the brawny attendant relaxed his vise-like grip. They led him, groggy and disoriented, to the communal shower and then to the dormitory.

Men were still filing into the dormitory when Ed lifted his slowly clearing head uncertainly and tried to take in the room where he was meant to sleep. A hundred men? More? There was shrieking and cursing. Caged windows, like portholes on a ship, lined the cracked plastered walls. Adult men rocked back and forth atop their bunks, talking to themselves or to someone not there. Others snarled and snapped. The quieter ones looked at the world through the eyes of a newly hooked fish. Glassy and stupefied.

Which one was he?

Ed searched for a calm and lucid corner of his mind. This was all wrong. He had to find a way out. Alerted to a sudden movement, his head snapped up in time to see a bug-eyed scrawny man darting between the cots. He landed in front of Ed.

"Give me, give, give me, give me," he bellowed. Thrusting an elbow into Ed's side, he clasped the fingers of both hands around Ed's frayed blanket and tugged. Ed's arms tensed, tightening their grip on the blanket. His assailant lost his balance and fell backward against a nearby cot. Wordlessly, he slithered away as quickly as he had appeared. Rob's thunderous voice, accompanied by a furious clanging sound, rang out above the din.

"Thimmer down. Thimmer down, or you'll get whacked." Glancing back towards the doorway, Ed thought he saw another attendant banging a piece of wood—maybe a baseball bat—against the metal frame of a cot. Clutching his blanket to his chest like a beloved teddy bear, Ed tucked his head and pulled his legs back atop the cot. An attendant came by and shouldered him.

"We've got you pegged, troublemaker," he grunted.

Had Ed heard right? He couldn't be sure since his powers of perception were blunted. He lay back down and stared at the ceiling. The mattress was thin and smelly. Ed recoiled.

The lights dimmed off, then on.

"Go to thleep, morons," Rob snarled from the doorway of the packed room of men. Like sardines, Ed thought. Or hogs in a pen. Hanging miserably in a long row from the crumbling plaster of the ceiling, naked light bulbs winked off. Ed pulled the musty blanket around him, turned on his side, and tucked his knees into his chest. He wrapped his arms over his head, like a soldier in a bunker being shelled.

## Chapter 16

# Letters from Home

*Dear Edward,*

*Mom said you were in the hospital, and I could come visit you. When you're a little better, she said. I hope you can come home soon. I miss you every day. I hope you can get better and come home in time for the church fair. I sure miss your root beer. We can have a party. But I don't want to invite Rosemary. She says mean things. She said you were a bad army man, so I shoved her and knocked her to the ground. Her dad told her the army made you go away to a funny farm. I asked Mom what a funny farm was, and she got so mad she whacked my butt with the spoon ladle three times! How the heck can a farm be funny anyway? Rosemary told her mother I hit her and, well, she told Mom. I was grounded for two weeks. That Rosemary got me into so much trouble. I hate her. But I know that's bad, so I guess I have to tell it in confession. But I still don't want to invite Rosemary to our party, and I'm not sorry I hit her. No root beer for her! Anna misses you. She cries sometimes at night. I tell her it's okay and not to cry. Mom says we have to have a stiff upper lip.*

*But I don't know what that means. I like my lips just the way they are. I don't want to ask her what she means and get hit with the soup ladle again. Dad doesn't talk much anymore. He mostly sits and listens to the news on the radio. Mario and Sergio got into a fight. Sergio said Mario cheated when they were playing handball and gave Mario a great big black eye! I don't think they would fight if you were here. You better come home soon.*

*Your little sister,*

*Mary Hohlfeld*

*p.s. I forgot. I won the spelling bee and got a ribbon! Aren't you so proud of me?*

*p.s. I tried to draw a cardinal, but it didn't come out so good. Not like yours anyway.*


*Dear Son,*

*I don't really understand what's going on, but I do hope that the good people at the hospital are helping you. The Army officer told your father you'd had some kind of breakdown after refusing to follow orders and getting into an altercation with an officer at the rifle range. Why, I don't believe it, I said to your father. Our Edward is sturdy, respectful of authority, and right-minded. But he said that's what the colonel told him. Or was it the major? Well, of course, you can imagine how very upsetting this turn of events is for us. I'm very worried about you, my dear, sweet boy. I think about you every day, and I've been saying a special Novena to St. Joseph for you at the church, and the girls light a candle for you every day. Your father refuses to talk with me, or with anyone, about the matter of your hospitalization. I think he blames me. He thinks I've had too strong an influence on you.*

*That I've made you soft-hearted. You know how he is. I dare not speak to anyone outside the family. I told Sam so. He agrees with me that it's not like you to get into trouble.*

*Oh, Edward, things are just going wrong all around since you left. Sam's hardly ever here anymore. He's planning to marry that Elsie girl. She's a Protestant. I don't know what he's thinking. I told him that, as sure as rain, if he marries that girl, I will have nothing to do with her, or him. My son should be marrying a good Catholic girl. She doesn't have to be from St. Anne's, but she has to be Catholic.*

*You must listen to the doctor, Edward, and do exactly what he says so that you can go back to the Army and make everything right again. I understand that you have some strong opinions about violence. Was that what caused the altercation? You can be stubborn sometimes, dear. I spoke with Doctor Windsor, and he said we might visit you soon, but it's not easy to get there. I will have to take the trolley, the El, and a bus, and it's a long walk to the hospital from the bus stop, and the weather is so bad now. Your father won't hear about going with me, so I'll probably bring Mary. Ronnie is busy with her new job and her boyfriend, and a visit to the hospital might be upsetting to Agnes. Mary's a sturdy little girl, though. I hope Sam visits you. I told him he should visit the brother he's always been so close to. He said he would think about it, but he gets queasy around hospitals. And this one's, well, a special hospital. Your father said that he would talk with you after you're yourself again. He's very upset and ashamed that you did so poorly in boot camp.*

*The doctor assured me they would do their best to get you well, but I mustn't get my hopes up because these things can take a long time. I told him that my faith is strong, and I know your faith is strong, so everything will be all right. You just need a little rest, I suppose, dear. I also told him you were quite the artist, and he said I might send you sketch paper and pencils. He thought that drawing might be good to occupy your mind. And, of course, your cigarettes and some of those Hershey bars you like so much. Please make them last. Times are hard, as you well know, and Sam's not helping out anymore. I hope they're feeding you well, dear. But I wish I could cook for you. You always need fattening up.*

*You are my dearest son, Edward, and my right hand. I miss and love you terribly and pray that God will bring you back to yourself and your family again.*

*Your Loving Mother*

## Chapter 17

# Corralled Crazies

Ed sat cross-legged beneath a window laced with metal rods. The jam-packed dayroom was dim, save for the bars of light seeping through. Naked or partially clothed bodies moved aimlessly in clumps like lost lambs. A hundred. Two? Some sat huddled together on the floor to generate warmth. The long, rectangular room was mournful and quiet. Loud and agitated. A continuous opera of wretchedness. Elbows and knees became weapons in the more aggressive ones. Others drifted like sleepwalkers with faces as blank as eggplants.

Days came and went in a fog of sameness. Mornings found the men funneled into a cavernous room with broken-down wooden tables and mismatched chairs. Harsh attendants prodded them. "In and out in less than ten. C'mon, loons. Keep the assembly line moving in and out, in and out." The attendant swung his arm back and forth like a saw, prodding a patient here, kicking one there. Breakfast was a plate of mush. "Maltex, get used to it," he snorted.

Ed saw a maggot's head peeping up through one of the bubbles. He shivered. Cockroaches darted from crevices in the floor and hovered in the shadow of the table leg. Bold and hungry. Patients guarded their metal plates, eating with their hands like greedy raccoons. Maybe because he had just been admitted, Ed was one of the luckier ones. He had pants, a shirt, and a spoon that he tentatively dipped into the bowl, removing the maggot with his fingers and tossing it to the floor. He tried to swallow without tasting. He had to keep up his strength. He had to get his mind clear. Lunch was the same. Maltex. Dinner consisted of watery, tasteless soup, a squished lima bean, and a slice of moldy white bread. Ed kept his spoon wrapped in the cuff of his pants. No one wore shoes. A few had socks. He glanced down at his green woolen socks, grateful for the small things.

For a few hours at night, Ed disappeared into a black hole of sleep and forgetting. Day always came back to claim him. More days and more nights until they spilled into one other, like storm clouds collecting into one ominous cloud. He lost track of how many. Three weeks? More? He had to try and keep track, but a creeping numbness threatened to overtake him. Trouble lurked all around him. He had to stay alert. Hold onto a slender reed of hope that he could come up with a plan and get out of this place.

In the dayroom he snagged a prized spot beneath one of the windows where bars of sunlight seemed to soften the rotting floor planks. He cupped his forehead and swallowed the hitch in his throat. Slid the two letters he'd read from his mother and Mary beneath his right knee. Can't feel now. Too dangerous. He would read them again later.

Swiping the moisture from his eyes and nose with the sleeve of his upper arm, he sensed a sudden movement. He glanced up. A portly-looking man with a tonsured head dropped his naked body next to Ed. Other patients started to follow, lured by the promise of the sunlight. Of day. Of air. They formed a half-circle. The naked man with the sagging stomach dipped his balding head beneath his arms and pulled his knees forward to shield his exposed genitals. He rocked back and forth and talked mournfully to someone only he could see. Another man came up behind him. Tattered pants, no shirt. He was bony but floppy as a scarecrow. The same man who had tried to steal Ed's blanket. Without warning, the scarecrow reared his leg and kicked the portly-looking man square in the back.

"You better move, asshole. That's my space. Staked it yesterday." The scarecrow narrowed his eyes and clenched his hands.

"NOOOOOOOO!" The naked man covered his face with his hands and cried. "NOOOOOOOOO, don't hurt me. Please, don't hurt me. Don't make me leave." In a feeble attempt to disappear or make the scarecrow vanish, the bald man squeezed his arms and pulled further into himself.

The scarecrow kicked him again. "Now!" He was aiming his leg for a third shot at the wailing man's body when Ed instinctively reached out and grabbed his foot, tipping him off-balance. He fell to the floor with a thud.

"Leave the man be." Ed spoke with quiet firmness.

The scarecrow sputtered and flapped his arms on the floor. "He knocked me down! He knocked me down." He jumped up and stabbed an angry finger at Ed. "He knocked me down." Other patients closed in and egged the scarecrow on, causing a ruckus as Ed watched helplessly. The attendant named Buster suddenly appeared. He pushed the scarecrow aside and told him to shut up. Then he charged at Ed.

"Whaddaya, causing trouble, loon?" He sounded strange when he talked, like his mouth was crammed with food or chewing tobacco. Buster pulled some sort of gadget from his pocket and started striking Ed on his shoulders and back. Thwack, thwack, thwack, thwack. Ed smarted. He raised his arms to protect his head and tensed his body to withstand the blows. No longer drugged, he registered the fact that he was being assaulted by a hospital attendant. He didn't cry out. Buster intensified the blows. Ed's body shifted. The second letter, its "Dear Son" salutation visible, slipped from beneath his leg. The scarecrow vanished.

"Not on my watch, mister, not on my watch." Spent, he finally pulled back, drawn to a different commotion some feet away. Beneath upraised arms, Ed eyed the attendant as he turned away, brandishing what looked like a length of rubber hose.

"Not on the wall, you sick bastard, you!" Buster ran toward the feces-slinging man. The fresh scent of shit wafted through the air. The chubby man whimpered.

Ed sat in the temporary shelter of his folded arms. His back and shoulders were smarting. Tears stung his eyes. How had his life been condemned to this barren, grimy, evil room no more than fifty by seventy feet? No chairs, no tables, no lamps. Nothing to touch or hold onto. Nothing to look at but ragged, desolate bodies. How many of them? Of us, he thought bitterly. Ed surveyed the peeling walls that were shit-smeared and different shades of gray. Broken floor planks soaked rotten with urine. Or missing altogether.

What kind of place was this? Who allowed this to happen? Who was in charge here? Had they sent him here to punish him for disobedience? How could he get out? He had to get out or risk going crazy. He studied the rusted and loosened locks on two of the dayroom windows, the cage of rods bent and likely unstable. Ed would have to watch his step, bide his time. Steer clear of the brutal attendant Buster. But he had to get out. He'd make a run for it. It was risky, a last resort. Maybe he wouldn't have to, if only he could talk to his parents and enlist their help, get them to understand his side of things.

His father . . . he'd have to talk with his father. His mother was a good woman, but she was fragile. She wouldn't, couldn't understand.

Ed rescued his mother's letter and re-read it. Then he stuffed it along with the envelope containing Mary's letter into his waistband. He touched the St. Christopher Medal resting against his chest. His mother's letter made it clear that his father had swallowed the Army's version of events. His father was ashamed. That's why he hadn't written. But he would come around. He had to. His mother was a simple woman. She believed in the authority of the military, the doctor, the priest, her husband. It would have to be his father. Ed would explain how he'd been railroaded. Visiting Sunday was just a few days away. He would speak with his father privately, make him understand. His heart flickered with hope.

*Chapter 18*

# The Plan

"This ain't right," the man shook his head vigorously. "It just ain't." He clenched and unclenched his hands. His taut body sat forward on the metal chair. Sat back. A chestnut and black pipe sat securely in the corner of his mouth. He pulled it out, tapping the cylinder twice to dump the tobacco in an ashtray that rested on a rickety card table. He sat back. Crossed his legs and filled his pipe with fresh tobacco from the pouch in his breast pocket. It smelled of molasses and licorice.

"It ain't right," he repeated, frowning. Lighting the newly freshened pipe, he glanced at the other men arranged in a circle and puffed. The Philadelphia State Hospital name card affixed to his right breast pocket read "Pete Wilson, CO Attendant."

Wind whistled through the cracks in the window casing and poorly insulated walls. Although the recent snow had all but dissipated, it was still blustery and cold, making it a fine night for the men to stay indoors and have their long-planned meeting.

"Yes, but what can we do about it?" another conscientious objector attendant asked. "We've no power to speak of, except with respect to the patients, and even that is minimal." A chorus of yesses and "That's so" swept around the congenial group.

Formerly a building for child patients, the men's dormitory was big enough to accommodate the rotating group of Byberry CO attendants approved by the U.S. government for alternative service. Personal storage space was limited. The men had to share a bathroom, but the cots were clean if not particularly comfortable. A card table with a handful of chairs and a broken-down ping-pong table sat in the narrow space between the conjoined dorm rooms. There was talk of getting double-decker cots if the hospital hired more COs. Most nights, they were so dog-tired the men fell to dozing before their bodies hit their cots. They chalked their cramped Spartan quarters and lack of recreational facilities up to necessary wartime sacrifices. Although their principles stood in the way of marching to war, they did not prevent the men from embracing their duty to country and take on their share of national sacrifice.

Pete's gray eyes found Walter's. The men had been railing against a growing list of problems at the hospital. Paid attendants were poorly trained or ill-suited to the work. There were shortages of the most basic supplies, and patients were manhandled by abusive staff and forced to live in unsanitary conditions. These conversations often trailed the men to Lester's, the local hangout where Byberry's CO attendants congregated on their free night. None of them owned a car, so the men sometimes pooled their money and took a cab. When the weather held, it was a manageable walk of two miles.

It was during one of their recreational nights at Lester's that Walter and Pete had decided to call this formal meeting of CO attendants, who were growing in number, along with the hospital's burgeoning population. Most were Quakers but some, like Pete, were Mennonites. The Mennonites sometimes lapsed into German when speaking among themselves. Walter and Pete became instant friends after Walter indicated that he, too, could converse in German. Walter's aunt spoke German with two of her sisters who were neighbors and frequent visitors at his uncle's Lancaster farm. Though he wouldn't call himself fluent, Walter picked up enough to get by. It was an overheard conversation in German at Lester's that led to this revelation and, eventually, the men's friendship.

"*Das Essen schmeckt. Nicht zu verachten. Probier mal den Hackbraten,*" Walter overheard and answered Frank's question about the food at Lester's. "The food is good. Really, not half-bad. Try the meatloaf."

"*Sprichst du Deutsch?*" Pete's head popped up from his root beer and hamburger. It was Saturday night, and Lester's was hopping. Couples were boogying in a semi-circle around the jukebox to the Benny Goodman tune, "Don't Sit Under the Apple Tree with Anyone Else but Me." Walter had been thinking about Sallie Mae when Frank lapsed into German, and he couldn't resist showing off his rusty language skill.

He tore his eyes away from the dance floor and the memory of Sallie's Mae's auburn hair to raise his glass of root beer to Pete and Frank.

"*Ja, ich sprech ein bisschen.*" Yes, I speak it some.

The Quakers shared a long history of non-violence with the Mennonites, adding to the commonalities between the two men. Like Walter, Pete was circumspect and even-tempered. But he was bound for medical school, not law school, upon the completion of his CO stint, a difference between them that Walter respected and appreciated.

Pete slapped Walter on the back affectionately and launched into a spiel in German. Walter was lost, having neglected to tell Pete that he could understand German but only when it was spoken slowly. While Walter struggled to keep up, Pete, oblivious, rattled on. "See, a good man . . . like one of us . . . not his fault . . . a Quaker. Ha, ha, ha."

"Don't Sit Under the Apple Tree" had wound down, leaving a lull in the room, and Pete's jubilant German outburst rang through the air like a siren. Heads turned and backs arched. From his roost behind the bar, the stocky owner-manager glowered at the COs' table. Most Americans did not distinguish Nazis from the German people and its rich culture, and America was in a decidedly anti-German mood. Sensing the downward shift in the air, Pete paused. Walter raised a hand in apology to Lester.

Unpopular with the locals, COs were welcome at Lester's because they spent money.

They were also quiet and kept to themselves, avoiding conflicts and shouting matches even when taunted by loudmouths. COs were accustomed to being called *wimps* and *yella bellies* and often, worse. Once, a local man approached Walter outside Lester's demanding to know why he didn't think it was important for him to die for his countrymen, Walter told him that he was serving his country in another, equally valuable way. Walter sensed it was a sincere question and answered in kind.

"Guess I'll have to think on that one." The man graciously stepped back and opened the door for Walter.

But many of the townspeople were rude and downright aggressive. Other local shops, like Joe's Drugstore, posted signs in their windows: "No Skunks Allowed" and "Conscientious Objectors, Keep the Hell Out of My Shop!" Lester, a kindly older man, took to the well-behaved COs. Since war rationing meant many slow nights, he was mighty glad to deposit the COs' spending money into his cash register.

In their excitement, Pete and Frank had forgotten how easily agitated the patriotic locals could become. Like Pete, Frank, a fellow Mennonite, was from Germantown. Their childhood bond continued into adulthood, strengthened by the men's shared faith and ideals.

"*Englisch*," Walter whispered, nodding toward the other tables. "*Englisch, ja?*"

"*Ja, in Ordnung einverstanden*," Pete whispered back. "*Na klar.* Yes, of course."

Walter picked up his glass to make a quiet toast, and the other men followed his lead: "To our soldiers on the battlefield. May God keep them safe."

"Yes, to our countrymen," Frank echoed. They tossed back their drinks and fell silent.

A strawberry-blonde woman in a flowery A-line skirt placed a coin in the jukebox. She sashayed to the dance floor to the energetic tune of "Basie Boogie." The tension in the room dissipated as she twirled her skirt and clapped her hands, beckoning a sailor at the counter to join her. He grinned and pointed to himself. She nodded. He jumped up, and they started jitterbugging. Short and muscular, he didn't look at all like the graceful dancer he proved to be. The sailor lifted his partner up and whirled her around, dipping her between his legs and pulling her up again. Other couples joined them, and onlookers encouraged the spirited dancers.

Exactly one month later, on a gloomy Sunday night, the same group of COs sat huddled in the dimmer atmosphere of Byberry's Cottage #1.

"Like Pete here said. It's a hellish business." Walter turned his wooden chair around and leaned forward, his forearms resting atop its chair back, his legs straddling the legs. "I think it's high time we begin taking matters into our own hands."

He paused and adjusted his Fedora, sliding it back and forth atop his head, waiting for others to weigh in. He wasn't really sure *how* they could take matters into their own hands. They'd be taking on a deeply flawed and complicated system. There were pitfalls, too. As COs they had no clout and were not well-regarded. They were hanging on the thread of Roosevelt's goodwill as it was. It would be crazy to infuriate administrators and endanger their own alternative service. They also didn't want to cause problems for the American Friends Service Committee and the Mennonite Church, the main source of support besides their families. But the appalling shortages and daily influx of patients showed no sign of waning. A crisis, it warranted action.

Frank, who had just rotated out of A ward, piped up. "Listen, fellas, this place is a cesspool. I can't believe I'm in the United States of America. Nobody cares. Nobody. There are not enough doctors here, and most of them are downright incompetent. It's a disgrace. The supervisors don't give a darn about the patients or the crumbling buildings. Toilets are overflowing. Ceilings are collapsing. Patients are filthy. Why, some are even dying. We don't have enough manpower to look after them, and most of these poor inmates are walking around naked. Naked. They have two bathtubs—TWO—for several hundred patients in a ward. And don't get me started on supplies. I'm sick and tired of asking. I mean, c'mon, soap? Disinfectant? Sheets? Clothing, for goodness' sake? The patients are little more than animals, defecating on the floor and whatnot." Frank pursed his lips and pinched his aquiline nose. "I, for one, plan to do my time, and get out."

"Frank's right," Louis nodded vehemently. A mild man with a cherubic face that belied his hardiness, Louis was, like his friend Walter, a Quaker. "I'm trying to get transferred out of this place myself. The paid attendants are brutes. Why, did thou know that

Buster is a convict? That other guy in reception . . . what's his name?"
He glanced over at Pete.

"You mean the toothless guy—Rob?"

"Yes, that's the one." Louis snorted. "He's disgusting and lazy.
Mean and dirty-looking fella, ain't he?" He tweaked his nose with
his fingers and grimaced. "Why, every day, he comes to work drunk.
Keeps a flask in one pocket and a piece of rubber hose in the other
to keep the patients in line. So does Buster. What do they mean by
hiring such people? Does this kind of thing happen at other mental
hospitals around the country, or is Byberry the rotten apple in the
barrel?" Louis uncrossed his legs. Slid back in his chair and shook
his head in disgust.

"They call them Bughousers." Walter observed. "Men like Buster.
Floaters. Should not be working in a place like this."

"It's the war, fellas," Frank added. "Part of it anyway. The shortage
of decent labor and supplies. Why, they're putting women to work
in the munitions factories. Did you know?" His tone rose a note,
matching his raised eyebrows. He was either shocked or impressed
by this development. Walter couldn't tell which.

"Hmm," Louis jumped back in. "Maybe, but I think there's
more to it than the hardships that come of war. Seems like this place
is plumb out of control. It's more like a concentration camp than a
hospital. A dump for throwaway people. Why, the people that pull
the purse strings don't seem to care about the patients at all. Takin'
plenty of money from the state, though, to keep them penned up.
I see more and more patients come in. Don't see any of them going
out. Don't see any of any getting better either."

The men fell silent. The wind rattled the thin windowpanes of
the cottage walls. Mike, a Quaker and recent hire, rose and walked

157

over to the main set of windows, securing the slices of newspaper that filled the cracks. The others shifted in their seats or studied the floor, waiting for someone to pick up the thread of conversation.

Walter shuffled his feet uncertainly. As one of the meeting's organizers, Walter felt the others waiting for him to speak. He was a reluctant leader. Sure-footed on the farm and in the classroom, he was less certain in his new role as an attendant. How much responsibility should he take on? He certainly didn't want to call attention to himself or cause problems for his family or church, but it was becoming clearer that action had to be taken. The mistreated, suffering patients tugged at his heart, like the infant he'd heard crying in the boarding house when he was a boy. This time he was a man and not a helpless child. He wouldn't turn away.

Walter raised his Fedora and pressed back his hair. He liked wearing it whenever he wasn't on the job. Indoors, outdoors. It didn't matter. Seemed to help him think. He cleared his throat.

"Quaker friend of mine at the Cleveland State Hospital says they're seeing some of these same problems. I suspect there are others as well. I suggest we start keeping a record, an account of sorts. Maybe reach out and see if other COs are interested in doing the same at their hospitals. We could put out the word that we're collecting information to come up with a kind of summary statement about shared problems, what to do about them, and so forth. We'd have to get superintendent Zeller's permission, of course."

"Hmmm," Frank added. "I've heard some of the same complaints from a Mennonite friend at the Norristown hospital. Claimed there was a doc in the women's ward there that was raping the patients. Superintendent didn't want to hear about it because there were only two doctors on staff."

"My word! How can that be?" Walter shook his head. Groans, sighs, and tongue-clucking swept around the circle of men.

"I don't rightly know about this idea," Frank said uncertainly. "Recording these things might just put the spotlight on COs. Get *us* into trouble with hospital administration or with our churches. We might lose our CO status with the draft board." He cast a sideways glance at Pete's face to gauge where he stood on the matter.

Pete didn't agree. He didn't disagree, either. He was leaning forward, his elbows propped up by his knees and his face resting on his right palm. He kept puffing on his pipe, his brows furrowed in thought. He shouldn't be smoking at all, he knew, but desperate times called for desperate measures, as he saw it, and he vowed to give it up when his CO stint finally ended.

Walter continued. "Well, Frank, I see that. I do. I have my own misgivings about rocking this here ship. This place has been operating for a very long time, and I suspect that many of the problems go way back. Looks like it might be the same at other mental hospitals, too. I'm not particularly crazy about the idea of sticking my neck out either, especially with my fiancé and future hanging in the balance."

"No offense, Walter," Louis interjected from the other side of the circle. "But really, is it our place to take on this, well, it's a huge problem, isn't it? Much bigger than us. We're just temporary workers, after all. Barely tolerated temporary workers. A lot of these people— supervisors and doctors and board members and what not—don't even want us here looking over their shoulders. They're glad to have our labor, but they don't respect us."

After Louis said his piece, the other COs turned back to Walter.

"He's got a point," Frank said.

"It's true, Frank. What Louis said is true." Walter removed his spectacles, thumbed his troubled brown eyes, and promptly replaced them. "There are many who mean us harm here. They resent us for our non-violent stance in this war. But see here." He eyed each of the men in turn. "We're here *because* we're men of faith and conscience first, aren't we? I have to believe that if we do the right thing, the rest will take care of itself. Won't it? My God, the suffering here is . . . well, I never imagined anything like it. Did any of us? And in our *own country*, as Louis said. Why, there are people in here who shouldn't even be patients at all. They're vagrants and soldiers and outcasts and whatnot, who found themselves on the wrong side of the law, is all. If they weren't crazy when they came in, they're sure to go crazy. There's no distraction, no recreation, no treatment plan. It's just not decent. How in the world can we turn a blind eye to it?" He searched the faces of his comrades.

"Uh, huh, that's so, Walter. That's so." Frank bit down on his bottom lip thoughtfully before continuing. "We do have an obligation to *try* and do something. Why, I talked to an older Negro fella just last week that said he was a vagrant with an outdated draft card. What was his name?" He scratched his head. "George, that was it. George Elder. Said a federal judge threw the book at him because his draft card was out of date. Can you beat that? Now, why would they put a man like that in a mental institution? Is that even legal?"

Another hush fell over the group. Between loud gusts of wind, the radiator in the far corner of the room vibrated and clanged, doing its best to beat back the drafty cold.

Walter removed his Fedora. Tilting it, his fingertips searched its soft inner lining for an answer. Then he placed it back on his crushed pompadour. "I do believe that if people had any idea what was going on in here, they'd be in the streets screaming bloody murder. This hospital is supported by tax dollars. It's a crying shame, is what it is. A crime. A travesty."

"Well," Pete started and just as abruptly stopped, as though he wasn't sure he wanted to talk at all. "Well," he said again, relinquishing his pipe and sitting upright in his chair, his thinking apparently done. "We came here to do a job, fellas. Didn't we?"

His question drew nods and grunts of agreement.

"But people have to know that we can't do our job because our hands are tied here, see, because of all these problems and shortages and the like. We can't do a damn thing about why they put patients in here. But there's something seriously wrong with how the place is run. How will the problems get fixed if people don't know about them? We have to start keeping a record, start documenting these shortages and abuses and whatnot, like Walter said. Put it all into some kind of perspective. Put this hospital and its administrators, hell, even some of these no-good doctors, on the spot. Begin comparing notes with our friends at other hospitals."

"Yep, yep," silent Mike, a Quaker, finally piped up, fueled by the others' testimony. "We're on the front lines here. We see what's going on." He pointed in the direction of the administration building. "Maybe they don't see it. They see ledgers and numbers but not the human beings in our care."

"Or maybe they do and don't want to be bothered," Louis added.

"So," Pete added, "we'll be careful. Sound out the superintendent on this here idea of a summary account to identify common problems and come up with ways to address them. To help new attendants do a better job. That's how we'll put it." He looked purposefully at Frank and Louis, his Mennonite brothers.

"Right," Mike added. "Not to point fingers but to identify common problems."

Pete nodded. "We'll start by keeping a record, as Walter suggested. And we'll contact COs at the other hospitals and get them on board with the effort. Maybe seek the guidance of our minister in Germantown to see what he thinks we can do about all this."

"A fine idea," Walter said with two taps to his Fedora, as if he hadn't suggested it in the first place.

*Chapter 19*

# The Boy

He was slumped against the wall in a drafty corner of the dayroom. His legs were splayed. Stringy black hair hung limply like tired strands of a dirty mop from his drooping head, obscuring his face.

Ed sidled up to him, uncertain. Is it him? The dark hair, tapered fingers, and slender body. It had to be. He leaned over and tugged lightly on his shoulder. A sliver of light peeking through a gloomy sky—something, someone, familiar. More certain, Ed tugged again.

"Joseph? Joseph?"

Ed had been pacing the perimeter of the enclosed room to keep the demons at bay. He asked about using an exercise yard he'd heard about but was told it was too cold and there were no jackets for patients. Misery reigned from one end of the room to the other, from one day to the next. The moans and shrieks blended into a single whirring machine with no off button. Even when he managed to block out the sound, Ed couldn't escape the stench of excrement and vomit and despair. It seeped into his clothes and skin. He tried to scrub it out in the cold water that dripped from the rusted tub's faucet once a week, the sliver of hapless soap teasing and mocking him.

Why here? Why am I *here?* The question, like a slow, steady burn in his gut, tormented him. He'd had to keep the question at bay and his emotions bottled up. The unexpected sight of the boy reminded Ed that he could still feel.

After a third tug, the boy shuddered and snatched up his legs, circling them in his arms.

"Nnnnnnn no, gggggggg get away, away."

"It's me, Ed. Remember? The soldier in the waiting room?"

"Gggggggget away. I told you to lllllllleave me alone. I don't wwww-wwwant to . . ." His indigo eyes, dulled and hardened, peeped between the strands of hair. For a long minute, they studied Ed.

Apparently convinced, Joseph muttered, "Wwwwwwwhere's your uniform?" He removed his arm to get a better look.

Ed's smile was slow and cautious. He couldn't remember the last time he'd felt this. . .this. . . he looked past the caged window for the word. Human? He crouched down like a catcher, placing himself on the same level as the frightened boy, and shrugged his shoulders.

"They took it from me." Ed's sad eyes trailed away. He rubbed his arms against the cold. A thin ray of light through the window threatened to vanish.

Joseph sat up. "Oh," was all he seemed to be able to manage. He pulled his floppy black hair back from his face, emerging from his stupor.

"C'mon," Ed urged. "Want to walk? Do us good. Attendant over there is holding my cigarettes." He gestured to the other side of the room. "Want a smoke?" Patients were permitted to smoke but only in the toilet room or outside during visits on Sunday.

Joseph blinked hard several times, as if he was trying to be sure it was Edward standing there, the nice man he'd met in the waiting room. Finally, he nodded and, leaning a hand against the soiled wall, pulled his lithe body up to a standing position. He swayed for a moment, weakened by the effort. He grabbed hold of Ed's elbow, steadied himself, and let go.

Ed guided the boy through the swarm of bodies. He scanned the room for the new attendant—the tall, nice one, while keeping tabs on Joseph. It felt good. Looking out for the boy rescued his bleak existence. Ed leaned over and whispered.

"Keep your eyes forward, Joseph. Don't make eye contact with anyone." To do so—to behave in a normal way, Ed was learning, was to court confrontation. Dangerous patients roamed the ward. He'd seen razors, probably pilfered from the shaving room where they were obliged to report twice a week to be shaved by worker patients. And nicked. Ed's fingers probed the still-smarting cuts on his cheek and upper lip from the morning's shave.

Then he heard it, the unmistakable voice of the prophet piercing the air. Ed placed his arm protectively in front of Joseph. The boy seemed unfazed, lost in his own world of pain, while the prophet screamed his doomsday warnings. Ed recognized his haggard face and tangled grey hair. The fierce eyes and booming voice. Between moments of absolute stillness, he exhorted his imaginary congregation to recognize his authority and prepare for doomsday. A husky middle-aged man they called the boxer danced around him and flailed his fists, riling some patients up. The zombies kept walking. All had a heart, and a soul, and surely someone, somewhere, loved them. Ed ushered Joseph away from the scene.

"Just keep walking, Joseph. I don't see the man yet, but I know he's here."

"Okay," Joseph said hesitantly.

Within minutes, another commotion was gathering steam alongside the wall. Buster was yelling at a patient who sat at the end of one of two benches in the dayroom where attendants parked trou-blemakers or sat for a break.

"Move, I said. What the hell is wrong with you, loon? Deaf or something?" He kicked at the bench.

The man was naked, except for the curly brown hair blanketing his chest and framing his groin. A worker-patient was trying to mop the floor beneath the bench where the distraught man sat. Collapsed into himself, the hairy man whimpered. Buster reared back, a strap in his right hand, and started whipping the man's shoulders. The man's head retreated, like the head of a turtle, into his chest of hair. The thrashing continued. The man yelped and squirmed, but he didn't move.

Indecisive, Ed weighed what to do. He didn't want to get caught in Buster's crosshairs, but he thought he might alert the other attendant, the nicer one. Should he try to find him, or try to distract Buster?

"Move your ass, Moron. Toldja, move!"

Why didn't the cowering man do as he was ordered? Instead, he screamed, his pitch rising with each thrashing of Buster's strap. Still, he didn't move.

A small mob had formed around the scene. Ed stood hesitantly on its outskirts, Joseph clinging to his shadow. Ed was just about to rush forward and grab the strap from Buster, thinking he might disap-pear into the crowd and drop it somewhere, when Buster suddenly stopped. Buster's thrashing caused the patient to twist his body defen-sively, exposing the strap that secured him to the bench. Fastened to the bench, the man hadn't been able to get up.

"Well, why didn't you tell me?" Buster ignored the fact that he hadn't given the terrified man a chance to speak. He turned, aiming his ire at the agitated onlookers.

"All right, show's over. Get out of here, or I'll show you how." He held the strap aloft and stepped menacingly toward the crowd. Patients slowly backed away. The worker patient resumed mopping around the legs of the tethered man. Buster strode off.

His heart hammering, Ed steered Joseph to the far end of the long side of the dayroom and close to the doorway where he'd last seen the other attendant. Danger lurked everywhere. The slightest provocation might bring a Buster down on your head or turn a meek-looking man into a raging maniac. Some attendants actually seemed crazier than the dazed and befuddled patients. Sunken cheeks, bent bodies, vacant eyes. Breathing, but dead. Ed shuddered at the prospect that, confined here long enough, he might become one of them.

They approached the end of the room near the locked entrance. Ed skimmed the room. Where was the man? He was tall and hard to miss. Had held Ed's cigarettes, the ones he bought with the privilege card he'd earned by shoveling coal. Coal was delivered at least twice a week to the hospital. It was filthy work in the freezing cold, but it released Ed from his dayroom-coffin for a couple of hours. He was able to smoke freely outside. Not free, though, with an attendant nearby keeping a sharp eye on patients.

Ed sensed his menacing presence as he sidled up to Joseph. A coiled slinky of a man, he leaned over and pressed his shoulder purposefully against Joseph who was walking alongside Ed. Copper thumbs tugged on the waist of his faded green pants. His fingers slid along his thighs and down toward his groin. He smacked his lips.

"Ready for me, kid?"

Ed had seen this worker patient before, trailing Buster like a cowed dog. Ed pulled Joseph away and shot an elbow in the threatening patient's direction. The man snorted before finally backing away.

Ed shook his head in disgust. "This happen often, Joseph?"

Joseph frowned and shrugged apologetically.

Ed finally spied the light brown hair of the tall attendant. He was zigzagging his way through the mass of bodies. New to the ward, he had a quiet voice, and he said "thou" instead of "you." A Quaker like Holmes, Ed guessed. He thought it might be a good sign that he didn't carry a strap or stick. The jury was still out, though. Ed trusted no one in here.

Ed raised his hand and made a motion with two fingers to signal that he wanted to smoke.

The attendant nodded, stopping to wrestle an agitated patient to a nearby bench. He thrust a finger of warning in the patient's face. The cuffs would be next if he didn't settle down, Ed heard him warn before he made his way to where Ed and Joseph stood by the latrine door. From his pocket, the Quaker produced a pack of Lucky Strikes. He shuffled the pack, and a cigarette popped out.

"Another for my buddy here too, if you don't mind." Ed gestured to Joseph, who stood quietly, like a character in a play with no lines.

The attendant hesitated, unsure. He looked both men over carefully. Then he shuffled three more cigarettes from the pack.

Ed remembered his mother's saying. Don't look a gift horse in the mouth. He nodded his thanks, noting the name "Walter Sinclair" on the nameplate above his shirt pocket.

"Thou know the rules." Walter flexed his thumb in the air. "Thou must smoke in the toilet room." He turned and led the way to the smelly toilet, leaving Ed and Joseph there with lit cigarettes before returning to the day room. They climbed a few feet up to a shelf situated under the single window in the room. The pane on the caged window was partly open so they could exhale the smoke and breathe fresh air.

Because Ed sensed Joseph was skittish, he started talking about himself to ease into a conversation. He told Joseph about his stretch at the CCC. About how being part of a crew with a shared purpose made him feel proud. He enjoyed the physical labor. Building bridges and roads made him feel like he was doing something that mattered. His hobby was sketching and painting, and he had a big family in Philly. He paused and inhaled, calmed by the nicotine and the attentive listener. Ed chuckled for the first time in months when he talked about his younger sisters. How Mary looked up to him, wrote him letters and drew him pictures. Explained how the sergeant beat him with his rifle when he wouldn't shoot it, and he'd ended up in this place.

Patients meandered in and out of the toilet room, ignoring the two men on the shelf. But a sudden clang drew Ed's attention to the metal utility sink where a worker-patient was emptying a bucket. He recognized the threatening patient-worker who had ogled Joseph earlier. He saw Joseph's limbs stiffen. The man relieved himself and rinsed out the mop. He gave Ed a sidelong glance and made his way to the door. Ed turned away in disgust and told Joseph it was okay. He was gone.

Slowly, Joseph opened up. Ed was surprised to learn he was seventeen because his small stature and soft features made him look so much younger. He came from an orthodox Jewish family. His father had thrown him out of the house because he wasn't "normal." Ed didn't ask him what that meant, but he had a good idea. It also explained why Joseph was a target on the ward and, probably, on the streets. Joseph was thirteen the first time he tried to kill himself. He'd been doing odd jobs and living hand to mouth ever since his aunt, who took pity on him when his father disowned him, decided he might be a bad influence on her own sons and asked him to leave. As he talked, Joseph's stuttering lessened. Ed listened attentively, like Father McGuire in the confessional. He nodded, saying little more than "uh, huh" and "I see" and "that sounds rough."

Joseph explained that the cops were the ones who brought him to Byberry. They found him in the bathtub of a flophouse, his wrists gushing red. The water spilled out of the tub and through the floor and leaky ceiling into the room below, tipping off the landlord. The landlord told them he was a pervert. His family didn't want him back, so the officers took him to the hospital and got him stitched up. Then they asked him whether he wanted to go to the state hospital to get help. Joseph agreed. He had nowhere else to go. Police told the hospital supervisor he was a danger to himself and society. They admitted him.

"Look, Joseph, the world can be hard on people who are." He looked up at the ceiling, searching for the right words. "I don't know. Different. Who don't conform. But there's all kinds of people in the world. All kinds. Believe me. Good people. And some are just. . . different." He remembered the Pittsburgh fellow he'd met at the CCC camp. A decent man. A Catholic even. He'd confided his fear of being tagged a homo to Ed, who was his sergeant. Was worried the others would find out and shame him. Just keep your head down, Ed had advised him. Ignore what other guys say. You're okay in my book. Just do the work you came to do, and I'll look out for you.

Ed clapped a reassuring hand on Joseph's shoulder. "You have to buck up and find a way to hold on, Joseph. See? Things will get better. I know it's tough. Believe me. I know. But out there, you have a shot. It's dark in here. It's way more dangerous. The worst kind of hell. Place like this can grind a man down to nothing." Ed took a long drag before lighting another and crushing the smoked one in the tin tray. He was talking as much to himself as he was to Joseph. Holding tight to his own thin thread of sanity.

"What's that?" Joseph asked suddenly, pointing to the St. Christopher Medal around Ed's neck.

Ed followed his gaze. "That? That's my St. Christopher's medallion. Had it since I was a boy."

Joseph's eyes widened. "A good luck charm?"

Ed smiled. "Kind of. He's the patron saint of, well, he, uh, he protects travelers. See?

He's carrying a child. Legend has it he carried this child across a dangerous river to safety. So, yeah, I guess it is a kind of talisman."

Entranced, Joseph leaned in closer and touched the Medal. "Oh."

Ed slipped the Medal from his neck and placed it around Joseph's head. St Christopher smiled back at him.

"No, I-I-I-I, it-it's yours."

"I want you to have it. A gift. For protection."

"Ok-k-k-kay." Joseph blushed. "Thanks."

"Listen, Joseph, you need to find a way to get out of this place. Tell them whatever you need to tell them to get released. If they won't let you out. Run away. You have a fighting chance outside. And no way they'll track you down." Ed knew it would be different for him. The Army had branded him a P.O.W. But first things first. Get out of this place, and then figure out how to get himself out of the jam he was in with the Army. "It's what I'm planning to do. Thinking of ways to get out. And when I do, you're welcome to join me."

Joseph sat back, hunched up against the wall, listening and twirling his unsmoked cigarette between his thumb and middle finger. The silver medallion glinted back at Ed.

Ed grew quiet. Took a long drag, pulling the smoke deep into his lungs before exhaling, enjoying the steadying feeling that followed. Talking with Joseph made it clear that running away was probably his best chance, too. Ed would wait for the right time to slip away. Find the unlocked door or broken window. There were plenty of those. Maybe he'd do it when he was unloading coal. Try to slip away when the attendant was yakking with the driver or distracted with another patient. No, that wouldn't work. His absence would be noticed too quickly, and he wasn't sure that Joseph would get the same assignment at the same time. Besides, it wouldn't give him enough time to make it to Port Richmond. He had to bide his time, find the right opportunity. Then he could explain everything to his father. Or maybe he should talk to Father McGuire. Yeah, he'd try the priest first.

"We could do it together. Plan it out. Slip away at the end of the day when they're moving patients from the dayroom to dinner." Joseph's head bobbed up and down as Ed, excited by the semblance of a plan, continued talking.

The boy's azure eyes looked troubled. "I'm not brave like you, Ed. Whaaaat happens iiif you make it out and I dddddon't?" His question registered like a clap of thunder.

Ed studied the fading winter sunlight through the window. Soon they'd be herded to dinner, then to bed and another black night. Who knew what horrors lay waiting in between? How could he protect the boy, or himself for that matter? He didn't know the answers. What he did know was that, with a little help from Ed's contacts on the outside, the boy stood a good chance of making it. Ed's hazel eyes swam in a pool of water as he clutched Joseph's shoulders.

"If you want to take the chance, you can run with me, Joseph. I just have to figure out some details first. If we make it out, I know of a place that's sure to take you in. A home for boys. St. Francis Industrial School. Run by an order of Christian Brothers. I did some volunteer work for them one summer. It's just outside the city limits, not too far north of here, just off Bristol Pike. If you make it out, get yourself there. Ask to speak with Brother Stephen Ryan. He's a decent man. Give him my name. Tell him everything that's happened. He'll help you."

Joseph shuddered. "I. . . .I . . . I'm afraid, Ed."

"I know. I know. But you have to hang on, Joseph. Hang on. We'll try to go together, but either way, you have to get away from here and get someplace safe. They're not going to help you here. Whatever happens, one way or the other though, I promise that I won't leave you behind." Ed hoped the idea of escape was not just a pipe dream.

"Oookkkay." Something like light returned to Joseph's eyes. "Me, too."

They shook hands. Ed put out his last cigarette and sucked in a long breath of fresh air.

The waning afternoon grew agitated, the wind huffing and puffing like the big bad wolf trying to blow the house down. Ed was amused by the thought. He wished it would blow this house down.

"We better go," Ed said, alert to sounds beyond the door. "They're rounding us up for dinner."

Joseph nodded. Ed picked up the tray of butts and ashes, intending to dump the contents. They were scrambling down from the shelf, Joseph first, when it happened. The door, which was supposed to remain open, banged shut. It was Buster. He stood, like a massive tree trunk, his bulk blocking the entrance. On the other side of the door, the patients were being ushered out of the dayroom. An eerie quiet settled over the room.

"So, it's the troublemaker and the pervert. What are you boys doin' in here, huh?" Buster sneered. "Up to no good, my spies tell me."

Buster rocked back and forth on his heels, enjoying the moment. He had a leather strap wrapped around his meaty hand. A pair of cuffs hung from his belt. A hunk of rubber hose peeked out of his pocket. Ed had seen him beat a patient almost senseless with it.

Buster had come prepared. Behind him, a shadow appeared. Buster's head turned slightly. "All right, you done your job. Get the hell out of here, now. Wait outside." The worker-patient backed up and shut the door.

Joseph stood, frozen. Ed stepped in front of him, his heart galloping in his chest. He had to think, to act fast. Divert him. Get Buster away from the doorway.

"Just having a smoke is all." Blood rushed to his head, but he kept his tone even. Couldn't let Buster see his terror. Joseph's fear trickled out of him, down the front of his pants, and into his pant legs.

"Just having a smoke," Ed repeated. "Time got away. We need to . . ." He pointed to the dayroom, his other hand grasping Joseph's shirtsleeve.

"What you need is to learn a lesson. You and your pal there." Buster unwound the strap. "You don't seem to learn, mister. Don't seem to know your place. Who's in charge. And you," he said, his black eyes boring into Joseph. "I'll show you what you're good for. Your friend can watch." He licked his lips and gestured menacingly to his crotch.

Ed did it without thinking. His arm sailed up, flinging the ashtray at Buster's face. It clipped his forehead, ashes raining into his eyes. Buster stepped sideways. He blinked and rubbed his eyes with the ridge of his palm.

"Run, Joseph, run," Ed pulled Joseph forward and shoved him to the doorway, willing him to safety. Immediately he sensed the futility of it. What safety? Where? Could he get the other attendant's attention? Would the other attendant dare to interfere with Buster? He had to. Hadn't he? Buster was out of control. But where was the other attendant? Ed panicked as he realized he was likely taking the other patients into supper.

"You . . . fucking . . . bastard . . . loon . . ." With one open eye, Buster swung the strap at Ed's legs with such force it knocked him down. Ed's body slammed against the side of the steel sink, his head against the wall. Blue-black dots swam at the front of his eyeballs.

He was alert enough to see Joseph find his legs a second too late. He had yanked the door open and was almost through the doorway when Buster's other arm shot out and clutched him by the hair. He threw Joseph to the floor alongside Ed.

"No!" Ed reached his hand up and gripped the lip of the sink. Wobbly, he struggled to pull himself upright and heave his body at Buster. But Buster kicked his hand away and clamped a giant work boot on his torso, shoving him flat to the floor. With amazing swiftness, Buster elbowed Ed in the neck. With his strap, he secured Ed's arms to a pipe beneath the sink. Joseph kneeled, cowering, alongside him.

Towering over them, Buster yanked the weapon from his pocket and started thrashing.

Ed tugged at the straps. Found no give. He drew his knees up to protect his body and clenched his teeth to steel himself against the blows.

Buster kept striking Ed over and over, and with such ferocity that the hose finally split and sent buckshot skittering across the cement floor. Buster, breathing hard, leaned over to gather them and re-tie the bag.

"Not . . . done . . . with you . . ." he said between breaths. "Then . . . take . . . care . . . your . . . little friend."

His body pulsating, Ed saw one last shot. Catching Joseph's eyes and motioning to the door, he pumped both legs, jamming them into Buster with all his might, throwing him off-balance. Joseph darted past Buster and through the doorway.

Like a befuddled giant, Buster stood upright with a roar. He picked up the hose and took another swing at Ed, this one catching him in the kidneys and making him gasp and sputter for air. He stuck a filthy blue- and white-checkered handkerchief in Ed's mouth. In a few large strides, Buster was out the door.

Ed shut his eyes, doubled over in pain. But Joseph got away. Joseph got away.

Within minutes though, Buster was back, his worker patient just behind him. With a triumphant leer in his eyes, he pulled Joseph back inside and banged the door shut. He held Joseph in front of him with a towel wrapped tightly around his neck. Joseph's fingers were struggling to free the towel from his windpipe. The more he struggled, the more Buster pulled, until his eyes bulged, and his fingers went limp.

A horrifying scream trapped in his throat, Ed pulled and twisted and kicked and pulled. But he couldn't get free. The boy's pants around his ankles, the slapping of skin on skin, the monster's thrusting and moaning, his hands clapped over the boy's startled mouth. Ed's sorrowful eyes reaching out and holding Joseph's while the monster split the boy open.

## Chapter 20

# Broken

Tim spied the drunken man on the other side of the street. "Hey, that you, Mr. Simzak. What in blazes you doin' there?"

Skinny as a starved turkey, his jacket wrapped around his knees, Harold Simzak was hanging onto the iron lamppost across the street from Willy's taproom for dear life. The massive oak doors, their lead-lined, stained-glass windows more suited to a church than the corner bar, stood ajar. An irritated, brawny man Tim recognized as the owner stood inside the doorway with folded arms.

"And don't be showing your mug in here again!"

Officer Tim McGee knew this was a performance likely to repeat itself the next day no matter what the bar owner said. "It's okay, chief. I'll handle this."

Tim's order was punctuated by a sweep of his right arm. The wind whistled and danced, kicking up debris. The front page of Friday's *Philadelphia Bulletin* flew up and draped itself across Harold's face like an errant scarf. Simzak was blind. He was also three-sheets-to-the-wind and unable to fathom the reason for his blindness. Tim tried not to laugh as he propped up the drunken man against the pole. He tore the newspaper from his face and helped him into his jacket.

"Well, Officer McGwee," Harold Simzak winked up at Tim. "Whatcha doin' here? How's the ole man? Wanna buy me a dwink?"

Tim chuckled. "Somehow, I think you're done drinking for this day of Our Lord, Mr. Simzak. Christ Jesus, ya tied on a good one. Didn't you now? How long ya been at it? C'mon, let me help ya home."

Just as Tim secured the drunken man's elbow and started pushing him in the direction of his house on Somerset Street, Simzak sputtered and belched. He let out such a noxious fart that Tim had to turn his head away.

"That was nasty," Tim complained to the whistling wind. "Ain't no way to thank me for not hauling your ass down to the station. They don't want you back in there now, Harold. And it's way too cold a night for me to leave you sleeping against the lamppost until your old lady finds you half-froze to death in the morning. C'mon." He helped Harold Simzak to his feet and aimed him in the direction of his house.

"Ah, hell, Offissssr, ya wanna get me killed?" He half-turned, casting a sorrowful look at the tavern, as if bidding a final farewell to a lifelong friend while being marched to the gallows. Despite being assaulted by the reek of sour beer, Tim managed to keep a tight hold under Simzak's arm as he escorted the stumbling man home. Within minutes, they arrived at the drunken man's stoop. Tim pushed Simzak up the steps, propped him against the white brick fascia, and rang the bell, dropping back down to the street so as not to get caught in the middle of a domestic skirmish. Mrs. Simzak opened the door in a rage. Broom in hand, she released a torrent of marital complaints.

"Did you spend it all, Harold?" she demanded, beating her hapless husband about the head and shoulders with the flat end of her broom. "Good for nothing son-of-a-gun . . . dinner freezing cold . . . wasting a hard-earned dollar . . . drinking up the grocery money . . ."

As long as Mrs. Simzak wasn't beating her husband with the broom handle, Tim figured Harold would be okay, and he was off the hook. Besides, this was a regular show at the Simzak house. Harold must have made peace with the broom by now, if not with the wife. Tim tipped his hat out of habit since neither one was paying much attention to him. He watched as Harold, arms raised to protect his head, staggered into the foyer, his body a drum to the steady beat of his wife's broom and volleys of insults. Tim, glad not to be acknowledged, turned toward Tulip Street and resumed his beat.

The wind shrieked and howled through the nearly deserted streets of Kensington. The pasty quarter-moon peeked wanly through denser clouds, as if afraid to come out. Well past suppertime, most families were settling into a cozy evening behind the tightly closed blinds of their squat row homes. But for the occasional drunk stumbling home from the taproom, or hooligans out looking for trouble, Officer Timothy McGee's Kensington-Port Richmond streets were quiet. It was home to friendly working-class folks, many of whom Tim knew by name.

Baton in hand, Tim pulled up the collar of his Navy peacoat and secured the top gold button. He cursed himself for not having grabbed his earmuffs. He'd come down with the pleurisy this time last year. His wife would surely kill him if he got sick like that again, with the holidays just over and no money in the pot for a doctor's visit. Well, she'd have a right to get huffy, he supposed, what with two kids, little Timmy and Rose, and a new one coming in six months. However steady, his pay didn't grow along with his family. Maybe the pressure was why he'd had that little tryst with the hot Ray Mar waitress. He winced at the recollection. That was all over now, thank God. He'd confessed his lapse to Father McGuire in the confessional and promised to do better. What a fool he'd been to risk his marriage for a little fun on the side. When all was said and done, Jeannie was his best girl, and he'd be lost without her.

Shoving the baton into his belt, Tim brought the palms of his hands together, raising them to his mouth and blowing warm air once, twice, three times. Cupped them over his ears before planting them in his pockets.

"Holy Mary, Mother of God, it's cold," he muttered. A loud bang and clattering sound coming from the railroad trestle answered him, dropping the curtain on his mental domestic drama and concern about the cold. Tim's body sprang into action. He hoofed it down the street to the trestle opening and peered into the murky darkness. Nothing. The sound of the wind huffing and slapping against the trestle convinced him the culprit had likely just been an alley cat or stray dog. Tim pulled out his flashlight and aimed it at the darkness. Sure enough, a scrawny tabby cat, precariously balanced on the edge of a barrel, yowled at the intrusive light before vanishing back into the blue-black night. Beyond the cat, on the other side, Tim glimpsed a shadow emerging from behind another barrel. The figure jumped up and loped into the semi-darkness.

Tim's baton bounced against his side, his flashlight leading the charge through the tunnel. By the time Tim reached the other end, the figure was gone. He scanned the street in both directions. Nothing but the headlights of cars and trucks rumbling back and forth on Aramingo Avenue. Must have been a bum he'd spooked with his light. But why bolt like that? A bum or drunk wouldn't have reacted so quickly and outrun Tim, weak lungs, or no.

His suspicions aroused, he holstered his flashlight and headed back through the tunnel towards St. Anne's church to make sure things were locked down tight for the night. There'd been a few break-ins recently, and the poor box had been robbed. Tim shook his head thinking about it. Sure, times were hard and bound to get a lot harder with a war on, but who would be desperate enough to rob the church's poor box?

Tim jammed his cold hands inside his pockets and made his way down Lehigh to Memphis Street. Ahead, St. Anne's loomed like a fortress. It sat on a square near the boundary between the two major working-class hubs of Kensington and Port Richmond. Tim's grandfather had told him that when the church was built by Irish immigrants in the late 1800s, it was meant to be a couple of blocks of solid brick, and walkways on its flat roof made it more defensible in case of attack. Granddad McGee told him that widespread riots years back led to the burning of Catholic churches throughout the city. Surveying St. Anne's seemingly impenetrable walls, Tim pondered that bit of Philly lore.

After ascending the 100 or so white stone steps, he tested the four sets of massive double doors to make sure they were secured. Satisfied, he made his way back down. He pulled his flashlight out again and threaded his way to the side entrance of the church and through the unlocked wrought-iron gate. He aimed the light up and down the darkened corners of the building and then cast it in the direction of the small cemetery. Tim's flashlight found nothing amiss. He'd check out the rest of the complex anyway, just in case. As he emerged from the side entrance onto the street, a gust of wind smacked him in the face, catching him by surprise. Wicked night to be out. Much better to be at home, wrapped around the soft curves of Jeannie's body.

After looking back once more at the darkened stone walls of the church and the school beyond it, Tim made his way over to the squat two-story brick building resting serenely on the other side. He aimed his flashlight toward the nun's home, swiping it from top to bottom, side to side. The first floor looked black and impenetrable, like the nuns in their black habits. A few lights peeked through the closed blinds on the upper floors, and Tim tried to imagine his 8th grade teacher, Sister John Anthony, in various stages of undress. His imagination couldn't get past the headgear, though, and the terrifying prospect that her veiled head might be completely bald underneath. What *do* they do on their own time besides pray? The priests played a round of golf or handball now and again, and they sure liked their Jameson. But unlike priests who moved freely in the world, nuns disappeared, ghost-like, behind the convent walls at the end of each school day.

Glancing in the direction of the rectory that stood adjacent to the church, Tim noticed that the first floor was lit up. The front door stood open, and a black-cloaked figure stood on the top step. Bathed in a corona of light, the figure looked around, left, right, left again, furtively, as though he were searching for a pet that had darted from the house. As Tim drew closer, he recognized a coatless Father McGuire.

"Evening Father," Tim called. "Everything okay?"

Stunned, John McGuire lifted his hand to his forehead, like he was looking out from the bow of a ship, straining his eyes to see in the darkness. "That you, Tim?"

Tim thought he heard a tremor in his voice. Or was it the wind that made it waver?

"Sure is, Father, my lucky night on the beat." Tim edged closer to the rectory to have a conversation that was less like a shouting match. "Saw something suspicious under the bridge and thought I'd check the church out, just in case. Church seems fine, though. All locked up. Everything okay here?" Why was the priest standing on the doorstep without a coat?

Father McGuire fumbled in his shirt pocket. He pulled out a cigarette and a pack of matches. He turned toward the half-open door and cupped his hands to light it.

"Oh, sure, Tim. Just, just, just came outside to, to have a smoke . . ."

Tim didn't buy it, but this was a priest he was talking to who had nothing to cover up. Tim had to stop thinking like a cop.

"Wicked cold night, Father." He chuckled. "Pastor won't let you smoke inside?" Reaching the steps of the rectory, Tim craned his neck upward.

John McGuire exhaled two clouds of smoke and smiled. He bent his head. Shook it back and forth. Placing the cigarette between his lips, he opened his hands and held them out.

"Guess you caught me, Tim, red-handed, as it were." He pulled the cigarette from his lips and then flicked it away, wrapping his arms against his chest. His upper body shivered. "Truth is, I just had an unsettling visit from a parishioner, a friend, really—well, used to be a—he was very upset, very distraught, not making a whole lot of sense. Ran away from the state institution. Told him to come inside while I called the authorities, and he, well, he bolted."

"A jailbird, Father?" Tim's back arched, his legs prepared to swing into action. Was this what he'd seen under the bridge—an escapee?

"No, no, not exactly, Tim. Not that kind, anyway." The priest scanned the sky, as if searching for guidance. "He's an awfully good man. He's, well, I think he must be ill. I don't really know what's going on. Seemed—I don't know—confused? Talking about a boy being in trouble that he had to help? Wasn't making too much sense. Had no coat or shoes, even. In this weather! Seems he's run away from the state mental hospital."

The priest clapped his arms twice against the cold, frost swirls coming from his mouth. "He's a soldier. Well, I think he's a soldier. Left a couple of months ago for boot camp. A week or so ago, his mother told me he was in the hospital—she didn't explain. Just asked me to pray for him, said he was ill. Makes no sense. The man was perfectly fine before he left for boot camp. I don't . . . I couldn't understand what he was saying, but he seemed to be in some sort of trouble. I told him I would call the hospital. Get it straightened out, but he, well, he ran off."

"Guy from this neighborhood, Father?"

"Yes, yes," he said. "Ed Hohlfeld. You know, the Hohlfelds on Somerset?"

"Ed?" Tim said, stupefied. Tim knew Ed pretty well. They had played on St. Anne's baseball team and manned a booth together at the church carnival a few times. Good man. Quiet but friendly. Did a lot for the Church. Tim thought Ed might go into the priesthood—sure seemed like that—but then he learned that Ed had gone into the Army.

Tim ran into his baby sister just the other day. She was carting the ice wagon home. What was her name? Mary, yeah. Mary. Sweet kid. Crazy about her big brother Ed. Tim told her he was sorry he didn't get a chance to say goodbye to Ed. Her sad eyes told Tim how much she missed him. Tim patted her on the head and sent her on her way. Tim felt bad he hadn't asked Ed to go for a beer before he left for boot camp. Truth was, Tim had avoided him. It was right around the time Tim got the thumbs-down from the Army because of his weak lungs, and he was feeling low about it. Tim shook his head. Makes no sense. What kind of trouble could a guy like Ed possibly be in?

"All right, Father. I'll check it out. He tipped his hat. "You'd better get inside before you catch your death."

"Right," Father McGuire looked at Tim as if he had just woken from a spell. "He's probably headed home. Then you'll take care of it for me? Good man, Tim. Good man." He slipped back into the shelter of the rectory.

Though he didn't know why, an image of Pontius Pilate washing his hands and telling the Jews he'd done all he could flashed before Tim. He wasn't religious, but he had listened closely, if reluctantly, to his catechism lessons. Every Catholic school kid who valued his life did. The unsettling image blew away with the next gust of wind, and Tim scampered back in the direction of the railroad bridge and over to Somerset. He made it back to Tulip in under fifteen minutes. As he turned and neared the Hohlfeld house, he caught sight of a Paddy wagon two-wheeling it around the corner on the far side of the house. What the . . . could it be they were going to the same place? Tim picked up his pace.

Two guys he didn't recognize from the 24th precinct, clubs extended, jumped out of the vehicle.

"Whoa, whoa, guys, slow down. This is my beat. What's going on here?" Tim held up his hands to announce his authority.

"Got a call from somebody," the first cop said. "Something about a guy causing a ruckus, run away from the Army or something? MPs here to arrest him?"

Tim looked at the cop, puzzled, and then turned his gaze to the second cop, who shrugged and threw up his hands.

"MPs? What the hell?"

Then Tim saw it—a military jeep parked several doors down on the other side of the street. "Stay here. I'll handle this, fellas," he ordered, incensed at the encroachment. Tim raced up the steps of the Hohlfeld house and leaned heavily on the doorbell.

Mrs. Hohlfeld, her apron pulled up and half-covering her tear-stained face, opened the door and led Tim to the back of the house. Good God! Ed was curled up, still as a statue, on top of the kitchen icebox. His head was tucked inside his arms. His socks were shredded. Water dripped from his violently shaking body. Tim almost didn't recognize Ed. He wanted to throw a blanket or overcoat over him and get him a stiff drink. But he had to wrest control of the situation first. The burly MP to his right glowered, his right shoulder leaned in threateningly toward Tim.

"We have orders to take this man back to the state mental hospital." He flicked his eyes away from Tim and addressed Ed's father. "Orders are orders. We're taking him back." Both MPs moved toward the icebox.

"Hold on, just a damn minute." Tim raised his baton. Without knowing why Tim sensed that this was all wrong. Something was amiss here. Mrs. Hohlfeld was sobbing. Ed's father stood guard in front of the icebox with clenched fists. The old man kept shaking his head. His thin lips were tight as a drum. The blue veins in his forehead pulsed, threatening to explode.

His heart thundering, Tim kept his tone even. "You're in my jurisdiction. You have no authority here, and you're not going to do any such thing until I get all the facts."

"Look at him," Mr. Hohlfeld choked. Tears welled up in the old man's eyes. "What did they do to my son? What did *you* do to him?" Ed's father turned and raised an angry finger at the MPs.

"Hey, now," the taller MP said defensively. "Attendant said he got into a fight. Hurt one of the other patients and ran away."

None of this made any sense to Tim. The cowering man on top of the icebox bore little resemblance to the man he knew, but he knew Ed wouldn't hurt a flee. He was a peaceful fellow. A regular church-goer. Did a stint as a sergeant in the Civilian Conservation Corps with his older brother. There was something amiss here.

"I'm sorry fellas." Tim glared at the MP to his right and the other to his left with all the authority he could muster. "I'm going to have to ask you two to leave until the family gets this straightened out."

"Sorry, sir," the taller MP said. "We have orders to take this man back."

A heart-stopping cry from the dark space atop the icebox stilled the room. "Mother, mother, please, don't let them." Ed's quavering voice pleaded, looking first at his mother, and then settling on his father's stern face. "What happened in there, Pop, I can't even tell you. It's too, too horrible. And what he did to Joseph—the man, the man is a monster, plain and simple. Please, please, don't let them. It's a wicked, wicked place. Pop, please don't let them take me back there. Mother. . ." The wounded voice collapsed into sobs that were echoed in his mother's keening.

Choking back tears, the old man glared at the MPs. "What did you do? What did you do to him? Look at him." His voice cracked. "That is not *our* Edward. He was fine before he went in. He was just fine." He slammed his fist into his other hand. "You *broke* him. Now, you can just take him back until you *fix* him."

His words came like a punch to Tim's gut. His shoulders and heart sagged as he watched the MPs cart the poor fellow away.

*Chapter 21*

# The Icebox

The lacey white hems of their flannel nightgowns danced up and down as the girls, careful not to slip through the crack between the aligned twin beds, sang out.

"Four little monkeys jumping on the bed/ one fell off and broke his head/ Mama called the doctor and the doctor said, no more monkeys jumping on the bed." Following several bounces to matching squeals of delight, ten-year-old Mary aimed her raised finger at cousins Alice and Catherine Connelly before landing on her younger sister Agnes.

"*No* more monkeys jumping on the bed!" With that, Mary sent Agnes off the bed and out of the game.

"Not fair," Agnes squealed. She folded her arms in protest and sat down on the bouncing bed with a resigned *harrumph*. "Why me? Why do I always have to go first? And who died and left *you* the boss anyway, Mary Hohlfeld?"

Undeterred, Mary and her cousins kept jumping. Between breaths, Mary huffed out an explanation. "Well, somebody has to be out first, and you're the littlest so . . . oh, oh, oh," she cried out as her left foot found a crack wide enough for her to slip through. Her leg, side, and arm promptly followed, causing the girls to burst into gleeful hysterics at the odd sight of Mary's lopsided, suspended body.

"Shh," Ronnie chided from the other side of the room, turning reluctantly from the page she was reading in *Little Women*. Ronnie's steely eyes glared at Mary. "I'm trying to read here in case you haven't noticed, and you guys are making way too much noise." Ronnie, older by five years, had no patience for Mary, the ringleader.

"Besides," Ronnie said, sitting straight up with the cool bearing of Sister Aloysius,

Mary's 3rd^rd grade teacher, "If Mom hears you, she'll come up and send us all to an early bed. Do you really want that?"

"Okay, all right already!" Mary pulled herself up and smoothed her brunette helmet of hair. Her cousins wordlessly slid to the floor and squeezed the two beds back together. While her cousins settled into a subdued game of checkers, Mary straightened the bedclothes. She sure didn't want Ronnie mad at her. She wanted an earlier bedtime even less. Mary watched her little sister Agnes climb into bed and snuggle next to Ronnie with a tattered copy of *Make Way for Duck-lings* in her hand.

Mary didn't much enjoy being the odd girl out. Her restless eyes searched the room for something to occupy her. They settled on the black and white copybook and No. 3 pencil sitting on a nicked-up end table against the far wall. Outside, the wind huffed and blustered. Inside, it was chilly. Mary grabbed her blue cotton robe from an iron hook on the closet door and wrapped herself inside it.

"There," she whispered. Feeling more settled, she dropped down to the threadbare rug in front of the two double beds and stretched out on her belly. Propped up on her elbows, her legs crossed and sticking up behind her, she tapped her forehead three times with the eraser top of the pencil, as she had seen her brother Edward do so many times. With the newly sharpened pencil point, Mary started to sketch the vague outline of the Arabian horse she remembered from Edward's big Art book.

"Start with simple things," Edward had instructed her. "With simple lines and with things that you know. The painting part will come after. First, you have to learn how to draw." That was hard for Mary because the horse that pulled the huckster's produce wagon through the cobblestone streets looked more like a mule than a horse. He had long, pointy ears and leather blinders for eyes. Her neighborhood never saw anything like the princely Arabian horse in Edward's book, so she figured the huckster's horse would have to do. She was sure Edward would approve. Tears sprang to her eyes as she pictured the perfectly arranged splashes of red, green, and gray of Edward's red-throated hummingbird.

The Christmas holidays had been terribly lonesome without Edward. She wished he didn't have to be an Army man and end up in a hospital. Her oldest brother Sam didn't have to go. He had the asthma. Mary secretly wished her brothers could trade places. Sam was a nice enough brother, but he didn't give Mary pennies for candy or make homemade root beer for the kids in the neighborhood.

A sudden pounding on the front door, followed by loud, gruff voices, made Mary's pencil jump, ruining her sketch. Her head shot up. It had been a long Sunday. They had just gotten back from St. Anne's and the last night of saying a Novena for the country's soldiers. Mary glanced at her big sister with a question mark on her face. Ronnie placed her forefinger over her lips. A hush fell over the room. Ronnie's ears strained toward the closed doorway. Minutes passed. After drifting up to the girls' bedroom on the second floor, the commotion continued down the hallway, ending in the kitchen at the back of the house.

"Who in the world could that be this late?" Ronnie asked of no one in particular. She slipped out of bed and padded over to the door. Opening it ever so slightly, Ronnie aimed her right ear toward the stairs. Mary stuck her pencil behind her ear, another habit of Edward's she had picked up. It signaled that he was stumped on one of his sketches and had to puzzle it out. With the pencil snug behind her ear, Mary pushed herself up and joined her sister at the door. Not wanting to be left behind, Agnes slid from the bed and sidled up to Mary and Ronnie. Their two cousins followed, all huddled together just inside the open door. Just as Mary was easing past Ronnie to get a better view, she spied her mother climbing the stairs. Her raised arms ushered the girls back into the bedroom.

"Girls, girls, please go back." Her mother's voice quaked. Her face looked wet. She lifted her apron and gave it a swipe.

"Mom, what's going on?" Mary leaned over Ronnie's shoulder.

"Never mind, Mary, dear." She waved the children back into the bedroom. "Please, Mary, take that pencil from behind your ear before you hurt yourself. Go back, girls. Back into your room. Don't worry. Everything is fine. Friends of your father's, stopping by for a visit is all. We weren't expecting them. Please, just return to your room. It's bedtime, anyway. Go." Her mother shut the door on Mary's face. "But Mom . . ."

Mary and her sisters knew better than to argue. The Connelly girls, grateful to have been taken in by the Hohlfelds after their father died and their mother went away to a hospital, obeyed without hesitation. Below, the voices lowered, and the girls tried to turn their attention back to their activities.

"What's wrong with Mommy? Why is she crying, Ronnie?"

While helping Agnes get back into bed Ronnie used her soothing big-sister voice to calm her little sister down. "Oh, Mommy's just fine, and grownups have their reasons. Let's just do what Mommy told us to do, okay? Come on. Shall I read you a story?"

Mary, whose heart was most closely attuned to her mother's, wasn't so sure. As soon as the others lost interest, she scurried through the door, closing it on Ronnie's perturbed face.

"Mary, wait, where are . . ."

Mary leaned over the second-floor railing. The downstairs hallway light blazed, which was unusual this time of night. The leftover aroma of spaghetti sauce from supper seeped from the partially opened kitchen door. Mary was stumped. Why is everyone in the kitchen? What the heck is going on?

The sudden buzz of the doorbell scared Mary backward and almost into Sam's empty room. A man's deep voice came through the door.

"Mrs. Hohlfeld . . ." Huh? That was Officer McGee's voice. Mary scooched back over to the railing, but all she heard was mumbling that echoed the length of their hallway and into the kitchen. Mary had to get to the bottom of this mystery. Cat-like, she crept across the landing and squinted into the semi-darkness. She slid her butt down the first two steps, hoping they wouldn't creak. Growing bolder, she stood up and tiptoed down a few more, pausing in case her mother stepped out of the kitchen. When she didn't, Mary grew bolder. She took two more steps. Three. The kitchen voices grew louder.

". . . the U.S. government . . . Mr. Hohlfeld . . . have our orders." Who was that man with the angry voice?

Mary slipped down three more stairs.

"Now, now, soldier." That was Officer McGee. Mary was sure of it. ". . . no need for that kind of . . . is their home . . . no authority here . . ." His words trailed off.

Why is the beat policeman in *our* house? Was her father in trouble? She pictured the nightstick Officer McGee always carried in his belt. "In case I run into any troublemakers, Little Miss Mary." Officer McGee had winked and chuckled when Mary asked him about it. She ran into him sometimes when she carted her wagon of ice blocks from Peg, the ice lady. The policeman was nice. He patted Mary on the head and made her smile when he told her that she was a good girl for helping her mother. In summers, he opened up the fire hydrant so the neighborhood kids could cool off.

But why was Officer McGee in her house? Someone must be in trouble. Mary leaned further over the banister and peered through the crack of the partially opened kitchen door. The blue back of the policeman's coat told her she was right. It was Officer McGee, his policeman's cap pushed far back on his head like it was thinking. His hand came up to rest on the shoulder of an Army man with a black armband. Another Army man leaned over and said something to the first one she couldn't hear. When Mary glimpsed her mother, she grew more puzzled. It looked like her mother was wearing her apron on her face. She couldn't see her father, who must be standing behind the doorway, but recognized his deep voice.

Mary stepped gingerly down the last few steps. She strained to see further into the kitchen, but her view was blocked by Officer McGee and the soldiers. She could tell they were facing the corner of the room where the icebox sat. Why was everybody looking at the Hohlfelds' new icebox? Mary pictured its polished new oak and the shiny silver letters on the front that read "Bay State Mfg. Co. Worcester,

Mass. U.S.A," but she couldn't figure out why in the world everyone was crowded around it.

A loud cry jolted Mary from her musing. "Mother, *please, please,* Mother," the voice, between sobs, pleaded. "Don't make me . . . don't . . . take me back to that place! I can't. . ." The voice collapsed into sobs.

Huh? Mary's head jerked back. That sounded like Edward's voice. No. Can't be. Mom said he was in the hospital getting better. Besides, Edward didn't cry. She had never even seen him get angry. But it sounded like Edward. What place? The hospital? The Army? No, that can't be Edward. Mom would have said if he was home. Who is it, then, and what are all those men doing in our kitchen? The voices grew louder. Angrier. Everyone was talking at the same time, and then her mother started to wail. Mary's heart hiccupped. Her brain froze like it sometimes did when she ate ice cream too quickly. Then she couldn't hear anything at all except a train thundering in her head. The soft whoosh of the bedroom door opening at the top of the staircase silenced the rumbling in her head. She looked up to see Ronnie's upper body poking over the stairway.

"Mary Hohlfeld," the angry head whispered curtly. "You get right back up here." Ronnie's sharp tone reset Mary's heart, drawing her back to the light spraying through the open bedroom door. She leaned on the cool, familiar wood of the banister. Rescued from the sound of her mother's wailing by Ronnie's order, she scooted back up the stairs and into the bedroom. She closed the door to the abrupt sound of her father shouting about something being broken that needed to be fixed.

Later that night, snuggled between her cousins, Mary woke with a start. She blinked herself awake, haunted by pieces of a dream in which her mother was hovering above her. Wearing angel wings, like the kind painted on the high ceiling of St. Anne's church, her mother was undoing the silver latch at the top of the icebox. Inside the small compartment where the block was stored, Edward was folded up like an accordion. He gazed at his mother with moist, shining eyes. In the dream, Mary was watching them from her place on the staircase banister. She was jumping and singing. "Three little monkeys jumping on the bed . . ." What in the world? Mary sat up. She rubbed her eyes hard and tried to make the troubling pictures disappear.

# PART THREE

*Chapter 22*

# Bottom of Sorrow

Where was he?

His head was heavy as wet cement. He dared his eyes to open. They refused. His wrists and ankles tugged at the straps securing him to something cold. The frame of a rickety cot. A prisoner-patient before, now he was a mouse clamped to a death-board and all around him a snake pit and the furies of hell. The tirade against God. The hurling of obscenities.

From the cot to his right, a hissing: "You demon, you. Back! Back! Stay away from me. I'll *sssssssss*, eat your *sssssssss*, eyes out. I will tear you into pieces and swallow them whole!" Hot spittle christened Ed's forehead. It slid down to the tip of his ear and settled in the lobe.

He'd made it *home, home,* hadn't he? Only to be brought back. No. Sent back, he thought ruefully. His body, a rigid rope of nerve and sinew and bone, tightened. He gritted his teeth and howled silently. Oh, father, my father, why hast though forsaken . . .? My own father does not *see*. How *could* he see what Ed's heart and words failed to tell? Could not tell. The silent howl was spent. His body slackened. His hand probed the cold slab of rubber on which he lay. The tips of his thumb and forefinger frantically dreamed the black beads between them, and the "Our Father who art in heaven" and the "Hail Mary, full of grace" ran over and over in his head. Dear God, are you in heaven, or are you here, now, with me in hell?

He inhaled the stink, his breathing ragged and shallow. Where was he? The realization came like a nail hammered into his heart. The restraint room. For a moment, it stopped. His heart. He felt a strange "kerplop" and then a brief reprieve from breath and the stink of brutality.

No more. No more, his heart said. Enough.

Without him willing it, his heartbeat returned with a frantic blip, blip, blip, blip, and a rush of blood stormed back into his head and lungs. Somewhere in the mist of memory, a picture. Jesus on the cross, arms and feet nailed. No hope. No escape. Our Father, who art in heaven, why hast thou forsaken. No, Ed would not stay on this cross. He was not a saint. He tugged and jostled the leather fasteners that bit into his wrists and ankles. He pushed back against the heaviness of his puffy eyelids. He felt his face ballooned with bruises. His bowels threatened to explode. Through the narrowest of slits, he confirmed what he smelled and heard. He was in the lodge. That's what the patients called it, or the dungeon. His eyelids drooped. A tickle on his cheek—as delicate as a woman's fingertips. Flooded with hope, his eyelids strained upward. He blinked twice before the waving mahogany wands and black beads of eyes registered. Panicked, he powered his concrete head upward, his face twitching and wrestling until the vermin fled from his cheek.

Events of the last weeks came tumbling back in bits and pieces. Buster's buckshot-filled hose wailing on him after the MPs had fed Ed back into the institution's angry jaws. Middle of the night. Just him and Buster. He should have been off duty. He must have waited. Where was the night attendant? Was there no salvation? No rescue from this devil? Home had been so close. The icebox. Home base but not safe. The faint smell of supper and mother's love, and father, my father, why has thou . . .?

"I took good care of your buddy," Buster had jeered.

Ed's arms were sealed to his sides, the ribs of the straight jacket biting his flesh through the tattered shirt. At the end of Buster's arm, the rigid rubber wailed on his defenseless face and shoulders and thighs, while Ed's mind flashed back to the boy sprawled helplessly on the bathroom floor. No! Buster was lying. Taunting him.

"Liar! Monster!" He propelled his body like a weapon at Buster, who stumbled and fell backward. Weakened from the effort, Ed fell to his knees.

Buster yelped and skittered back. Then he slammed the thick soles of his angry boots into Ed's chest and leered.

"Ha, ha, ha, wanna have at me, soldier boy? That it? You stupid bastard. You're mine, now." He regained his feet. His body loomed over Ed, a wingless damaged bird on the cold tile floor of the holding room.

"You worthless piece of lily-livered shit. Disrespect Buster, will ya?" A thwack across his cheek and another across his shoulder. The salty taste of blood trickled between his lips and down his throat. Ed's snaggletooth loosened. His tongue worked to press it back into his gum.

Joseph, where was Joseph? What had become of the boy? What would become of all of them trapped in hell's forgotten pit? He'd reached the bottom of sorrow. He was sure of it. There couldn't be more beneath this.

"Animal! Monster!" Ed squirmed and tried vainly to right himself.

Sidestepping him, Buster sneered. "Thought you could outsmart me, huh, soldier boy?" Suddenly, he stepped back, his face drained of menace. Tears surprised his eyes. He shook his head at some invisible injury. "Buster never gets no respect. Buster's ugly. Buster's dumb. Buster has to lay down."

A wave of unexpected compassion swept over Ed.

Buster's Adam's apple bobbed. His moment of melancholy vanished. He aimed his arm like a gun in Ed's direction. "No respect. None. Show me up, will ya? That it? Stinkin' yella belly eloper! I'm better than you. See? I'm the guy in charge. And I gotcha now. Thought you could get away? Show Buster up? You're bought and paid for, see? You belong to me now. Who do you belong to?" he shouted. "Who do you belong to?"

You, Buster, I belong to you.

After the beating, Ed fell into a hazy twilight state, vaguely aware of being dumped into a tub of freezing water with the rubber throttling his neck. When the shuddering finally stopped, his head sank forward. He woke, sputtering and coughing, yanked out of the tub by someone clapping his back. An unfamiliar voice.

"Yup, Buster said we got to keep this one under wraps. Said he caused a scuffle and tried to run away. Eloper." Next stop, the restraint room.

Unable to hold back any longer, Ed's bowels exploded, releasing more toxins into the dank air. Dark, wet matter spread beneath his buttocks and dripped down his leg. Tears found a crack and climbed into the corners of his eyes. They dripped down the side of his face and nestled, finally, in a crease in his neck. Ashamed. Hopeless. He willed his soul to leave his body, but it resisted, his body still tethered to the cot. In a pool of stinking wet.

"Aww, ya loon. Whaddidja go and do?"

Ed turned away from the accusing attendant and the bowl of gruel in his hands.

"I ain't got time for this. Barely time to feed you, so you just stay in your stinking stink." He leaned over with a spoonful of gruel and aimed it at Ed's mouth.

Ed tightened his lips. The gooey substance stuck to his lips and dribbled down the side of his mouth.

"No time for games, pal. I got 22 others to feed. Open up, or I'll jam the spoon in your mouth and ram it down your fucking throat."

A cackle came from the cot beside him, followed by a string of gibberish. Another language. Slavic or Russian, maybe Czech. He'd heard it in the neighborhood.

The attendant swiveled. Kicked the foreigner's cot.

"Shut up already, stupid loon can't even speakadeEnglish. C'mon, open up." He threw an elbow at Ed's head. Clamped his hand on Ed's jaw, trying to muscle it open. "The hell with ya." He poured the gruel over Ed's frozen lips.

The pasty goo dribbled down his cheek and chin. Ed tongued his eyetooth that was still hanging on for dear life.

## Chapter 23

# Something Like Hope

After the failed escape attempt, Ed's days sleepwalked by. A fog hung over him. He tried shaking his head, hitting it with the flat of his hand. Nope. Not going. Get used to me, it said.

He kept an eye out, but there were no signs of the boy. He'd lost him. Not in the dining hall. Not in the dayroom. Not in the toilet. He would keep searching, even though hope was as elusive as an exotic bird. Maybe, though, just maybe, the boy had grown wings and flown away. A bird. Some day he would draw the delicate bird. His sluggish heart quickened. If only he could draw his sorrow, make it visible.

Sunday. He tried to remember what it used to be like. Coming home from Mass, the Sunday *Bulletin* under his arm. The smell of bacon wafting down the hallway, a fresh pot of Maxwell House percolating on the stove. He didn't know what was worse, forgetting or remembering.

The dayroom hummed with mania. A jarring of sounds, like vying stations on a radio. His mind tried tuning the dial to the static between them. He sat down, cross-legged on the floor, his shoulder hugging the wall just beneath the window. Hiding in plain sight. But there was no hiding from himself. No getting away from his tortured conscience, the torn and smelly pants, his naked torso. Tears stung the back of his eyes. In this moment, being shirtless felt like the worst thing in the world. He shivered, the curls of dark chest hair standing at attention.

Startled by a tap on his shoulder, his neck swerved. The stately bespectacled attendant with a shock of sandy brown hair looked down at him.

"Thou has visitors. Mother and sister, I believe. Edward Hohlfeld, is it?"

Ed summoned his voice. "Yes," he finally said haltingly. "Do you know what happened to the boy? Joseph? The one I shared my cigarettes with?"

Walter looked puzzled. "I'm sorry, no. There are so many patients to keep track of here."

Edward nodded.

"Please come with me to the reception area. Thou must clean up. I'll find thee a fresh uniform and a jacket. It's damp and chilly." The man's kind voice felt like a caress.

Ed shrank, reluctant to face his visitors. His stomach flip-flopped. Bees buzzed in his head. He stiffened and examined his emaciated body. A fraction of the man he once was.

Walter Sinclair eyed Ed sympathetically. "Thou must come. They are waiting."

The attendant had cuffs attached to his belt, but he did not carry a weapon. No hose or broom handle. Ed stood up warily, the relentless fog hovering above his head. Time was a riddle, the past swallowed up. And the future? He stared into the mouth of a cave.

On their way to the locked dayroom door, Ed clung to the man's white uniform like a shadow, his eyes peeled for crazies with weapons. Any encounter might be a fatal one.

Minutes later, he was christened by sprays of warm water over his head and face. He lathered his body with harsh brown soap. He glanced down at his thin legs, the droplets of water swirling around them. The water slid down to the cracked, moldy tile and into a rusty drain. He was sure now his father would never come. He prayed his mother would not see the wasting of his body. The horror his life had become. What to tell her? *How* to tell her? He could find no beginning or end to an explanation. No. It was better this way. His mother must not be tainted. She must be protected. He must bear it alone.

He pulled on the clean pants like a man going through the motions of life, grateful for the miracle of clothing. For glistening skin and shampooed and combed hair. Visiting Sunday offered a small respite. He wrapped the cloth belt twice around his waist and cinched it, leaving the tails of the shirt to balloon outside the baggy pants. The attendant beckoned him to a chair in front of a basin and handed him a razor and a ragged towel. He scraped it evenly across the foamed skin. Through the mirror, other bodies were being prepared for visitors. He steadied his gaze. A gaunt face and vacant eyes stared back at him in the cracked mirror. He tried to concentrate, to put on a face suited to the upcoming visit. He winced, recollecting the clumsy, dangerous razor of the worker attendant that nicked and ran roughshod over his cheek and jawline. He cupped water from the spigot, splashing it across the smooth skin. He tongued the loosened tooth and felt its fall from grace. After cleansing the bloody tooth with cold water, he pitched it into the waste can.

The attendant handed him a pair of shoes and led him to the supply closet where men's jackets hung from a wooden bar. "Let's find one that fits thee."

Shoes. No socks, but still. Of course, the shoes would be taken back once the visit ended. He bent down and slipped on the black shoes, his trembling fingers fumbling with the laces. A rack of empty coats stared at him. He wondered what had happened to his Army jacket. Was it stowed away safely somewhere like his life that waited to be re-claimed? The attendant removed a black pea coat from its hanger and held it up for his approval. Ed nodded vaguely, slipping his arms into the silky lining of its sleeves, stunned by the luxury of its warmth.

"Follow me, please." The attendant led Ed through the locked door, down the stairs, through a tunnel, along two corridors, and past the reception area to the outer door, the one through which he'd first been sucked into hell. Nervous patients milled about, waiting for their visitors. Like him, they looked normal. They had clothing. They wore jackets. Visitors were not privy to how inmates lived day in and day out. They saw only this visiting Sunday performance on a picnic bench outside the hospital. Ed's eyes settled on an older man. His head was completely bald except for wisps of hair at the nape of his neck. He had no eyebrows, and he was talking to himself. His fingers moved back and forth like spiders drifting in the air. Ed shuddered. *There but for the grace of God . . .* will that be me? *Is* that me?

He trailed the tall attendant out the door and into the chilly dampness. The sunlight shocked him. He raised his face to the palest of suns. At midday, it hung, proud but uncertain, from the sky's peak, eyeing the path of its sure and steady slow-motion descent. Maybe now the fog would go away. Ed hoped so. But no, there it was, trailing him, determined to block the sun's thin rays. It would not be detached. Could not be eluded.

"Trouble you for a cigarette?" he asked of the man's back. A stalling tactic? The sound of his own voice startled him. A whole sentence. An interrogative sentence—he remembered from his school days.

Walter Sinclair stopped and turned, shuffling a cigarette from his shirt pocket. "Is it true that thou are a soldier?"

Taken aback by the normalcy of his question, Ed was slow to answer. Finally, he shook his head.

"I suppose I am." He tapped the cigarette on the back of his hand to secure the leaves and placed it between his lips.

"Nervous?"

The attendant struck the match and cupped his hands. Ed inhaled deeply, avoiding the attendant's gaze, and shrugged.

Ed's clouded eyes scanned the grounds until he found the long, elegant drive. It was awash in cherry blossoms. Early spring. It beckoned him. A flair of hope, like a comet in the night sky before it disappears into the endless black. He'd run once before, hadn't he? As soon as he thought about it, he knew. He had no place to run *to*. A hard lesson. But there it was anyway. The road, and something like hope. He couldn't pretend it wasn't.

"Just over there," the attendant gestured toward a rickety picnic table beneath a towering maple tree. Not thirty feet away, he eyed another picnic table—stick figures stationed around it—and yet another on the other side, on all sides as far as the eye could see.

"I'll be back for thee in an hour." The attendant escorted Ed to the picnic table where his mother and Mary waited.

Ed took a few last drags and exhaled. Flicking the cigarette to the ground, he walked woodenly toward the family he once knew. That knew him as he once was. He swallowed hard, pausing to crush the cigarette with the sole of his shoe as he surveyed his mother from a short distance. She held up her hand in a wave, like a child. She lived on hope. On faith, really. And ignorance.

"Ignorance is bliss," he remembered her saying. In his mother's world, he guessed it was.

## Chapter 24

# Visiting Sunday

"Philadelphia State Mental Hospital," the bus driver blurted, his cap pointing to a large wooden sign. From her seat at the front of the bus, Mary leaned forward to peer through the driver's window. She didn't see much of anything beyond the sign except a winding road that disappeared into a long row of trees on both sides. She followed her mother's labored movement down the bus stairs. At the bottom, she reached for her mother's hand. Mary pinched her nose when the bus burped black smoke as it pulled away.

"Where's the hospital, Mom?" Mary couldn't wait to see Edward. It had been such a long time.

"See where the others are walking?" Her mother pointed the way with her elbow. A black pocketbook hanging from her arm, she grasped the handles of a large brown sack. "We'll follow them. It's a bit of a walk, I'm afraid."

Mary tried counting the other hospital visitors to pass the time. She'd counted fifteen so far, but it was hard to see the ones that were pulling ahead of them. Her mother had to stop every few minutes to rest her puffy legs and catch her breath. Mary's legs were itching to run, but her mother admonished her to "slow down, Mary. Slow down. We'll get there soon enough."

When the hospital finally came into view, Mary couldn't believe her eyes. She'd never seen so many buildings or such a big lawn.

"Jiminy, is this where Edward lives now?" Her mother didn't answer.

"Now, mind, Mary, dear," her mother said as a tall man in a white uniform led them to a picnic bench to wait for Edward. "Don't pester your brother with a lot of questions. Remember, he's . . ." She looked around as if for help. "Edward's not well." After setting her pocketbook next to the bag on the bench, she bowed her head, whispered a prayer, and blessed herself. Looked up at Mary. "Do you understand me?" The pat on Mary's head did not make up for the sternness in her voice.

Mary nodded even though she didn't understand at all. Shouldn't they go inside the hospital? When her grandfather was in the hospital, he was propped up in a bed. It moved up and down in the room that had a big window with trees on the other side. She was about to ask her mother about this when she spied her brother walking toward them. Like a jack-in-the-box, Mary popped up.

"Edward! Edward!" She waved and ran to greet him. She threw her arms around his waist, half-expecting him to pick her up and twirl her around. Instead, he patted her on the shoulder and said softly, "Mary." Then he gently nudged her away. He felt all bony through his shirt. He smelled funny, too. Kind of like a wet dog. She scrunched her nose and flashed scrunched eyebrows at her mother, busy dabbing her eyes with a handkerchief.

"Son." Her mother stood up and threw her arms around Edward's neck. Gray hairs Mary hadn't noticed before strayed from her mother's tidy bun. Edward pulled back and motioned for them to sit down. His mouth turned upward, but his eyes didn't smile.

Edward sat on one side of the picnic bench while Mary sat alongside her mother on the other side.

"Edward, guess what? Mom and I had to take a trolley and the El and a bus to get here. Then we had to walk a long way from the bus stop. But see? We brought you cigarettes and Hershey bars, and guess what else? You'll never guess. Your sketching pad and pencils. What do you think? Are you pleased?" She grabbed the shopping bag of goodies and pushed it across the table.

Edward lifted his hands, as if warning Mary to stop. His hands were shaking and his cheek, where his dimple was, kept jumping like there was a frog in it. He spoke so softly Mary could hardly hear him.

"Yes, very nice. Thank you." He reached over and removed the sketching pad from the bag. He rubbed his thumb across the paper. He slipped it back into the bag and reached for the cigarette carton. He opened it and took out a pack of Lucky Strikes. Mary fished out a pack of matches and handed them to him, pleased with herself for thinking of it. He undid the cellophane, pumped the cigarette out, and tried to steady his hand as he lit it. After a long drag, he twirled the cigarette between his two fingers and watched it burn.

Mary was full of questions. Had Edward gotten her letters and pictures? Why wasn't he talking? Why didn't he seem happy to see them? She guessed it was because he was sick. But sick where? How? She didn't see any bandages. When she had asked her sister Alice about it, all she said was that Mary should stop asking questions. She was too young to understand. Alice was so mean. Meaner even than Ronnie.

Edward looked up from his cigarette to face Mary's mother. "Pop?" His voice was so quiet.

Like two little birds, her mom's hands fluttered up to the bun that had loosened during their long walk from the bus stop. She gathered the stray hairs and secured them with bobby pins. "Well, dear, you know your father. He's not much for, for . . ." She waved to the huge brick building behind Edward.

"For seeing his son in Bedlam?"

"Huh? Mom, what's bed . . .?"

"Mary," her mother said sharply.

Mary's question hung in the air like a sneeze that wouldn't come. She closed her mouth. Her long-awaited visit with her big brother, whom she loved more than anything in the world, wasn't turning out the way she expected.

Edward's shoulders drooped. A line of cigarette ash plopped to the grass. Mary followed his sad eyes across the grass to the other tables spread around the huge lawn and beyond them to the roadway. Was he looking at the road or the trees? The cherry blossoms were awfully pretty. On their walk up to the hospital, Mary had wanted to pick a few, but her mother 'tsked and said, "No."

Mary was not liking this visit at all. Edward was too quiet.

"Well, Dad's been awful busy," she piped up. She glanced at her mother for permission to continue. Her mother nodded. "He's working on, well, he's been looking for a job, and he's fixing a lot of things around the house. Sam doesn't come around much anymore to help. Did you know he got married?" Mary brushed some leaves from the table. "But we didn't get to go to the wedding." Mary frowned. "Elsie's not a Catholic, and Sam didn't even get married in the church." Mary harrumphed, echoing her mother's complaint. But Mary was awfully disappointed. She had so wanted to be the flower girl. Agnes was younger so it probably would have been her anyway.

Mary's mother quickly changed the subject. "The hospital said it was okay to visit you, Edward, dear. But the doctor didn't have time to talk with me. He was so nice the first time I spoke with him on the phone. Now I can't seem to reach him at all. Did you get the cigarettes I mailed to you?"

Edward's chin tilted upward. That was a yes, Mary guessed.

"How is the treatment going? Does they have any idea when. . ."

Edward reached over and patted their mother's hand before she got the question out.

Huh? What treatment? Mary scratched her head but held her tongue.

Her mother pressed on. "But what does the doctor say, son? Does he think you can come home soon? Is everything all right now, with that, that mix-up with the Army?"

Mary's head bobbed back and forth between her mom and Edward. They were both talking funny. What the heck was going on?

Edward waved his hand like he was shooing a fly. "Nothing much to be done, mother. The die, as they say. . . How are things at home? Have you spoken with Father McGuire?"

"After Mass, yes, I did. He's just fine. The pastor has been ill, and Father McGuire is a very busy man these days. With the war on and so many men away, he doesn't have much help at the church. That's probably why you haven't heard. . ." She gulped, as if she suddenly remembered something.

Edward's face turned red. Mary reached over the table to touch his hand. He pulled it back.

"We're getting along as well as we can, dear. Everything's rationed, you know. Meat is even harder to come by, but we're happy to make sacrifices for our soldiers . . . for the war effort, I mean."

Edward closed his eyes, his jaw jumping like crazy. He opened them. "What about the girls? How are they?"

"Well, Anna is the same. Getting bigger and a little harder to manage. But Mary's a big help." She reached over and patted Mary's head. "Ronnie's quit school and got a job to, well, to pitch in at home."

Edward's face drooped, as if her mom had just slapped him.

"Edward, dear," her mom said, folding her hands like she was praying. "It's not your fault . . ."

"Don't say what's not true, Mother." His chin shook.

"And Agnes . . .?"

This visit was going all wrong. She had to do something. Maybe if she changed the topic? "Oh, she's such a brat, Edward. You have no idea. Just yesterday . . ."

"Mary!" Her mother chided. "Edward doesn't want to hear about your silly quarrels."

Mary sank back on the bench and folded her arms across her chest. Edward was sad and talking funny, and her mother was getting crankier by the minute. Ever since Edward had gone into the Army, her whole house was topsy-turvy. Nothing was right anymore. She was determined to get to the bottom of it. She had to fix it. But how? For one thing, she would pray a lot harder. She would do her best to be a good girl, and she would light two Votive candles at the Blessed Mother's altar with the pennies she'd gotten for her birthday. She just knew that if God would hear her prayers and make Edward better, everything would be okay. She tilted her head back and looked up at the sky. She sure hoped God was listening.

## Chapter 25

# The Attendant

*1943*

*Dear Sallie Mae,*

*Hiya, sweetheart, how's tricks? I'm wearing the blue and green sweater vest thou gave me for my birthday. Somehow it makes me feel closer to thee. Boy, oh boy, the day thou waltzed into my life, I hit the jackpot. Thou are an angel from the breath of God—sweet as nectar and true as the North Star. I look forward to the day we will be married and won't have to live apart. When this war is over and I've finished my work here, we'll start our new life together. I'll finish my schooling so I can get a decent job, and one day buy thee that country house I promised—somewhere in beautiful Bucks County where the cows moo and the hills roll green.*

*I read that book by Khalil Gibran. "The Prophet?" Surely does have some beautiful verses. Maybe we can read it together sometime.*

*We had such a good time at Lester's. Didn't we? In my heart, I'll be forever dancing with thee to Bing Crosby's "Night and Day." He sang it for us, sweetheart. I sure loved slow dancing with thee,*

216

and I regret that I have two left feet when it comes to the jitterbug. I was green with envy watching Pete jitterbug with thee. I'm glad thou do like my best friend, though. He's a swell fella, even if he is a Mennonite who can dance better than me (ha, ha).

How's the new job working out? I'm so proud of thee. A fully fledged RN! I'll have to hurry and catch up once I've finished the important work I've started here. Law School will just have to wait a while longer.

On that note, the American Friends Service Committee finally approved our plan! Pete and I and a couple others met with Superintendent Zeller. He understands what we're up against, with 148 attendants doing the work of 800! He's also the only one here that supports us COs. He said that as long as we don't give the hospital or any particular administrators a black eye in public, he'd support our little newsletter. He even gave us some space in one of the cottages to do the typing and printing and whatnot. Can thou believe that? We're calling it "The Attendant." We'll mail it to all the COs working at mental hospitals around the country. The idea is to share information about our common problems working at mental hospitals and improving our service to the patients. Zeller also agreed to let us consult experts in the field!

The second part of our plan will be under the radar for now, but it's bound to blow the lid off this hospital and all the others like it. We won't be able to make that public for a while, maybe not 'til after this war is over. We have to bide our time. My preference would be to get information out to the public sooner to put the pressure on those in charge of these disgraceful institutions. We just have to find a back-door way of doing that so as not to *endanger "The Attendant" and those who sponsor us. Why, when people find out what's going on in here, they will be up in arms. Guaranteed. Pete and I are working on something that's hush-hush and a little risky. I'll tell thee all about it in due course.*

*But enough about work. How are thy folks and little brother? Tell that rascal he owes me a letter. I hope thy dad's health has improved. I feel badly that I'm not around to help him fix that roof of his. I sent thy aunt Harriet a note of thanks. That was awful generous of her, and with the $2.00 she sent, I can finally get my eyeglasses repaired.*

*Two more fellas got married and brought their wives to live nearby. Mike's wife is a nurse who started working here, so she can live with him on the hospital campus.*

*I know the next question, and the answer, sweetheart, is we have to think long and hard about it. It would be wonderful to have thee here, and the Lord knows this place needs more nurses, along with just about everything else. Conditions here grow worse by the day. More and more patients are coming in. TB is becoming a huge problem. They had to open a new building just for TB patients. Lack of food and unsanitary conditions—all the things we've been complaining about—have led to the disease's spread. (Don't worry. I've been extra careful.) The list of problems here goes on and on. Damaged buildings and locks that don't get fixed, so we can't keep our patients safe. One fellow got out and wandered around the grounds until he fell dead from a heart attack. It's freezing cold in winter, and bugs galore in the hot months because of all the broken windows and missing panes. Plaster ceilings in the dayroom and dorms are caving in on patients' heads. I've been keeping track of each and every repair that's needed, believe me. They can ignore my requisitions, but they can't deny my records.*

*The worst thing is that patients are left with nothing to do and nowhere to go. Those in the worst shape are kept in lodges— bare rooms, no furniture, dark as night, no windows, save for a small square of window on the door. It's such a desolate life! The suffering here—well, it's unspeakable, really, and not a fit place for a human being. And that's the thing, Sallie Mae. These patients are human beings. We have so little time to spend with them in a caring way, but I do try to get to know the more lucid ones. One fella is a soldier. A good-looking, youngish man who told me he was an artist. He's a depressive. Chart calls him a schizophrenic, but that seems to be the catchphrase here for most all the patients. We have quite a few soldiers in here. Well, they come from all walks, really, all walks.*

*But there I go—talking about work again. It's a wonder thou don't get tired of me! It is a good deal on my mind, and I thank thee, sweetheart, for thy indulgence. I don't know what I'd do if I couldn't open my heart to thee. There's many a dark day in here, but when I picture thee in that green dress standing in the glorious sunshine at the bottom of my ladder—well, I am reminded that though there be evil in this world, it will surely shrink in the sunlight of love and beauty and goodness. The Lord blessed me that day and every day since.*

*Ours is a young love, but I do look forward to putting this place behind me and embarking on a new and kinder world with thee.*

*I am forever thine*
*Walter*

## Chapter 26

# "Oh Long May It Wave"

*1944*

"Now, then, Henry, leave that fellow alone. Thou must calm down." Walter muscled Henry, a bully and inveterate troublemaker, away from George who was pinned against the wooden post supporting the ceiling beam. Walter had spied the fight in the dormitory when he was threading his way through the jammed cots trying to track down a nastier-than-usual smell.

"What's that sonofabitchin' nigger doin' in here anyway? He's got no business being with white folks," Henry shot back, making another lunge toward George. Walter yanked him back. Henry's fists were clenched, and angry veins like crisscrossing subway lines popped through the skin of his forehead.

"Don't want no trouble, Mistah Walter." The whites of George's eyes bulged. "No, suh. Don't want nooooo trouble from this here white man." He shook his head to punctuate the point. Broad in the chest with large hands and muscular arms and shoulders, George was built for farming. Walter recommended George for the hospital's patient-worker duty, and good reports from the farm manager suggested that the arrangement was working out well. Although he cut an imposing physical presence, George was a soft-spoken, easy-going man. Walter couldn't understand why he had been thrown into Byberry in the first place, and the violent ward at that. George's explanation was puzzling. "That there judge didn't like me, Mistah Walter." He had a habit of shaking his head over and over again when he wanted to be clear. "No suh. My damn draft card was out of date, and I didn't want to fight Roosevelt's damn war."

With his feet planted behind the troublemaker, Walter tightened his grip, keeping the man's arms pinned behind his back. Walter glanced at his watch. It was a little after 7:00 p.m. Buster had already clocked out. The other night man had called in late. Pete was busy getting patients to bed in another dormitory. Walter was on his own. Around him, manic patients, jockeying to get to their cots, shoved and taunted the depressed and catatonic ones. Such territorial issues plagued the ward, and Walter was prepared with a pair of cuffs attached to his belt in case his preference for firmness and cajoling failed.

"Henry, I've warned thee. I don't want to put the cuffs on, but I will if thou won't settle down and leave the man be." Bubbling over with rage, Henry twisted his torso and his elbow shot out and caught Walter in the face. The force bent his spectacles and caused an abrasion where the metal clung to the bridge of his nose. Not again! Inside, Walter was shaking. He couldn't show fear or insecurity, though. A patient such as Henry would feed on it and gain the upper hand. Dodging a backward kick to his groin, Walter quickly secured Henry's elbow behind him. Tightening his grip, Walter lowered his voice.

"I don't want to place thee in the restraint room, Henry, but I will if I have to." The magic words. Henry sputtered and squirmed

221

for another minute until, finally, his body quieted. The veins on his forehead retreated beneath the skin. While being dragged away, Henry narrowed his eyes at George and hissed. Repeating his warning, Walter steered Henry to the other end of the room. Assured that the man's rage had subsided, he left him sprawled out on his cot.

Walter examined the crowded dormitory for signs of trouble as he made his way back. He rubbed the cut on his nose and removed his spectacles, straightening them out as best he could. They'd already been broken by a patient who'd swung a broken piece of floorboard at Walter's head. Fortunately, his head remained intact. The spectacles, not so much. Keeping order while moving patients from one location to another posed challenges. Thus far though, Walter had resorted to using the cuffs a handful of times and the restraint room only as a threat.

He knew that paid attendants like Buster often used harsher methods, as evidenced by patient complaints about him and the sawed-off broom handle and hose stuffed in his pockets. When he took it up with the ward supervisor, Walter got a shrug and stern reminder about how shorthanded they were. Such brutality was unconscionable. But that wasn't the end of it. The entire situation was a disgrace. Attendants were thrown onto wards with little to no training and preparation. There was no manual of "Dos and Don'ts" and "What to Expect." Walter was sure they could do better. Pete and their fellow CO attendants agreed. The supervisor be damned. The COs started training one another and were coming up with new ideas for reform. Right now, though, Walter had more pressing matters.

After getting Henry settled, Walter returned to the task of tracing the source of the unusually nasty odor. As he laced his way to the back of the crowded room, the smell grew so intense he placed his handkerchief over his nose and mouth. Then he saw it. The naked, rigid body of a patient lying face-up alongside an empty cot. Walter felt his legs quake. He leaned over and closed the man's eyes. The gut-wrenching image of a stiff cow lying on its side in his uncle's pasture, its eyes open in horror, came rushing back. Walter thought he'd herded them all safely into the barn in anticipation of the storm that raged for two days. In the driving rain, he'd lost sight of the animal and left it behind.

Walter turned his head away from the awful sight. He coughed to settle the bile that rose from the pit of his stomach. He turned back, sucking in his breath while he leaned over to more closely examine the patient's dead body. His eyes, face and belly were engorged and distended. He thought he recognized the man, but he wasn't sure. There were so many of them, with more coming in every day. It was too hard to keep track. How long had he lain here like this? The smell suggested it had to have been at least a day, maybe more.

His hairy chest and belly were covered in welts and sores. Matted brown hair curled angelically across his forehead. A woman bore this man, Walter thought. Somebody loved him. No human being should have to die in such a desolate way. Walter bit his lip and coughed, resisting the urge to keel over. "Lord, bless this man," he said aloud. Then he followed the man's marbled eyes upward in search of the apparition that had so transfixed his gaze. All Walter saw was a leaky ceiling. On the floor beside the dead man's cot was a mildewed piece of it. Walter looked at the nameplate at the base of the cot. "Cot #151. Paul Burton. May 5, 1909."

Walter glanced at his timepiece. It was late. The supervisor was likely gone for the day. Walter knew the coroner would make his report, but Walter would also write his own as well before he left. He would personally notify the supervisor of this travesty first thing in the morning. He had a sick sensation that Mr. Gerald Frank wouldn't much care, though. Maybe no one would. After closing the man's eyelids with thumb and forefinger, he stood in prayerful silence amid the restless moaning and cursing that whirled around him. In spite of the handkerchief shielding his nose and mouth, the wicked scent bludgeoned his nostrils. He had to have this body removed. How had the other patients in the dormitory tolerated it?

He glanced around. Two cots over, a man sat atop his cot, his legs folded. He held a piece of his sheet over the lower part of his face. A sketch pencil between his fingers, he appeared to be writing on a large pad that rested on his knees. The man's name escaped him, but he vaguely remembered him. He'd held his cigarettes for him in the dayroom and escorted him to his family one visiting Sunday. Brooding man. A soldier. Intense hazel eyes. Kept to himself. Spent a couple of weeks in the restraint room. The man looked over at Walter who nodded. The patient raised his chin slightly in response. Walter made a mental note to speak with him after he'd seen to the removal of the deceased patient.

On his way back to the office to call the in-house morgue, Walter calmed down several more agitated patients, urging quiet and coaxing them to go to sleep. Even though his shift had ended, he would wait until the morgue orderlies arrived so he could show them where to collect the body. The commotion was likely to stir patients up again, but that couldn't be helped. Buster had skedaddled. The night shift attendants should be clocking in soon. No matter. He felt an obligation to wait until the man's dead body was decently covered and taken from the ward. He turned on the overhead office light and locked the door behind him. He'd catch up on his rest later.

"Hello," Walter said after five rings and a gruff greeting of "Yeah," followed by a garbled name on the other end. "This is Walter Sinclair from B ward calling to report the death of a patient." After ten hours of being on his feet, his legs ached. He sank into the wooden chair behind the broken desk. With the flat of his hand, he caressed the solid, finely grained oak. Ink-stained and nicked and scratched from years of use and neglect, it could be made beautiful again. All it needed was tender loving care, some sanding and re-finishing.

"Time of death?" the man demanded at the other end of the line. He didn't catch his name—Mack Morley or Torley—something like that. He sounded annoyed. Maybe Walter had woken him up from a nap.

"Can't say, but it looks like he's been gone upwards of a day, possibly two." Walter glanced at the flag hanging from a stand in the corner. It was crooked and close to touching the floor. He got up and righted it. So much injustice over there and over here.

So long may it wave, he said with a mental salute and sat back down.

A snort at the other end of the line. "That's nothing. Record's three days."

Walter wasn't sure how to respond to the man's remark. "Well, can thou come and see to him?" He tried to keep the annoyance out of his voice.

"Oh, you're one of *those*, huh. Are *thou* sure he's dead? Got my hands full down here. TB outbreak and all. Just me and one other guy at night, see? And he's busy rat-catching down here." He inhaled loudly to demonstrate.

Walter wasn't sure which was more alarming. He knew about the TB, but rats in the morgue. The man couldn't be serious. He had to be pulling the CO's leg about that one. Walter let the "you're one of those" comments whistle past his ears like an errant arrow. Walter had grown accustomed to the snide remarks, the kicks, the shoves, and sometimes outright threats. He was a Conch, after all, so he'd had to grow an extra layer of skin. Most times, he bore the abuse reasonably well. Right now, exhausted by a particularly trying day topped by the discovery of a dead man on the ward, Walter had the urge to reach through the phone line and sock the guy in the nose. Walter chuckled at his non-violent self. Obviously, the place was starting to get to him.

"You still there, or what?" Morley or Torley demanded. "I have lot of work down here."

"Yes, yes, I'm here. Of course, he's dead. The poor fellow smells to high heaven, his body is stiff, and he has no color or pulse. It's outrageous. The man must be seen to. It's unsanitary!" Regretting the obvious irritation in his voice, Walter collected himself. "I'm happy to help thee." Walter sat forward in the chair to indicate his willingness. "I'm off duty in ten." He reached up and smoothed his hair down, missing the ballast of his Fedora.

"All right, all right," the grumpy voice replied. "Give me a few."

"I thank thee. I'll be in my office. Ward B," but the phone on the other end had already clicked off. Walter sighed. The dead body would have to wait a little longer.

*Chapter 27*

# The Bond

Where was the man? Walter drummed his fingers on the office desk to hasten his arrival. The desk was a mess. Patient records, requisition slips, requests for repairs and supplies. What a joke. There was never money for any of it. Newsletters and directives from hospital administration—another joke—since they didn't have the manpower or resources to follow official recommendations. "Recreational exercise" and a "healthy, nutritious diet" amounted to so much bull crap. Walter guessed that such official directives were intended to placate some administrator, hospital board, or state overseers, but they had no bearing whatsoever on day-to-day conditions and operations. The exercise yard was too small to accommodate the ever-increasing number of patients. In bad weather, it was impossible to take them out of doors anyway, given the lack of suitable clothing.

The *Philadelphia Inquirer* headline staring out at him from the bottom of the pile of papers disturbed Walter's mental tirade. He slid it out. "US FLEET ATTACKS TOKYO; Waves of Carrier Planes Hit Capital." He skimmed the day-old article. The Allies were on the move, and the chessboard was changing. The Yanks were making a difference. Hitler and Hirohito were finally being squeezed. But thousands of Americans were dying, and killing, of course. War-related news roused an odd mixture of horror and national fervor in Walter, along with a measure of guilt. After all, he was safe on the Homefront while kinsmen his age were dying. He thought his internal debate was settled when he became a CO, and in the truest part of his heart, he knew he couldn't have taken up a rifle. Still, his country was at war against the vilest of villains. He sought solace in his mission here at the hospital. If only it were run like a hospital.

The office door squeaked open. Walter looked up hopefully. "Pete?"

"Notta lapst time I checked." Rob pushed the door open.

"Oh, my mistake. I expect Pete to be coming along soon."

Rob shrugged. After clocking in, he whisked his keys from the wall and grunted hello to Walter. He seemed annoyed to find Walter behind the desk. He'd probably planned on putting his feet up and catching a few ZZZZs.

"Just doing some organizing." Walter picked up a stack of papers and held them aloft. "Waiting on the fellow from the morgue for the dead patient in B. Know anything about that?" Walter eyed Rob carefully. "Looks like he's been there since yesterday, maybe the night before." When Rob had been on duty, Walter thought but didn't say.

"Woo mean anoder dope wup and died?" he lisped. "One wess to wurry about—ain't it?" It wasn't a question.

Walter 'tsked in disapproval.

"Nah," Rob finally shrugged. "Don't know nuffin about it."

"But weren't you on duty last. . ."

Rob answered Walter's unfinished question with the thud of the door as he strode back out of the office.

What a strange fellow. Walter tossed *The Bulletin* into a pile meant for the trash and returned to the task of organizing the papers on the desk. He kept the other papers crucial to the COs' investigation of mental hospitals safely secured in a cabinet in *The Attendant* office.

It was Monday. On Sunday, his day off, he and Pete had started cataloging the statements and reports coming in from hospitals around the country. They'd put the call out through word-of-mouth in their various churches. Overcrowding, patient abuse, supply shortages, repair needs. There was no end. Different players, different hospitals, and yet always somehow the same issues. Walter winced, recalling one report about a doctor who claimed it was too much trouble to remove a patient's inflamed gall bladder. Stuck a drain in the man's stomach and closed it with a single row of wire sutures. The CO attendant had been a medical student. Knew the procedure needed at least three rows of sutures. Should have removed the entire gall bladder in the first place, the CO reported. The patient was dead the next day. The doctor shrugged it off. Astounding, and all too common.

Patients were dying left and right—eight a week in Byberry alone. Another Delaware hospital CO trained as a bacteriologist discovered that 75% of his patients were afflicted with diarrhea. He tested the milk and found it to be contaminated with human feces. After two more tests, he registered a complaint with the supervising doctor. The doctor didn't want to hear about it. "They all get diarrhea from time to time." He ordered the CO to do the job he was hired for and keep the patients in line. Walter shook his head at the recollection. How could a man who'd taken the Hippocratic oath be so callous?

State mental hospitals were a disaster. No, Walter thought. A travesty. They hired ex-cons and drunkards, fired them only when forced to, and then rehired them at another hospital, and sometimes even at the same one. Walter suspected Buster of falling into that category. According to a New Jersey CO attendant, a patient complained to his wife about being picked on and choked with a wet towel by an attendant who regularly came into work drunk. After the attendant was reprimanded by his supervisor, he persuaded some other patients to gang up on the man for having reported him. His wife reported the abuse to the supervisor, and the attendant was fired. Six months later, the rehired employee, bent on revenge, terrorized the poor fellow until he jumped off the hospital roof to his death. And on and on and on.

Walter shook his head. Shuffled some papers. Picked up the phone again. It rang five times. He slammed the receiver. Where was the man?

The dead man in the ward below was just another in a long list of horrors. They haunted Walter. They also hardened his conviction that the COs would have to find a way to take matters into their own hands. A Mennonite fellow by the name of Frank Wright had the same idea about collecting CO attendants' testimony. The men decided to team up. Walter's lawyerly bent came in handy. He stressed the importance of being methodical and accurate with their collected testimonies. The men agreed. First, they'd collect the evidence. Then they'd try to work within the system. Go up the chain of command. If that failed, they'd bring it to the public's attention. Let the chips fall where they may.

Walter wasn't too hopeful about the plan to work within the system. Doc Windsor barely made it to B ward once a week. Stayed five, maybe ten minutes, tops. Why, that wasn't enough time to look after over 300 patients! Many of the patients never saw the doctor for months at a time, and then only for five minutes. When the doc finally made it to Walter's ward, he was defensive and prickly. Completely uninterested in Walter's suggestion that they stop tying patients to their beds as a form of punishment and control. The doctor also dismissed Walter's concerns about persistent illnesses and injuries owing to the ward's unsanitary and unsafe conditions.

It was left to Nurse Tasker and her assistant to put Band-Aids on ailments, give shots, and so on, but she had limited skills and no authority to speak of. Supervisor Gerald Frank had plenty of authority, but he rarely visited the ward. Sat in his big fancy office in the administration building, issuing futile directives about patient hygiene and the benefits of exercise. Same as the inane training lectures and films on patient care. The "treatment of mental illnesses" training was nothing more than pie-in-the-sky bromides entertained in medical schools with little bearing on the real problems attendants faced every day. Why, they needed resources, not more futile directives! Such concerns fell like a thud on Gerald Frank's obtuse ears.

Two weeks before, Mr. Gerald Frank finally showed his face on Walter's ward. Demanded to know why so many of the patients were naked and huddled in groups on the cold floor, as if he himself weren't partly responsible. Why, the unmitigated gall of the man. Pranced through the door in his fancy black Wingtips, worsted wool suit, and red bowtie. Wispy blond hair was combed forward to camouflage a widening bald spot.

"What's the meaning of this?" Frank launched into a tirade with a grating, high-pitched voice. "Miss O'Hara from the governor's office will be here in four days to do an inspection. This does not look good at all. Why are these men naked? I want them cleaned up and clothed. And those walls. Is that, is that *smeared* feces?" He grimaced. Pulled a perfectly starched pocket square from his suit jacket and covered his offended nose before escaping back out to the corridor. Two minutes on his own ward was the maximum he could stand.

Did the man think Walter had a magic wand he could wave to clothe patients and clean the walls?

"Why, yes sir, it is." In the corridor, Walter leaned over to trap the man's pale blue eyes. He had a good four inches on the supervisor's rotund frame, and he meant to use every inch of physical dominance to make his case. "It's not just the lack of clothing, Mr. Frank. We don't have enough soap or disinfectant. Or mops, for that matter. The ward is bursting at the seams with patients, and we don't have nearly enough staff to manage them."

"Don't we have patient-workers on the ward to help with the, uh, with the mopping and cleaning and so forth?" Mr. Frank waved his hand, his gold cufflinks glinting.

His supercilious air rankled Walter. "Well, sir, yes, we do. But we need supplies—soap, lye, and whatnot—and more attendants on the ward to supervise those patients." He strained to keep his tone respectful. "The ward is stuffed to the gills, as you just saw. More keep coming in every day. And there's no end to the list of needed repairs to this building."

How could Frank be so ignorant about conditions in his own ward? He knew he was probably testing the supervisor's patience. Given this rare opportunity to speak to the man in person, Walter intended to make his case. When was he likely to have the man's ear again? He led Frank back to the dilapidated office. Showed the man the supply closet, all but empty except for a small stack of underwear riddled with holes.

The supervisor eyed the office and near-empty closet blankly. He cleared his throat. "War's on, as you know. Shortage of supplies, you see. My hands are tied." He tugged on the white cuffs of his shirt-sleeves, first one and then the other, to emphasize how tied his hands were. Cleared his throat again.

"Well, then," Gerald Frank turned away from Walter's steely gaze. "Well, then, we'll have to, ah, we'll have to fix some of these things in advance of the inspection." He finger-combed the wispy strands of hair on his balding head. "Thank you, Mr. Sinclair. You may go back to your duties. You'll be hearing from me."

Mr. Frank's frantic tone suggested he was genuinely worried. Walter was hopeful. Mike, from Ward A, said he'd heard something about the state Secretary of Welfare's upcoming visit. Maybe they'd finally start providing the supplies and resources needed to care for the patients properly. Maybe that's why the Secretary of Welfare was coming to visit. Walter was buoyed by the flurry of activity that followed over the next three days. The crumbling ceiling in the dayroom was patched. Not very well, in Walter's view, but at least it would hold until they properly repaired the roof. Assuming they would. Extra attendants, and maintenance men armed with mops, buckets, and gallons of disinfectant, magically appeared. They cleaned the floors, walls, tub, and toilet room. Why, it felt like Christmas on the ward, especially when an assortment of clean shirts and pants arrived! Walter couldn't wait to tell Sallie Mae about it in his next letter.

His hopes were dashed however when, almost a week later, Mr. Frank returned for the planned inspection with Miss O'Hara and Doc Windsor. The very next day Walter and Buster received orders to collect the patients' newly dispensed uniforms and send them to Mr. Frank's office. Walter discovered that the same uniforms were to be sent to another ward in preparation for Miss O'Hara's next inspection. And the next. And on it went.

Walter reached for the Fedora. Realized it was not there. Their little newsletter was not going to be enough. The COs would have to focus on plan B.

Dick McSorley tapped twice on the door before sticking his head into the office and announcing himself.

"Hold on, just finishing up." Walter set the last stack of papers aside and looked down approvingly at the neat, well-organized piles.

"Ain't got all night. Gurney's out here."

"Right with thee." Walter pushed the chair back and set it neatly in place. Hitching up his pants, he stood up and strode to the doorway. He adjusted his bent spectacles again, trying to ignore his aching legs and the burning sensation at the back of his eyes.

When he entered the hallway, Walter sensed McSorley sizing him up. Apparently deciding he was an okay fellow for a Conch, he started talking freely.

"How long you been here?" He didn't pause for a reply. "Me? Going on three years now." As he chattered, Walter led the way to the elevator at the end of the hallway as Dick steered the gurney from behind. "Some job, eh? Crummy hours and pay, but it beats being in the Army. I hear some guys are being sent to the Pacific. I never been anywhere but Philly! But heck, I was sure glad they didn't want me. Too old anyway. Would you believe I'm almost fifty?" Not pausing for Walter to answer between questions, he fluffed up his full head of ginger hair and flashed a toothy grin. Freckles swarmed his baby face, on which time seemed to have left few calling cards.

"That so?" Walter muttered when Dick stopped chatting long enough for him to reply. The weary elevator squeaked to a stop and lumbered open.

"Didn't mean to be so huffy before." He looked vaguely chagrined. "This job gets to a fella."

"Was thou serious about the rat problem down there?" Walter held the door as they steered the gurney in.

"Oh yeah, huge problem. HUGE." He held up his hands as if he was showing off a prize Marlin he'd just caught. "Why, I got some stories would knock the socks off . . ."

"Walter, Walter, wait up," Pete called from the other end of the hall just as the elevator door was about to close. "What's this I hear about a dead body? Need any help?"

"Well, thou are a sight for sore eyes," Walter grasped Pete's hand when he reached the open door. "Dick, this is Pete. Pete, Dick." The two shook hands. "Yes, it may be good to have a third man. We're likely to rile up the patients. Thanks, Pete."

"Have you seen Rob? He's supposed to be on night duty as well."

Pete snickered. "Your guess is as good as mine."

The lift shuddered to a stop and spilled the men out on the terrazzo floor of the dank basement where the dormitories were located. Fearful of stirring up the patients, they fell silent as they approached the door. Walter produced the heavy ring of keys from his pocket. Holding them to the dim overhead light, he found the correct one for the dormitory. The wood was split on the side, so key or not, someone could easily muscle the door and get out. He shook his head in exasperation and pushed it open.

"Body's all the way at the back on the left side. We'll just get in and out as quickly and quietly as possible."

"Yeah, yeah, fine by me. We're in your territory now."

Pete nodded his agreement.

Walter flipped the switch, and the light flickered three times before deciding to stay on. Ignoring the grumbling and rising level of patter among the patients, Walter led Pete, with McSorley and his gurney behind him, to Paul Burton's body.

"The stench of this place," McSorley grumbled under his breath.

The patients lay curled up on their bare cots. One was wailing and praying. Another was engaged in a heated debate with himself, his neighbor telling him to "can it, already." Taking his handkerchief back out of his pocket, Walter motioned for Pete to do the same. Then he placed it on his face and tied it at the back of his head. McSorley came prepared with a surgical mask, which he promptly slid on.

"So, how do we do this?" Walter gestured to the dead man's body.

"Why isn't he on the damn cot?" McSorley seemed annoyed. "Sucker's going to be heavy to lift from the floor. Good thing that other fella's here."

At the moment, Pete was intervening in a fight that had broken out several cots over.

"Well, let's have a look." McSorley squeezed the gurney between the rows of cots, where it waited patiently for its cargo. He bent over the body to get a better look. "Not much room here to maneuver. Guess I'll lift him up by the shoulders." McSorley positioned himself at the head of the body. "You take the feet and legs. Other guy can help us get him onto the gurney. Watch out for that puddle, there."

"That may take a minute." Walter beckoned to Pete, who was on his way, having just calmed the unruly patient.

"Well, then," McSorley said, "Let's do it. On three: one, two, three . . ."

"Oh, *mein Gott! Hör auf!* Oh, my God! Stop! *Seine Haut! Seine Haut!* His skin!" Pete shouted as he neared Walter and McSorley, who'd just begun to raise the body. Pete's alarmed hands emphasized the urgency of his directive.

Walter's head snapped up. He immediately released the man's legs. He looked at McSorley, whose face had gone ashen.

The skin of the dead man's back was stuck to the floor.

Walter followed Pete's eyes and leaned forward to examine the body more closely from the side. While gently probing the man's underside, he was thrown backward. A swarm of maggots and other insects scurried out.

"Well, this beats what-all to hell!" McSorley snickered.

"Mein Gott." Pete clapped his hands over his ears in disbelief.

Walter's stomach somersaulted at the sight of a man's skinless back. His ears buzzed. He leaned over and coughed into his handkerchief. All around them, bugs hopped and scrambled in every direction like patrons at a speak-easy raid scrambling toward an exit.

Walter stood up and stepped back from the body. He slumped against the gurney, grateful for Pete's reassuring hand on his shoulder.

Shaken but mindful of McSorley's presence, Pete spoke loudly in German. *"Mach dir keine Gedanken Walter, wir she'n, dass sas an die Oeffentlichkeit kommt. So wie die andern Faelle, die Geschichte von dem armen Kerl muss ans Tageslicht kommen!"* Don't worry, Walter; we'll make sure this atrocity sees the light of day. This is the last straw. This poor man's story must be made public. *All* these nightmare-stories!"

Walter shook his head and groped for words. "A disgrace, a disgrace."

Around them, patients started clamoring, stirred by the commotion. The stillness of one patient drew Walter's attention. It was the soldier-patient who liked to sketch. He sat cross-legged on his cot. He was shaking his head, his pencil working furtively on the paper before him. Walter straightened. He stepped across the aisle with a curious Pete close on his heels.

"Can I help thee?" Walter asked when he drew closer to Cot #298. The tiny label read: Edward F. Hohlfeld July 22, 1914. He was astonished when the man replied in German.

"*Vieleicht kann ich Ihnen helfen*," Ed said, his voice low and steady. Maybe I can help you. He held up the sketch. Pointed to his brown sack holding other sketches.

Walter blinked in recognition. At that moment, in the deepest part of himself, he knew. Here was a kindred spirit. A new bond formed. An agreement made to rectify this travesty.

*Chapter 28*

# David and Goliath

*1945*

The men spoke in hushed tones in the alcove between the connected dorm rooms. It was long past midnight at the end of another grueling day. The men had just put the month's newsletter to bed. Part of the targeted CO-devised mental hygiene program, *The Attendant,* drew on research from doctors and leaders in the mental health field, thanks to Byberry superintendent Frank Zeller's approval. They had to hold their punches, though. Zeller supported their efforts only so long as COs didn't present the institution in a bad light. Their newsletter was a success, far better than Walter and Pete ever dreamed. *The Attendant* was the beleaguered CO attendants' Bible, even though its reach was hamstrung by politics and lack of funds. With it, they established much-needed credibility in the mental health field, and Eleanor Roosevelt sent them a commendation letter for their work with the mentally ill. But for all it did do, their monthly newsletter could not remedy the hospital's concentration camp-like conditions that remained hidden from the world, stored securely in the institutional closet. At the base of it all, state laws governing institutions for the mentally ill did nothing to help. They were either arcane, or else simply ignored by administrators.

Walter was sure now that more muscle was needed to open that closet door to public scrutiny. Where did the money allotted by the state legislature for repairs and the construction of much-needed buildings go if not to the hospital? How did administrators get away with running the hospital at 75% over capacity, with 180 attendants doing the job of some 1,000 men, and most of those unfit for the work? With the war starting to wind down and CO stints about to come to an end, the fate of Byberry's patients would be left in the hands of these same corrupt and morally bankrupt administrators. No, something else begged to be done. Who else but men of conscience to do it?

"Time to act. We've seen enough." Walter shook his head in disgust. "And thou saw the soldier's sketches. I don't think he imagined those, those . . ." He stopped, unable to describe them. "Horrors."

Pete clucked his tongue and grunted in agreement. He shifted from his left to his right foot and looked away to give Walter privacy.

Walter cleared his throat. He lifted his eyeglasses slightly to thumb the moisture away from his eyes, recalling the stomach-churning pictures the patient had drawn. The bug-infested dead body. A beefy man's penis jammed into the naked buttocks of a young man whose transfixing eyes broadcast his terror. A half-naked man smeared with feces cowering under an upraised arm holding a pipe at the end of it. His arms strapped to a bench, and his head bent in abject surrender. Rats stalking the dining hall and snatching food from patients' bowls. The dead man's skin peeled from his back . . . and on and on. Some sketches were disturbingly fragmented. An arm here, a torso there, as though the artist had perfectly matched form to its grotesque subject. Since he'd first clapped eyes on them, Walter had tried erasing the images, but they refused to be banished, even in sleep. Especially in sleep, as nightmares and night sweats became constant companions.

"We're *seeing* it. This man is *living* it, Pete."

Pete lifted his head and placed a reassuring hand on his friend's shoulder.

Walter pressed his fingers against his temples. He shook his head. "The man is depressed, sure, deeply depressed, and there may be some distortion there because of the trauma. But it squares with everything we're observing. Doesn't it? We *saw* that man's skin on the floor, for pity's sake!"

Pete nodded, removing his hand. "All the patients are living it, Walter. But there's only so much we can do. We're so few in number. The administration's happy to have us, but they don't respect us. We're a necessary evil. They need us, but they hate us. Well, maybe the superintendent appreciates the work we do. He did what he could by supporting our little publication."

"Where does all the state money go, though? No." Walter said with finality. "He *should* be doing more." His mind was still fixed on the sketches, considering how they might use them. He remembered that Pete had stopped looking at the sketches after seeing the one of a bound boy being sexually assaulted, his legs at impossible angles and his mouth agape. How *many* patients were being abused in this way?

Pete sighed heavily, emitting a sound like a low whistle. "Hey, Walter how about we write to Eleanor Roosevelt? We'll ask for an audience and give her an idea of what's really going on. Seems like just the kind of issue she'd take up." He threw his arms open, as if he'd just thrown a Hail Mary pass.

Walter caught it. "Good thinking, Pete. That just might be the way to start the ball rolling. But people need to see it for themselves. They won't take our word for it, especially with administrators doing their best to hide the dirt. Thou saw what happened with that phony state inspection. The only way we can pull this off is to become snoops. Get a camera in here. I got that little Agfa camera Sallie Mae gave me for Christmas, and that fellow, Ed, his sketches . . ." Walter paused. "If we can use those sketches and maybe take some photographs of our own and get them out to the public. Wouldn't that be hard evidence?" He paused and waved his arm. "That would be proof of how bad conditions are in here, the kind of proof a journalist needs. If we could get a national magazine, let's say, *Life,* to publish, maybe, just maybe, it would blow the lid off this place. Well?" He eyed Pete, the more cautious of the two, to gauge his reaction.

Pete snorted. "*Life?* That's a long shot, Walter."

"For that matter," Walter offered, "Eleanor Roosevelt is a long shot."

"Yes, well," Pete hesitated. "We can write a letter to Mrs. Roosevelt. She answers folks, but how are we going to get the attention of a hotshot journalist at some big-time magazine? And who is going to care about the deranged pictures of a mentally ill person?"

"I don't know, Pete. I don't know." Walter's eyes drifted off, remembering the soldier bent over his sketchpad sitting atop his bunk. "The man is sullen, no question, and his pictures are dark. Strange thing is, though, the fellow seems sane enough. Don't he?"

Pete nodded in agreement. "Mistrusting, though. Traumatized. Can't blame him." He paused, grasping the significance of what he'd just implied. Individuals becoming mentally ill in a hospital intended to heal the mentally ill. "Just like that Negro fellow. Remember? One who got thrown in here because his draft card was out of date? Maybe it's something like that put him in here. Other soldiers also told me they're in here because of insubordination or some such. Why doesn't that just beat all? Makes no sense whatsoever." Pete placed his pipe back into his mouth. "Are you sure about this, Walter?"

"I don't know what put this man in here, Pete. But I know this," Walter shot back. "It's not right. So many things here, well, they're just not right, and we can write summary reports 'til we're blue in the face, but a national black eye? That might just do the trick. We'll write letters 'til they're coming out our ears. We'll make phone calls, too. Boy, wouldn't it be something if we could persuade Eleanor Roosevelt and she could get some hotshot producer to make a movie? Wouldn't that be a great way to get the message out to the public?" As he spoke, Walter grew more animated. The prospect of a plan, of taking more direct action, lifted his spirits.

Pete chuckled. "Whoa, slow down there, Walter, one thing at a time."

Walter grinned. "Yes, I suppose thou are right, Pete. But I am not about to slow down. We'll do what it takes to get someone's interest piqued. Photographs and sketches to a journalist, that's our best bet, and as thou said, this may be the kind of social justice issue to get Mrs. Roosevelt to do some flag-waving in her *My Day* newspaper column."

As if he'd finally run out of steam, Walter slumped back against the wall. He rolled up his shirtsleeves, his armpits dripping with sweat. Walter badly wanted a shower to scrub off the stink that had seeped through his clothing and into his pores. He wondered if he would ever be able to wash it off. The stink of this place. He was bone tired, too, somewhere beyond exhaustion, and yet he'd never been more focused, more alert or determined.

"You sure about this, Walter? It could go sour, come back on us."

Walter's head was bent, like a priest in the confessional, his hands folded in front of him. He rubbed his chin with his thumb and forefinger. He reached up to press back his Fedora, signaling his decision was made.

"Yes, yes," he said, almost sorrowfully, "I surely am."

Pete placed his hand on his friend's shoulder. "Well, Walter, I don't mind admitting that I'm a little scared. But the right thing is always the hard thing. You're the brains of this outfit. What should I do?"

Finally, a plan. A sense of direction. Walter felt a surge of energy that defied his exhaustion.

"Since he understands German, speak to Hohlfeld, discreetly. See if he has any reliable contacts on the outside—a town or city official or church leader he can trust to show his sketches to. He mentioned a trusted priest friend of his. Maybe the priest could help persuade a journalist to get on board. I'll take some photos on the sly. We'll have a two-pronged attack."

The war metaphor was not lost on Walter or his friend. They stood on a battlefield as real and menacing as the one their Yankee brothers in the European and Pacific theatres were fighting on.

"All right, Walter." Pete extended his hand. "I'll talk to the other fellas. Bring them up to speed. Get them on board with the plan." They shook hands and clapped one another on the shoulder to seal the pact, like blood brothers in a schoolyard.

Walter knew they were about to take on an institutional Goliath. All they needed now was the faith and shrewdness of David and a mighty powerful sling.

*Chapter 29*

# The Sketches

He couldn't dodge the horrors of the dayroom. Its cracked feces and urine-stained cement walls. The putrid smell of despair. The man flapping his arms and screeching like a buzzard. Another picking at his skin until the blood trickled down his arms and legs. The child-man, naked and tucked into himself like a terrified turtle. Lost bodies locked in hopeless space. The inertia, the pacing, the circling. The attacks. A sudden kick to the groin or fist in the face, a shoulder to the back. They came like thieves in the darkness of daylight. In and gone. Damage done.

Ed was stabbed twice in the side with a shaved-down spoon. A phantom attacker, there and gone in a breath. Metal ruptured his skin and found the bone. His blood gushed out like water from a newly opened fire hydrant. He was lucky. One of the CO attendants happened to be on duty. He hustled Ed to the infirmary. The nurse was distracted. She absent-mindedly directed him to a chair. Her fingers searched the cabinet for iodine and gauze, a telephone receiver nestled between her shoulder and chin. Her voice was crisp. Control with a hint of accusation.

"Well, doctor, this *is* the 4th day . . ."

A man bellowed in pain from the adjoining room. Someone shouted for him to "Shut up already. Ya wanna wake the dead?"

The nurse shook her head. "Yes, I realize patients run high temperatures, Doctor, but 105 seems awfully . . . all right, but this is the 4th day. At what point do you . . .? Doctor, doctor?" The nurse examined the receiver in disbelief before slamming it into the cradle.

Poor bastard, Ed thought, then laughed to himself. All of us poor bastards.

The harried nurse turned her attention back to the wounded patient in the chair. Her nametag read Mrs. Tasker. She was a tidy woman. Her dark brown hair was bobby-pinned under a starched white cap. Her hands moved adroitly over the open wound. She said she was sorry if it hurt. Ed couldn't tell her he didn't feel it. Why alarm her?

"What happened?" she asked, tenderly pressing a cool white bandage on the deep, ragged gash.

As if it mattered. Ed bent his head toward the wound and shrugged.

He tried to keep to himself. In his head, not in space. Space was crammed with desperation and the constant thrum of crazy. He clung to the outer wall while pacing the dayroom. It afforded a better view of the danger that came from all sides. Away from hard benches with their strapped-down patients. Straps made him shudder. So did the hanging heads of misery and the tales of patients who'd frozen to death when they'd made a run for it.

And yet, like a trapped animal he held on, waiting for something. For what, another opportunity to escape? Just thinking about it made his breath quicken. He knew he wanted to live, to return to his life. He wasn't ready to risk dying, but for the life of him he didn't know why. Hoping against hope for a sign, he supposed.

He'd studied the locks. Knew which ones were rusted and broken. Windows, too. But the rumors of bodies frozen and buried on the grounds gave him pause. Could they be true? Still, Edward had managed to find his way off the property once. Might he bide his time and try it again? Maybe they wouldn't come for him this time. He had been stronger then, though. Less foggy in his head. No, his last chance lay in the sketches and Walter's plan. Besides, where would he escape *to* now his family assumed he was crazy? His father and mother certainly thought so. How could he blame them? They'd come home that fatal night not to their son but to a crazed, terrified animal crouched atop their icebox.

He couldn't blame them for what they didn't understand. If he'd known what his choice on the firing range would come to, the damage it would cause, the hell it would send him to, would he make the same choice? Why not just shoot the damn rifle, go off to war and be done with it? *Bless me, Father. I'm sorry. I'm sorry. I am so, so sorry.*

The nurse's clean hands applied the bandage with a tenderness that sent a shock through his system. That forgave him.

"You'll have to wait here until someone can escort you back to your ward." She finished up her handiwork with a tidy flourish. A woman's hands. Soft and reassuring. He almost cried when her hands released him.

The moaning in the room continued. Three other sick or wounded patients waited in their safe metal chairs. A man Ed judged to be about his age was sweating profusely, a thermometer dangling from the corner of his mouth. The other, a bit older, was bent over. He clutched his bloodied face, a gash just visible on his forehead beneath his fingers. He was talking to himself in a raspy voice.

Under her breath, the nurse muttered. "There's just too many of you and too much of this. My Lord, I've only two hands."

Ed hoped the attendant would take his time getting back and returning him to the dayroom. The infirmary was small and cozy, the room contained, and the patients restrained by their physical ailments. He leaned back and shut his eyes, remembering.

Ed hadn't seen Dr. Theodore L. Windsor since the day of his arrival. When he saw him the second time, Ed was in the cold, cramped art-therapy room sketching with a handful of other patients. The pencil kept him alive. He wasn't sure for what. He smelled the musky cologne before he saw the man.

The doctor's crisp, tailored suit loomed over Ed's shoulder. "Pvt. Hohlfeld?"

Ed glanced up.

The doctor checked his watch. "Your mother's been badgering my office." The doctor spoke tightly. "She's concerned about you."

His mother's badgering. Ed was sure it was the only reason he had access to his sketching materials and this room. He returned to the textured sheet of paper spread flat out on a table, a brown bag filled with sketches stored safely beneath his other arm. He was ready to do battle to protect it. It gave him purpose. Conscientiously objecting didn't always work. After sensing the doctor's approach, Ed deftly slid his hummingbird sketch on top of the one he'd been working on.

The doctor leaned over to get a better view. His ears jutted away from his head like errant children, something Ed had not noticed the first time.

"Lovely bird." The doctor stood back up. "Very good. Your mother said you had a knack for drawing." He smiled tightly. A gold tiepin gleamed from his starched blue shirt. Two middle buttons strained to open and free the balloon of his belly.

"I understand your, uh, your depression has worsened." The doctor glanced at his watch again, and at Buster standing dutifully behind him, his heft and rubber hose a silent warning to Ed. Buster shrugged his shoulders and looked around. "Is the, uh, the sketching helping at all?" The doctor peered at Ed over the rim of his glasses. "I've granted special approval for that, you know. At your mother's request. She's a rather insistent woman."

Ed tapped his forehead with the pencil. One true thing.

"As I explained to your mother, we might try insulin shock therapy, but we're, uh, we're short of insulin these days. The war, you see. Don't, uh, don't know when we'll have more. In the meantime, let's just keep up with the sketching, shall we?"

The doctor's hands reached up and tightened the knot of his tie that was already Windsored into place. He nodded to the attendant on duty and hastened through the doorway, retreating to the world of sanity on the other side. Hadn't seen him since.

Ed placed the hummingbird sketch in the bag and thumbed through the others. His hands grew clammy. Each sketch, a reminder, a heartbreak, a tragedy. Joseph. He imagined the boy safely on the outside, but was he safe or was he dead? The not knowing tortured him.

Nurse Tasker touched his clammy forehead, startling him and interrupting his reverie. "Take these." She handed him two aspirin and a cup of water. "You have a fever, and this will help with the pain."

He swallowed the tablets and closed his eyes again. What if his mother and sister didn't come again this Sunday? Who was the person who had come the previous weeks pretending to be Mary? Could the visitor have been Mary? She looked so grown up. Certain it couldn't be Mary because she was not accompanied by their mother, Ed had sent her away. Now he was worried. He had to give his sketches to someone he trusted. His mother and sister had to come. He had to get the sketches to Father McGuire.

Ed was sure . . . he thought he was sure . . .Father McGuire would help. That's what he'd told Walter.

"When he sees . . . when he knows . . . Yes." Ed had assured Pete. Ed trusted that the priest would be willing to deliver them to a journalist. But so much time had passed . . . and the last time. He winced, remembering the last time he'd seen the priest. Freezing and hysterical, and yes, desperate, and out of his right mind.

"But the sketches . . ." Pete asked warily. "The sketches will get the priest's attention . . . will persuade him to act? To assist in our plan?"

They've got to, Ed thought. They've got to. He owes me that much.

Ed felt a tap on his shoulder. It was the same CO who'd brought him. After being escorted from the infirmary back to his cot, Ed lay down with his eyes open. A gaping hole in the ceiling stared back at him. Rats scuttled back and forth. He shuddered and turned onto his side, cuddling the brown bag as a child would its precious blanket. Tomorrow was visiting Sunday. This was it. There was a part of him that didn't want to part with his sketches. They contained evidence of injustice, and of his life and what had become of it. He had to share his sketches with the world and help Walter and Pete with their plan. If the right eyes would only see.

His St. Christopher Medal was gone and put to better use and Joseph, somehow miraculously saved. Ed imagined the beads between his fingers and prayed that his mother would come.

*Chapter 30*

# Little Miss Mary

Mary lost track of how many times she and her mother visited Edward after Sunday Mass when her mother suddenly stopped going. Just couldn't do it anymore, she said, so Mary was getting ready to make the trip to the hospital for the fourth time by herself. The other times, Edward didn't even recognize her because of all the makeup and sent her away. Mary returned home, having failed her mission. But her mother didn't give up.

Mary sat in front of the oval mirror at her mother's vanity, trying not to sneeze from the plume of bath powder her mother patted across her chest. The nylon stockings bunched into her sister's brassiere felt itchy and wrong. Mary screwed up her face and pleaded with her mother.

"Please, Mom, I hate this. I'm thirteen. I don't want to look like I'm eighteen.

"Please sit still, Mary, dear. When I'm done with you, even your own father won't recognize you. You have to do this for me and for your poor brother, Edward. I can't . . . I just can't . . . I'm not strong enough anymore. Your father won't do it. Someone has to go. You've gone with me so many times. You know the way there. You're my rock, Mary. Remember that."

In the vanity mirror, a stranger stared back at Mary. Her hair was arranged in a French twist. She had ruby-red lips, rouged cheeks, and long, black eyelashes. It was a pretty face, but it wasn't hers.

"But when is Edward going to get better and come home? Why does he have to stay at that stupid old hospital anyway? You never tell me anything!" She blurted it out, not meaning to, and immediately wanted to take it back. She knew, without knowing, that Edward's being in the hospital was shameful, like Anna's slowness and Sam's marriage to a non-Catholic. Things never to be discussed or asked about.

In the mirror, her mother raised the hairbrush at Mary. "I've told you. Edward is sick." She pointed to her head. "It's up to the hospital to say when he's better and can come home." Her eyes were filled with tears, but her voice sounded mad. "I can't explain it to you. I've told you. Now, I don't want to hear another word about it. *Not another word.*"

Hours later, on her fourth solo visit, Mary sat across from her brother at a picnic table. Edward eyed her uncertainly. This time, he didn't demand to know who she was, and he didn't run off. It was windy, and the bench was damp. Mary was glad when the sun finally peeped out of the clouds. The grass glittered from the morning's rain, and the air felt shiny and clean. Spring sat around the corner like a cat in front of an open window, alert and ready to pounce. Mary buried her pale arms inside her mother's black shawl when the wind shifted, and she tucked the skirt of Ronnie's dress beneath her legs. The belted blue and violet-patterned dress hung loosely around her hips. Mary slipped off her shoes and toed the dewy grass with her stockinged feet. Then she got an idea.

She pulled out a tissue from her pocket and started to rub the lipstick off her lips.

"See. Edward? It's me, all right! Your little sister Mary. I brought you your cigarettes and candy, just like always." She slid the carefully packed bag of Lucky Strikes, Blackjack gum, and Hershey's bars toward him. Her mother had also included a few Sunday *Bulletins* and clippings about parishioners that got married or died. Edward didn't seem interested, not even in the cigarettes. He just sat there holding a brown sack against his chest. Mary couldn't see what Edward's jumping eyes were looking at or looking for. She tried to follow them. A little boy raced back and forth across the grass, trying to get the breeze to lift his blue kite. Its silver stars winked at the sun. A woman sat nearby. The boy's mother, Mary supposed. She was bouncing a baby on her lap. She held the baby up, coaxing the man across from her to play with him. The man ignored her and the baby. He stared at something on the ground that Mary couldn't see. The woman finally gave up and cradled the gurgling baby on her lap.

"Mary, is it really you? What's wrong with Mom? Why didn't she come? Is she okay?"

"Kinda, but not really. Mom said she just can't do it anymore, Edward. The trip takes too long, and she's awful worn out. With Alice and Ronnie and Sam gone, and Dad not getting around so well, and Anna getting bigger and harder to manage."

Edward made a loud sucking sound, like he couldn't catch his breath. "All because of me. All my fault. Got to make this right," he muttered.

"No, Edward, oh no. I didn't mean . . ." Mary didn't know what she meant or what Edward meant. She just knew she didn't want her brother to feel bad. His eyes were so droopy and sad. Her fingers reached across the table to touch his arm. She felt his arm relax. For

253

a moment, the anchor of worry that hung from her thin shoulders was gone. Mary was little again, and Edward was walking her home from the trolley stop, her small hand nestled safely in his. When he suddenly pulled his arm back, the picture vanished.

He shook his head from side to side. "I can't believe Mom let you wear those clothes and that, that *paint*, Mary." His finger traced a circle around his face. "What was she thinking?"

Mary felt her cheeks flame beneath the makeup.

"Mom wanted to be sure the hospital would let me see you by myself, Edward. That's the only reason. I had to look like I was 18. I'll wash the rest from my face as soon as I get home. Honest, I will." For the first time in Mary couldn't remember how long, Edward smiled. It startled Mary. But where was his eyetooth? The wink of a smile passed so quickly that Mary thought she must have imagined the gap where his eyetooth should be.

The spell was broken. Edward scrunched his eyebrows.

"Listen, Mary, you have to do something for me? All right? Since Mom wasn't able to come, I need you to do something really important for me." His hands jerked, and he pulled his brown sack up onto the table and pushed it across to Mary. Mary's eyes darted back and forth from Edward to the bag.

"What's in it, Edward?" She started opening the bag handles.

"Never mind what's in it, Mary. Don't look inside." Edward reached over and secured the handles. "Just get this bag to Father McGuire for me. See? On the way home, stop at the rectory and ask for Father McGuire. Nobody else. Please don't look inside the bag, Mary. Do you understand me? It's important. I'm counting on you. Okay? Just don't look inside the bag." He pointed his finger at her and said it again. "No looking."

Mary heard him the first time, but she was still confused.

"Okay, Edward. Okay, I'll take the bag to Father McGuire, I promise." During visits with her mother, Edward spoke quietly, if at all. Now he was giving her orders. Before-hospital Edward wasn't sharp and bossy, or gloomy and sad. He was kind and loads of fun. Mary sometimes imagined that hospital Edward was a fake and the real Edward was still in the Army. She waited for him to come back and be his old, nice self again.

Mary nodded. "Okay, Edward. I understand. Go to the rectory and give the bag to Father McGuire and don't look." As she said this, her throat swelled, and her ears closed up. She recognized the sensation. Tears were on their way. She trembled. The makeup burned her wet eyes. A sudden gust of wind caught the front hem of her skirt, and she yanked it back. She hated this stupid dress that was way too big for her.

Her brother's eyes widened, as if he was seeing Mary for the first time. "Oh, I'm sorry. So, so sorry, little Miss Mary. I've . . . I didn't mean to scare you. I . . . I didn't mean . . . any of this . . . It shouldn't be you. I thought Mom . . . I hoped . . . You're a good sister, Mary. Honest." Edward reached over and lightly touched Mary's cheek. Then he let out a long sigh and looked away.

Following Edward's eyes, Mary found a blue jay balanced on the branch of the maple tree. His fingers on her cheek had brought her beloved brother back to her, even if just for a moment. He was home, sketching a bird in his art studio. Her throat relaxed, and the tears retreated. The blue jay chirped and winged away.

"Ten more minutes," a man in a white uniform yelled as he walked by. He edged closer to their table. Mary recoiled. He had spiky blond hair and two fat whiskery chins. He parked himself behind Edward. He screwed up his eyes at Mary and grinned. "Are you causing problems for this beautiful young lady, Hohlfeld?" He poked his finger into Edward's shoulder. "Cause we can't have none a 'that nonsense." He swung his hips back and forth and fingered the keys attached to his belt.

Mary folded her arms in front of her body. She didn't like this man.

Edward bit his lip, but he didn't say anything. He shook his head no. The ugly man threw his head back and laughed as he tromped away.

"Time to go, Mary," Edward whispered. He pointed toward the bag. "I'm asking you to do something very important for me. It's a lot. I know. Don't open the bag and don't tell anyone. Okay? Just deliver the bag to Father McGuire like I said. Will you be sure to do that for me?"

Mary would do anything for her brother. If only he didn't look so sad. "Okay, Edward, but what should I tell him?"

"Nothing, just tell him you're delivering it for me. He'll know. There's a note inside. Remember, don't look inside the bag, Mary. Don't you dare look inside. Understand?"

Why did people keep asking her if she understood when she didn't understand anything? Mary shook her head yes. "Okay, Edward. I will. I promise."

"Good. Good girl," Edward said. "I'm counting on you." He reached his arms across the bench as he stood up to leave and held Mary by her shoulders. His eyes got wet. Mary had never seen her brother cry before, and it gave her a sick, sorry feeling in her stomach.

Mary trudged to the bus stop as if in a trance. The bus somehow delivered her to the El train. She got off and found her way to the trolley stop. Her mind started to wake up. She'd completed the mission for her mother, only to get a new one that she couldn't tell her mother about. She watched the trolley lumber to a stop and climbed aboard. Mindful that one of the handles had torn slightly when it got caught on the arm of the turnstile, Mary clutched the pasty-brown paper bag closer to her chest. The trolley sputtered and wheezed forward. Mary tottered down the aisle in her sister's high heels and slid into a window seat, the heavy-duty paper chafing her chin. A gray-haired man, who had been quick to steady Mary with a hand under her elbow when she lost her balance, grazed his eyes in her direction as he passed. His tongue flickered, moistening the upper lip beneath his gray handlebar mustache. He flashed Mary a look that burned through the paint on her face. She swallowed her tears, ordering them to stay put. Through the reflection in the window, she watched the man slide into an aisle seat several rows behind and across from her. She concentrated on making his image disappear in the parade of trees saluting the bits and pieces of grayish-blue sky that peeked through. A nun in a black habit with a stiff three-pointed veil resembling a sail, sidled in and settled in the seat next to her. Mary immediately felt safer. Her mind wandered back to her visit with Edward.

What had Edward said to her exactly? "Do not, under any circumstance, look inside that bag. You understand me, Mary? Do you?" His eyes had found hers and didn't let go. The severity of his tone caused a momentary hitch in her pattering heart. He repeated these directions three times. During visits with their mother, Edward was sad and quiet. His eyes drifted somewhere behind them. Although the white cord around his waist was cinched, his puke-green uniform sagged. It gave him a sloppy appearance that was not at all like her neat and smartly dressed brother. Worse still, Edward no longer smelled of Ivory soap and Old Spice. Mary couldn't identify it, but the scent reminded her of Mr. Harris, the elderly, crippled man in their neighborhood that she and her mother delivered food to. Mary chided herself. Edward wasn't at all like old man Harris.

The trolley whistled and drew to a stop. It jolted the dozing nun into wakefulness. Her prayer book slid from her lap and onto the floor. Mary promptly placed Edward's bag down and bent over to reach under the seat in front of the nun to retrieve her prayer book.

"Here you go, Sister." Mary used her most polite Catholic schoolgirl voice. She swiped it once to remove the dirt particles. As she did so, she felt the nun inspect her appearance.

"Well, thank you, dear." Sensing Mary's discomfort, the nun politely drew her eyes away from her smudged, made-up face. As she took the prayer book, she pressed her rose-petal fingertips lightly against Mary's hand.

"You're welcome, Sister." Mary watched the nun rise and make her way to the door, the angel-like wings of her head gear disappearing down the steps. When Mary turned her attention back to Edward's bag, she saw that it had fallen sideways, and several of the drawings had slid out. When she leaned over to place them back into the bag, she couldn't help but peek. Her eyes widened, and her body stiffened. The palm of her hand flew up and settled like a clamp over her mouth. Her breath came in short, rapid bursts. Finally, her eyes willed themselves away from the startling images.

"Don't look in the bag, Mary," Edward said. "Don't look." She hadn't meant to, and she didn't want to see them again, so her mind pressed them down, down, down, somewhere deep inside her. She closed the door and locked it.

*Chapter 31*

# "Proof Through the Night"

*1946*

"L ookie here." Pete waved the May 1946 copy of *Life* magazine in Walter's face, his long legs sprawled atop the battered desk. "How about that? We finally did it!"

Walter sat on a stool in a corner of the cramped office where the COs churned out their monthly newsletter, *The Assistant*. His Fedora was pushed back on his head, his pompadour crushed from the frenetic pressing of his hat back and forth as Pete read aloud for the second time from the article, "Bedlam, 1946: U. S. Mental Hospitals a Shame and a Disgrace."

It was well past midnight. Any other night this clear and balmy would have found Walter scanning the heavens for the twinkling upside-down kite of the Big Dipper. But not tonight. He was too elated. He was also anxious about the institutional fallout that was bound to follow the *Life* exposé. Eleanor Roosevelt had been skeptical of the COs' story at first. When she finally agreed to meet with Walter and Pete, she expressed disbelief that the atrocities they described could be happening in a U.S. hospital. But the photographs served as hard evidence, bringing Mr. Maisel and his months-long investigation to their door. Mr. Deutsch's local *PM* articles had been steadily chipping away for weeks, but they hadn't made the national splash that the *Life* article did. The truth was finally out. They couldn't close the door on visual evidence. Couldn't hide behind denials and excuses. The question was what would happen next, and how soon.

"My Lord," Walter clapped eyes on Pete. "*Life* magazine!"

Pete chuckled and shook his head in response, turning back to page 102 of the article.

"Says here, '*Yet beatings and murders are hardly the most significant of the indignities we have heaped upon most of the 400,000 guiltless patient-prisoners of over 180 state mental institutions.*'" He paused to whistle. "See, Walter, our institution may be one of the worst, but it's not the only one. Why, it's a doggone systemic problem. You always said that, Walter. I bet Eleanor Roosevelt will be getting up on her high horse now. She as much as said so, Walter, didn't she? If she could come around to believing it. Said if these things were true, she'd push any reform that was needed."

"That's so, Pete. "That's so." He still couldn't believe their letter-writing campaign had gotten an audience with the first lady. Was sure sorry he had to show those disgraceful photos to such a kind and stately woman. He cringed, picturing Sallie Mae's reaction. He was glad he had prepared her. Mrs. Roosevelt just kept saying, "My word, my word. This can't possibly be true."

Walter returned to Pete's excited voice.

"*. . . jam-packed men, women and sometimes even children . . .* Mrs. Roosevelt's bound to clamp on that, Walter, ain't she? *. . . into hundred-year-old firetraps in wards so crowded that the floors cannot* *be seen between the rickety cots, while thousands more sleep on ticks, on blankets, or on the bare floors.* Well, well." Pete finally tore his eyes from the magazine page and peered at Walter over the top of his glasses. "*Bedlam.* Isn't that something? Maisel sure found the right word. Didn't he? If this doesn't get Governor Martin's attention . . ."

Just then Frank, with Louis close on his heels, bounded through the doorway.

"Better be on the lookout." Frank strode over to Walter and clapped him on the shoulder. "Buster and a few paid attendants from the other wards are out for blood. They got wind of this article. Calling us rats and squealers and the like."

Louis found an uncluttered end of the desk and plopped himself down, twisting his neck to scan the article.

"They can't get away with doing us any harm, not now." Though confident, Walter's voice betrayed an undercurrent of alarm. "Besides, most COs will be going back to their lives in due course." Because of the severe staffing shortage, Walter and Frank were among those that had agreed to stay on a bit longer than the CO stint required. Walter understood that he had been in the company of good men. The best. The kind he might never meet the likes of again. To work in a place like this and hold on to their humanity against such odds, well, he was right proud to be numbered among them.

"To tell the truth, I'm more worried about how Buster and the others might take their anger out on patients. How in the world do we protect them until the people upstairs get things sorted? Realistically, it could be months, maybe even years." Walter searched the faces of his compatriots, realizing none of them had considered the weight of their actions from this angle. Truth was, they hadn't been able to protect the patients before the *Life* story. That's why they had taken such desperate measures in the first place. Still, Buster on the warpath? That was a frightening prospect.

Pete finally placed the magazine on the desk and rubbed his chin thoughtfully. It was if the hot air balloon they'd been riding in suddenly sprang a leak.

"Do what we've been doing. All we can do, ain't it? Hopefully, they'll get some inspectors in here soon, and heads will start rolling." Pete reached for his smoldering pipe in the ashtray. He added some tobacco and struck a match to light it.

Frank and Louis nodded simultaneously.

"That's right," Frank snorted. "And I'd like to watch them roll right on out of here."

"But who will take their place?" Louis looked from Walter to Pete and back to Frank. "It's bound to take a long time to turn this behemoth around. We might be long gone by then."

Walter sat up with a start. He looked as if someone had just shot an arrow between his eyes. "What about the soldier? Ed Hohlfeld? Thou don't think Buster knows . . .?"

"No, no, I don't think so, Walter. We were careful. Spoke only in German." Pete sat up in his chair and took two furious puffs from his newly lit pipe. "I don't think Buster ever got a look at the man's sketches." His black eyebrows met in the center of his forehead, a signal that Pete was deep in thought.

Walter was skeptical. "We don't know that for sure. I sure wish I knew how to help the man. Thy Elder spoke with the priest before he spoke to Maisel?" Walter eyed Pete. "Did he offer any information about Mr. Hohlfeld's background?"

Pete squinted and scratched his head. "No, not much, Walter. Said Ed was right as rain before he went to boot camp. Didn't get past boot camp, though. Wouldn't shoot his rifle. Didn't believe in violence or killing. A pacifist without CO status. Had an altercation of some kind with an officer about it. Didn't make any sense to the priest that he ended up here."

"A conscientious objector?" Walter sat upright and set his Fedora on the desk. "Is that why they threw the man in *here?*" His eyes narrowed. A brother not *in* arms but a brother who'd shunned arms. "That poor man." He shook his head and glanced first at Pete, then at Louis and Frank. "*There but for the grace of God . . .*"

"Go all of us," Pete added, completing Walter's thought. The two men had grown to be as close as twins.

"But why is he *still* here?" Frank asked. "The war's over."

Walter shook his head. "Only a few of them *do* get out of here. They languish and get worse, and maybe the military just lost track of him, war on and all."

Frank grimaced. "Well, we've also seen how patients that aren't mentally ill in the first place—vagrants, misfits, and the like—become traumatized. They get sick. Those that *are* sick don't get better. Do they?"

Walter sighed and shook his head. "No, not that I have seen."

"There's only so much we can do, Walter, you know that. We did what we could." Pete searched Walter's worried face. "You think Buster might take his anger out on the soldier, Walter, don't you?"

"Yes, I do, Pete. Could also be that Buster got wind of his involvement somehow."

"Well, if so, the soldier never said anything to me, Walter." Pete gripped the cup of his smoldering pipe, absorbing Walter's unease. Pete's mastery of German made him the better carrier pigeon when it came to communicating with the patient about using his sketches in their plan.

"No, but he wouldn't. Would he?" he eyed Pete. "He's quiet. Takes it on the chin, that one. Doesn't complain. Turns it all inside." He stole a glance at his watch. "Who's on tonight besides Buster?"

Pete shrugged. "Louis, do you know?"

"The new fella. Mack, a paid attendant but not a bad chap." Louis cast an inquisitive look at Pete.

Walter half-stood and reached an arm toward Pete. "I need that."

"What, the magazine?"

"Yes, I want to let this fellow know in case, well, to warn him and to thank him for doing his part with the sketches. They helped make the case now, didn't they? Let him know we pulled it off. Then I'm going to see Zeller. Buster's days of running roughshod have to end." Walter glanced back and forth between Frank and Louis, his clouded eyes finally resting on Pete. "That story Ed told us about the young man Buster assaulted. The brutal and disgusting things he did?"

Pete shook his head. "I know. I know, Walter. Tip of the iceberg."

Walter's voice cracked. "Zeller has to listen now."

Pete frowned, hesitating before he handed over the copy of *Life*. "Be careful, Walter. Frank and Louis just told us that Buster's irate. Might not be the right time."

"Might not be, but something's telling me otherwise." He snatched a flashlight from the desk drawer and made his way to the door.

"Walter, wait." Pete grabbed his friend's Fedora from the desk. "You forgot your hat!"

But Walter was already bounding through the door and down the hallway.

## Chapter 32

# Mirrors and Memories

*1947*

Mary examined her face in the foggy medicine chest mirror. Tilting the mirror slightly to get the best angle, she turned her head to the side. She pursed her lips and raised the arch of her left eyebrow. Mary had a habit of lifting it whenever she was annoyed or couldn't quite believe what she'd heard. She liked that it made her look older. Knowing. She thought it wasn't half-bad. Her face. Her blue eyes were turning hazel, like her brother Edward's had. Mary examined her eyes again. They went nicely with the Veronica Lake hairdo she'd adopted. Even Ronnie said so. She turned the water faucet on and then lazily lathered the Ivory soap onto the cloth before pressing it against her face. Was that a pimple on her cheek? A knock at the door startled her and prevented her from seeing to the suspicious-looking blemish.

"Can you hurry it up in there?"

Agnes was such a pain. "Yeah," in a couple minutes, okay?" She heard Agnes harrumph as she stomped away from the door.

Mary wrung out the wet cloth and set it aside. She returned to the mirror and smiled. Even though it was barely noticeable, the slight separation between her front two teeth nagged at her. She practiced smiling with her lips pressed together to hide it. Her closed-mouth smile highlighted the dimple on her left cheek. Edward's dimple was on his chin, not his cheek, but his smile showed his long eyetooth. They shared a dimple and a flawed smile.

"Oh," she said aloud. Her body sank against the sink. She pictured Edward's hospital-face in the mirror, her eyes suddenly stinging with tears. She picked up the cool cloth and pressed it against her eyes. Memories of Edward came out of nowhere, as if to spite her forced forgetting. She grabbed the lip of the sink, aware that her breath had gotten stuck in her chest. She took a deep breath and blew it out a few times until she was breathing normally. Mary examined her body for missing limbs, suddenly fearful she'd lost something precious. Nope, all there. She touched her forehead, her chest, and her left and right shoulder. Then she felt for the Blessed Mother Medal around her neck and pressed it to her lips. Edward had given it to her for her First Holy Communion. Her will may have banished Edward's image from the mirror, but her memory had a mind of its own. Mary felt a sudden twinge of guilt. Working and going to school kept her busy, and she hadn't been able to visit the hospital for weeks.

"Why? Why? Why?" she whispered to the ghost in the mirror. "Why are you more ghost than brother now? Kind of there and kind of not?"

The mirror didn't answer. There was no answer, or at least not one she knew of, not now, not yet anyway. But someday, when she got old enough, she would figure out the mystery that her brother's life had become. She knew her parents hid things from her. She remembered how, months before, she heard her mother sobbing and shouting on the other side of her parents' bedroom door, her father silent on the other end. She was sure it had to do with Edward. It always did.

"That awful night . . ." It was her mother's voice. "You . . ." Mary strained to hear the words. "Why didn't you . . .? We should have listened to Officer . . ."

Her words jolted Mary, reminding her of the time her Connelly cousins were still living with the Hohlfelds. The girls were playing in the upstairs bedroom. They heard loud voices below. Mary had sneaked downstairs, surprised to see an Army Man in their kitchen. And Officer McGee. Her father shouted about something being broken. What was broken? Then, Edward's voice. Crying. It had been him, after all, hadn't it? Her mind strained to recall that night, but like a butterfly with a secret message, it flitted in and out of view. Her mother's pitiful sobbing behind her bedroom door brought Mary back to the strange night, years before, when she had crept down the stairs. It was a memory that made no sense at all. And yet. . . Mary suspected her mother's recent sobbing quarrel with her father had something to do with that night. And with something else that stood out in Mary's memory.

It was months ago on a rainy Saturday afternoon. Mary felt like drawing. She went into Edward's art room in search of sketch paper. Instead, she found a copy of *Life* tucked between some old newspapers. The cover photo of Broadway actress Margaret Leighton caught Mary's eye. Curious, she wanted to read more about her. That's why Mary had noticed it in the pile of old newspapers in the first place. She couldn't care less about newspapers. They just reminded her of war and of Edward. She picked up the magazine and thumbed through it, past the Dixie Cup and Orange Crush Ads and the article about Emily Post. The Pond's cream Ad stopped her for a moment. That's what her sister Ronnie used to keep her skin looking young. Mary turned the page. She was still looking for the Margaret Leighton story when she saw something that brought a hitch to her throat. Instead of a beautiful actress, she saw pictures of skinny, naked men in what looked like a dungeon. They were strangely familiar. They reminded her of something, but what? Shocked, she covered her eyes. Her heart hammered inside her chest. Maybe the pictures were from one of the German concentration camps she'd heard adults talking about. She flipped the pages. No, it was something else. What the heck is this? "Bedlam," she read out loud.

"Mary! What in tarnation are you doing in Edward's studio? Give that magazine to me at once, young lady." Her eyes blazing, Mary's mother swooped into the room and snatched the magazine from Mary's startled hands.

"Geez, Mom, I was just looking at . . ."

"Never you mind." She shoved Mary through the door and into the hallway with such force that Mary almost toppled over. Rolling up the magazine, she clapped Mary on the shoulder with it.

"Ouch, Mom, that hurts." Mary ducked and backed away from her mother's fury. "I was just looking for sketch paper in that old pile of newspapers. What's the big deal?" Mary had never talked back to her mother. She didn't dare. But her mother's sudden outburst shocked her.

"You know that's Edward's art room, and your father and I don't want you girls in it. If you want something from the room, ask me. I am very disappointed in you, Mary Hohlfeld."

Her mother's disapproval silenced Mary, but she'd also uttered the unspeakable in the house, her missing brother. The empty art room was a constant reminder. Mary's shoulders drooped. She ran up the stairs and into her bedroom. She threw herself on her bed and wept. Why was her mother so mad? Why did those awful pictures seem familiar? Her memory flickered, and something started to come back into focus. She was on the trolley. She had a bag filled with Edward's sketches to bring to the priest. They slid from the bag. Mary gasped, remembering. She clapped her mouth. No. She refused to see. With all her might, she pushed and pushed and pushed the memory back down into the dark. She refused to see what she couldn't understand. Not now. Maybe not ever.

# PART FOUR

## Chapter 33

# The Farewell

*1949*

Sallie Mae had finally gotten her way. She was a stubborn woman. Walter pecked her forehead and cradled her head. She was spent after another long day on the woman's ward. He knew the feeling. Walter was proud of her. Against all his objections, she decided to use her nursing skills where they were most needed. Her sacrifice made it possible for Walter to sign on for two more years at Byberry. The dust from the firestorm of the *Life* article had settled, and things were improving. Well, they were improving slowly and in small increments, if truth be told.

Buster was finally gone, arrested, and charged with manslaughter for beating a patient to death. All the patients were clothed now, and essential supplies were coming in. Family members were now permitted inside the hospital to visit their loved ones. Attendants had been fired, and new ones were being hired every day. COs like Walter, who had extended their alternative service, were training them. Their Mental Health Hygiene Program had won national respect as well as the approval of the American Psychiatric Association. There was still a staff and money shortage, and many repairs and conditions yet to be addressed. A lot more work to be done and a long way to go yet. A long way. But at least things were out in the open now that the conscientious objectors had made the public see Byberry's horrors for themselves.

"Another month, sweetheart, and we'll be moving on to greener pastures." Walter regretted having to leave his patients, but he also knew that he and Sallie Mae would have to move on with their life together and address his long-delayed plan to attend law school.

Sallie Mae chuckled and poked him playfully on the shoulder. "Thou are referring to that tiny apartment we put a deposit on in center city?"

Walter winced. "I promise, sweetheart, once I finish law school, it *will* be back to the country for us."

"Walter Sinclair! Don't thou know by now when I am teasing?" She stood back and surveyed him with folded arms. "We made a pact. We're in this together, through thick and thin."

"And thou are sure about working while I . . ."

"If thou bring that up again, I *will* have to be angry." She kissed his cheek and ruffled his Pompadour.

"Hey!" Walter reached up and patted his hair back into place. He grabbed his Fedora from the coat rack and placed it on his head.

"What? I thought we might have dinner together now my shift is over." Sallie Mae loosened her nurse's cap and released her long hair from the bobby pins.

"Can it wait a bit, sweetheart? I'm off to make a visit to the sick ward. Back soon."

"The sick ward?" Sallie Mae raised her left eyebrow.

"Yes, I won't stay long, and I promise to keep my face covered with my handkerchief. See?" he said, producing it from his pocket.

"The soldier? The one you've been worried about?"

Walter nodded. "We'll be leaving soon, and I need to say goodbye to the man, Sallie Mae." He rested his hand on her shoulder. His new wedding band smiled up at him.

Sallie Mae folded his hand into hers. "Go."

With her blessing, Walter strode out the door.

Fifteen minutes later, Walter found himself on the sick ward, zigzagging his way through the packed cots. The fevered man had shrunken. Bones protruded from his skull, and his arms were sticks. He clenched a blood-spattered handkerchief in his hand. Sketches of different kinds of birds lay strewn about him on his cot. They seemed sad, their heads tucked, their wings folded.

"Mr. Hohlfeld? Ed? It's me, Walter."

A look of recognition flashed in Ed's eyes as he strained to sit up. "Walter," he managed before being stymied by a fit of coughing.

"Whoa, whoa, take it easy. No need to sit up." Walter gently pressed Ed's shoulder back onto the bed. His wedding ring glinted in a slant of sunlight streaming from the window.

Ed may have declined physically, but he was alert. Ed's voice was raspy and strained. "So, *thou* went and did it, huh? Got hitched?" His right hand weakly motioned toward his head.

A salute, Walter guessed. Walter managed a hearty laugh.

"I did, indeed, and I'm a lucky man for it." He had been listening then. On previous visits, Walter had told him stories of home and Sallie Mae. Ed had seemed far away, lost in a world of physical distress and, no doubt, painful memories, and Walter never knew how—sane wasn't the right word—*lucid* Ed was.

"We're, ah, we'll be leaving soon. Me and Sallie Mae. My time here is coming to an end, and I wanted to say goodbye, Ed, and wish thee Godspeed." Walter felt the catch in his throat. For a decent man to suffer such a fate and for Walter to be so helpless to do anything about it. "I won't forget thee, and what . . ." Another fit of coughing ensued. Walter stood there reverently, steadying the shoulder of the comrade he had come to know on this hellish hospital battlefield. A man he would gladly call friend.

## Chapter 34

# Working Girl

*1950*

Mary straightened her white apron and secured her cap with bobby pins before she skipped through the swinging double doors to start her 4:00-11:00 evening shift. She hooked her hands on her hips and did a quick check of the red counter that stretched the length of the diner.

"Hiya!" Kathy waved as she slid past her and made her way to the door. "And By-ya, Mary. Gotta run to the butcher's before I head home." She smiled, revealing small creases along the sides of her mouth and between her thin eyebrows. She removed her cap and whisked through the door.

"Yeah, see you tomorrow. I lit a candle for you at church this morning."

"Thanks, kiddo," Kathy called from the other side of the door. "Guess it can't hurt."

Kathy wasn't a Catholic, but Mary felt a kinship with the older woman who'd made her a confidante on coffee breaks during their shifts. A good listener, Mary learned that her thirty-three-year-old friend had lost her Navy husband, George, to a battle somewhere in the Pacific. Heartbroken and saddled with three kids and a rent she couldn't afford, Kathy had to move in with her husband's parents. Mary felt sorry for Kathy. Except for her husband's parents, she had no family, having lost her own folks in a train wreck when Kathy was just fifteen. While living with the in-laws kept Kathy and her kids out of the poor house, it brought a different set of problems that included a meddling mother-in-law and an alcoholic father-in-law.

Mary did a quick scan of Raymar's Diner, her second home now that she had quit school after finishing her junior year at Hallahan High. Her dad couldn't work at all anymore, and her oldest sisters, Alice and Ronnie, were married and long gone, as was their brother Sam. She enjoyed being able to chip in at home. It made her feel more grown-up. She liked her job where the people she worked with treated her like family.

Mary surveyed her new home. The diner gleamed. Red-topped bar stools were lined up neatly in front of the white counter like soldiers standing at attention. Alongside the outer wall was a row of cozy booths with red upholstered seats rimmed in polished stainless steel. Most of the noisy kids who always stopped in after school had cleared out for the day. The place was nearly empty, except for a couple smooching in the corner of a back booth.

Within the hour, the place would be hopping. The Vets would saunter over from Mel's Pool Hall across the street, looking to score with one of the cuties that stopped by Raymar's for a burger or a piece of pie after work. Although the war was over, the race to the altar, or at least to the backseat of a smooth-talking fellow's jalopy, was on. Raymar's was living up to its reputation as the number one pick-up joint in the K & A neighborhood. Mary sighed. Her own future was a question mark sitting on top of her head like a big, empty block. No letter from the postman with an answer to her application to the convent meant that Mary's childhood dream of becoming a nun was just that, a dream and nothing more.

The busboy with a narrow hangdog face finished mopping the last squares of the glossy black-and-white checkerboard floor at the other end of the diner. When Joey lifted his head and saw Mary, he grinned, revealing two prominent front teeth on his pimply face.

He waved. "Hiya. Just finishing up."

A sweet boy more than a year younger, Joey was, well, too boyish for Mary to be interested in dating. Besides, she was pretty sure God wanted her to be a nun. Or that is what she *had* thought. She still hoped to hear back from any of the three different convents she applied to.

"Whaddaya want me to do next?"

Mary examined the napkin and condiment trays. "Did you check the bins, Joey? Everything filled up and ready to go for the rush hour?"

"Yep, I think so." He squeezed his mop out one last time and hoisted the bucket. He headed toward the swinging door to the kitchen and paused. "I topped off the salt and pepper shakers on the counter. Booths, too." He smiled broadly and waited.

What was he expecting? A wink? Mary knew Joey liked her, but she didn't want to be one of those girls that led boys on. She made a point of being friendly but not too friendly.

"Great, thanks, Joey. Floor looks swell. Mickey will be pleased."

"Yeah?" Joey's eyebrows arched.

"Yeah. Gloria in yet? I didn't see her in the kitchen."

"Nope." Joey shook his head.

"Hey, youse two," Mickey shouted from the opening between the short-order grill and counter where Mary hung her ticket orders. "Rush hour coming soon. Quit your yapping."

Muttering something under his breath, Joey scooted past Mary and disappeared into the kitchen. Mary made a fresh pot of coffee and restocked the sugar containers. Then she dipped her hands into the sudsy water of the stainless sink and began washing the glasses.

Mickey did an awful lot of barking from his kitchen outpost. He'd scared the dickens out of Mary in her first weeks on the job. Then she figured out that the grouchy short-order cook, and sometime manager was a big old softie. He had a round head that was mostly bald, a fat, vein-lined nose, and reddish cheeks. A salty-looking old seaman's face. He teased Mary in a gruff, grandfatherly way. She understood that this was Mickey's way of showing affection. Whenever she shouldered through the double doors into the kitchen, grumbling about a nasty customer or an order that was held up, she had to listen to him recite the nursery rhyme "Mary, Mary quite contrary" over and over until he got her to giggle.

Mary was glad to have Mickey in her corner. Edward was still sick, and it didn't seem he'd be coming home any time soon. Maybe not ever. Mary shook her head to wipe away the horrible thought. Mickey wasn't anything like Edward, but he was protective of Mary, especially when the cocky young servicemen made passes at her. If one of them got too frisky with his mouth or leaned in too close, making Mary blush and stutter, Mickey would pop out of the kitchen and flash him the evil eye.

"Don't be bothering this girl, fella." His voice was raspy and phlegmy, from years of smoking and booze, according to Kathy. Mary was certain that it was exactly what Edward would do if he were around to see Mary growing into a young lady who was out in the world mixing with men. But he wasn't, and he didn't, which made Mary sad to think about, so she tried not to.

Oh, there it was again. The familiar pang, like a nagging toothache that you could forget about when you were distracted but was always there, and it couldn't—no, wouldn't—go away. Memories of her brother came in waves with a mix of guilt and sadness. She missed Edward. The solidness of his fingers around her small hand, the back of his head when he was sketching or painting, his hearty laugh in the kitchen while drinking coffee and talking with Mom. Edward haunted Somerset Street, so Mary tried to stay away. She was escaping into the world of work like her sisters and brother had. Anything to avoid feeling the terrible rush of heat that blasted through her arteries and veins and into her head until she felt like she might just burst from grief.

The Edward she visited in the hospital wasn't the brother she knew, the brother she remembered, the brother she longed to have come home. She felt guilty about that, but there it was. She snatched a dishcloth from the steel sink and wiped down the counter and then the booth tables. Automatically, she whispered the same old prayer for her brother. A prayer that hadn't been answered yet, but she said it anyway. She would try to visit Edward after church on Sunday. The last few times they sent her away because he was still in the sick ward. She would bring him a present. Use some of her pay to buy him a new set of paints. There, she felt better.

The front door opened with a long squeak. It brought a blast of warm air in with it. The fans whirred, fighting off the heat that spread through the length of the diner. Relieved by the interruption, Mary glanced up to see two smartly dressed young women spill through the open door. They were probably secretaries that worked in one of the nearby offices. Their high heels clattered across the gleaming tiles of Joey's newly washed floor, and they settled into a booth in front of the kissing couple. Mary glanced down self-consciously at her saddle shoes and turned-down white bobby sox. The woman with the red beret signaled.

"Be right there." Lifting two sets of silverware and a pair of menus, she hurried over.

Whispering conspiratorially, the women flipped through the jukebox selections. The one with the red beret was as tall and skinny as Popeye's Olive Oyl. She dropped in a coin. Within minutes, more customers streamed in. Three Marines sat at the counter. She served them coffee and pie. Several couples made their way to open booths. Mary looked behind her. Gloria still not here? Whipping into waitress mode, Mary pretended she was Gloria, the seasoned waitress, and tried not to panic.

"What can I get you?" Mary approached the booth. She pulled her pencil from behind her ear and leaned on her ticket pad, unconsciously humming along to Bing Crosby and the Andrews Sisters' "South America, Take It Away."

The short, plump one with Shirley Temple curls ordered a burger—hold the onions— and two Cokes. But someone will be joining us in a few. I think he'll want a dog. With relish and onions. Won't he?"

Red Beret pulled out a pack of Viceroys and lit up a cigarette before she finally nodded. "Uh, huh, Billy will want a Hot Dog and fries."

"Right up." Mary jotted down the final items.

"Oh, and a coffee." Red Beret tore her eyes away from the menu and glanced up at Mary, as if seeing her for the first time. Then she dropped them, settling on Mary's saddle shoes. "Thanks."

Her haughty smile revealed a lipstick stain on her front teeth. Mary instinctively tongued her front teeth, remembering how hastily she'd applied her own lipstick in the break room.

The sudden stream of customers meant the evening rush was officially on and Gloria, who shared the shift with Mary, was now more than twenty minutes late. After hanging up her first ticket, Mary shifted into third gear. She scrambled from the counter to the booths and back again to take orders, hang tickets, and serve drinks. She didn't think. She moved, her hands and arms and legs like synchronized motors. Thankfully, Joey left his mopping-up in the kitchen to come out to the counter and help her out. Mary flashed him a thank you smile as he helped her refilled coffee cups, pour Coca-Colas and Ginger Ales, and scoop ice cream into glasses. Between taking and delivering orders, Mary started a fresh pot of coffee.

Mickey stuck his head through the opening and thundered to no one in particular. "Where the hell is Gloria? Half-past 5:00," he exaggerated. "Shoulda been here already!"

Within minutes, Mary saw Gloria hustle into the doorway as if she'd just heard Mickey's thundering call. With a shrug to Mary, she stuffed her handbag under the counter and grabbed a notepad and pencil. Not that she needed them. She seemed to remember every order down to the last detail.

"What can I get you, Hon?" she asked the man in a blue and white bowtie who was tapping impatiently on the counter. Then she half-turned toward the opening to the kitchen. "I know, I know." Above the din of jukebox music and customer chatter, she held up her hand to stop Mickey's oncoming verbal traffic. "Kid was sick. Had to get him to the doc's. What can I say?" She winked an apology to Mary.

Mary didn't mind. Broad-shouldered and mouthy, Gloria was also bossy. Mary liked the way she didn't take guff from men. Gloria took customers' teasing in stride, and when they gave her a hard time, she just gave it right back to them in spades. "Give it a rest, will you, Mister? Meatloaf will be up soon. Mickey only has two hands, last time I checked. How about another coffee on the house to go with that cigarette? Get your hands off my behind unless you want a knuckle sandwich with that grilled cheese, Pal." Gloria usually chased her quips with a wink and a smile. The customers sipped their coffee, lit up, and shut up. They also tipped her well. Mary hoped to be as tough and confident as Gloria someday.

When Mary first started working at Raymar's, Gloria's no-nonsense, hard-edged manner made her stomach quiver, especially if Mary dropped a glass or got an order wrong or failed to put on a fresh pot of coffee after using the last cup. Almost a year into the job, Mary was a lot easier with her duties and with Gloria, who, like Mickey, was more bark than bite.

Red Beret and her friend were enraptured with Billy's story about a fight in the pool hall across the street when Mary returned with their order. "Yeah, and Golden Gloves wasn't having it. You know? The Navy vet socked the guy. Told him never to disrespect a soldier in a wheelchair again and threw him out the pool hall!"

Mary cleared her throat. "Anything else I can get you?"

"Hey, sorry, sweetheart. Just telling them a story. You sure have beautiful eyes. How come I haven't seen you here before?" His slightly crooked front teeth were stained yellow, but he had a pleasant face and brown curly hair that looped in front of his forehead.

Red Beret aimed her hot eyes at Mary. Her friend tried to distract her by asking for the Catsup. Red Beret grabbed the bottle and shoved it in her direction.

Mary blushed. "If that's all . . ." Mary said uncertainly, ignoring Billy's question. She added up the items on the check, placed it on the table and turned to go.

"So, Billy, are you still planning on meeting up later at the dance?" Red Beret's voice was tight. She lifted a butter knife and pointed it at Billy.

Billy's arm popped out of the booth and grabbed Mary's elbow. "You can't leave me now, sweetheart. I just found you. Billy, Billy Haas. Group of us going to the club later. Wanna join us?"

Mary's ears buzzed, the way they did when she'd won a race or a spelling bee at school.

"I'll be needing this arm to deliver my orders." Mimicking Gloria's coolness, she pulled away.

He clapped eyes on her nametag. "Okay, then, Mary. But think about it."

The evening rush flew by. Mary didn't have much time to think about Billy Haas. When she did, though, she felt a warm feeling she did not recognize spread throughout her body. It was nice, but it felt wrong, like she was somehow violating the vow of chastity she one day intended to take. That was the plan, anyway. Then again, her grand plan to become a nun was growing dimmer and dimmer by the day. She might just have to accept the fact that she really didn't have a vocation after all. The last time she'd broached the topic, her mother told her to take the lack of response as a sign. "Give it up, Mary, dear. No answer is your answer. God must have other plans in store for you." She figured her mother must be right. It was a hard pill Mary had to swallow. Ever since she was a little girl, she'd dreamed of being a nun.

What was the harm in taking an interest in boys, then? In dating one, if she wanted. Billy. Billy Haas. She liked the sound of his name. Out of the corner of her eye, she watched him get up and saunter to the door with Red Beret and her friend. He said something to make the cashier laugh when he paid the bill, catching Mary's sideways glance at him. He winked. Behind the counter now, Mary blushed and overfilled her customer's coffee cup so that the dark liquid splashed on the saucer and onto the countertop.

"Hey," the older man jumped back from the counter. "Watch it, why doncha, Missy!"

"Oh, I'm so, so sorry." Mary couldn't help smiling.

Just then, Gloria sidled up to her. "I toldja, Mary." She chuckled and winked. "You're a looker. You better watch out for them fellas."

"Hey, what the hell's going on out there?" Mickey's chin jutted through the kitchen opening. Mickey's eagle eyes never did miss a trick, even if he was a few beats late.

## Chapter 35

# A New Man in Her Life

M ary had seen him before, but only from a distance on his way in or out of the diner. He was one of the fellas who hung out at Mel's Pool Hall and sometimes stopped by the diner for coffee and Raymar's signature lemon meringue pie. She thought she caught him looking at her a few times, but she was too embarrassed to confirm it by returning his gaze. He was a snappy dresser. Handsome, too, more handsome even than Edward. He was older. Twenty-three? Twenty-four? She slyly examined him through her compact mirror. The band had just stopped playing to take a short break. He was cradling his beer at the bar, his head thrown back in laughter. He wore a snazzy brown bomber jacket, and his dark wavy hair was neatly combed to the side.

"So how about a Sloe Gin Fizz, baby?" Mary's mind snapped back. She and Billy were sitting at a small candlelit table at the Midway, an after-hours club in the neighborhood where young adults met to drink and dance.

"Huh?" Mary slid her compact back into her purse.

"A Slow Gin Fizz. C'mon, live a little," Billy pleaded. He opened his hands and leaned across the table.

"Are you kidding? I shouldn't even be here! I'm not dressed right, Billy. I don't know why you insisted we come. I thought we were going to catch a movie at the Cameo." Mary scrutinized her straight, navy-blue skirt and pink chiffon blouse. The two young ladies at the table next to theirs were all dolled up. Both wore fancy dresses and black patent leather pumps. One of the girls had a single string of pearls draped around her bare neck. The other had dangling earrings that glittered when they caught the low light. Mary crossed her ankles beneath the chair to conceal her plain Loafers. She tugged her earlobe, imagining a fancy earring hanging from it and her hair all doodied up.

"What are you talking about? You're the prettiest girl here." Billy reached over and squeezed her hand. "C'mon, one drink. Your mom will never know."

Mary pulled her hand away, imagining her mother's disapproving eyes.

"My mom will kill me if she finds out I'm here." The truth was Mary wasn't sure if she was more concerned about her mother or annoyed by her shabby appearance. When Billy told her about his plans for the evening, a part of her was excited and curious. She wanted to experience what everybody else did, especially now that her convent dream had evaporated. She was also tired of being her mother's dutiful daughter.

"She won't find out, baby. Come on." Without waiting for her answer, Billy lifted his hand and beckoned to a nearby waitress. "A Sloe Gin Fizz for the lady, and a Jameson's and water for me."

"Sure, in a jiff." A rectangular tray hung from a strap around the waitress's neck. Her stockinged legs looked lean and long beneath her short, red-hemmed black skirt. A matching black hat, tied under her chin, sat jauntily on the side of her head. Mary couldn't decide if she was envious or embarrassed for her.

They had come in a group. George worked with Billy at the plumbing company, and Sissy and Nancy waitressed at Raymar's with Mary. Billy and George were bragging about how much dough they expected to make as owners of their very own plumbing business. Sissy told Mary she was sure George was the one for her. She was crazy about his blond hair and sky-blue eyes. Mary suspected that a man with the prospect of a decent living sure didn't hurt. Her friend Nancy enjoyed playing the field. Nancy winked at Mary when she returned to their table, escorted from the dance floor by a tall, tawny-skinned man in an Army uniform. Mary sucked in her breath and turned away. She didn't want to be reminded of Edward just now.

Mary studied Billy as he pulled a cigarette from the pack of Vice-roys in his breast pocket and aimed it towards her. Billy was a good guy. He took Mary to nice places and treated her well. He also made good money. Still, she wasn't so sure he was the one for her. He held out his pack to Mary, while Nancy, who sat beside him on the other side of the table, whispered something in his ear. Nancy flirted with Billy, but it didn't really bother Mary, a sign that she wasn't as crazy about Billy as he was about her. Mary declined the cigarette Billy offered her. When the waitress came by with their drinks, though, she scooped up the Sloe Gin Fizz, determined to be like everyone else. She took a sip and winced at its bitterness.

Billy shrugged and put his cigarettes back into his pocket. He angled his chair away from Nancy so he could watch the band that was just starting back up.

At Kathy's urging, Mary had tried smoking once, only to end up in a fit of coughing. She hated the taste, but the smell reminded her of home. Edward bent over his newspaper in the living room, his cigarette smoke curling down the hallway. Gosh, everywhere she turned, she bumped into another reminder. She just couldn't cut the painful ribbon of memory.

"Excuse me, pretty little lady, I wonder if I might have this dance."

Mary started. It wasn't a question. More like a mild order. She picked up her drink. Put it back down.

Before she even looked up, Mary knew it was the handsome, happy-go-lucky guy she'd seen yakking it up at the bar. She turned toward him. He smiled. His teeth were sparkly white and perfectly even. Instinctively, her tongue found the space between her front teeth. People told her it was hardly noticeable, but still. For a moment, Mary thought she might disappear in the ocean of his eyes. Her mind went blank. She regretted that she hadn't freshened her make-up. She flushed. Mary reached up and fingered the silver comb-barrette she'd borrowed from Kathy to keep her wavy brunette locks in place. She thought about her black Penny-Loafers. She shook her head. "I'm sorry, no, I can't."

Besides, Kathy had warned her that boys didn't like girls that were too easy. She regarded Billy, who raised his eyebrows and shrugged. She wasn't sure what that meant. She knew he liked her better than he liked Nancy. He'd as much as told her so. But what did she feel? She liked the attention Billy gave her and the movies, milkshakes, and big tips he left for her on the counter. She turned around to confirm that Mr. Snappy Dresser still stood behind her chair. He flashed his broad smile. Her head felt hot. She pulled her legs further under her chair to steady herself. She felt his hand tug at the back of her chair. The band started playing "Cement Mixer." Like Nancy, Mary enjoyed jitterbugging, but Billy wasn't much of a dancer. She waffled, unsure of what to do. This fellow was certainly insistent.

"How about it, beautiful?"

She turned back. She felt rather than saw the flat of his hand reach toward her. She secured her legs under the table. She was shaking her head and saying, "No, thank . . ." when she felt herself being lifted from her seat and guided onto the dance floor.

He flashed her a smile. "Nobody says no to Buddy Joyce."

Did he really just say that? Who did this guy think he was? Mary's temper flared. The nerve! She wanted to pop him right in the nose. As quickly as the match flared, it subsided. He was cocky, sure, but sweet, too. There was something about his self-assurance that pleased Mary.

He removed his jacket and tossed it with a purposeful flourish across her chair, like an exclamation point at the end of a sentence. After he swooped Mary onto the dance floor, the other dancers and tables dissolved in a swirl of flickering candlelight. Mary was swept up by his strong arms. Taut muscles stretched the arms of his cream-colored shirt, fashionably rolled up above his elbows. A wide-swing tie, patterned with swirls of light brown, green, and ivory ovals, lay snug against his shirt with a silver pin. He lifted Mary up and swung her around. His two-tone brown wingtips slid her Loafers gracefully around the dance floor. Charm oozed from him. His eyes twinkled and held hers. When the band's singer began playing Perry Como's "Prisoner of Love," he pulled Mary's slender body into the curve of his arms and crooned the words into her ear. His smoothly shaven cheek grazed hers.

"What's your name, beautiful?"

Mary was so glad that Ronnie had taught her how to foxtrot. To herself, she kept repeating, "Slow, slow, quick, quick; back, back, side right, close left foot to right." She was concentrating so hard that she almost forgot to breathe. "Mary," she finally managed.

His raised eyebrows approved. "A beautiful name for a brunette beauty of a girl."

Mary was taken aback by his cockiness. But another part of her liked his self-assurance. He was a swell dancer. His good looks sure didn't hurt, either. She'd figure it out later—if there was a later. Right now, she didn't much care. Right now, she felt a little punch-drunk from the warm feeling that flushed through her. She was closer to happy than she'd been in a long, long time.

At the end of the dance, Buddy escorted Mary to her seat. He looked into her eyes and placed his hands over his heart. "Well, Mary," he said, his voice buttery, "when you're ready for me, I'll be waiting." Then, with a wink and a smile, he sauntered away.

## Chapter 36

# Sweet Dreams

*1951*

Ed blinked hard. It was difficult to see through the sweat that dripped into his eyes. "Pop?" Somewhere behind him, he glimpsed his mother leaning heavily on Mary. A grown woman now. Beautiful, too, as well as sweet. Or was he dreaming? He'd been seeing things lately that weren't there. He couldn't tell what was real anymore.

"Son," his father choked, his voice muffled by the cloth covering his mouth. "I, I . . . We didn't understand. This place . . . had no idea. What could we . . . Army said . . . we thought the doctors knew what was best." He stopped talking and wept. His father wept.

Real or imagined, his father was there, and he saw, and he was sorry. It's okay. Pop, it's okay, Pop. Not your fault. Nobody's fault. The words he uttered in his head couldn't find their way to his throat. He managed to lift his arm and pat the woolen sleeve of his father's worn jacket. Pictures swam in his head. Not the ugly ones. Older ones. He was swapping stories and drinking beer with Chappy. Lifting a sledgehammer in the camp alongside his brother. Mary was leaning over his shoulder to watch him sketch in his art studio. Coming home to breakfast after Sunday Mass. The birds came then. They twittered just outside his window. They begged him to come and sing with them. Angels hovered above the trees. I'm coming. I'm coming, he said, as he flew up and out of the icebox.

*Chapter 37*

# A Life for a Life

Mary studied the swollen legs extending from her ballooned belly and tried to calm herself. She pulled the flowered pink blanket back over her legs, picked up the sodden white handkerchief, and blew. She had not been able to stop the steady flow of tears. Just eighteen, she was newly pregnant with her first child. Doctor Nelson said that her baby might not make it, and she had just learned that her dear, dear brother Edward had died. Worse, because of her condition, she would be unable to attend his funeral.

"I'm placing you on complete bed rest, Mrs. Joyce. I don't know if we can save this baby or not, but there's a chance *if* you follow my orders." His thin brown hair was combed neatly to the side, and a thick mustache masked his upper lip and moved up and down when he talked.

She had been on bed rest for a week when Buddy broke the news to her that Edward had passed away from T.B. Now Buddy and the rest of her family were at Holy Sepulcher cemetery burying her brother, while Mary sat alone with her grief in the cramped third-floor apartment of Buddy's parents' house on Elkhart Street. Edward was gone for good. This was the second time her brother was gone, just like that. This time there would be no visiting him. No hoping for his eventual return. She ran her hands over her belly and pictured the life stirring within her. Edward would never come back, and her baby would never know the brother she loved. She was grateful that her husband had met him, even if the Edward he met was but a shadow of himself.

A few weeks after they started dating, Mary finally told Buddy about Edward. She was worried. Unsure how he might react to her family's secret shame and the puzzling circumstances around Edward's hospitalization, which Mary was slowly unraveling and piecing together.

It began with the one-sided telephone conversation Mary overheard between her mother and Aunt Maureen. At the time, Mary had just quit school to work at Raymar's. She remembered that her mother's voice was testy and tired. "The shame of it, a mental hospital. Well, it's a cross God gave us to bear." A pause followed. "No, he still refuses to discuss it." Pause. "He won't hear anything about. . . and that awful magazine article . . ." Pause. "How can such things . . . in a hospital . . .?" Pause. Of course, we didn't know. "It can't possibly be, can it?" Pause.

Her mother still refused to talk about Edward except, apparently, with her aunts. Mary suspected that the "awful magazine article" was the same one that Mary had accidentally come across in Edward's art studio. The pieces were beginning to fall into place. The fight between her parents, her father's refusal to visit Edward, this overhead conversation. What tied them together were the heart-stopping photos in *Life* that Mary had shoved into the basement of her memory. The door was open now, if only a crack. What was the title? She thought it began with a B. Beelum? Birdlan? Bedlam? Yes, Bedlam. Photos of naked men in a dungeon or prison of some kind came back into view, along with the glimpse she had gotten of Edward's eerily similar sketches.

On the day she shared these bits and pieces of the puzzle with Buddy, they were sitting on a park bench in Pulaski Park with a view of the Delaware River. It was a Saturday. It had rained earlier, but the sky had finally cleared. Long rows of identical, spiral-shaped cotton-ball clouds drifted across the powder-blue curtain of sky, lit by a golden hue behind them.

"What do you see, Buddy?" she asked, pointing to the clouds. It was a game they sometimes played.

"Hmmm, let me think." He squinted, scanning the horizon. "A quilt?"

Mary scrunched up her eyes. "Oh, yeah, I can see that. A blue-and-white quilt with streaks of yellow to keep heaven warm."

Buddy burst out laughing. It was a hearty laugh, much like Mary's. Mary thumped Buddy on the shoulder. Then she relaxed and joined in, until both were shaking with laughter.

"You're awful damn cute, honey."

Mary was happy. They did have fun together. The war had taught them that life was short, so both were eager to marry and start their new life together. Getting Buddy to settle down and give up his bachelor ways would be a challenge, but Mary was up for the job. She had a strong will. Now that she was sure God was calling her to marriage instead of the convent, she was determined to be the best wife and mother possible. That meant Buddy had to be the best husband. She'd just have to figure out how to make Buddy think he was doing it all by himself.

It was earlier in their courtship when they sat together on the park bench, Mary struggling with how to begin the conversation about her institutionalized brother. "So, Buddy." Mary's heart thumped. "I've been meaning to talk to you about something."

"Uh, oh. Am I in trouble?"

"What? No, silly. Oh, you." She thumped his shoulder again.

Buddy pretended to fall back from the force of her blow. "Ow! You sure do pack a mean punch, lady."

"Well, I'm serious, Buddy. This is serious. Can you stop horsing around for a few minutes?" Nervous already, Mary was impatient to get this difficult conversation about her brother over with.

"Okay, honey, sorry. I'm all ears. See?" He cupped both ears. "Shoot."

"You know how I spend some Sunday afternoons after Mass visiting sick people at the hospital?" Mary guessed that Buddy was relieved that she had regular Sunday plans because it got him out of going to church with her.

"Yeah, what about it?" He tossed his head back and sniffed the air, as if sensing danger.

Mary kept her gaze steady, even though her heart began galloping the way it did when she was in the confessional. "Well, it's not actually sick *people*. It's one person."

Buddy screwed up his face. "What do you mean?"

Mary sighed and looked away to collect her thoughts. An older couple strolled by hand in hand. They smiled at Mary in a knowing way. Did they see her and Buddy's happy future together? She sure hoped so. In the distance, a young, shaggy-haired boy, who was tossing a football with his friends, yelped when a black Boxer started chasing him. His friends laughed and started to chase the dog. It was a three-ring circus of running, barking, and laughing.

"Mary?" Buddy lifted his hand to chase a fly away from her nose.

Mary took a deep breath. "My brother . . . it's my brother, Edward. He's in the Army, like I told you. Well, he was in the Army. I don't really know if he still is. He's been in the hospital for a while now. It's not a regular hospital. It's the state hospital." Mary had come to understand that people avoided talking about this *special* hospital. It was for people who were sick in the head, which meant that Edward must be sick in the head, even though Mary still couldn't believe that.

"In a what? Why?" Buddy sat up. His playful smirk vanished.

"Well, that's just it. I don't really know why." She clenched her hands. Unclenched them, trying to release the red flush of shame she felt travel from her ears to her cheeks and into her neck. The word "ignominy" came to her mind. Where had she heard that word? In church, she guessed. Her heart sped up. What if Buddy didn't understand? Would he hate her? Judge her family, or think horrible things about her beloved Edward? It didn't matter. She had to tell him. Get it out and trust that he would understand.

"All I know is that everything was fine before Edward went into the Army. The next thing I knew, me and my mom were taking the El and the trolley to this out-of-the-way hospital to visit him and, it was so horrible. . ." She couldn't finish her sentence any more than she could stem her tears.

"It's okay, honey. It's okay." Buddy pulled Mary into the shelter of his arms.

Between sobs, Mary explained. "Edward used to be fun. He was happy. Now he's. . . I don't even know how to describe him. He doesn't talk much or smile, and we had to visit with him outside at a picnic table and my mother stopped visiting him and . . ."

"Whoa, whoa, hold on there now, honey. Are you talking about Byb . . .?"

But Mary wasn't about to stop. She had held in so much for so long. "It's an awful place, Buddy. I never see any doctors or nurses there. I don't know what's wrong with Edward or why he doesn't come home, or why Mom and Dad and my sisters never want to talk about him. It makes me so mad sometimes I can hardly breathe." She paused to dab her eyes and blow her nose with Buddy's handkerchief. "It's like they all just want to forget him, Buddy. But I can't. I won't, and I'm so sorry. I know I should have told you before."

Buddy had grown quiet. He released Mary from his arms and sat forward, his gaze focused on the river. Mary noticed a crease between his eyebrows. Was he shocked? Disappointed? Angry? She couldn't tell.

"And what," he glanced back at her. "You thought what? I would hold this against you. Seems Edward's sick, honey, and it's not his fault. It's not yours." His eyes caressed her, and then drew away. They were looking at something she couldn't see. "Remember Joe—my oldest brother—the one you haven't met?"

Of course, she remembered. Buddy had one older brother, Tom, who was a priest, but his oldest brother Joe, like Buddy, had served in the Navy. Buddy talked more about his five lively sisters that fussed over him, the baby of the family.

"Well, Joe came home from the war all messed up." Buddy pointed to his head. "You know? All messed up in the head."

"Oh," Mary managed to say. Was that how it had been for Edward? Had he gotten messed up in the head because of something that happened in the Army? Mary caressed Buddy's arm and waited for him to continue.

"Joe was captured by the Japanese and held as a prisoner of war for over a year. When he came back, he was a different man. They tortured him in there. Lost most of his teeth, had burn marks all over his body. Other stuff I can't even. . ."

Mary squeezed his hand. "That's horrible, Buddy. The poor man."

Buddy reached into his top shirt pocket for a cigarette. After placing it between his lips, he took out a pack of matches. His hand was shaking. Mary reached over, took the matches, and lit the cigarette for him, just as she had done for Edward in the hospital.

"Yeah, it is." Buddy took a long drag, removing the loose tobacco from his tongue with his fingertips. "Kept him in a cage for months like an animal. I have some choice words for them, but I won't say them in front of you, honey." He leaned forward, smoke swirling around his head like a halo.

Mary squeezed the shoulder she'd just thumped teasingly minutes before. She imagined how hard it must have been for a Golden Gloves boxing champion like Buddy Joyce not to be able to protect his own brother from the bad guys.

Buddy flicked his cigarette to release a line of ash. He lifted his head to face her, remembering.

"Like I said. When he came home, he was, well, he was nuts, and it was sad. I mean, nuts. Ya know? He got into fights with everybody, even me. My parents were scared. I was the only one who could control him, but I couldn't be with him all the time. He'd get into fights down at the bar, in the neighborhood. You name it. Got into fights for no good reason. He was just, I don't know, out of control." He inhaled deeply.

Mary didn't know what to say, so she listened with her heart as well as her ears. She realized that there were so many things in the world she didn't understand.

Buddy exhaled the smoke with a long sigh. "Sweetest guy in the world too, our Joe, before he joined up. I couldn't believe the change. Had a fiancée. Beautiful girl. But she couldn't take it. Called it off. He scared my parents and my sisters something awful. And then, you're not going to believe this, Mary, and then the cops charged him with assault and battery, and the judge ordered him to be locked up in . . . well, in the mental hospital just outside the city. Byberry, they call it. I mean, I think that's the same hospital where your brother is."

Like a baby bird, Mary opened her mouth and then closed it. Her mind was struggling to make sense of what Buddy said. It was like trying to read the jumble of words and lines on the blackboard from the back of the classroom without her eyeglasses. Was Edward *nuts* like Buddy's brother Joe, then? Had he been out of control and gotten into fights? She couldn't wrap her mind around that idea. She shifted her gaze toward the horizon. The perfectly formed cloud spirals were unraveling and scattering, the sunshine sweeping them away, creating a new picture on the sky-canvas.

"Byberry?" she finally said. "Is that the same as the Philadelphia State Mental Hospital? Do they call it Bedlam, too?" Mary's stomach churned. Ed's sketches, the magazine. The door opened wider.

"Yeah, Mary." Buddy flicked his cigarette into the grass. The boys' football landed a few feet away from them; the gasping dog was not far behind. Buddy jumped off the bench to retrieve the ball and throw it back. The dog turned in the opposite direction.

When Buddy sat back down, Mary slipped her hand into his. "So, does that mean we both have brothers who are in the same hospital? I can't believe this, Buddy. It doesn't seem possible." As she said this, she realized something. Both she and Buddy had brothers they loved, but it was like their brothers were taken away and kept in a lost and found department where they couldn't be claimed. Maybe that's why God had brought Mary and Buddy together. To find their brothers.

"Go figure," Buddy shrugged. "Now, here you wanted to have this big talk with me, and I end up telling you *my* sob story." He kissed her forehead and gave her the slanted grin she loved, revealing a dimple on his right cheek.

"Now, give. I want to hear everything. How long's your brother been in the hospital? Was he in the war? I think you said he was Army, right?"

"Well, yeah."

"Was he shipped overseas?"

"I don't know. I don't think so. At least, nobody said that. Just bootcamp."

"Are you sure? That doesn't make any sense. Tell me more."

Mary told Buddy everything she remembered. Her story came in fits and starts, and Buddy didn't say much. But his eyes listened closely, especially to the part about her secret mission to deliver Edward's sketches to the priest.

"You're the only one I've told, Buddy. You're the only one, besides Fr. McGuire." She continued, admitting to having accidentally peeked at them even though Edward had warned her not to look at them. She felt so badly about disobeying him that she pushed the creepy sketches out of her mind for the longest time. Then she came across the *Life* magazine article that reminded her, but she still refused to think about what the sketches meant.

"No, honey. You shouldn't," Buddy said protectively. He kissed the top of Mary's head. "But wait. Back up the wagon a little. Tell me more about what happened at boot camp."

"I don't know more, Buddy. I was young, and we don't . . . I don't know. My family doesn't . . . we never talk about it. You know?"

"Yeah, the Irish way," Buddy added. "So, nobody knows how he got from boot camp to Byberry?"

Mary shook her head. "Well, maybe my parents do, but if so, they're not saying."

"No friends that knew him in the Army?"

Again, she shook her head. She was about to say no, and then she remembered something. "Wait a minute. Ed had a good friend in the neighborhood who went to boot camp with Edward. He used to tease me. He had a funny name. What was it? Chappy. Chappy Lafferty." She raised her eyebrows and looked at Buddy. "Do you think he might know something?"

"Do you know if he made it back?"

She shrugged. "I don't know, but my other brother might know." Mary hadn't seen much of her older brother Sam since he'd gotten married. His Protestant wife was not welcome in their home, so her brother had drifted away from the family. Although Mary was on friendly terms with them, she didn't get to see him or his wife much.

Buddy threw his head back decisively. "Well, sweetheart, I think we should try to track that fella Chappy down and have a talk with him. Let's go see your brother and find out."

It was a short and awkward visit, and Sam was not willing to talk about Edward with Mary and Buddy. But he did tell them that Chappy had made it back after serving in the Pacific and they might find him at Tony's Tavern in Kensington. A bunch of ex-Army guys from the neighborhood often got together there on Friday night. Buddy thought it would be better if he went alone to talk to Chappy, man to man.

"Absolutely not," Mary said, stomping her foot. "It's *my* brother. I'm going."

A couple of weeks later, after some small talk about the war and a couple of rounds of beers on Buddy, Chappy started talking.

"Nah, Ed didn't ship out with us. Refused to shoot his weapon." Chappy paused and pressed his thumbs against his eyebrows. "Your brother was stubborn, Mary. He refused to fire his rifle on the firing range. The sergeant almost had a stroke. Got so pissing mad he beat Ed over the head with it. Sent him to the base hospital. After that, I don't know what happened."

Chappy stared into his beer mug, avoiding Mary's stunned eyes. "Sorry to tell you this. But it's the truth. God as my witness." He raised his hand and shook his head. "Your brother was in the Army, but he didn't want to kill anybody. That's a fact. When I came back, I told your parents what happened on the firing range. I honest to God don't know what happened after."

Mary's heart sank. Edward, who was kind to everyone, beaten? She wanted Chappy to tell her more about the brother she knew and didn't know. She pictured herself as a little girl leaning over Edward's shoulder while he read his newspaper in the living room. She wanted to know what he was reading. What had he said in response? Something about guys who didn't believe in shooting or killing. "Guys like me," she remembered him saying. He pointed to a caption in *The Catholic Worker*. Mary couldn't remember what it said.

Mary sipped on her rum and coke, waiting for Chappy to continue. Buddy held out his pack of Luckies for Chappy to take one and ordered another round of beers.

"Ed was respectful to the Sergeant, see? Didn't give him lip or nothing. Whole platoon was on the firing range that day. We all saw. Knew it was wrong. What could we do? The Sergeant—he wasn't a bad guy. Just doing his job, I guess. Had it in plenty for Ed before

that, though. Thought he was a coward. Ed wouldn't back down."
Chappy looked up from his beer. His words started to slur. "Yeah,
principled. I guess that's what you'd call a guy like that, Mary. Too
faithful to his principles for his own damned good, if you ask me. I
told him that, too. He didn't believe in violence, and he wouldn't back
the hell down. Neither would the Serge. Maybe the Serge thought
Ed was showing him up. Who knows?" His eyes shifted from Mary
to Buddy and back again.

"Was he?" Buddy asked. "Showing him up?"

"Nah, it wasn't like that. Ed wasn't like that. He was a good guy.
The best. Just doing the right thing, you know? According to what
he believed in and all." Chappy shook his head and threw his hands
up in the air. "What the hell could I do? He was my buddy. I tried
to warn him. I did. When he got beat up, I felt really bad. A lot of
the guys did. Never saw him after that. Didn't know what happened
to him 'til I got back and heard the rumors."

"But wait." Mary looked quizzically at Chappy. "How did he end
up in Byberry?"

"Beats the hell out of me. He was right as rain in boot camp, just
worried about having to kill." Chappy shook his head and stared
glumly into his beer mug.

Mary hugged Chappy when they finally said their tearful good-
byes outside the bar, thankful that he gave them an important piece
in the puzzle of her brother's life.

Back in the present, she turned away from her recollections and
glanced up at the grandfather clock in the corner. A sob caught in her
throat. Edward was in the grave now, while she was newly married and
pregnant. It felt all wrong and all right at the same time. The apartment was strangely quiet without Buddy's whistling and the steady

hum of voices of family members in the rooms below them. Mary didn't know what to make of such stillness. Of the loss of one so dear, balanced against the new life stirring within her. Her faith had taught her to believe that death was not the end. Mary vowed to hold onto that belief as fiercely as she would hold onto her brother's memory.

She cried softly into her cupped hands. She'd never visit Edward again. Never see him get well. Never, one day, bring him to her home as she and Buddy had planned. But one day, when she was stronger and could face it, she would rewind Edward's story. She would answer the niggling questions: why had Edward been sent to Byberry in the first place, and why wasn't he ever released? Clearer now that some terrible injustice must have occurred, she was determined to unearth the other puzzle pieces. She would find a way to rectify it. She wouldn't rest until she did.

Not now, though. Not now. She had a baby to bring safely into the world and a marriage to get on with. Mary leaned forward to stretch her spine. She was reaching for her water glass on the end table when she heard a whooshing sound, followed by a thump, in the open window behind the sofa. She lifted the lacy white curtain. A hummingbird lay against the window lattice. Mary thought for sure it must be dead. But then it started flapping its tiny gray-green wings, and its ruby throat started to chirp.

"It's okay, little bird," Mary said soothingly. "I'm not going to hurt you." She resisted the urge to cradle the tiny creature in her hand and kiss its beautiful head. Nature just had to take its course. And it did. Within a few minutes, the bird extricated itself from the window, and its quivering wings made their way into the welcoming sky. Mary thought she might try to sketch it later. For Edward.

## Chapter 38

# The Metal Box

*1971*

Mary was trying to put Bart down for a nap when she heard the rustling and banging sound coming from her and Buddy's bedroom.

"What in the world? Jimmy, Jimmy?" Alarmed, she kept her voice low so as not to awaken her sick, fussy baby. What is that boy getting into now? Mary took a few long, deep breaths to keep her temper, as Father Sullivan had suggested.

The week before, in need of encouragement, Mary waited to speak with the priest after the 10:00 a.m. Sunday Mass.

"You don't know what it's like, Father." With Bart in the crook of her arm, she leaned her weight on her left hip to relieve the ache in her back. The infant would be hungry soon, and Mary hadn't brought a bottle with her. A few minutes with the priest was just the thing she needed to jumpstart her day. "I try my hardest. I do, Father. But seven boys are a handful. They would try the patience of a saint."

Father Sullivan looked at her earnestly. "Well, no one's expecting you to be a saint, my dear. No one's expecting that. But in those moments of trial, just try to take deep breaths and say a little Hail Mary or two. Can you do that?"

"I'll try, Father. I will."

"Is your husband not helping, then, Mrs. Joyce?" He stooped down to pat the baby's feathery head.

The baby gurgled and fussed with the sun in his eyes. Mary lifted him from her hip and up to her shoulder to shield him from the glare.

"Oh, Buddy's crazy about his boys, Father. There's no question about that. But he's better at horsing around with them than he is at disciplining them. Sometimes he's the biggest kid of all."

Father Sullivan guffawed. Recovering, he folded his hands prayer-like over the tip of his nose.

"Well, he's a good man, your Buddy, but we have to do a better job of getting him to Sunday Mass now. Don't we, Mary? I could work on him from my end." His eyes twinkled.

Mary shook her head. "He's working day and night, Father, to keep clothes on their backs, shoes on their feet, and food on the table. It's not his fault. On Sunday, he likes to take a little break. We're both working on the weekends. Catering. It helps us make ends meet." She strained her neck to eye the Buick station wagon where her restless older boys were waiting for her. She'd left her enfeebled sister Anna at home with her husband, so at least Mary didn't have to worry about her. It looked like the boys had gotten into a scuffle as usual, but she didn't see blood, so she guessed they'd last another two minutes without her intervening.

"Yes, yes, it's a hardship, I know, Mrs. Joyce. But God blessed you with beautiful children now. Didn't he?"

"Of course, Father. I'm grateful every single day."

The priest touched her forehead and blessed her. "You're a good girl, Mary Joyce."

It was something her mother had always said to her, except her words were, "You're *my* good girl, Mary dear. I can always count on you to do the right thing." She'd been talking about her sister Anna, of course. Mary promised her mother she would take care of Anna when their mother was gone, her father having passed some time before.

On Monday, Mary was home alone with the baby and her sick four-year-old, Jimmy.

"Okay, Bart, time to close your eyes, time to close those little peepers," she cooed. The baby was almost asleep when the banging and rustling sounds from the other bedroom suddenly stopped. But for the rattling of the old heater furnace and the now-familiar Sesame Street tune blaring from the TV, the house was silent. More reason to worry. She stepped lightly towards the open door, the baby falling slack in her arms. She called out softly. "Jimmy, Jimmy Joyce. What have you gotten up to?"

No reply.

Bart's eyes flickered, once, twice, three times, until his tiny body finally surrendered.

"Thank God." After laying him down in the crib, she stole away from the room and closed the door behind her, her ears on full alert. She'd left Jimmy in the family room watching *Sesame Street* and playing with his Tinker Toys, grateful for the relative quiet that would last until the older boys got home from school later in the afternoon. This kind of quiet smelled like trouble. Jimmy trouble. She scooted down the hallway. A glance at the empty family room confirmed that her instincts were right. The boy must have gotten into something in her bedroom.

She rushed to the master bedroom.

"What in the world? Jimmy!" Mary covered her mouth with her hand. "What a mess you've made!" She remembered what the priest had told her. She took two deep breaths and kept herself from yelling and waking up Bart.

Startled, the boy's eyes widened, snot dripping from his nose. He sat on the floor of her closet with opened hatboxes and shoeboxes strewn all around him.

"Look what I found, Mommy!"

Thrilled by the discovery of his newfound treasure, Jimmy held up a long chain with a St. Christopher Medal hanging from it. He clutched a fistful of German and Irish coins in his other hand. An upturned gray metal box sat beside him. Old photographs, letters, coins, and documents lay scattered on the floor. It was the box Mary's mother had left behind for her, with instructions not to open it until after her death. Mary had not had the heart to open the box to the past. Not yet, though more than two years had passed.

While Jimmy examined his treasures, Mary wiped his nose with her hankie and leaned over to get a closer look at the medallion in the boy's hand. She was sure it was her brother Edward's. He was wearing it the day he left for bootcamp. Had Edward given it to her mother? And what's this? She picked up three yellowed envelopes wrapped in two rubber bands. Mary gasped. The letters were still inside, and they were addressed to Mary Hohlfeld. Three letters from three convents. One had a tiny note attached to it in her mother's hand.

*Dear Mary, I hope you'll find it in your heart to forgive me for not giving you these letters. I hope you will understand that I needed you more than the convent did. Who else could visit our poor Edward and take care of Anna after I'd gone? You've been a blessing to me, my dear child. Love, Your mother.*

A quick glance at the short letters, each one written in elegant handwriting with a gold cross embossed at the top, told Miss Mary Hohlfeld that she'd been accepted at the three religious orders she'd applied to. They awaited her reply. A reply that would never come. She wasn't sure how she felt. Deceived? Robbed? She imagined herself in another life. Sister Mary kneeling alone in a chapel, or standing at the front of a classroom, her hair shorn, and her women's body hidden inside the sacred robes.

Mary shook her head as if to awaken herself. No, that wasn't right. There was no other life than this one. Her married life. God had not intended for Mary to be a nun. That was a just a schoolgirl's dream.

Mary turned the metal box upright. She was placing the rubber-banded envelopes and letters back inside the box when her eyes were drawn to two other pieces of stationary under the crook of Jimmy's knee. It was as if they had been waiting for her. What now? Her chest tightened. She picked up the letter and started reading.

*Dear Mrs. Hohlfeld,*
   *You don't know me, but I was a friend of your son Edward in Byberry some years back . . .*

"Oh, my God." Mary collapsed on the beige carpet alongside Jimmy. She held the writing paper between her thumb and forefinger. Her mind raced back to her childhood. Edward promising that he would try to write back to her the day he left for the Army. She and her mother on the trolley to visit him at the hospital. Silent Edward seated at the picnic table. His eyes far away, the nub of a cigarette nestled between his yellowed fingers.

"Mommy, Mommy, what's the matter?" Jimmy tugged on her apron. He was still wearing his bunny pajamas, and snot kept dripping from his reddened nose.

Ignoring his question and stifling a reprimand for making a mess, Mary wiped his nose again. "It's okay, honey. Blow, Jimmy. Blow into this."

Mary held back the tears that swelled in her throat. She wondered if she had the courage to finish reading the letter addressed to her mother. Was she willing to dredge up the painful past? She rocked on her heels and tried to decide. Exhausted, Jimmy finally curled his small body in her lap. He placed an arm around her neck and settled his head in the crook of her shoulder, his breath ragged and raspy. He was chastened. Of all her sons, he was the one most attuned to her moods, just as she had been to her mother's. She kissed his warm forehead. Her heart pounding, she lifted the letter and read.

*I've been meaning to write you for some time but didn't for a couple of reasons. Fear, I guess, was the main one, at least at first. Maybe shame, too. Then I couldn't track you down. Ed told me his family lived in Port Richmond. Said you and his little sister, Mary, or Maureen, I can't remember which, wrote him letters and visited him. His sister drew him pictures. He'd taught her how to draw. The way he smiled when he talked about it. Well, it meant a lot to him. I finally hired a private investigator to track you down. He found an address in Philly, but after my letter came back from the post office unopened, I kept trying 'til I got your forwarding address there in Fairless Hills. At least, hope this is the right address.*

*It was a long time ago, and I was just a kid then. I didn't know Ed very long, Mrs. Hohlfeld, but there's not a day that goes by I don't think about the man and his impact on my life. He was a good man. A good, caring man. If it wasn't for him,*

*I would surely be dead today. He gave me the idea that it was okay for me to live, even when everyone else was mean and hateful and told me something different. I held onto that until I learned to believe it myself. I ran away. Got out of that place, just like he told me to. I don't know why he was in there. He wasn't crazy, that's for sure. I know the Army had something to do with it, and he was awful depressed. Awful depressed. I didn't really understand that at the time. I was depressed myself, and I didn't understand a lot of things. I found out later that Ed never got out. That he died in there. TB, I guess, like a lot of them. I wish I had gone back to the hospital to see him before he died. To thank him for what he did for me, but I couldn't do it. I was a coward, I suppose. Afraid if I went back, they might recognize me and throw me back in because I ran away, see? I couldn't take that. I couldn't survive. I don't want to go into details about what happened in there, but it was an awful hellish place. Ed gave me a tip about a Catholic orphanage just outside the city, named St. Francis Industrial School for orphaned boys where he'd done some volunteer work. He said that if I got out, I should go there, and they were bound to help me, even though I was Jewish. Well, he was right. It had its own set of problems. Most such places do, I suppose. But the Christian brothers took me in. I got a new start and learned a trade, and now I'm a typesetter for a local newspaper. It's a solitary job, but it suits me. I don't know why God made me the way he did, but I know that my heart is good, and Ed was the only one who saw it back then. He tried to protect me in Byberry, and I'll never forget that. That doesn't make a whole lot of sense to you, I know, but that's all I can tell you.*

*Well, I don't really know what more to say, except that your son was a good man. He saved my life, and I thought you and your family should know that.*

*Sincerely,*

*Joseph Myerson*

*P.S. I thought you should have this St. Christopher medallion your son gave me. It helped me get through some rough times.*

There was no date at the top and no matching envelope with a return address.

Jimmy snored softly into her chest. Tears trickled down her cheeks. Mary brought the Medal to her lips and kissed it. Then she placed it back on the boy's chest, thankful he'd finally fallen asleep. She swiped her face with her apron. She stood up and lay Jimmy on the bed before returning to the floor and her long-delayed reckoning with the past.

## Chapter 39

# Edward's Honor

*Present Day*

Life is a freight train on its own timetable, and it doesn't slow down or stop when you want or need it to. It keeps chugging forward. It takes you into long dark tunnels with no end in sight and across heart-stopping bridges with a view of heaven, and there's no getting off.

After bracing herself and examining the contents of the metal box in 1971, Mary burrowed into the past to re-assemble the pieces of her brother's ill-fated life. Because she was having babies and raising a family, it took years. She plied her sisters with questions. She scoured newspaper archives and the card catalog at her local library for information about Byberry. She talked to anyone and everyone whose relatives had also been patients there. She read about the conscientious objectors who served in mental hospitals and how they had labored, against all odds, to expose and improve conditions at the notorious hospital. She came to understand that, like them, her brother was also a conscientious objector who hadn't been able to avoid the Army draft. This time, she made herself examine the horrifying photos in the *Life* article that were so like Edward's sketches. The very ones she had delivered to Father McGuire. She discovered that the good, decent men who worked so hard to bring Byberry's evils to light had been few in number but mighty in spirit. It was an inspiring crusade, but by the time the conscientious objectors working at Byberry had attracted Mrs. Roosevelt and the country's attention, it was much too little and far too late to help her brother.

There was no end to the sad, grim tales associated with Byberry. Its horrifying conditions, mysterious deaths, corruption, and incompetence. All the terrible things were going on behind the doors of the hospital Mary had so faithfully visited. And yet, she never had a clue, even though the evidence stared at her from her brother's vacant eyes.

Time and time again, her husband warned her to stop. To stop searching. To put it away. To bury it for the sake of her health. But she couldn't. Wouldn't. Didn't. In her heart, she knew her brother had been treated unjustly and that her family had failed him because shame trumped love. Her brother had died in an insane asylum. He was a good man who had been disgraced. She had to find out why the military sent him to Byberry in the first place. A crucial missing piece. She had to get to the bottom of his story, only there seemed to be no bottom.

She tried to track down Father McGuire, who had left St. Anne's after being promoted to Monsignor, only to discover that he had died several years before. Most everywhere she turned, she ran into similar roadblocks or dead ends. The hospital released Edward's death certificate, but there were no notes from an attending doctor on Edward's treatment. She was told that the information was not available. When she reached out to the Pennsylvania State Archives, she learned that the medical records for the years 1941-1951 had been lost in a fire.

After months of calling and writing, of being shunted from one department to another, she also ran into the same stone wall at the U.S. Army.

"Sorry, we can't tell you anything, ma'am. The military records for the soldier in question were lost in a fire."

Two convenient fires and no records of the whys and wherefores of Edward's Army or Byberry life.

At first, the Army representative had refused to acknowledge that Edward was in the Army during the time that he was a patient at Byberry. But Mary persisted in her crusade to learn the truth about her brother. She wasn't a little girl who could be left in the dark or an inexperienced young mother who could be dissuaded. She was a grown woman with an iron will. Her determination paid off. She discovered that there were no discharge papers for Edward. The Army spokesperson finally relented, and said, yes, Edward F. Hohlfeld had never been dismissed from the Army, and that his pay had been re-routed to her parents. So, her parents had known? He could not, or would not, though, provide any other information. At Mary's insistence, the U.S. Army finally sent a letter admitting Edward's military status at his death. They also provided a long overdue headstone at his gravesite that identified her brother as Pvt. Edward F. Hohlfeld. Then, the pay-off. Through a back-channel connection to a mid-level government worker in Philadelphia, Mary uncovered the ultimate document that lay at the base of the mystery of Edward's hospital imprisonment. The document showed that Edward F. Hohlfeld had been remanded to Byberry as a POW—a prisoner of war—a U.S. POW.

Although her brother and sisters stayed mum on the subject, Ronnie finally admitted that Edward had escaped from the hospital once. This confirmed Mary's vague memory of the night the beat policeman showed up at their house. The same night she crept down the stairs and thought she heard Edward crying. Edward had been gone a couple of months, Ronnie said, when their parents came home to find him hiding on top of the icebox in their kitchen. There was a big commotion. The military policemen showed up with orders to take him back. The beat policeman tried to interfere, but their father would not have it. He said there was something wrong with Edward. That the Army had broken him, and the Army needed to fix him.

Why had her father said this? Done this? Why had her family been so frightened, so ashamed, so secretive? Why hadn't they pressed the military authorities? Did Edward's POW status have anything to do with her father's German ancestry? Why hadn't her parents ever challenged the doctors or attempted to have Edward released?

Why did she grow up too late to do any of these things?

She had no answers to these disturbing questions. Only one thing was clear. Edward had gotten caught up in a vortex of events and circumstances peculiar to that time that were outside of his control. As had she. Someday, she would have to forgive her family for failing Edward. Someday, she would have to forgive herself. She would try to make it right. She would tell Edward's story to the world.

Maybe then, just maybe, she would finally set things right. Restore Edward's honor and rectify her heart.

\* \* \*

# Note to Reader

*The Faithful Ones: A Novel* is a work of fiction based on a family story. It originated with Mary Hohlfeld Joyce's warm recollections of her brother and was bolstered by research. Through interviews with Mary and her older sisters, and in the absence of certain verifiable facts, I stitched together a portrait of a man of faith, whose principles ironically led to his own undoing. Jimmy Joyce—son of Mary, and nephew of Edward—approached me about writing his uncle's story on behalf of his mother. In addition to facilitating my research, Jimmy participated in many productive conversations with me about Edward and his pacifist principles in a pro-war world and how he may have navigated it.

Most of the principal parties on which the characters in this story were based are long gone. Fortunately, however, I was able to track down Quaker and former Byberry CO Warren Sawyer, aka, the fictitious Walter Sinclair. Aged 92 at the time of our email and telephone conversations (2013), Mr. Sinclair's recollections were amazingly vivid and his mind, incredibly sharp. Mr. Sawyer did not remember Edward per se, but he reported that there were many such soldiers in Byberry during the war years, some of whom were there for disciplinary reasons. (This is corroborated in the personal papers of Warren Sawyer that are housed in the Peace Collection of the Swarthmore College Library.) In the absence of Army and hospital records, it could not be determined why Edward was never released from Byberry after the war. Caught up in the war and its aftermath, the military may simply have lost track of him. Moreover, confined to the violent "B" ward, he was likely traumatized on a daily basis, and with no hope of release became institutionalized. Indeed, at the time, few patients were "cured" and discharged. Many were simply lost and forgotten.

The incident in bootcamp that prompted Edward's incarceration was witnessed by his neighborhood friend and fellow draftee, Chappy Lafferty. Mr. Lafferty witnessed the drill sergeant's alleged brutal beating of Edward on the firing range after he refused to use his rifle. Mr. Lafferty reported the event to the Hohlfeld family following his own discharge from the Army. Edward's escape only to be returned to Byberry by the military police is also factual. According to Mary's older sisters, his parents discovered him crouched and terrified atop the kitchen Icebox following his escape from Byberry. Also true are the scenes in which Mary visits Byberry alone after being made up by her mother to pass as an eighteen-years-old woman. Vivid in Mary's memory were Edward's instructions to her to deliver his bag of Byberry sketches to her mother and father, then to be passed along to the parish priest. (I tweak that scene in the story, removing the part about her parents.) I could find no evidence that the sketches were, in fact, delivered to the parish priest and used in the *Life* exposé and no evidence of the sketches; however, Mary feels strongly that Edward's sketches did play a role. I was unable to confirm this, although I suggest as much in the story to soften its bleakness.

Although it may be difficult for the reader to imagine the Hohl-feld family's passivity and compliance with military and hospital authorities, especially in light of today's emphasis on institutional accountability, I would offer a caveat or two. Many Americans of that generation, including my own parents, had a blind trust in authority figures, beginning with the Church and extending to other authority figures and institutions. Patriotic fervor during the war years was heightened, and Edward's actions were very likely viewed as shameful for him and his family. Shame, of course, leads to secrecy, and shame and family secrecy—and the unwillingness to talk about disturbing matters openly—played a huge, if unwitting role in this family tragedy. Moreover, mental illness was a scourge for any family at this time (and maybe still is today). "Deviance"—a lack of confor-mity to social expectations—was labeled a mental illness at the time, and mental illness was something to be ashamed of and hidden away, as evidenced in the high number of people locked away in Byberry during the 1930s and 40s who were deviant but not, necessarily, mentally ill. In one testimony I came across, a *deviant* Slavic woman who was unable to speak English languished in Byberry for years, though she had no mental illness.

The Hohlfeld house still stands in Port Richmond, although the neighborhood is in decline, and the makeshift playground is gone. In the early stages of this process, I spent time walking its streets and studying its contours and ethos. I visited St. Anne's, the hub of the Hohlfeld family life. The school is closed, and the church is under lock and key and preparing to shut its doors altogether. I was able to get inside and see the altars where Mary and her mother lit votive candles and prayed for her brother's safe return. My own earliest years were spent in a similar northeastern Philadelphia neighborhood and parish, and I have many family members still living in the area. I drew on this cultural sensibility in the writing of this book, including my own memories as they related to patterns of speech, stories I heard growing up about Byberry, and the attitudes and values of my parents and aunts, uncles, and cousins. It would not be an exaggeration to suggest that many who grew up in the Philadelphia metropolitan region have had a family member, or have known of someone who was locked up in Byberry, which finally closed its tainted and scandalous doors for good in the 1990s.

I hope I do justice to the heroic efforts of Byberry's CO attendants. Alfred Q. Maisel's *Life* 1945 article excoriated the hospital's horrid conditions, as did investigative journalist Albert Deutsch's newspaper series, *The Shame of the States*. As referenced in the novel, the COs actually did win an audience with Eleanor Roosevelt in 1945, although she did not at first believe the authenticity of the horrifying photographs they showed her.

Charles Lord was the CO whose photographs were published in *Life*. The character of Walter Sinclair is based on a composite of COs Charles Lord and Warren Sawyer who are both discussed at length in Stephen Taylor's exhaustive and illuminating study of COs during World War II: *Acts of Conscience: World War II, Mental Institutions and Religious Objectors*, another source I consulted for my project. Housed in the peace archives of Swarthmore College is an invaluable collection of artifacts from the era, and I was privileged to read COs' personal papers and correspondence. Walter's fictional relationship with the fictional Sallie Mae in the story was inspired by the many personal letters I came across in the peace archives.

Several sources, including Warren Sawyer, confirmed that the dayroom into which Ed and other patients were corralled was no more than 40 feet by 70 feet, that its floors were torn up, the walls were stained with feces, and they had no chairs to sit on. Also true is the fact that they were often manacled to benches in the dayroom and that the more disturbed patients made weapons out of spoons and anything they could get their hands on.

Superintendent Zeller did allow the COs to consult with reformist psychiatrists for their newsletter, *The Attendant*, recognizing that COs were committed to training themselves in order to improve patient care. However, they had to do this work on their own time and did so in spite of excessively long work weeks. They also had to assure Mr. Zeller that the publication they distributed to COs at mental hospitals around the country, would not make the institution look bad.

J. P. Webster's *The Philadelphia State Hospital at Byberry: A History of Misery and Medicine* found there were eight deaths in a single week at Byberry in 1941, pointing to a disturbing pattern of unexplained and unnecessary patient deaths at the institution. Bodies of patients had to be claimed within 36 hours, and many went unclaimed. In 1940 the so-called "slugger of Byberry"—and the basis of the character Buster Keating—was a brutish bully and a former boxing champion who beat one patient to death. He and another attendant were eventually charged with involuntary manslaughter. Unfortunately, it was not uncommon for such men, once fired to be then re-hired at other mental institutions during the war years. Although "Philadelphia State Hospital Patient Necrology" identifies some of the more "gruesome" patient deaths from abuse and neglect on its website, estimates of patient deaths are actually much higher.

According to Albert Deutsch (*The Shame of the States*), by 1938 there were as many as 600 deaths per year in Byberry. 180 attendants were responsible for the care of 6100 (or so) patients; Byberry was running at 75% above capacity by 1941, and only 14 on-site physicians and 41 nurses were on duty at any given time. Republican Governor Edward Martin and Secretary of Welfare S.M.R. O'Hara—who did make a personal visit to Byberry, as shown in the novel—spurned Deutsch's exposé that was originally published in a series of articles in *PM* (formerly, the *New York Star*). O'Hara also criticized the COs for their "distorted" complaint letters. Likened to an 18th-century asylum, or pest house, Byberry went through a series of incompetent superintendents. Moreover, in spite of a wartime treasury of $200,000,000.00, the state, which had taken Byberry over in 1938, did not allow this money to find its way to the hospital that was badly in need of repairs and supplies.

> *As I passed through some of Byberry's wards, I was reminded of the picture of the Nazi concentration camps in Buchenwald. I entered buildings swarming with naked humans herded like cattle and treated with less concern, pervaded by a fetid odor so heavy, so nauseating, that the stench seemed to have almost a physical existence of its own.*
>
> (Alfred Deutsch, The Shame of the States, 41-2)

Because the family was unable to obtain Edward's military records, it is unclear by what legal authority he was transferred from boot camp to Byberry. I suggest that a federal judge must have remanded him and so fictionalized that aspect of the story.

I created the character of Joseph Meyers, the scene of his rape, and Ed's role in trying to protect him. His victimization is based on ample evidence of physical and sexual abuse of Byberry patients. Edward's family members remembered Edward as a kind and gentle man who would be quick to step in and protect the weak, and this scene gave me the opportunity to illustrate that and highlight the rampant abuse of patients.

War-related developments and events serve as the backdrop of this story—a reminder of the "good war" being waged abroad and an allusion to the just and invisible *war* against institutional evil occurring on the Homefront.

Ed was a proponent of Dorothy Day and her social justice causes. Although the scene is imagined, the newspaper article that Edward reads from *The Daily Worker* about violence and the merit of conscientious objection is based on an actual editorial. I accessed it in the Peace Collection of the Swarthmore College Library, a treasure trove of information about Byberry, conscientious objectors, and Civilian Conservation Corp Camps and Projects. Its private collections, which included letters written from and to conscientious objectors, inspired the letters between Walter and Sallie Mae in the story. I fabricated letters from Mary and Edward's mother to Edward in order amplify the letter-writing trope and capture their perspective. In addition to creating characters and inventing scenes, I have also compressed the time frame to strengthen the story's dramatic structure. The substantive facts, to the best of my knowledge, are true.

Although this project exposed me to a dark and shameful corner of American history, it also introduced me to true American heroes and exemplars of honor, moral courage, and compassion.

Kathleen Joyce Waites

# Acknowledgements

When my cousin, Jimmy Joyce, asked me to write this family story about the uncle he never knew, I wavered. From the other end of this undertaking, I am thankful he persisted, entrusting me with this hidden away, split-your-heart-open gem of a family story that took me on quite a personal and creative journey. I appreciate Jim's unwavering support and collaboration throughout the project, as well as his helpful ideas for the book cover and title.

My aunt, Mary Hohlfeld Joyce, inspired and set this book in motion. She opened her heart to me, sharing cherished artifacts as well as vivid memories that helped me piece together the tragic story of her long-lost but never-forgotten beloved brother. We could not have imagined, however, that it would take ten plus years for this book to see the light of publishing day. I regret not the hours of labor and bouts of doubt in between, but the fact that she did not live long enough to know she had, at long last, accomplished her mission with its publication.

Many thanks to Lynn Wolf for her love, support, and unflinching encouragement. I am also grateful to Steven Alford and Suzanne Ferriss for their literary counsel and abiding friendship, as well as the many rejuvenating hikes they led me on in the wilds of the northwest.

(The nightly wine and soft pretzels also definitely helped.) Heartfelt thanks to Thomas G. Waites and Lisa Greenfield for their steadfast belief in me even when I doubted myself, and to Joseph P. Hearty III for his expert introduction to the M1 Garand rifle at the heart of the story. To feel its weight and heft brought me closer to the man who refused to shoot it. I am deeply indebted to fellow author and dear friend Deirdre Fagan for patiently holding my hand throughout this arduous publishing journey. She generously shared her knowledge and hard-earned tips on how to navigate agents, the publishing industry, and social media platforms.

To my cherished daughters, Sonya and Kirsta, and grandchildren Amber, Bryce, and Khalil, thank you. You make me want to do and be better. I hope this story deepens your appreciation of family love and loyalty and inspires you to find your own north star.

Thank you so much for reading *The Faithful Ones*.

If you've enjoyed the book, we would be grateful
if you would post a review on the bookseller's
website. Just a few words are all it takes!